Ohm

Ohm

A RESISTANCE TO FAITH

Prakash Sharma

PARTRIDGE

A Penguin Random House Company

To order additional copies of this book, contact
Partridge India
000 800 10062 62
orders.india@partridgepublishing.com

www.partridgepublishing.com/india

CONTENTS

My generation is born in just the perfect time of peace and love!

Thus my foremost dedication is to the fact that I am living in a time where I need not be worried about the issues of the ice age, scorching heat of the Sun thereafter, floating inside the ocean for years, the age of heresy, or for that matter the world war era.

I further dedicate this piece of thought to the wonderful people whom I keep meeting every now and then. They inspire me to think as to how and why do they profess the defined procedures per ancient scriptures.

I personally dedicate this to my family for raising me like a nomad, giving me an interesting ability to tune my brain, especially the left cerebral hemisphere, helping me logically question the events around me.

I would be ungrateful if I do not dedicate this work to my wife who has been bearing my sarcasm so efficiently. She has been smart enough to act as a great editor and a contributor to this book. Though she censored a lot of hard hitting anecdotes... aaarrrgh!

Lastly my favorite and ever young English teacher, Bannerji ma'am... I don't know where she is, but wherever she would be, I am sure she must be spreading happiness with her contagious smile.

CHAPTER 1

Incubation

"Hey come, let us go to the *naala*?" I asked Rahul, my neighbour. He also happened to be the first person I could call a friend.

"No Om! it's chilling out. Dad would get up and he would expect me inside the house. Also he has warned me about the landmines" he replied.

"Don't worry, anyways the tap is frozen. We have no water at home" I smiled and continued "The boiler hasn't been repaired yet"

I saw his smile approving my reason. I then added "All mines have been removed and no one has been hurt so far."

We both did not know what mines were, but were sure that if a person lands on it, it tears the body into numerous uncountable pieces.

"Ok but promise we would be back before the sunset"
"Sure. Say *om alakh* and we will be safe as always... now come along."

Then I remember having sat for comfortable toilet, spreading our legs on the two banks of the small sewage canal.

Also I recall that we discussed the shitty race happening in the open gutter, and I cannot forget the gust of wind blowing from all sides of my body especially from under the feet arc and that gives me goose bumps all the time.

Those were the early years in Rajourie when we enjoyed the sun in our backdoor garden, racing with *naala* water or climbing up the snowy peaks.

I belong to a family which is from a so called superior caste called Brahmins and I see almost everybody busy in prayers at any time of the day.

That day, I remember my father planning about a visit to *Vaishno Devi*. As always I could see everything being filtered out, as what is pious allowed and what is not, what has to be carried, who can wear what and so on. I watched him closely talking to my mother about the pilgrim. He was ironing his *kurta* and my mother was closely watching him. He was tall and always looked the strongest to me.

My mother was of short height and even though my father was sitting on the chair, my mother was just managing to match her shoulders to his head. I did not know about the classification of days, months then, but I did know that this was Saturday and thus my mother was done oiling her hair. It smelled mustard. Now she was giving my father a head massage to help him relax before the journey.

I was finding it difficult to keep my eyes opened now, the sleep was hitting it hard. My sister, who looked just like my mother and had the strength of my father, was sleeping next to me.

My brother was busy running his toy car on the wall and I could manage to add all these views and just hear my father mentioning the divine place we were to visit in the Himalayas.

With the excitement of the visit, I slept making my personal plans.

However I woke up suddenly out of my sleep following a bad dream. As always my father recited a nice mythological story to get me back to sleep. This time the story was about *Devi Trikuta* who was promised by Lord Ram that in the next Vishnu re-incarnation, when he takes birth he would marry her. He said that she still resides in *Himalay* waiting for the promise to be fulfilled.

I would often become one of the supporting characters of all the stories that my father narrated. If my father was not around me, I would re-iterate *shree ram* hundred times, not knowing what that number actually meant, but I knew that it had to be a very big number which doesn't stop until I sleep.

Next morning we were all ready to start the trip. My mother looked nice in this new red *saree*. She now approached me to do some clean up. I was dressed in this new white *kurta*. She finally added a black *kaajal teeka* on my forehead.
I can still feel her fingers on my eyelids. Though the procedure brought tears but her touch felt nice. She would then not forget to say that may God protect me from all the evil, especially the witches. She would then smile with her face flashing the feeling of being contented owing to her selfless efforts to protect us.

How did we start with the trip? I don't recollect, but yes I do have that vague collection of tired feet, beautiful hills all around, cold breeze, serene atmosphere.
Yes there was that clean but very cold water passing from just under my feet…
I managed to walk through that low lying cave. I could see my feet through it. How was I still walking? The feet should have gone numb.

Also, there was this crowd of believers running here and there. But I wondered why was everybody shouting so hard? As far as I could recall, that might be the first question I raised against the procedures laid down to show faith. Then I myself developed an argument which justified the distance of Goddess above the hill to be a reason for the shout. They were mainly focusing towards some special gate, behind which rested something or someone very important.

I was very surprised to see the Goddess still, she wasn't moving, blinking. I had envisaged her to be as reactive as my mother, but she was quiet and was placed like an idol. I too had a glimpse of the idols, they were beautifully dressed. I also have a sharp image of that small flame lit in the earthen lamp, placed just in front of the idols, which was generating a soothing glow to the faces of those idols.

"zor se bolo, jai maata di" was again the shout from the mob, everybody either repeated that sentence or followed the person shouting that slogan. I did not know why but I felt happy being a part of the devoted troop and that I was contributing to their synchronous shout through my murmur.

I wish my brain had accumulated some more snapshots of J&K. I am not sure if my brain had fully developed then, but whatever mass was inside my skull did store the feelings that are capable of giving me chilling sensations and are powerful enough to close my eyes.

CHAPTER 2

Crack In The shell

My father was transferred to New Delhi where I was enrolled officially to a school. Since the beginning I was not a very diligent or bright student, but I did understand what I was studying.

We stayed in a place called Palam which was relatively far from my school in R.K. Puram and thus the bus journey helped me connect to the city.
The bus used to drop us near a subway and from there, my brother and I had to walk for around 10 minutes to reach our quarter.

I heard my mother talking about some distant relative who had passed away at the age of hundred and twenty one. I am not sure if he even had a birth certificate, but the whole village knew he had done enough good for the village and had participated in the independence struggle against the British.

So this great grand old man had died and my family had got this rare black piece of *naada* for me. This is a thread tied across one's waist to keep away evil and negativity. As per the elders in our society, the person wearing this *naada* gets a share of that longevity and maybe some luck too?

My mother is a very caring lady and she double protected me by bringing few ashes and charcoal paste from a *baba* who sat just outside *Nizamuddin* mausoleum. Now I had a *naada* with a *taweez*!.

I was back from school and was dropped by the conductor at the same very spot where I got down daily. Today I did not see Mummy around. I had to walk back to the home alone. That was roughly a kilometre. While I was walking from the bus-stop to our quarters, there was this lady wearing dusky clothes and not very clean. Her hair strands had stuck together to form a thick brown muddy tress. She must be much older than my grandparents. She was leaning forward, maybe due to some problem in her waist or vertebrate. She started looking at me and slowly she started to follow me. She was now walking fast and parallel to me. She was still five to six yards away and her breath was loud just like her laugh.
I knew from some inner voice that she is what may resemble as a witch. The more she stared at me the more I was frightened. I closed my eyes and was now walking much faster than her. Closing my eyes reminded me of that *taweez* inside my *naada*. I turned to my right to see her not very far from me, she was opening her mouth to chew something... I couldn't recall what was she eating. I finally took the *taweez* out and flashed it towards her face. It worked!

Maybe the lady somehow understood I was nuts, so she moved ahead her way. Or was it some fear in her for this black thread? I had that feeling of victory and jubilation. I then narrated my bravery to the family to become a laughing stock for everyone. My mother may have also laughed at me, but she was happy that I had applied my minds to use some secret weapon that was given to me by her. She hugged me to celebrate my courage and was sorry for not being present at the bus-stop.

I was a being trained with all *'good'* things that every young Brahmin boy gets during early days. Daily we used to have evening prayers at home. I still remember the fumes of incense sticks and various small and large idols arranged properly in a corner of the room. This was kind of work around for a temple, I should say.

I used to feel good seeing these people who have been moulded into idols, and were given so much respect due to the fact that they are invisible but are potent enough to drive our lives... moreover they have been empowered to keep all bad away from us. I was fond of these godly idols.

Now we were planning to visit a very holy place called *Haridwar* close to Delhi.

This is on the banks of river *Ganga*. Its holy water has served the Indian subcontinent for millions of years. It has also helped flourish vegetation and some of the biggest cities under its huge network of rivers.

I have half memory of how my father narrated me the story wherein mother *Ganga* is pouring down from lord *Shiv's* tress and that flow, according to him, never stops. I wondered how the water ever went back to the sky or the clouds. I read about the water cycle much later to clarify the doubt, but had been charmed by the capability of lord *Shiv* to hold all the water so easily over his head.

One very strong image of Haridwar also resides in my brain from a very popular Hindu belief which again was recited to me by papa. He said that few drops of *Amrit*, the divine *nectar* fell from the pot while Jayant, the son of lord *Indra* travelled over some great cities of that time; Haridwar, Nasik, Prayag and Banaras. My father told me this but I forgot why the fight was, how high the drop fell from, was it a big drop when it slopped over the edge of that container? Also I wondered if the single drop split itself into multiple small drops while it covered the long distance... did wind help it to travel such widely distant cities.

Whatever happened, my father says that very thing made the whole city very pious, and the pilgrims visiting this place equally gained from a part of that tiny sacrosanct drop. Thanks to papa for actually imbibing in me some sense of mythology, else I could never have related to this place and forgotten that visit just like numerous other trips I had done in my life.

Starting a trip is referred in most parts of north India as *jatra*. For many Hindus it's just *Shri Ganeshaya namah* which would serve the purpose of initiating a good journey, but not at my place.

We were not allowed to ask directly where we were going. That question was considered as omen and often would need some serious prayers by mummy to avert the negativity caused by the query.

My mother would be ready with curd; sugar to make sure the start is good.

Even if the curd was sour or putrid, we had to gulp it in one shot and I would be under the mental pressure that if I don't have this then it will cause something very bad for my family... I never understood that something. I loved my family, my parents and for the safety of everybody, the superstition lived long in me.

Next was the superstition that no utensil while leaving should be empty as an empty utensil represents bad fortune hence it was filled with water. Elders would spend half an hour filling all the vacant utensils, before we could actually start the journey.

The best of all was the belief that seeing the teeth of a washer man was the best precaution one can do before starting the journey. My father was in Army and we lived in well-organized quarters where we don't see stalls or laundry shops. I being the youngest kid was forced to go to an army washer man, *Havildar* L.K. Jha's house. He lived around 200 meters away near Army wet canteen.

I would just say hello to him so that he opens his mouth to reply with a smile, if not then I would somehow break that schedule he was busy in, by my jokes or some news update until I had the view of his teeth.

That may sound funny but I did continue that for long time.

We started the journey in this hot summer using a matador van that looked like a chameleon. It was painted dark green and its wipers looked like its eyes. Every one loaded inside with clutched spacing for knees and head touching the ceilings of the van but we had to complete the journey with the greater cause of mental peace by visiting religious places. Hence we had no silly reason to complain.

"What is this place called, papa?" I asked
"Darya Ganj"
"I have heard this place or maybe seen it on TV" I added
"Where, what? He wondered how I knew this.
"*Doordarshan*... they show pictures of kids and some ladies too from here. Mummy says they are lost and police here helps the families by finding the lost people"

He pressed his lips, maybe to appreciate my memory.
The itinerary had one important stop; *Shri Shiv Mandir* at *Dilli* Gate, *Bangla sahib* before finally stopping at *Har ki pauri*.

"We will see lord *Shiv*" My father said and talked about this temple's recent blessings on few people by which the devotees had made good money and some had had miraculous health benefits.

I liked lord *Shiv's* idol a lot, its colour, its stature and the reptiles around his body.

"My teacher calls him lord *Shiva*" I said pronouncing the name of lord with extra "a" in the end.

"She may be right from her point of view but I have never and will not be referring Shiv as Shiva as that I feel is misleading" I did not understand much of what he said. I was staring his face for more explanation. He continued further to add "...and I have never understood why our English literature refers all Hindu deity names suffixed with an 'a'."

In the school, I had just started learning alphabets and their pronunciations. I could understand a bit of what he was saying. Then he started talking to himself. I did inherit that quality from him.

"Is it wrong to call lord Shiv as Shiva or lord Ram as Rama, we see in books?" I asked

"No, not wrong. But yes this may be per the convenience of the foreigners. But then, we also don't call John as Johna or Smith as Smitha. Right?"

Who were John and smith? I did not know them, had never read or heard about them in any of the stories. But he explained that we should call that idol as lord Shiv and not Shiva.

So we reached this ancient temple and as always my task was imitating the elders. The reason was simple or maybe I was searching for a reason to justify my acts, without there being a solid reason of what I was doing. Maybe there was no reason at all? My maturity or urge to question would be overridden by the fact that parents are supposed to be unquestionably super correct always!

Most of the idols looked same as what we see in other temples, but I came across a unique idol that day. It was dark coloured statue resembling lord Shiv, who was holding a bottle in his hand. This looked like the bottle which my father often sits with during the evening snacks. My mother tried to resent that act of drinking. I would often see her throwing away the bottles secretly in the garbage. Papa referred that bottle as Whisky and sometimes as Rum.

My query to myself was why this fusion of modern bottle of whisky with ancient saucer full of poison. May be people like to see new things in the idols. My father says this is *Kaliyug* and people have gone bad, very bad.

May be they have transformed the idol or want to see God in some new avatar more understandable by them. Was that lord a different version of lord Shiv who asks people to drink the new age whiskey? I did not ask that seeing the fear and some anger that was developing on my mother's face. She was trying to take us away from that idol as fast as possible.

I was in the assimilation stage of my life and had no stand of my own. I had the primary duty of observing the events around without judging those events.

In Shiv temples, few things that I always noticed was a black or blue coloured statue of lord Shiv, a cobra in a *kundali* around his neck, a crescent of moon and a fountain of river Ganga flowing out of the long tresses of hair. Two other important things which I could always spot in Shiv temples were the *Shivling* and a *nandi* bull.

That small pillar like structure was referred by all as a Shivling. I did not know what it meant.

"Is that some raw material used to build the idol of lord Shiv?" I asked my father.

"How? I mean what makes you ask that question" My father wasn't comfortable talking about it. He was fumbling while replying to my small query. I then continued

"It's looking exactly like the clay center that we build using pottery wheel" I was excited to see that solid stone, the one that we were given in school would always be soft and wet clay.

"You are correct in one sense, that center is the energy which is helping this whole world grow... and be fertile" I looked around to see if somebody is there who would be spinning it on a wheel, but people moved ahead hence I had a limited time to dig more about it. While I walked ahead I gave it one more look and then a new idea came to my mind.

"Papa" I ran close to him to hold his fingers

"Yes Om"

"Could that Shivling be the hump of that bull, see there" I showed him the *nandi* bull idol.

"So we just see the hump... where is the bull buddy" He asked controlling his laughter.

"The priest of this temple is busy right now, he would soon build the bull with the hard clay he has. Next time we come here we would see it full" My father laughed at my imaginative story.

After we were done paying respect to all the idols, we came back to our van.

The journey was boring me now so I closed my eyes and laid my head on my mother's lap. I covered my face with her new printed *saree*. Nothing is as soothing as mother's lap and bonus if her *pallu* can be used as a pullover. Though I was not talking to her, but this feeling from her to me had an unheard language for sure. She is so soft and caring; a single stroke of her hand on my forehead was enough to send me to a different world.

I could now see myself in the valley surrounded by huge snow covered and lush green peaks on both sides and my feet slipping over shallow snow cover over green deodar leaves.

I was seeing a huge figure wearing tiger skin and covered with ashes and his fragrance gave a mixed smell of ashes and coconut. I suddenly started approaching the hazy figure but was blocked by a white calf having beautiful black eyes and equally dark eyebrows.

The calf wanted to talk to me but when I saw the tail of the calf, I could see no hair at the end tip of the tail which was weird.

I tried holding the tail and the hump of the calf but it was so soft that my hand just slipped and had no grip over any thing that I was seeing.

The calf then vanished from my eyes and now I could see a figure resembling Shiv, smiling at me.

Lord Shiv... but I was not able to open my mouth to even say anything or ask any question to him, though I had many queries juggling inside.

"Om get up *beta*." My mother had applied coconut oil and its aroma left an impression enough to transcend into my dreams through my sleep.

I sat back and noticed people dressed more traditional and their Hindi sounded closer to *khadi-boli*. Normally we talked in Hindi at home, in English while in some party. This language was what my family used to interact with people coming from our village.

"We have almost reached Haridwar." Hearing papa I rubbed my eyes and stood straight.

"What does that mean papa?" I asked about the name of this place.

"It means the entrance to God's abode" He wanted to be lucid in his explanation so he continued...

"*Dwar* here refers to the entrance to *Badrinath*, where lord Vishnu resides in a divine cove called *vaikunth*" He looked at what I understood and got no response. I did understand that it was some gate.

"This place for has two important motives; first to visit the holy river *Ganga* for a dip." Papa tried to explain the two important reasons why we were there.

"We will be bathing in the river... Is it very deep?" I asked with full excitement.

"Nah, don't worry. That dip will help us clean away with all our sins, which we may have committed knowingly or unknowingly"

My mother then added "Mother Ganga helps the pilgrims to be exonerated... She is very warm and all the water around the world comes from her."

That again was fascinating to hear.

"All the water in this world? I mean the rain drops, the ponds, the well, and the lakes... all of them?" I asked and my mummy closed her small eyes and replied by nodding her head.

"Second reason is a very important practice where our great grandfathers would come and get their family tree documented here" Papa continued.

"We will write all the names. Why?" I asked.

"So that in future if someone from our family wants to enquire about his origin then these documents would give a clue" That was again sounding like a great job.

"My name also... and Tipu's name?" I asked about our pet dog's record which was replied negative as he was not a human. I felt sorry for our dog. Poor guy would not be able to clean his sins and may not even know who his parents or grandparents were.

I realized that we had now reached the bank of the holy river. Without thinking for a second, Papa just jumped in the water and called out my name to join him. I was shivering due to my fear of bath, not due to the fear of fast running water current.

He closed his eyes and took a long dip, finally coming out to loudly shout some hymn, uttered a hymn. I think I had heard it often from his mouth. As per mummy, the hymn was requesting the gods to forgive the whole family tree... he kept repeating it loud. I was not sure if God was giving him some sort of energy to stay for long in this cold water:

idamapahh pra vahata yat kimm cha duritamm mayi
yadvahamabhidudroha yadva shepa utanrtam

None of us knew what it literally meant. I went quiet during the prayers with a fear of offending my family or some God who is constantly watching my acts, and is waiting for that single moment when I commit a mistake and he punishes me through some magic. I was thus keeping quiet thinking the hymn to be something really serious. While my father kept reciting, I tried sometimes to repeat those words but they were too difficult for me to listen and bring out.

With much repulsion, I too had a dip in the water with other members. As I did not know how to swim, so I held tightly the iron chain, one end of which was tied to the shore. The cement stairs at shore were slippery and the water was chilling cold. I did not lose the grip of that chain with my right hand and with my left hand tried to close my ears. I managed to come out happily from the water and stood in attention position for few seconds, then ran to my mother to change my dress quickly.
The breeze was flowing from all directions touching my skin and making me shiver. However the excitement of cleaning all my sins was even more thrilling.
I did not know what my father meant by 'sin', but I had my own definition of sin like any other kid of my age would have had. Not telling the truth, arguing with elders, stealing health drinks from the kitchen were all candidates of crime for me.

My mother wiped water from my hair and body with papa's towel and changed my dress. She then held my chin and combed side partition as always. I watched my sister and elder brother going for that dip and felt happier about the reason that now my entire family is all clean. No crime records whatsoever and this feeling of being pious and clean could not be expressed by me, so a tear rolled down expressing that happiness. I was seeing that some pilgrims were just inserting

15

their feet inside the water and coming up to ask for forgiveness. I wondered how they managed to clean their wrongdoings by such a partial, half hearted effort.

"Come *jajman,* let us offer the evening prayers" was a stern and baritone voice from a young priest who had appeared in front of us from nowhere. Was he following us all this time, and waiting for us to just complete this informal way of prayers. He had no expressions on his face, yet he had a persuasive body language, maybe he was assigned by God to take us to the specific portion of river bank where he held the prayers.
"Who is he?" I asked my father
"He is a *panda*" He replied. I had seen the pictures of panda to be a cute black and white bear like animals and this guy was a human. I was confused and my father looked busy in some discussion with my family. I did not disturb him but kept looking at that man's face.

My father thought for few seconds of how he should be denying the offer. The offer to me was more like a command, than a request.

"*Panditji!*" my father said, while moving closer to that priest. "Let me first congratulate you that we are also *Brahmin*" My father ran his palm showing us. I felt happy to see that hand pointing towards me as well, though for a fraction of seconds, I enjoyed my special status. While he said this, I could see the feeling of pride and happiness coming on my father's face. Was this an attempt to bridge that anonymous gap between the *panda* and us?

The *panda* smiled asked "Which *gotra?*"
Maybe he wanted to know what exact class of lineage of Brahmins we fall into. I did not know how that would have helped him.
"*Bhardwaj*" said my father.

The panda then just passed a sarcastic smile. Not sure why?

"Come let us see the *bahi*".
"What is that papa?"
"*Bahi* is supposed to be the family lineage documents." He replied and I could recall that this was the second reason papa wanted us to visit this place.

We followed him till an old monument behind the *Krishn* temple. This religious office looked like an abandoned cave of bats. It smelled very unpleasant and had minimal light. Maybe the idea was to keep away artificial lights or electrification, which could damage such important documents. The *panda* asked us all the details of village, district, my grandfather's and great grandfather's name and their old addresses.
He spent hours searching the documents, while we sat on few bricks and were waiting for him to surprise us. Finally he came running towards us; he had few papers in his hand.
"Naini, Allahabad? Hrishikesh Bhardwaj son of Indreshwar Bhawdwaj, son of..."
"No *panditji*" My father stopped him.
That wasn't exact address of my grandfather. The panda tried convincing that the found records were ours. However despite my grandparents' name being correct, my father was sure that my grandfather never lived in Allahabad. My father thanked the priest and felt sorry that we couldn't get any details of our great grandfathers. He too looked disappointed. Had he found some record, we would have felt so happy to append further the details of the family tree in the same document. With this, we had no other choice than to leave.

"*Jatha Shakti tatha bhakti*" We heard him shouting from behind. He rubbed his index finger with his thumb, asking for his fees. His statement in the local language was an indirect order asking my father to pay as per my father's capability. My father gave him fifty one rupees and suddenly I could see some anger in the *panda's* eyes. He asked for at least 100 rupees more. Now was the time for my mother to jump in and show the exquisite bargaining capabilities she had.

My mother gave several unrelated logic bundled with couple of old sayings in the same dialect which I don't remember. She finally gave the *panda* ten rupees more and took leave from the search team inside the cave. The panda stood still, he did not react to this. We walked till the exit gate.

"Stop *jajman!*" came a little loud voice from behind.
"I should be paid my dues and if you don't then I would give a *shrap* bound by the holy water of mother Ganga, that curse could not be washed off by any priest."

Why was everybody looking worried, all of a sudden? What logic did that sentence make? Why did he warn us to curse or spell some negative tantr on our family?
My father knew the importance of what would happen if a Brahmin gives a curse, so he replied to get more out of this *panda.*
"*Kshama panditji,* but we have paid you sufficient and would have paid you more had you shown us our lineage books" He was averting any altercation.

My mother asked us to ignore this *panda* and was now calling him a fraud. May be she was correct and would have understood the priest's tactic to get an unprofessional increment.

"One Brahmin's curse cannot be put on another Brahmin and hence we are safe. Come let us go" She gave some weird logic that the curse of the panda would not work on us... I did not know how true that was, but I had faith in my mother's sayings.

The panda knew that his attempt to frighten us had not worked. He walked towards us and took an exit while chanting some *mantr*, he ran towards a group that had just started with the holy dip. There was no deficiency of clients for this guy.

It was already sunset and we thought of heading back to Delhi. Mummy too looked tired so she suggested us to have the dinner somewhere midway. The return journey wasn't very troubling and the breeze after sunset acted as a catalyst to help my brain signal to my body for hibernation.
I was enjoying this wind, cool enough and all coming to me after touching mother Ganga. There was some warm breeze as well; maybe it was the wind that touched hot metal parts of the van.

I took my palm outside the window and tried to figure out what if the Panda was really a magician or what if he had some wicked power in his mantr. What if he could cast a spell to force all the traffic to suddenly block our way and bang a large truck with our van?

"We've reached home!" I heard my mother again and could see her looking at me with all that love and calmness that the dream just gave me. Had I stared at her beautiful eyes for some more time, I could build that beautiful world over and over again. But where was I? Before I could slowly bring myself back from the dream, Tipu ran to me and started licking my cheeks. He would have missed us the complete day. I looked at his bowl and he had not had his food. Tipu was a short and plump Labrador. His eyes were wet at the corners and I cursed myself for leaving him alone. I lifted him up in my arms and took the bowl in my left hand. I took him for a walk, but he was enjoying the free ride and I was the one walking around the quarters. He was just five months old and had the same level of love for the family as I did.

I felt years passing by adding inches to my height. Once in a while distant relatives paid short visits to our place. We had no permanent place to live, may be that was one reason which kept them away from us. However whenever they came, they often looked at me with a surprise to see the speed of my growth. I was now gaining more sense to ask questions… but the irony was that I did not understand the answers most of the times.

Sunday, and we all sat together this day to watch TV, but this box mostly showed some programs on brave soldiers and epics of ancient India. Papa called them the *itihaas,* the rich history of ancient Indian civilization. It was much later that I actually understood the stories to be well directed excerpts from Hindu mythology.

"Papa why does lord Shankar wear that tiger skin? Did he kill that tiger?" I asked showing him the bright yellow black tiger skin on TV, on which the lord was sitting.
"I don't know the exact reason son… but I do know that he was very brave and that skin may be just one small token to hint his bravery?" My father tried to convince me.
"Brave! So does it mean he had killed that tiger and then plucked its skin to wear that dress?" I asked again
"Again… I apologise Om, but I am sure he would not have killed that tiger just for his skin. There must be some deep reason to it" He did not want to give up that easily so he added "But also understand that he stays in a place full of snow mountains, *Kailash*?" My father reminded me of lord Shankar's abode, which is amidst Himalay.
"Yes… I have seen that place on TV. It's very beautiful"
"That tiger skin not only shows his valour, but also keeps him warm"

I did not get any satisfactory answer so I thought I would better watch TV. May be some day they would show me the reason why lord Shiv wears a tiger skin?

It was that phase of life which taught me waiting for answers. I was keenly observing everything around me, developing questions inside and then waiting for elders to hear me.

"*Pranam Chachaji*" my father was greeted by a guy whom I saw for the first time. He had lost almost all his hair but a thin tuft of hair was hanging down, right from the center of his head. He also had a badly trimmed moustache which was sometimes running inside his upper lip. He was looking at me after every few minutes and I couldn't understand why he was doing that. While talking to my parents, he would sometimes go slow and then suddenly become agitated shouting slogans or some *mantr*. I started getting a bad feeling from this guy.

"Om *beta*, please touch the feet of Kamal *bhaiya*" My mother asked.
It looked to me that my family was showing respect to this guy unnecessarily. I still obliged to my mother's request and went close to touch his feet. I saw his feet, and they were too clumsy. He was wearing a rubber slipper and his toe nails were long enough to come out of that slipper area. The color of his feet was brown owing to the layer of mud over it, or maybe he hadn't washed his feet in years. I got up after touching his feet and then observed his dhoti. Has this guy come directly from village to search for a job? My father often called people from his village and gave them too much of respect. I did like some of them but this guy seemed bad to me. His dhoti had yellow blots and interweaved patches. It smelled awful, so bad that I stopped breathing in. I felt like running back.

"*Ayushman bhav!*" This guy gave me his blessings by rubbing my head, but that spoiled my nicely combed hairstyle. My mother had done that style after so much of effort. I tried to fix my hairstyle and moved back. He kept his bag on the chair and went to wash his feet and may be his body too. He badly needed that shower.

"Who is this guy papa?" I asked in a very low voice, going close to his ears.
"Om, he is Kamal Jyoti Pandey. You must be meeting him for the first time." He looked up to recollect something and continued... "Yes, he is here for the first time, right?" My father then looked at my mummy and she nodded her head to say yes.

"He is the senior most leader of *Hindu Raksha Prachar Sena*"
"I've never heard of it. Is that also some kind of army?" I asked hearing the last word *'Sena'* which meant an army. I had seen *Ramayan* on TV and knew very well what Sena meant.
"It's a body to protect the Hindus and propagate this faith to all, across the world." My father replied.
"Propagate means?" I asked.
"To let others know... I mean help them know"
"But you always say this world is created by lord *Brahm* and how is it that others in this world don't know about such a big God?" I was surprised.
"Very nice questions Om *beta*..." That filthy guy now came close to me wiping the water over his moustache. He then looked at papa and held my shoulders tight and in a way erected my body to look straight into his eyes. I was afraid now.

"Not everybody has the *Brahm gyan*... people have been brainwashed. We need to forward this deep knowledge and secret of Hinduism and *sanatan* to the world outside" He said. I kept quiet for some time as I did not understand the meanings of some of the words he used.
"We at HRPS go places, we travel a lot. We see the world and then realize how ignorant the world is!" He looked down and was sad at something now.

"What is it that they don't know? And the people of 'other' world... who are they? Where do they live?" I asked

"Outside *Bharat maata*... they live far, but not very far. Once they know it, they will come back to where it all started" He was feeling good about something now. He looked hopeful. He now stood straight. But I was happy he was far from me.

"Where does *Bharat maata* start and where does it end?" I asked, I considering it to be something like Delhi.
"This is the problem *Chachaji*... they don't teach about *Bharat maata* anymore? They teach about India, they teach about planets, they teach about aeroplanes, they teach *twinkle twinkle*, they teach *cobbler cobbler*... but..." He turned around and went close to the window. He held the iron bar of the window and continued..."They don't teach about our mother for whom we have been shedding blood since ages"
I was now getting some of the things he said. I had learnt the rhymes he just quoted, but still did not know what had that go to do with his mission.

"It's our motherland Son... we live here, we grow our paddy here, we build our houses here, and we drink the water of rivers flowing through the heart of our mother"
He did not make sense again; maybe I was too small to get to his matured talk.

"You mean it's bigger than Delhi?" I asked to bring him to my level.
"Yes Delhi is part of it, we have similar places where we stand tall and pay respect to our motherland. We have Kanpur, we have Kashmir, we have Calcutta, we have Bombay... so many places and so many lives together constitute this place... *Bharat*" He lowered his voice, but had some anguish burning inside.

Okay, now I was somewhat able to understand. But the queries in my mind were multiplying many folds now.

"*Bharat maata…*" I said

"Yes Om… correct… *Bharat maata…* our mother" He was happy at my slogan.

"Then what is *Dharti maa*?" I asked

"This soil spread from one country like Bharat till other countries like America, the air, the water, the trees, the mountains they all constitute the *Dharti maa…*" He said

"So *Dharti maa* is bigger than *Bharat maata*?" I had a simple question

"Yes… but we should give more respect to the place where we are born, we are earning, we are living and finally we will die" He was quick.

"Dharti maa also has the ignorant people whom you just talked about? I mean those who don't understand the correct *gyan*… what did you say?" I was forgetting his word.

"Brahm *Gyan*" He said

"Yes, so why is it that not everybody knows it the way you know it?" I asked

"Did you see his attitude? He will be a big revolutionary one day." He looked at my father and picked me up in his arms. He smelt bad and I wanted to get down so I started moving my arms and shoulders. He let me down after some time.

"I know the power of a Hindu, I know the power of lord *Brahm, Vishnu and Mahesh…* I want the world also to know it. They should leave their ignorance and come to us"

"How many people are there *bhaiya*?" I asked about the count of people whom he wanted to change. I assumed that he must have a big target.

"Several *crore*... spread all over, they kill and eat mother cow, they produce several children, they propagate that obscene culture and nudity... aah!" He lowered his head.

He did not answer or may be answered but I did not understand what he wanted to say. His eyes showed that anger. Sometimes they went red and bulged out and he would search for things to hold and hold really tight. I was not happy to see this guest.

He took bath and had the lunch with us. He then went to take some rest and I looked at my father to tell me more about this fellow. My father was already busy in his work so I ignored and went to the balcony to see kids playing in the park below.

Suddenly something hit my brain, that curiosity maybe? I checked the bedrooms and saw everybody sleeping. I then walked fast to the drawing room and found that his bag was still there, on the chair. That fear in me asked to check again, I quickly ran my eyes on all corners but found no one. I then slowly started opening the bag.

There were some papers and several magazines which had very small fonts. I could not read them, so small were the fonts. I was able to recognize that it was in Hindi like script but did not know what was written on it.

While I was turning the pages of the book to see if it had some pictures which would help me understand who this guy actually was. The bag suddenly slipped from the chair and fell on the ground making a noise, not very loud, but high enough to break the sleep. I looked again but no one was disturbed by the noise. From the snores that were reaching my ears, I was assured that somebody was fast asleep, not sure if that somebody was my father or Kamal bhaiya.

I slowly put my hand inside the bag. I felt some object. It was heavy and rough. I touched the corners and took out the thing.

It felt like a stone, may be some utensil gone rough, used to prepare *chutney*?

It was heavy but I managed to pull it out and started seeing it all over. It was white but most of it had a thin cover of blackish grey smoke or maybe that was years of dust that had layered up on one surface of the stone. It had fine lines with curve, it may be some brick. I looked around the kitchen and saw a ventilator brick similar to this. I thought this may be some gift for us. But how can someone give an old item as a gift. Mummy says when we think of gifts, we should always buy a fresh item.

This brick looked old and was giving an impression of a used, stone owing to its weathered corners. On a careful look I was also seeing a broken edge and I thought it got broke after its fall from the chair so I started searching the corner piece under the chair.

"Keep it inside" I turned back and was shocked to see Kamal *bhaiya* behind me.
He then snatched the brick from my hand and kept it inside the bag and adjusted the other papers well. He went close to the TV and there was a hook which was out of my reach. He hung it over there.

"Do not tell anybody..." He fingered his lips and continued...
"We broke that structure, it should have been destroyed long back" He was talking to himself now.
"The root of every problem is this brick.... bricks like this used to construct places like mosque and churches..." I couldn't understand what he said. But I was too afraid to ask him, so I kept quiet.
"Oh lord Ram, I am sorry that such people have taken birth, but we are your true followers and we would give our lives to protect *Ayodhya*" He said.

I had heard this name... yes it was in Ramayan, lord Ram's kingdom. Was this guy from that place? If so, then how come I had never seen him on TV. Moreover he looked too bad to be a part of that royal army of lord *Hanuman*.

"Have you seen lord Hanuman, is he also in your army?" I asked and this took away some of my fear.
"Yes *beta*... you are correct, he is always with us to fight against the demons... these Muslims, the rich Christians.... they are demons.... with the blessings of lord Hanuman and the power vested in us by our sages, we will defeat all of them"

He was now regaining his anger. Why is he always annoyed at something or the other? I had no answers to his behaviour.

I stepped back and was afraid to ask further. He kept looking at me and using his fingers movement did warn me to not tell anybody.
I did not.
May be I forgot to tell anyone. May be I was afraid to tell about that brick to papa as the 'demons' would attack us. I have not seen the demons so far but I could imagine their pictures.

Days passed and I was having a normal life now, without any guest. There were festivals every now and then. In those days, I often slept early after assisting my mother in her daily set of *pooja*.

"Get up... get up baby" This was my mother and it felt so good to get up hearing her voice over and over again. Many a times I would have lost the sleep and would be fully awake but would want her to come to me and wake me up with her sweet voice.
"You should not sleep this late... get up my cute *langoora*" She called me *langoora*?
Oh! Now I got it.

That part of the year was the *Kanya Poojan* time. I would join with several girls from the neighbourhood and visit few places where *Durga pooja* was celebrated. The girls would mostly be of my age and very few would be taller than I. But it was good to be a boy in the gang. Every year only younger girls were allowed to be a part of the ritual. I did not understand what age had to do with worship but I was happy that I was leading the gang. Often the group of girls would change but I would always be the boy in the pooja. I was also given good food and nice *prasad*. I would sometimes go to neighbouring regions with girls without informing my parents, but would bring some prasad to bribe them. I liked the fruits that were served those days.

"Mummy, why do you call me *langoora* only during the *pooja*?" I asked her.
"*Beta*, *langoora* is the guard, the protector who always stays with Durga maata. Just as you stay with us and protect our family" I was happy to hear brave notes about me, but little did I know that this was again reflecting some hypocrisy.

The Goddess who is considered to be the strongest form of power needed a *langoora* to guard her? I did not understand it but mummy then continued again.
"One day *Maata Vaishnavi* was in her cave and there was a surprise attack from *Bhairavnath*"
She made that expression to frighten me and she did succeed in it.
"Then?" I asked with my mouth wide open.
"Then what? The brave *langoora* stood in front of the gate and fought a great battle..." I was now thinking myself at the gate of some cave in which my family lives. However I was not able to imagine how *Bhairavnath* would have looked, but he did sound dangerous.
"Just like our batman... he is always there to protect us" I said and my mother smiled at my stupid analogy.

We were to leave Delhi now, years passed and Tipu was also a grown up adult. We decided to leave him with the new owners who were allotted our flat. Tipu had so much of attachment with this home that it would have been lethal to give him that pain. It was my father's decision; I was recommending him to hide Tipu in a suite case to our next transfer location. No one agreed and with a heavy heart I hugged him for the last time. His eyes were so beautiful; looking at them brought tears in my eyes too.

Thanks Delhi for brightening up some memories, making them sharper to recall. Thanks for letting the bird come out of that hard shell... But as I was moving ahead in life I turned back to see one half of the shell facing me, positioned as a cosy bed. Was it calling me? I did not want to go back... at least for now.

CHAPTER 3

Hatched In God's Own Country

My tryst with my inner self started here in Kannur, Kerala. During early 90s my father was transferred to this beautiful place in North Kerala, called 'Cannanore' by the Army. Kannur was a place surrounded by sea from all sides, some low lying shores and some sharp cliffs with sudden acclivity. Fortunately my father's office, our quarters and my school all were in the radius of around 5 kms. From that height, It was fun to see the sun rise from one horizon of sea corner and finally set from the other angle with its crimson shade spreading all over the aqua green surface.

"Did you take bath?" My mother asked
I said no and as usual with much reluctance went towards the bathroom to finish up that difficult task. I would often throw water around the bathroom walls and came back with wet hair so that she can dress me up quickly. This time she wanted me to get ready for something new, some work for me.

"Take this and sit on the small stool and recite it line by line." She then made a serious face and continued... "Do not stop or go out, even for loo... got it?"

My mother gave me a thin book on some Goddess. She had come to know about her importance very recently and had now started fasting formally for some important wishes she had.

"Who is she? She looks like *Lakshmi maata*" I said and she laughed hearing my silly question.

I had a reason to ask as all the pictures we had looked same. Sometimes even the pictures of lord Krishn, lord Ram, lord Shankar had the same face cut, same expressions. What changed were just the get up and color. Sometimes the background changed too with some new weapons.

I was also happy that my mother had given me the task which may improve my reading skills as I often got punished in the school for that.

"She is *Maa Santoshi*" She said and I was hearing this name for the first time. Literally it translated to a mother who helps satisfy all our needs.

"Om, she is the daughter of lord *Ganesh*" My father said. He has always known a lot about the relationship between various Gods and Goddesses.

For me this sentence complicated few things. I asked myself as to why are we worshipping the same God's family members, when worshipping the head of the family can solve the purpose? I was ignorant and I was referring here to the ultimate God Shiv.

"And...?" I asked

"Ok I will tell you but first tell me who the son of Lord Shankar is?" My father asked and my mother looked at him with some pride. She knew this was a great education being imparted to me.

"There are two. Lord Ganesh and lord *Kartikey*" That one was easy.

He smiled at the quick reply and then further asked "Who are the sons of lord Ganesh then?" I was confused; I did not know the family tree that long so I gave up.

"*Kshama and Labh.* Their names mean 'to forgive' and 'to gain' respectively" He said, but immediately asked another question. "Do you know the name of Lord Shankar's daughter then?"
"He had a daughter too?" I asked
"*Jyoti...* meaning light" I got the names, they were easy.
"Om I know you like the festival *raksha bandhan?*" He asked and he was very correct. That would be the day when my sister would tie a string on my fist to give me some spiritual power to protect her. She was older than me, but still she had a hope that I would protect her. I did not know how a small kid like me could protect a grown-up girl, but that's what is infested to all... the girl, however strong she is needs to be pushed down in the society to make her realize the need to protect her. Maybe I was wrong but I was suddenly not liking the reason behind that festival.

"Once Jyoti was tying the *rakhi* to lord Ganesh. Seeing that *Kshama* and *Labh* also felt like having a sister. Why?" Papa asked
"So that they also have someone to protect, some girl to tie that thread?" I answered but did not like the label of 'protection' dumped on sisters, however strong they were.

"Correct. Like we fulfil all your requests, lord Ganesh and his wives *Riddhi* and *Siddhi* also did a magic to bring in to this world a powerful Goddess, their daughter"

My father failed to explain what that magic was in detail, but he told me whatever he knew.
"Thus Maa Santoshi was born?" I was charmed.
"But Papa, why do we have so many Gods, so many sons, so many daughters all of them are again Gods, Goddesses?" I

asked after keeping quiet for a while. The reason why I asked this question was my bad memory. It was not very capable of remembering all these names and the respective powers and the details about their birth.

"Because we have several bad people in this world, demons... Gods stop them"
"But we never fold our hands and ask Gods to stop them, I always ask for sweets and I've heard mummy asking for peace to all, prosperity to all"
"You will know it when you grow up. God is needed all the time" He said and adjusted my seat to continue the *fast* for Santoshi maa.

"Have you seen her?" I gave my final shot.
"Yes, when I was young like you, there was a movie produced about her. In that movie I saw her for the first time. She did all amazing things to make us happy. The best part was that we all had to take out our slippers and sandals before entering the cinema hall" and my mother laughed at this recalling her movie trip with papa. I too smiled and continued reading the book.

"Place the gram and jaggery in the plate..." I asked mummy. The pre-requisite was clearly written on the book. "Oh! There is no jaggery..." My mother was in all shock as if the God is in her house and she can't offer the desired food to the God.
"Mummy can we place sugar here. That is also sweet no? Moreover it looks better and clean too" I tried to bring her out of panic.
"No, it's written we need to use jaggery and... oh my God now what...?" She started sweating and her forehead was shining wet now.

"Got it" was the call from my father. He had managed to quickly find it in the kitchen. Finally it was brought and kept in the plate. They closed their eyes and folded hands to apologize to the God for delay in the *prasad* material. This looked serious, so I was also under some fear now but I started reading the lines.

"There was an old lady who had seven sons. Six of them had a job while the seventh was jobless. The old lady used to prepare nice dishes and serve the six boys while the leftover was given to the idler."

I was feeling bad at this behaviour of the mother. My mother always gave me tasty food and never ill-treated me. I read the whole story and I had to pee, it was strong call from the nature. I controlled and after we all dispersed, I ran to the washroom and came out relaxing.

"Mummy does she not like any sour thing... like pickles, tamarind, lemon, oranges..." I asked my mother after finishing the story. They were all relaxing and watching TV now.

"Don't use such names on Friday's..." My mother said, she then continued and looked at my father.

"Why do you tell him to ask so much, look my mouth automatically developed the saliva hearing pickles and tamarind... this is a sin" She said and my father smiled and came to me. She went to the kitchen to spit the saliva.

"It's so good that you know so many sour names... but some days we should keep away from some good things too. It's not about the God liking a thing or not, it's about restricting as a pledge from few things. God demands abstinence" My father replied.

His words were now going all over my head and I went out and spat. I was developing that god-fear which had categorised the saliva in my mouth as a sin...

"But papa you say these things..." I did not name them but continued my query "... have vitamin C and nutrition too?"

"Yes Om, but like I said, we have pledged not to eat it, so on Fridays we will not take their names or eat them even in school... okay?" He got an assurance from me and I focused on the TV, but then again I went to him and asked.

"But you also say that God has created this world and everything in this world, the plants, the fruits, the flowers, the sea, the rain, the light, the fire... everything?"

"Yes"

"So why would God not like a thing which he had made for us to use it... we use it while preparing salad, or a juice. Right?" I asked

"No. A carpenter may prepare a lot of tables, chairs and some other furniture but he may not like all of them. Maybe he would not be comfortable sitting on a chair which is itching or rough." Saying this he tickled me and kept coming close and I laughed and he followed and we then ran out in the porch to play games.

"Listen..." My mother then called my father in the drawing room and instructed him in low voice that from next Friday onwards my father would recite the story and not me.

I felt outcaste. She felt I may unknowingly breach the pledge. I did not like that loss of trust on me. I wanted to read the whole story for months but I was so afraid that I stayed away from such sour fruits and vegetables and also asked my friends to not show it to me as I may tend to eat them. I never asked again why in the story maa Santoshi punished the lady and her family who had sour fruits. A God is always there to help us, to protect us, to guide us... this is what my father always taught me but his recent lectures had developed fear inside my heart for my actions and my questions.

Mahatma Gandhi said that human mind should be so open that it always accepts the good things about any new place but at the same time not lose the values that we have been carrying since long. This was in some funny ways obeyed by my Mother.

She has travelled a lot with my father by the virtue of being spouse of government personnel. However to all the places she went, she used to adapt the superstitions, Godly figures of that region. May be she compelled herself to start exercising new local superstitions. The possible reason could be the very fact that she did not want to miss any opportunity to make sure her loved ones stay healthy and prosperous.

In Kannur there was this God referred to as *"Muthappan"* having dedicated temple and religious saints. Few of our *Malayali* neighbours followed him religiously.

My mother having befriended those ladies, used to go to curiously ask about the miracles and stories associated with that God. The ladies used to visit a dedicated temple of this local deity every Friday. It was around 30 minutes drive from our place.

"Get ready fast, wear the new brown shorts and yellow full shirt" said my mother.
I hated shorts, but was forced to wear them. I longed to wear a full trouser but in my family that was considered only for the big boys. Also from an aunty who was from Bihar, my mother had picked up saying "full shirt" and "half shirt".
So I was ready that day wearing a 'full shirt' and a 'half pant' as she had started calling it.

With a gang of Malayalam speaking ladies, my mother and I somehow managed to reach this temple. I was a great devotee then, of almost any figure which was respected by my mother. I looked at the person who was meeting the followers one by one. We moved slowly in that open area and my legs had started to pain walking at that pace. I then had a look at the central character in that temple. I was shocked. He was a live person.

So *Muthappan* was actually a human with some yellow paste on his forehead and other make-up painted on his face. I had imagined him to be a static idol but it was good to see a human. I had never read about this God in books... who was he? That very moment I had several questions running in my brain.

This so called God had a very long queue of followers. Some were just seeing him and getting emotional. Some were touching him; his feet and then suddenly I saw one of them going flat on the floor. People ran to wake him up and sprinkled water on his face. Few well built guards lifted the devotee and took him somewhere inside.

"Why did he faint?" I asked my mother. I was wondering if that guy was ill.

"Did you touch his feet? He must have had some mystic experience and we should respect such souls" My mother wanted me to touch the body of that person. Yes she was right, there were people who came running to his body and I was wondering if they would lift and help him but saw everybody was touching him, taking some blessing and walking away. He was not in the sight now and the queue had rearranged itself to show that discipline to the God who may not like the disorder. People had come here with flowers, coconuts, incense sticks, money, sweets etc. But few had wrapped in wet leaves what smelt as dried fish. I was seeing fish as an offering for the first time, but this place was different and so could be its practice.

Finally it was our turn and we reached quite close to this God. He was very chubby. He must be of the same age as my father. He was blinking his eyes continually. I was not sure if that was a problem or some exclusive method adopted by this God to convey the problems of the pilgrims to some other God or higher command. Was this blink some miracle?

The procedure to make a wish was to speak it in his ears and my mother asked for some wish in Hindi, but I couldn't hear what she said. However the reply was what I can never forget. *"Muthappan ko yaad karo…"* He asked us to recall God Muthappan.

I thought we are in front of the God and the answer to our problems was just to recall this God?

He was talking full length to Malayalam speaking people, maybe due to his limited stock of Hindi words; the God chose to smartly reply short. I wasn't happy over the extensive efforts we had put to reach here and then ask him the solution to our problems. Maybe he had a limited jurisdiction and our problems could be better solved by the bigger Gods which we see on the Television?

Whatever happened, I still respect that person who was painted well to look like some divine figure. I was seeing people losing their distress and some gaining confidence to walk back smiling. He said something to them which made them feel happy. It was in the local language which I had not yet learnt. Like every other temple we were given *Prasad* which this time was boiled grams.

Once I went to the Army Canteen to buy monthly grocery items for our family with my mother and there I could see this beautiful white temple whose architecture was referring to some ancient heritage building with white marbles.

I asked my mother as to what was inside and she, being ignorant about any other religion lightly replied *"waha Sikhon ke bhagwan hain."* She described that temple to be a place where a 'different' God lived. I was curious to see how that new God looked.

Now my routine was very much fixed as I would get up early, and walk to the school which was just 5 minutes away from my place. After having the lunch with friends I would visit the same *Gurudwara*. I loved its architecture. Inside the Gurudwara I would gaze at the top of the dome. I would look all over the place. So what was preached there? Mummy had informed about some God of a different religion, however I struggled to see idols. I would keep quiet and collect the prasad, which normally would be sweet porridge prepared in *shuddh ghee.*

Until I was in Kerala I had never known anything about Sikhism or for that matter any other religion. I had slowly developed a great friendship with the religious teacher inside and he used to talk to me about the current system of education in schools. He also recited to me various anecdotes and brave stories of Several Gurus of Sikhism.

He was lean and tall. His beard was all white and his turban would be often orange or yellow in colour. He had a very soft voice and I would sometimes try to focus on the belt around his shoulder running down till his waist. It had a knife like weapon.
He mostly talked about Guru Gobind Singh, the tenth Guru of Sikhism. I did not understand all of his stories but the stories did sound brave.

I was also fascinated by his expressions and his voice when he talked about Gurus.
He would often laugh and smile at my silly questions about the miracles which I expected God to perform. He helped me discover a new faith without which the Indian diversity would be incomplete. He never talked about fasting or offering items to that temple to request for a wish. He was leading a happy life while obeying so different set of principles.

Babaji, as I called him, would come close to my ears and sometimes take help from me to walk around the *Guru Granth sahib,* the sacred book of the Sikh religion and what he referred as Guru. His stories never had a magic, but his voice did had that charm which signalled me something very special he possessed... what was that?

My favourite anecdote was when *babaji* recited to me the decree passed by Guru Gobind Singh which said that all human are equal.
"So everybody around, the cobbler, the washer man... everybody is equal?" I had asked him. I was silly but that was the most important lesson I had learnt from him.

"Guru Gobind Singh ordered us to shun division on the basis of caste, creed, color and..." He took a deep breath. I made him talk too much.
He continued... "Second thing is that the women in this world should share the same status as men"
The latter was even more powerful in the time when I would see many of my father's colleagues hitting their wives. I would hear the news of some young ladies traumatized after marriage. Life had taught me to consider women as nothing but second grade human being. While he was teaching me morals through stories from fifteenth century, I was reading similar efforts in my books. I was reading in my books about the hardships taken to bring drastic reforms in the Indian society.

One day I went close to babaji and wanted to know about why he called himself and the community as Sikh. I could never forget how he gave that smile and walked back to his closet slowly. His reply was "I don't know, but I am still searching for who I am..."
He was sometimes so difficult to understand, but his expressions would be often loud and clear. He then turned back and asked.
"I've never asked you your name..."
"Om" I replied

His eyelids opened a bit wide and I could see the eyes shining more with lubrication from some fluid may be. He just said one thing *"kirpa rahe waheguru di jee"* to bless me. He was a warm and very quiet person but I did not understand as to why was he so surprised and his eyes wet on hearing my name.

"Get ready everybody, the jeep has come" Papa said.
"But where are we going?"
"Om, today is *Vishu* and we would all go together to the market and the park"
Oh the festival *Vishu*. This was very famous in Kerala. I used to relate it to *Diwali* as that festival also had same enthusiasm around crackers, sweets and new clothes. That was the spirit of my family. We are ever ready to adapt to religious and social celebrations.

We were all dressed up nicely and we reached in the market and it was amazing to see many elephants lined up and ornate for the festival. We all roamed around in the fair and could see the joy spread in the air. In the park I went close to kids who had crackers. I walked long that day, pointing out differences between the elephants.
There were some ladies sitting on the footpath and were selling some local food.
"What is this *amma*?" I asked one of them.
"Mambazha pulissery" She replied and offered it to me in a small cup made of leaves. I enjoyed it and asked her how much did it cost.
"No no... *Prasad*.... no money" She smiled and opened her right palm to face me. She must be blessing me, I was puzzled why did she bless me. I did not even touch her feet? I instead had some food which she might have prepared with so much of effort.
I walked away from her but liked the *prasad*, it was tasty. I had now set a target of coming to that very point to meet *amma* and ask for the same *prasad*. *Vishu* was now a reason to wait.

Next day was Monday so usual routine began with my father bringing me the ironed school dress? I was polishing my black shoes and noticed my brother already dressed up. I was now under the pressure to get ready quick. My father had this style of combing my hair by holding my chin with his left hand tight enough that I don't move my head and with his right hand he created the side partition with just two strokes of comb and I was ready. He never wasted time like mummy, and the way he held my chin did give me some pain.

I was waiting for the lunch to get out of the school and visit Babaji. The lunch bell rang and I ran to the *Gurudwara*. I covered my head with the orange cloth and sat in the corner. I was waiting to see Babaji. I wasn't seeing any familiar face. It was high time now and I went inside the room attached to *Gurudwara* to search him. I saw few soldiers sitting there.

"Excuse me sir, do you know the Babaji who sits here, I used to see him every day... can't find him?" I asked to the person sitting on the cot.
The reply came late and his voice had regret, it was low and sad. He also looked like a priest and while he wanted to speak a word, I could see his eyes getting wet.

"*Puttar....*" He hugged me and then held my shoulders to continue... "last evening Babaji had a severe chest pain and he ran to the Gurudwara from his closet."
"Is he fine... I want to meet him" I asked
He stood up and hid his face from me.
"We asked him his health but he ignored and sat inside the Gurudwara. His health got deteriorated till he went unconscious"
"Then?" I was still asking...
"Finally we forcefully took him to the Military Hospital.... we waited for hours to hear some good news. He was loved by all... left us with his unforgettable memories"

"What?"

I was shocked to see someone go away, never to come back. This shock was hurting me from within. I had started knowing and understanding this person, it sometimes felt I knew him since long.

I looked around and it was all quiet and painfully silent outside and within me. I still regret I never asked him his name. I slowly walked seeing down the ground, but not knowing whether I was headed to home or to the school or the beach. It was just ten minutes walk from the Gurudwara to my classroom but I seem to have no memory of what all happened and how much time did it take to reach the classroom.

A part of me was lost with Babaji. In my books I had kept two peacock feathers adjacent to each other. The feathers were given to me by Babaji. They resembled his eyes, white boundaries, then black circles, deep blue core. Sometimes I gazed at the cashew trees. The leaves looked still, though there was breeze trying to play with the trees.

Was that experience an illusion? At times I was confused with the distance between my feet and my eyes in terms of height. Was it fluctuating to make me feel tall or a midget? I don't remember.

I stopped visiting the Gurudwara. Some fear had built within. Even if I passed through that Gurudwara I would seldom collect the courage to turn my face towards the marvellous architecture as my eyes would have started the search for someone they knew since ages... that invisible entity was no more?

I was a worshiper of lord Krishn. I remember having left a painting of Krishn in our quarter in Delhi. I had assumed that the next family who gets this quarter would respect and love this painting. I did not know if that painting would still be there?

I had got a lot of appreciation for that piece of art, from the school as well as at home. So much that I tore the paper from the book and glued it to my room... no it was the drawing room... yes!

I had to channelize my wandering attitude, so I had developed a new routine. In the evenings I had started visiting a Hindu temple of lord Krishn. I was so enthusiastic that, some days I would miss my football match to attend the evening prayers at the temple, sharp at six. This temple was again run by a different unit called DSC. This was a different corp. than the one in which my father served.

This priest would often brief me about various incarnations which lord Vishnu had taken to save the mankind. His sayings were strengthening my roots. I was relating to what I used to hear from my father. The revelation of holy *Geeta* was done by lord Krishn and my father would often take its references while giving me some moral teachings.

Once I was sent outside the classroom for discussing some irrelevant topic while George sir was busy taking his serious lectures. From outside the classroom I could hear few giggles and murmuring on how idiot I acted. Then I heard one question for my rival in the game.

"So Nishad what is the lesson we have been learning in history today?"
Nishad was weak in English and had a typical Malayalam accent like most of the native boys.

"Sorry saaray, enniku Harappan civilization onnu mansalay illya"
He replied that he was not aware of Harappan civilization, but
the way he apologized made all of us laugh. He did sound
very funny and innocent. George sir was very impartial and
particular about what to speak and how to speak.
The class was hearing scolding given to Nishad by George sir
and after a lot of arguments the final say was a fine on Nishad
for speaking Malayalam instead of English. That incident was
funny; the reason why he was punished was not the prime
reason why he was scolded.

While I was standing outside the classroom gazing the coconut
trees and their reason for standing so tall, I could see a group
of ladies walking towards the classroom. One of the ladies was
wearing a bright blue saree with golden borders and her face
was looking familiar too.

I realized that the lady was no other than my mother. My
classroom was few hundred metres away from where I stayed
and it was also midway to the Army Canteen. Now I had to
quickly drop the idea of stressing much on how the coconut
water reaches inside a coconut and that too 60 meters above
the ground. I rather thought investing my mind in covering up
my face. I quickly turned towards the classroom wall with my
back facing the road. I heard her taking my name, but the way
she took my name was not the way I could be called, maybe
she was talking about some incident to the ladies. I closed my
ears too and requested lord Krishn to save me. I had learnt
from my mother that a boon is never granted for free so I had
to offer the lord a bribe... what max I could have given to the
almighty. I thought and promised him to spend the Sunday
as well in the temple to conduct the morning prayers. Sunday
would otherwise be reserved to watch cartoons, but I was okay
with that small sacrifice.

The voices were more distant now indicating that the ladies had left and it was safe for me to stand normally. However my sigh of relief did not last long as the bell rang signalling the end of the period. I wanted the ears of my mother to close, so that she doesn't hear the bell. She finally did not turn back.

The class was getting ready for Gracie miss as she was the one who taught us moral science. She was a Christian by religion and taught us stories and tales not only from the Bible but also from various Hindu religious books. I would often wonder if the conviction in her narration came from the fact that she was seeing these stories in front of her eyes or was it her style.

She had a great command over her vocabulary and the words she chose were worth hearing. Even more fascinating was her accent. Her hair would always be oiled and braided with a center partition. She wore her elegantly ironed cotton saree neatly, just like my mother. I would like the way she opened minimal area of her mouth while talking. Sometimes I would not be able to spot her lips move.

She had often talked about her visits to the US and her ancestral farms in France. I always remember my first interaction with her was after I heard her speaking English. For a minute I couldn't believe that she stayed in India, especially because of her white skin and glowing charm. I had recollected my guts to go to her and start a conversation.

"You come from America to teach us? I've heard... the students talk so."
"My great grandparents were a native of France. Somewhere around the eighteenth century they settled in India. But my parents then moved to the US" She had so much to talk but wanted to keep it short.

Then she added "But I love this place; I see life here, vibrant colours, rich diversity… why should I go to France if I can cast my vote from India?"

She further explained how she and thousands of her acquaintances in Pondicherry had the right to vote in the French elections. How was that possible?

George sir had taught us democracy and I knew the casting of votes is done by citizens. Citizens per my understanding were only the people residing in that territory. How did she do that for a foreign country?

May be due to that reason her accent was a little different. It did not sound Standard English though, however when she wrote it on the black board it would be perfectly same as what we had interpreted. I don't know why but I was in her good books and she was a motherly figure who tolerated my early questions about life, faith, civilization and so on.

"*So is Om ain't comin to the class?*" She asked and by the time she ended her sentence I had reached the entrance of the class room with my right hand stretched perpendicular to my body and I asked "May I come in Miss?" and she smiled and just nodded her head.

She had given us homework to write an imaginary story.

"Remember it should be nowhere documented in this world and…" She walked towards the board "It should inspire us to love God."

Everyone wrote something or the other and my workbook was blank. Why? I don't remember. May be I was too busy thinking that story and when it came to documenting it on paper I slept or maybe I found the story not good enough to inspire many. May be the word God was not understood by me at all?

She came to me and did not look happy with the blank page. She asked "*Om You ain't done nothin bout it?*"

I said "Sorry miss, I thought on this topic a lot but couldn't pen it down and I am really not sure why?"

"Okay so Om would narrate an allegory of an ancient Greek God Phoebus." It was my punishment and this was going to be difficult. I looked like a parrot asked to speak an alien language in front of the guests. I was embarrassed as well, I had never learnt about the very existence of a God by this name from my father.

I started thinking back to force my brain bring out some line to me... something please.

Yes... I started walking towards the blackboard and this name was sounding familiar to a new girl "Phoebe Joseph" who had recently joined our class. I remember having asked her the meaning of her name during the morning assembly prayers. What was her reply? Yes, she had said "light, shining light" and also added that it was taken from some Greek word.

I was now the centre of embarrassment as the whole class was looking at me with their mouth wide open. Students knew from my body language that I am blank. I didn't remember the complete lecture miss had talked about this God.

I kept staring at Phoebe, how could I have described her by just knowing her name. She looked beautiful. I wanted to talk, but I was left startled to see her eyes, until I was brought back to the real world by Gracie ma'am. Students laughed at me, except one pair of eyes.

There were several stories which were narrated to the classroom by the students one by one, each lasting not more than a couple of minutes and they were all inspired by either local deities worshipped in Kerala or were taken from the Sunday Mass, I guess. I was hearing them seriously and finding some correlation between the supreme deities of Hindus and the other faith. That was one of the most interesting sessions of moral science class.

Getting up early on Sundays and running on the beach at around 4 AM was a hobby that I had recently developed. The high tides normally left a lot of shells of starfish, conch, big snails and cranks, hence this time suited the best.
Just before the sunrise, I would be there running across the beach and collecting these shells. The atmosphere was filtered from man-made noise and what I heard was just the waves, coming from far away.

Their huge volume of water which sometimes gave birth to a small wave and then... some waves reaching the end of their lifecycle on the shore. There was a clear transition in the music produced by the shores of different amplitude. Also it was fun to compare the races between multiple waves created at almost the same time in different corners of the shore. In the morning the length and area covered by the waves was almost double of where they reach during day time.

Every Sunday I would collect these shells and some *kauris*, which were used as currency in ancient India. I had seen the images of these kauris in history books.
I would often be very tired to come back from the shore. Running across the sea shore was a little difficult. My legs would find it hard to grip and the moist sand would often increase the weight of my feet. Other hurdles were the cute crabs, running here and there; some peeping from their tiny burrows and others running from wet to the dry sand. I had to make sure I did not step on them. Finally going back to home was a boring task, until I had done the task of bathing.

"Why do you run away to the dangerous shore and that too so early when it is dark?" asked my mother.

"Mummy, it isn't that dark and the shore is flat and long. There's nothing to fear. Also I don't want to lose the beautiful shells by reaching late on Sundays"

My mother would find no logic in collecting these dead shells which were once the cover of a sea animal. She would keep them away. Also the smell of freshly collected shells was very pungent so I used to store them in my room in the last row of the almirah. I liked to see their pattern and the strength. Some had a soft and polished cover with sudden sharp edges. I was always amazed with the way they were designed or born. The effort in building that pattern on a shell would be next to impossible by a machine too. I thanked lord Krishn for designing such beautiful creatures.

I had to get ready as I had promised to visit Krishn temple this Sunday. So wearing just shorts and my tee, I ran to the temple and skipped the breakfast. The morning *aarti* normally started at seven thirty sharp and I managed to reach there on time. The *pujari* was very happy with my daily attendance. That day he gave me the prayer bells and asked me to guide others with the *aarti*. I was very happy as this was like becoming a monitor of my class and in the temple I was leading hundreds of soldiers.

By that time I had mugged up most of *aarti* and *hymns*. I was thanking lord Krishn for being kind on me and saving me from Principal's wrath and also for giving *guidance* to George sir so as to forgive me.

Once the aarti was over, the Pujari called me up close to the idol as always. The Pujari was happy to hear my last name. His quick reply showed his profound knowledge of the last names adopted by various sects of Brahmins. I remember him praising my surname and saying "You have a strong lineage and it is highlighted by some of the best scholars ever produced on our motherland."

"Like?" I asked

"Birbal, about whom you must have heard a thousand times whenever it comes to applying common sense and presence of mind. You must know that he was a great mind, a gem in Emperor Akbar's courtyard" He was quick in replying and that impressed me. I never verified if he was true, I believed his expressions.

"Also *Hrishi Bhardwaj* was himself the son of God *Brihaspati*." He added.

"Brihaspati... means planet Jupiter?" I asked

"Yes... that is what you call that Godly planet in English."

What the heck? I had heard only one name from that great planet, *Saboo,* the accomplice *of Chacha Chowdhary.* Now the priest's knowledge had inferred that even I was a descendent of Jupiter. I was still surprised and not very confident of what he spoke. It did sound good though. I kept thinking about how people would have survived on Jupiter millions of years ago, how we would have slowly migrated from a planet that far.

I came home and narrated this at my home during the lunch. Others in my family were least bothered and it looked as if they knew they have a high quality blood in their veins. I was resilient but still kept that pride in me and went back to check the shells.

CHAPTER 4

Nestling In Fear

While strolling through the school ground one day, I heard that loud voice.

"Why are you not present for the Independence Day march past?" This was Mr. Srinivasan, who was a very strict P.T. teacher. He was also very rude, or the rudest?

I wasn't feeling well and was pretty weak to go ahead and lead the drill for my school-house.

In my school, we had four divisions which were referred to as houses. These were named after all great kingdoms of the past which had ruled the Subcontinent.

Mine was "*Chola*" house and I was a very enthusiastic athlete. I was keen to participate in cultural events as well as athletics.

Today was not my day. My legs were not coordinating with my brain. I apologized to Mr. Srinivasan "Sorry Sir! I am not keeping well."

"What?" He had bent his upper half to be too close to my ears. "I have caught flu and I am feeling very dizzy and weak" I added while rubbing the ointment on my nose.

Mr. Srinivasan was a retired *Subedar* from the Indian Army.

He must have served for more than thirty years before he could develop that tummy.

It would have developed only after his retirement. He hardly did any exercise in the school. His hair had gone all white and the most irritating thing about him was the way he did that itching on his thin lined moustache.

"You bastard! Is cough and cold an ailment?"

I was shocked. Never in my school or at home, has someone abused me with that authority?

Was he annoyed at something else which came out on me? I was quite hurt. Though my parents were strict as well but the petty language used by this teacher was very unacceptable.

"Sorry?" I replied to let him know what he spoke... was it a lapse.

I wasn't his servant or a junior reporting to him. I was son of a soldier and had a self-pride which forced me to reply.

"I take my name back from the parade." I was haughty too.

Without waiting for his reaction I turned back and started walking towards my classroom.

"Common cold cannot stand tall. Strengthen your will and come over!"

Was he motivating me? I did not feel like replying to him so I kept walking till his voice had lost the intensity to reach my ears.

The classroom was all empty and I was upset at what had happened few minutes back. I also had this bad feeling for not being able to participate in the 15th August events. I just closed my eyes and lay down taking the support of the desk. My head was feeling very heavy and my nose was out of control. The tears from my eyes and the water from my nose were competing now. This was gave me a gross feeling. I fell asleep.

Next day I wasn't feeling better either but I still walked to the school. Today was the day when the British left the reigns of governing the Indian subjects to the hands of Indian leaders; At least that was how George sir described the day. George sir had taught us again and again, the speech given by Jawaharlal Nehru, addressing the people of India on the eve of independence. I still remember the speech word by word and the expressions for each word on George sir's face, ignoring the itch on his forehead.

People of Kannur too celebrated this with a great pride. In all corners of roads, you could find small stalls distributing free *Payasam*, a sweet porridge made of milk and rice. At the main square, I saw a tall pole installed right at the center. I wonder if I saw this pole last day... No it wasn't there. It felt nice to see the Indian tricolour being hoisted on this pole. Usually, there is a lot of enthusiasm in the minds of people on this day. Patriotic songs praising Indian culture and martyrs could be heard in almost all the shops. I too was enjoying the one I was hearing. I looked around and felt good and healthy to go to the school to attend the parade. It was a very important event as various dignitaries and senior officers in the school administration would have come to pay their tribute today.

In the school ground, I saw a boy of section B was given the responsibility of leading the march past with house-flag in his hands. The chairman was Colonel Thomas Matthew who had hoisted the Indian flag in the school campus. He happened to be the commanding officer of my father's unit as well. I cheered the parade and was sorry that I did not lead it instead of having prepared for it since last few weeks.

After the ceremony was over, I collected the sweets and was tired standing in the sun. The sun rays were making me feel bitter and my skin was fighting with each ray of light.

"Om, why weren't you leading the march past today, is everything alright?" I heard this familiar voice from behind me. I turned to see the chairman. I could hardly look into his eyes. He had that British accent and wore a lot of shiny medals on his chest today. Col. Matthew was standing tall and bent a little to hear my low voice.

"Good Morning Sir. I was just not feeling well and thought of taking some rest today" I replied.

"How do you find the school in terms of other activities and facilities?" He asked again.

This question wasn't as simple as it sounded. Any negative reply could lead to the school management facing repercussions.

"So far all is set and we are doing well. We have great new infrastructure this year, including the new basketball court" I then added "There is never a deficiency of the sports equipments"

While I was replying, I saw Mr. Srinivasan coming on to us. He seemed to have a strong feeling that I must be complaining about his last day's nonsense. His walk was not smooth.

I then heard a thud! Mr. Srinivasan hit his boots on to the muddy ground.

"*Jai hind Sahib!*"

"At ease Teacher" said Col. Matthew.

Though Mr. Srinivasan was retired, he loved wearing his dark green uniform with nicely polished boots and shiny lustrous stars on his shoulders. He did this more often during the special events like that.

"Sir, you should not listen to this lad" He shouted with a weird look towards me. I was surprised and so was the chairman.

"What is the context?" asked Mr. Matthew.

"Sir this chap is a weak nincompoop with no ribs to carry the Indian flag. He sees no glory in the tricolour and the lion capital. His weaknesses led me to use some stringent words against him last evening."

"Well *Subedar sahib*, you've said it all. You are here to serve the purpose of a teacher, not train recruits. I hope it is crystal clear that you are not training the Defence Academy recruits, not anymore."

I was all quiet and uttered no word to explain my case. He was embarrassed and asked to leave for some other engagements.

Months passed and that flu did run for long. My parents had gone to Delhi for some work and we were just three people at home; me, my elder brother and my elder sister.

My brother was busy studying and my sister was preparing the food in the kitchen.

I was not much into the books so I sat on the porch, looked at the stairs, the jackfruit tree and the tall grasses around. Suddenly I could hear a lot of noise coming from the grasses. The sound resembled as if someone is cutting the grasses and hurling something in it. Out of curiosity I followed the noise which was like few feet away from the stairs.

It was an hour since the sun had set in the horizon leaving behind the crimson sky and pale blue sea water. Beyond the grasses it was sharp downfall of the shrubs, finally meeting the shore. I then spotted a tail of some creature moving around. While I was busy thinking what it could be, just a meter away I saw two tall plants cuddling and I was confused. Suddenly a beam of light fell on one of the stems and I was startled. Our quarters were amidst bushy vegetation and in this part of Kerala it was common to see rain forest creatures crawling close to the fence.

Amazing! For the first time in my life I was seeing two big snakes, which were capable of standing tall to about a meter. One of them had a big hood and was continuously trapping the second snake which had a smaller hood and a U shape over it. The larger was a king cobra much larger than the snake figures I had seen one trapped around Lord Shiv's neck and the smaller was a black cobra which has a print of lord *Krishn's* wooden Patten.

I was childish and hence was finding it difficult to understand why king cobra with no print on his hood and that has never met lord Krishn can defeat the cobra which later got blessings from the greatest God of Hindu mythology?
The king then turned his hood towards me and I could see that life in his eyes.
His eyes were wet and the fangs... too long, much longer than my palm. I stared at the king but kept moving back slowly and very cautiously. I could not take the risk to attract either of them inside my house. I went inside the house and closed the exit door which was facing the ground.

The quarters we lived in were actually very old but very robust and beautiful. The architecture too was what would suit a rain forest area. The walls and flooring were very old too. These and many similar barracks were built by the British and were now being used as army quarters.
My father often explained that there was severe reconstruction of India done during the British era. He would cite examples of the Parliament, several other government buildings, railway stations, railway lines, the India Gate and several other monuments.

The area in front of the main living room was a big veranda like an atrium and was very accessible to the outer world. Our house did not have very high boundary walls. "Come over Om. Rakesh you too join in for the dinner. Study after a break, come on!"
I heard my sister's call and started running towards her. She cooked equally good food. At times she would get upset for not being able to prepare a round and thin *chapati* as mummy did.

However the taste of the vegetables cooked by her matched the flavour of my mother's food.

She looked at me and had a question mark on her face as to why be I so scared.
She came close to me and smiled
"Mummy?" She wanted to know if I was missing mummy, which was not the case.
"Nah" I replied and saw her cheeks bulge out when her lips stretched to pull her shot chip up. She looked like papa and would often make faces like him. One good thing she got from mummy was her beautiful long hair. Like her, she too was fond of coconut oil and made those long thick braids in her hair, just like my mother.

We were ready to have the dinner prepared by our sister and suddenly we could hear some noise in my parent's bedroom. Empty boxes fell from above the storage boxes and under the almirah. There was something hitting the walls of the metal almirah. I went close and bent my body down to see what was producing the sound.
To my greatest shock, this was the same huge king cobra under the almirah and the hiss produced by this serpent was so loud that my sister ran from the kitchen and pulled me to the other room.

She got so worried for us. She shouted and asked how did a snake come and asked me to open all the doors. My brother ran to open the doors which would help the king in exit.

"Go and stand on the bed" She wanted us to be safe at a place out of reach of the king.
She did not know that this snake was much taller than her and even papa.
I could see half of Cobra's body encircled and had thick uneven shape.

What was that? Did he just eat my pencils?

My sister was in panic and yes, we were afraid too. We could see the king cobra peeking outwards from the almirah. My sister started praying to some Hindu God with a very quiet chanting. Her eyes were closed but she did know that she had to throw away the danger out of the house.

I ran to my room and got the cricket bat which was approximately one third of the length of this king cobra. My sister went a little closer to the almirah and inserted the bat under the almirah.

Hissss was the reply!! I and my brother were taken aback.

So we sensed that the king had no intention of leaving and neither did it want to attack. It looked lazy and wanted to just rest under the almirah. My sister then asked me to bring the badminton racket and she tied one end of the badminton racket to the cricket bat and thus the length was now safer to push the king.

After around 15 minutes of constant tension and fear the king was annoyed.

It started doing something which I had never expected. His neck was moving fast and it looked as if a bull is shaking his upper half to frighten us. We were now seeing folded tail of the cobra coming out of the king's mouth. It was a disgusting and bizarre scene. So this was the food the king wanted to digest?

My sister shouted "Oh My God! Rakesh please go and call the neighbours. Ask them to call some other people to help". Hearing the orders, he could sense that it was something serious and started running out of the house. I was hiding behind my sister and watching the action carefully. After few minutes, the king had vomited complete cobra and now the king might be relieved. I did not know if this was the waste which had been vomited or it was still an undigested dish?

I guess the king was agitated over the loss of its prey and the continuous disturbance to it by my sister. It started coming close to us and then taking its hood back. My sister then took the badminton racket close to the cobra hood and tried to hit it. The king attacked with a force but its venom teeth and fangs got trapped in the badminton net. My sister was quick to drag it straight towards the exit. I ran to the kitchen and got some heavy metal utensils. Then I looked around and found my brother's books, I threw them as well on king's head.

The king was damaged out of repair and then she started pulling it slowly out of the house and now we were seeing its full length.... too long for us to lift it completely.
The body in the air was almost the same height which was rubbing the ground.
It looked heavy too as my sister was now using both her hands to tightly lift the badminton racket. She wanted minimal touch of poison on the ground.

She walked till the fence and threw the badminton racket as well...
I used the cricket stumps to lift the dead cobra which was vomited by the king.
This looked so small and its body was burning miserably bad. I followed my sister and while she had disposed the king and turned around she was little surprised. I too threw it at the same spot.
She wanted to stop me but then she stopped herself and felt happy. My sister hugged me and cried. My elder brother came with few people for help but the matter was already sorted. We sat and talked about the whole episode again and again. We all had lost the hunger and did not have the meal that night. The kitchen utensils were also thrown out by my brother.

The next morning our parents returned and couldn't wait to tell them the story. I added all kind of spices I could, to make it look like a heroic act.

"And then *didi* and I dumped them in the backyard". I ended smiling with pride.

"Oh my God! What you guys have done?" Mummy exclaimed not looking pleased. This was a totally unexpected response which disappointed me. She rather reported everything to Papa who started thinking gravely. I was made to feel guilty of doing something wrong unknowingly.

"We will have to do a *havan* to ask for forgiveness from lord Shiv and serpent kings.

We need to pray to seek their blessings to keep our family safe in future." Mummy was ready with the solution. And likewise was done.

The whole episode left me confused. I thought I and my sister had been brave to protect ourselves and we would be rewarded. But this whole havan thing made me think was that snake so pious? Had we accidentally killed a Godly creature? What if that sin is levied on us? These questions never got a satisfactory answer.

I had now entered the *teen-trivia* and this was the time when my concept of goodness revolved around prayers and touching the feet of elders.

The kids who did not satisfy the above two rules, were not appreciated by me much.

I had moved to the next class and grown taller.

We were once standing in the morning assembly prayer. As usual the PT teacher was closely observing all the students.

"Hey where is your badge?" asked the PT teacher.

Ravi replied "I've put it on the tie, sir. Is it not correctly done?"

Ravi used to stand just before me as he was just few inches shorter than me.

"Don't you know that the badge has to be exactly six fingers below the tie knot?" Ravi was actually a very thin guy and his fingers were small too. I am sure that would have miscalculated the place of the badge.

"*Thhhadd*!" was the voice heard by a sphere of almost thirty metres.

The students in the adjoining lines also turned towards us to see what was happening. I could not see the facial expressions of Ravi but I am pretty sure he must have been pissed off by the slap received for such a silly reason.

"You lazy lump of corruption! See this..." said the Mr. Srinivasan and started measuring the distance of the badge from the tie knot. He had distinctly obese fingers. How could poor Ravi match the distance with his thin fingers width? He of course, cannot cut the fingers of Mr. Srinivasan for measuring his badge position. I was fighting his case in my mind.

"Sorry sir I would fix it right now" said poor Ravi. I was getting the heat in Ravi's mind about how he wanted to slap back for the nonsense caused by the PT teacher.

I mean once we set a tie knot and pin the badge on it, we hardly disturb the arrangement.

"Get out of the line and 5 rounds of the football ground, NOW!" shouted the teacher.

Ravi quietly moved towards the football ground which was not very close. I am not sure if he really completed 5 rounds or just sat and cursed Mr. Srinivasan. The assembly was yet to start and hence there would be no one to check his punishment.

Now it was the time for us to fold our palm in *Namaste* position and start with our regular prayer starting with the hymn "*Asato maa sad gamaya, Tamaso maa jyotirgamaya, Mrityumaa amritam gamaya...*"

I did not know the meaning of the verses but I definitely had the interest in knowing what I was praying. Thanks to the impatient pathogen inside me.

"*Thaaat!*" we heard the second slap.
"Don't you know we need to join our palms while we are offering prayers?"
The victim was Nishad. Doing prayers in Sanskrit must be an alien act to him. He did not even speak proper English. Mr. Srinivasan used to verify the problems in our uniforms and now he was developing that habit of pointing every act, even if that was not in his jurisdiction.

"Sorry sir" said Nishad joined his palm.
I was shocked seeing two consecutive absurd acts by Mr. Srinivasan within half an hour or so. I was hundred percent sure that Mr. Srinivasan would not be aware of the meaning of the hymn for which the posture of *Namaste* was advocated.

That evening I did not go to my home rather I directly went to the temple.
"*Pranam panditji*" I greeted the religious teacher.
He was happy to see me as I was the only non-serving army personnel who was a regular visitor to his temple. Though he was given an army rank, but this priest was actually never seen in uniform. His duties were limited to prayers and offering *prasad*. He may be the only person in the unit to have gained a belly. He often wore a white dhoti and kept his upper half nude. No, he did cover his upper half with some sacred thread which I have seen on my father as well. He was bald and had a circular face. He kept chewing some *masala*, I don't know may be cardamom.
But his jaws were big and often pressed his cheek muscles to produce a visible line outside.

"Is it mandatory for all people in this world to offer prayers by closing eyes and joining hands" my question was subtle and straightforward.

"No Om, it's not the way we pray, it is about whom are we preaching" He replied while stopping his chewing for some time. He wiped his lips which looked red.

"So whom are we praising?" I asked promptly. The *pandit* took a long pause staring straight in my eyes and just said "*Parameshwar*"

It seemed to me that he wanted to keep the reply as short as possible so that he can engage himself in the *Godly* duties.

We continued with our prayers and I had the *manjira* that day. I kept playing it in monotonous style but could not sing the *aarti*. My mind was full of questions and with that melancholy; my brain just guided my fingers to play the manjira without the zeal. May be it was a noise today and without a co-ordination.

The prayers were over. Everybody had the *Prasad* and marched back to their barracks. I however waited for the pandit to get free so that I could take out that anxious curiosity from my mind.

"Then panditji who is *Parameshwar*?" I asked with a sigh.

"The almighty who has created us" he said and inserted one more cardamom inside his mouth. His denture was all rotten but there was no smell when he spoke.

"And how did he do that? I mean did he create all of us at once?"

He then started talking about various books explaining how millions of years ago lord Brahm created us and imparted us knowledge in the form of books. He wasn't specific and was giving general statements which did sound like made-up.

I then asked "Then how Nishad does doesn't know about Brahma at all or neither does he know about the other books you referred to?" Before he could reply I added "or the *aarti* that we do?"

I forgot to give an introduction of Nishad to him. But the pandit was smart; he had an answer for that. He could make out that Nishad sounds Arabic or Muslim.

"Everyone was a Hindu once and later some bad people came and propagated their religion and bad lifestyle" He replied.

His reply was difficult to be related to my history books.

He later went on to explain that every individual from root is a "*Sanatan*" and later on they chose for some or the other reason to profess a different way of life.

So I asked "So do the books of other religions also mention at all about the supreme Gods of Hindus that you just described?"

"No. But they are all inspired from our rich heritage, our manuscripts, Ved and then they built other religions for their convenience."

But that reason did not satisfy my question.

"But our religion, which you called as Hinduism is full in itself, right?"

"Yes"

"So what could be the purpose of shifting to the need of other religions or other lifestyles?"

The pandit was not feeling comfortable now or maybe he now wanted to run away from further questions. He then replied with some anger

"There are different people with different mind-sets and some are constructive while some are destructive. Hinduism doesn't stop anyone to profess any new way of life like Sikhs, Jains, and Buddhists. But that does not mean they are no longer Hindus, they may follow a different way of life but on larger scale they are Hindus"

This was difficult to digest as every religion was now becoming a subset of Hinduism as per the pandit and I was moving away from his knowledge base. I had talked to Babaji in Gurudwara and he had never talked about any decree which forced humans or followers to perform some aarti or observe some fast.

"How many Hindus are there panditji?" I asked
"Billions" His reply was quick but vague.
"And what about those who don't follow this way-of-life you refer to as Hinduism?" I asked.
"Don't know, must be billions again. But they will soon understand the power of Hinduism"
"So they either don't know about Hinduism or they have gone away from this religion you mean?" I then made the question more precise.
"No"
"I mean billions in this world don't preach Gods, no idols, no mantr, no deities?" I was tensed
"Yes... they don't know this great knowledge yet" He replied.
"If so, then how are they happy, living their life, discovering new things, doing scientific research, contributing to humankind, doing inventions...?"
I recalled that I was recently taught about inventions. All the scientists I was reading about were either from Europe or America, leaving few Indians. The science teacher had explained to us about the unexpectedly poor environment where some great scientists like Michael Faraday, Louis Pasteur and many others who had spent their lives researching about ways to improve human life. So I was now confused as to how were they doing this without praying lord Krishn?"

The pandit lost his cool and now just wanted to show me his greatness so he stood and shouted
"I am a *Brahmin*, I have lived a celibate life, my father, grandfather and several generations have done this and you are questioning my knowledge?"

I felt bad but I did not mean that, I corrected myself
"I am sorry panditji, I am not questioning rather I want to benefit out of this huge knowledge that you possess... what is that *gyan* you always talk about?"

He wasn't happy now and he ended the conversation by saying "You are a child and will come to know the truth as and when you grow up. For now, just remember that you should be proud to have taken birth as a Brahmin. Be proud that you are *Sanatan*, the mother of all religions."
"Thanks" I kept it small.
"But that does not stop you from becoming a demon. They were also from our religion only" He was harsh on me now.

I could not buy that logic. That guy has lost the respect I had in my mind for him. I slowly started walking back. After a few minutes I stopped and turned back to walk towards the *pandit* and asked
"Do you really understand what you teach or is it just to get paid with a handsome salary so you continue these prayers?"
His eyes started bulging out with red linings clearly appearing from the anger. His blood must have boiled at this statement. I continued.
"I think Indian army has all sects, all kinds of religious communities and if you have been commanded by God to just serve the Hindus, then I am sorry to have come to this place."
The pandit now had understood that I was not an easy target to brainwash. So with all his anger, he shouted at me
"Go away and do not enter this premise again."
He was shouting to call the regimental police to hold me. I managed to get out of the premise before anyone could respond to his call.

I was hurt but happy too that I did not become a target of his fanatic philosophy.

I then pledged to myself not to go to this temple or any other temple from that day!

I had lost the fear from the idols and age-old customs. I had gained such a confidence which I had never experienced before this day. That was the day when I had spread my wings for the first time and the happiness was ineffable!

While I was having my bath, it felt like an ablution which washed away the slightest of fear and faith I had in the idols. The feeling was so intense that I could see even wet hair working hard to get erected over my arms, behind my neck, over my shoulders. That was a moment of great strength.

"Hey kid, take this milk" The milkman called me and pointed towards the cold and cornered bucket. It was quite evident that that milk was already adulterated and can be either given to anyone who is in hurry to take the milk home or would be later sold to small time restaurants. I was instructed by my mother to never take that.

"No, I need the fresh one" I said with a sense of smartness and some ego, as if the fresh milk would be in its purest form. "Why did your mother not come today" asked Mrs. Banerjee. "She had to visit *Satyanarayan pooja* at Shukla madam's place" I replied.

The milkman filled his bucket with water and marched towards milking the cows. I followed him.

"What happened, can't you sit on the cot outside" he asked. He wasn't concerned about my comfort; he actually just wanted me to stay from the site of action.

"No I want to see how you milk the cow." I tried to be diplomatic this time to rule out confrontation.

This was the first time I had visited the *khatal.*

Many a times, I had seen pieces of "cow dung" or plastic in the milk that was delivered to us. I would ask mummy, but she would be okay with the cow dung in the milk, as she said anything coming from the back of the cow is good. That statement would just spin my head.

The milkman then tied the legs of the cow with a small rope and started applying something looking like oil on the nipples of the cow. This was a weird moment for me to see. I felt something very indecent was happening but the people sitting around had acclimatized to this process so well. The nipples looked somewhat erected now. Maybe it would be a signal for the readiness to be milked. Anyways I was bothered about the adulteration. So I was trying to be sharp, observing his hands and the bucket. He then washed the adjoining areas of the nipples with water he had carried in the bucket and threw away the rest of the water.

"Release the calf" He asked his son.
The son then brought the calf close to the cow, and the little calf started having some milk. The moment the baby calf was trying to quench his hunger by his mother's milk; the milkman pushed the calf aside and took control of the ready-to-milk nipples.
This looked outrageous to me.
How can someone exploit kid-mother instincts for his commercial purpose?

I asked "Do you feed this calf after the milking is over?"
"No, anytime during the afternoon the calf is free to go out to graze fresh grass in the fields. He is free to have the milk then"
This did not answer my question at all. I was still being very diligent.
The milking procedure had started, though in the background I could hear the poor calf yelling at the milkman which was unbearable. The calf was white and had big black eyes. He wanted to stretch his neck and reach the nipples. I was seeing a permanent scar on his neck owing to this regular exercise. There was some water coming out from the corner of his eyes.

Poor creature was shouting and cursing the milkman. The milkman's son pulled the calf back to some shed far away.

I focused on the bucket again. I liked the froth that was created by the speeding milk inside the bucket and that made it look so fresh and authentic. The milkman was also changing the nipples every now and then when the first pair dried out. The bucket had filled to almost fifty percent. Suddenly the cow started spreading her legs.
I did not understand what it could be? Was she not well?
I was thinking to myself that this pervert milkman would definitely be hit someday by the cow or her calves.

The milkman moved closer to cover the bucket.
Then came a jet of urine. I immediately moved back.
This seemed a daily hurdle for the milkman; he wasn't taking any concrete step to obstruct the sprinkles from entering the bucket.
I could now understand why I could see some yellow patches and sometimes solid substances while filtering milk at home.

Mrs Banerjee watched at the cow urine and felt happy as if some Godly activity has just happened. She closed her eyes to read out some prayers. I could just see her lips moving and no voice, she did it so low as if it's top secret which no other person in this world should know. May be she did not want to share that special privilege of Godly connect?

This site of cow urination reminded me of a *"Satyanarayan katha"* that I had attended last year at our neighbour's place. The person conducting the pooja again knew me by my last name *"Bhardwaj"*. I sometimes felt that last name to be too heavy for me.

After the prayers everyone was served the Prasad and *panchamrit,* meaning the five immortal nectar. I could get a taste of basil leaves. This taste was similar to the tea prepared at my home for someone with fever.

"Why do we get this drink only after this pooja? What is this?" I asked the neighbour who himself was dressed as a priest.

"This is a liquid prasad which has five important sacred elements of life; curd, honey, sugar, ghee and cow milk" He said

I asked then why am I getting a salty taste on the basil leaves, this was weird.

He then explained me the importance cow urine, which he had put in a very small quantity. I felt like vomiting after knowing this but I wanted to listen to him.

Maybe my quest suppressed that vomit call.

"This is prevailing since thousands of years." He then asked "You are a Bhardwaj so you must know Hrishi Bhardwaj?"

"Yes I've heard his name... ancient saint."

"He has elaborated the importance of cow and *panchgavya* or the five cow products." He was sure of what he was doing. The guy then also stated one mantra which still runs very fresh in my mind:

Goumutre tridinamsthaapyay visham tena vishudhyati!

Which roughly meant that the consumption of cow urine, if done for three days, has the power to clean toxins from our body? It was hard to believe but this gentleman had such an old documentation to prove his statement.

I had to rush early as it was going to be sunset soon. I took milk and walked back towards our quarters thinking about the poor calf. He had once looked at me for help, but why did I not say a word? Why did I stand helpless, just like others? I felt sorry and wanted to get rid of that helplessness in me.

I looked up and saw a bright cashew hanging quite low. The fruit of cashew happened to be one of my favourites. I thought it wouldn't be tough to get that and I would still be able to make it before the sunset. I kept the milk container aside under the tree and climbed the cashew tree. I threw my slippers down as I trust the grip of my legs.

I had almost reached the top and was getting rid of the leaves coming on my way. The branch holding the cashew was thin and out of reach. I extended my hands to reach there and took hold of it but suddenly I heard some buzz near my right ear and I pulled my left leg to get away from this menace.

It was looking like a honey bee but there was no honey comb nearby. I stretched again and was fighting with the gravity.

I tried to balance by weight on just the big toe of my right feet. My left hand now held the cashew apple. I started pulling it tightly and then... *oouchh*!

I could feel pinch of a strong bite. Was this some snake? Could it be the bee? I did not know. This was intense pain.

I was so unbalanced now that I gave all my weight to the cashew fruit and my feet slipped. I could see my transient journey towards mother earth. I have no memories of this short sleep or what did I dream now, but I managed to open my eyes soon.

My back was paining and my head was spinning but my mind was alert checking if I was breathing.

My mouth was open, my nostrils were open. I checked with my fingers and there was no blood, still I wasn't able to suck that air inside. The height wasn't much but the angle of my fall was not safe. I was finding it hard to breathe. I closed my eyes and started dreaming about all good things that had happened to me so far. I slept or was I unconscious?

There was complete silence and then I heard horn of vehicles passing by. I opened my eyes slowly. I was safe. It took time but lifted my body slowly, giving all the weight to my right leg. I folded my hand to feel my back, it was swollen.

Could the cow urine inside my milk container save me from this poison?

This was best time to test it. I limped and then walked towards the container. I opened the cap and had the raw milk as if I was the calf of that cow. I drank it all.

I then sat for some time concentrating on the pain. A lot of time had passed and the pain did not reduce. I proved myself to be a fool instead!

I did not have a watch but it looked very late right now. I could progress from walk to slow run now. I was back to home with pain in my back. When asked about the milk I gave a lame excuse that I fell walking and spilled the milk.

I continued having pain for next three to four days and the more pain I had, the more confident I was to go against the orthodox practices around. This was my learning which any other person could not have taught me directly. I was gaining knowledge from experience and understood it one by one.

CHAPTER 5

Revolting Wings

"Om let us go for a visit inside the cantt."
We had been transferred to eastern India's largest cantonment, Danapur.
I was habituated now to get up early enough before the sunrise.
"Ok papa."
We then moved on to see the cantt from within.
"This cantt. is one of the oldest in the country."
"Nice!" I was happy to hear the information. The structures were beautiful and spoke of century old traditions of the Army.
"This was built by the East India Company in the 17th century"
Papa said with much pride in his eyes.

Papa further said "In your history course, did they teach you about *Patliputr*?"
I started missing George sir as he was very nice in explaining history through his innovative ways. He often added his funny touch to an incident and we used to link his act with the portion of history to memorize it. I missed him more for his interesting anecdotes. He made us visualize the history running through our brains. He made us all a part of that history.

"Not yet. Anything special about that place?"

"Everything!" Papa had the smile with a content that he has moved to a historical place. I could understand why I liked history so much, this is the gene pool!

However, I did not limit the history to the scriptures which mostly talked about mythology.

"I should highlight that this place has been the capital of Ashok and Chandragupt Maury. Those were the golden years of Indian history"

I liked the feeling of pride in his voice while describing this.

Papa took me to the unit library which had a huge hall. It looked more like a church than a library. I walked to one section and went through the books arranged there. It mostly had stories and autobiographies of some key Generals of the Indian Army. I looked up and read an inscription on the wall that read

"If a man says he is not afraid of dying, he is either lying or is a Gurkha - Field Marshal Sam Manekshaw"

I have heard stories of Manekshaw from my father many a times, but here I was ignorant about the word *Gurkha,* so I had to ask papa about that.

"Om you should make a note of asking in detail about *Gurkhas* to your history teacher." He asked me and then added.

"By the way, they are bravest of the lot and Indian Army is proud to have Gurkhas serving the motherland. For now you can understand that GR or the Gurkha Rifles is just like our unit and they are natives of north-eastern part of the subcontinent, touching Nepal"

He paused for a minute and then continued again

"In 18th century there was this accession attempt by a big unit of the British Army in North Eastern India and Nepal and few hundreds of Gurkhas gave a tough fight to a big battalion of British. That tells all about their bravery."

I had developed quite a bit of interest in the GR and wanted to know more. But it was time to return to our quarter, so we started walking back.

"How did you come to know about them?" I asked

"In my training days as a young recruit, I made few very close friends and one of them later moved to GR. His name was Timshik Dorjee. I have fond memories of that group of friends but I am not in touch with any one of them now."

"Tell me more about him" I liked him talking about his friend, he hardly mentioned any.

"He was brave and the best in all categories of sports" I saw some shine in his eyes now.

"He was great in the war classes, but the best part was his cry to bring us back from fatigues"

"What was that?"

"When our batch would be tired and exhausted, then Dorjee would stand up and shout the slogan in his highest pitch... *Jai mahakali, aayo gorkhali* and we all would get up and be ready to fight"

We were done with the stroll around the cantt and its heritage library. Papa promised me to take out to neighbouring landscape, which looked so very beautiful from his office.

One fine day, it was a beautiful drizzle that had covered the mist forming a hazy rainbow outside. The monsoon had just struck the eastern parts of India.

I could see thousands of cranes flying all over and sitting on the marshy wetlands close to the cantt. The birds were running from one palm tree to the other. The chaos had a charm. They had such a nice formation and it seemed as if they had some relation with this place.

"Papa what are these birds? They look nice."

"Om, they are Open Bill storks who have migrated from various parts of the world to our Cantt." He was amazed at the sight too. Then he continued "I have this strong feeling that they are the souls of thousands of martyrs who laid their lives in this very cantt. during the British Raj."

Now I could see papa coming out with that Hindu rebirth philosophy of soul, and had added his military touch to it. Papa still thought me to be that 5 year old kid sometimes. I thanked him for taking out time to show me the surrounding areas. I had the privilege of enjoying my parent's company as my siblings had shifted to Delhi for their higher education. I was alone but got more time to spend with my parents.

"Om there is a call for you... get up Om."
Mummy was trying to pull me out of the dream.
"Yes mummy, what's the matter?" I asked while rubbing my ears and fixing my hair.
"Someone is on the phone. He is asking for you... some *Madrasi*."
I walked towards the living room and picked up the telephone receiver. I did not have a clue about who that person could be.

"*Adaa Om, anganey da nee?*" The person asked about me in Malayalam. This was none other than Nishad, from Kannur.
"I am fine yaar, tell me about school and other developments in the school, also about George sir." I asked him.
It must be more than 2 years that we had talked. I was glad he had saved my father's number that I gave to him long back.
"All is good. George sir also good *daa*. He talks about you. Gracie miss has left the job. Rest same weather, same time pass.... yes but the PT sir.."
"Yes what about him? Did he beat you up or some other student? Tell me what happened yaar?" I was worried about Nishad
"No man he passed away... few days back, some disease I don't know, all say some... swine flu. He had changed and had started talking good to us."

77

"Oh…" Nishad himself had been a victim of several tortures given by Mr. Srinivasan, and I was hearing him condole.
Though I did not personally like that man, but a fit man's death due to flu was shocking news. I still have fresh memories of the scolding and punishments this PT teacher gave to all. After that we had some general talks before I ended that call.

I later read in the newspaper about the pandemic caused by some virus. At this very moment, I was not able to recall hundreds of people who were nice to me in Kannur but I had a clear memory of Mr. Srinivasan and his scolding. Maybe because he taught me one trait of human personality which one should not possess. He must have under-estimated the flu and that laxity may have caused his… I too felt bad.

This place was different, the best part that everybody knew Hindi, or they knew just Hindi? Unlike Kannur, this place had some bone chilling winter and getting up early became even tougher. I failed to understand whether the nights were longer now or the sleeps? I had now cultivated the habit of getting up early and by myself. I had also been inspired by my father to take cold water bath. He was so punctual in bathing just with cold water, even in winters. I was out of the bathroom and was getting ready for the school.

"Here, take this, your DM" papa threw a heavy box to me.
The box was heavy and opening it did leave me in great surprise. Boots!
It was already shining black, brand new. I was still not getting its name.
"Thanks… yesss… but why do we call it DM?"
"Maybe because it's D-shaped Military shoe" and he smiled.

That was sturdy, heavy and strong boot. Another advantage of this boot was its three inch heel which made me stand tall and equate my height to papa. He could not have guessed why

I smiled after wearing the boots but I cherished that growth. I had started wearing them to the school daily and this made me the tallest boy in my class. I now had the privilege to stand last in the assembly queue.

"Move to chapter five, we would study the evolution and creation of earth as per science"
This was the shrill voice of Sumona madam who taught us Biology.
She would always put a long line of vermillion from the center of her forehead till the end of the bridge that held her thick spectacles.

Sumona madam never entertained us; rather she bored us with her monotonous teaching style. I would've ignored the voice had there been a good coverage of the material she taught. She was always in a hurry to finish her lessons up.

Hearing her sentence I got a little restless and raised my hand.
"As per science?" Why did you refer to the lesson by that name madam?"
"Because this is just one of the hypotheses."
"I am sorry madam but I fail to understand how science becomes a hypothesis?"
"A theory which can't be proven... just a theory" she said and I could see the *'no more questions'* lines on her forehead.
"I beg your pardon madam, but why are we taught just a hypothesis and not the exact way in which this Earth got created? We all would love to know that" I looked around and no one gave a positive sign or a signal to agree to my interest.
I asked this as I had heard many a times about the creation of Earth. The stories had various versions and all fascinating.

"Om may I request you to sit down and let me continue the lesson!"

"Sorry madam" and I had to sit and listen to her boring lecture. She was talking exactly what was typed in the book. She was done with a lot of topics and I was finding it hard to just sit and hear it.

Finally I kept staring at her with a gesture of confusion, my mouth open and puzzled to force her to call my name.

"Hmmm... What?" She asked

"So you mean everything was made up of dust and gases... I mean rocks, planets... everything?"

"Yes" she was prompt.

"You just talked about the Big bang... what according to you could have led to that? Was it inspired by God?"

My query may have sounded like a satire. Most of the girls started staring at me as if I have done some crap talk. I could hear whispers all around. Only Surya was the one who started giggling and hid his mouth with his right hand.

"I don't know. I can just teach you what this book says." She held the book straight in her hands. She was short heighted and she would always wear a green saree. She wasn't very young but her skin and height made look much younger than her age.

"You should not bother much about the cause of it as no one will ask you that question" She was correct, my queries would never be asked in the exams.

"But I ask that to myself?" I replied with conviction to know.

"Okay class, that's all for now." She ignored me and ended the chapter. She gave us some homework which would not be hard for a third standard kid to find from the books.

I sat down with despair.

"Tomorrow we would discuss the best start of our Solar System, that is the Sun and also cover the death of a black hole."

I knew she should not to be blamed as she was doing her job the way every teacher is expected to. Just close the doors to any question which is not in the books.

"Hey have you gone mad? What made you ask that silly question?" That was Surya. He then added "Just read what is written and pass the exams... move on."
He was my best buddy in the class. Maybe he was right.

"Yeah, tomorrow she will teach about you, *Surya the Sun*" I replied to him.
"Hey Surya, you are the class monitor and the star of the class. Your weight would be 100 times more than the Sun right? So does it mean you have hidden your black hole somewhere?" I was pulling his leg as Surya was the most obese guy in the school and almost five times my weight and width. His face was small though, but his curly hair made him look chubbier. His ears were big and he had that weird habit of shaking his ears without using his hands. He could control left and right ears simultaneously to dance through his muscles. He did that funny act and I looked at him to say something.

"Yes I am a black hole, I will suck you.... come ..." and I had to run away from Surya else he would have squeezed me before the next lecture. No one messed with him. He would often press that person against the wall or on the ground until that victim cried out loud for pardon.

My bedroom ceiling and the lateral walls had the stickers of solar system, which lighted up in the dark.
Thanks to papa for pasting the stickers on my room's ceiling. I watched them for long and thought about the motion of the cosmic bodies. After the lights were switched off, there was a shimmering light that always came from across the window. Maybe it was the moon light? The single beam added a blue tinge to the shining planets.
I would switch from one planet to the other, from one tiny start to the adjacent one.
But every time I looked at the starting point I felt that it had shifted few centimetres apart. Then I would be confused as to

what these bodies communicate to each other and if they do then how?

I was also wondering what the small celestial bodies of this infinite universe would be feeling when they meet after so many light years of separation?

In no time I was fast asleep.

Next day we had to start the day with that irritating voice again.

"So do we have a question about the Sun before we move ahead?" Sumona madam wanted none of us to ask so that she could quickly complete her lecture.

"Does Sun really have 7 horses, as we see on Television?" I asked and the whole class laughed at this. Did that laugh mean NO?

"No Om, stop being childish, that is mythology"

"What is the mythology about Sun? We all watch Sun in the Television riding seven horses." I was intentionally trapping her in her bookish knowledge and her actual brain.

"That is per the Hindu mythology and not science. But now that you have asked, the seven horses of the Sun can be related to the seven colours of the rainbow. Does that analogy make any sense to you?"

"Yes it does. However, I would again have to defer with you madam."

"Why?"

"I think we now know that this world doesn't just have seven colours but hundreds of colours which on intermingling in different proportions can give birth to millions of other colours. So why not million horses madam or millions small horses, pony?"

"What?" She was annoyed at the logic.

"Madam, I have heard few hymns from my father. I don't understand the complete meaning of it. But with the superficial Sanskrit knowledge I have, let me recollect it"

I looked at her; she had made a poker face now. I then read out
vi jananchyavahh shitipado akhyan ratham hiranyapraugham vahantah

"As per my father this roughly means that the Sun is drawing his chariot with golden yoke and white footed horses which has then manifested light to everybody."
"So?" She asked
"Why would the Sun be driving his white footed horses? Isn't it too hot to burn the poor horses?"

"Om I don't think I have the slightest insight of the scriptures. Even if it's written like that, please don't take it literally. Haven't you read about the experiment of Sir Newton?"
"Which experiment?" I asked
"The one where he demonstrated that white light constitutes all the colours? May be the writer here wants to convey that, though not literally? The white horses might be symbolizing all the colors"

That did not make sense to me. Surya could not control his laughter now and started to cough. He hit hard with his elbow to pull me back on the bench and let the lecture finish. While his right hand was busy pulling me, his left hand was on his mouth controlling his laughter.

"I think you are bothering the complete class with this mediocre behaviour."
I just said thanks and sat down.
"Why is this guy creating so much of trouble? He doesn't understand that Sun is *Surya Bhagwan,* having holy powers to generate all colours… idiot!" That was the super intelligent Rajlatha in her Tamil accent and she was infamous in the class for her love for books, so much that she never talked of anything outside the books. I just passed a smile to her and she ridiculed my smile by raising her eyebrows. She had a decent

face cut, but her hair would never be organised. She would often whirl a patch of her hair with her left hand while her right hand was busy writing.

"Sorry madam, I just wanted to differentiate mythology and science but..." I apologised

"Om there are hundreds of beliefs and all of the religions have a theory about life, earth, sun and science is a common thread between all the theories" She made a valid point now.

"So does that mean that to explain logically the sayings of a religion we need science?" I asked

"I don't know." she closed the conversation.

"Sorry madam, I just wanted the myth to be busted by none other than the person who understands science better. I am sorry to have hurt you"

I really did not mean that. I was smiling within, I certainly did not mean to apologise to her.

When madam left, I unknowingly followed her. Maybe she wanted to go to the library and I wanted to visit the washroom, which was just before the library.

I saw Shamita madam coming from the front. She taught us geography. She was wearing her shirt and a short jacket. She always dressed up like an executive.

Most of the boys would often fall for her. She was tall and somewhat on the healthier side. Her waistline would often bulge a bit out of the shirt. But her coat would cover that up nicely. She had a file pressing her chest and had folded both her hands to hold the file. She was brown and beautiful, but she never applied lot of make-up to give her that unpleasant lustre. Her eyes were small but her eye-lashes were long enough to make her eyes look curved like a deer's eye.

I went inside the washroom and while doing the pressure job, I turned my head left to see the ventilator window broken enough to give me the view of the discussion happening just outside the washroom.

"Good afternoon Shamita" Sumona madam wished the Geography teacher midway on the ground. That place was just few meters away from the boys' toilet.

"Good afternoon, all's well?" Shamita madam wanted to know because of the contours on her forehead.

"Yeah, so far all is good. However have you noticed something about Om?"

"Who Om?"

"The one in the ninth grade"

"Oh yes, he is good but bugs a lot" She laughed.

"What does that mean? Don't you find him weird?"

"Yes, sometimes"

"You know today while I was explaining about the life of Sun, he dragged me into mythology." She pressed her lips to show her worry.

"Isn't this the age to question?" Shamita madam asked while holding her ear rings. The rings were matching her tall stature.

"Yes of course but the questions should not be irrelevant and outside the book, right?" Sumona madam explained her worry.

"I would say just ignore his questions, but don't reject them if possible. Rejecting may lead to further search and loss of faith in your explanations about the subject."

"Maybe you are right. I would try to stop entertaining him"

One day while I was walking after the assembly, I could see a very familiar face walking slowly towards me. That face had so much known affection. I couldn't believe what I saw. Was I dreaming???

I pinched myself. Ouch. No!! She came close to me and kept smiling at me.

Then she opened her mouth to say something... but then said nothing and decided to express her feelings through her eyes. She might have aged, but her eyes... still looked the same to me.

She hugged me and moved her fingers through my hair to make me look a little decent. She bent her head to her right a little and scanned me from top to bottom.

Finally the words came "How are you?"

I was feeling so happy. This was Gracie miss... err Gracie Madam.

One more change that Danapur brought in me was referring teachers as Madam and not Miss.

She was looking elderly and weak now. She spoke very little, almost kept quiet.

"How are you madam? How come you are here? I hope everything is fine with you? So many years..."

I had so many things to ask her but there was shortage of words... or words were ready in my brain but were not coming from my mouth?

"Fine" she said just one word and hugged me again like a mother. She made me more emotional by not talking much. She then asked about the Principal's office.

"Come madam, I'll take you to the staff room" I escorted her to the staff room which was close to the Principal's cabin.

She was walking so slow that I could barely manage to be at par with her with smallest possible steps. Anyways it felt nice to walk with her!

I just said thanks and walked away. I was wondering why was she here?

Why did she ask me about the principal's room? I had no clue. Days passed and I could no longer see her coming to the school.

Last time, Shamita madam had taught us about the *supermoon perigee* when the moon is closest to the Earth. She had described that moment as the best time to see the moon, splendid was the word she used. Was that the exact event which made early humans think that Moon was a bright God? Was it the high tides created during full moon in those days led the coastal people believe that moon is not just a calm God, it can destruct as well? I did not know.

"Good morning students, let us study about the rocks today." Shamita madam said while pulling her spectacles from her purse. She kept her files and some books on the same purse. That day she taught us in detail about all kinds of rocks, their forms, their creations and finally the use of such rocks. The lecture had come to an end.

"Any doubts or questions?" I don't remember a day when she had not answered my queries with full conviction and that too with a beautiful smile. The latter was the reason why I liked her and the former was the reason why I respected her.

"Just one small query madam" I raised my hand. This habit of mine was killing my classmates and they certainly cursed me a lot through their expressions for extending the lectures. "Yes Om?"

"Have you been to *Amarnath*… in Jammu & Kashmir?"

"No, but please be relevant in asking your specific question and keep it short" She pointed her palm towards the classroom, showing no one else was interested.

"I have a faint memory of the visit to that place… however I saw the news last evening and saw the video of the giant *Shiv ling*."

"So?"

"Today after you taught the limestone caves, I have this small query."

"Please come to the point."

"What is the possibility that the Shiv ling in the cave of Amarnath is a stalagmite?"

"Possible" She was quick, but then she did not look sure. Then she added her logic to it.

"...as it's a cave. But we can't question the belief around the Shivling. It is giving confidence to live to millions of people around the world. Makes sense?" She asked

"Yes of course madam. I feel that the early civilization was already preaching Shivling and when they moved to the areas around glacier they would have noticed that gigantic structure created by droplets, maybe?"

"Then?"

"This might have been propagated throughout the mainland and thus the faith might have developed in hundred years of information. Excavations have proved that the Indus valley did preach forms similar to Shivling and the bull."

"What an idiot. He is again mixing science with God, foolish guy! Why is madam not sending him out?" This was Rajlatha again and she had the "hmm..." support of some of her nearby benches.

"Om go slow... one by one." Madam asked me and then continued.

"I don't think I am teaching philosophy or history here." She smiled

"Normally stalactites and stalagmites develop in limestone caves and in pairs. I mean if there is a stalactite above then at bottom we can see a stalagmite..."

"You are right"

"In Amarnath, I don't think we have two structures facing each other, and I am not sure what kind of cave it is."

She then rubbed the blackboard, started packing up her items and moved out of the class. I ran to her and managed to break my speed just few inches behind her.

"Madam I have a small request"

"Yes but please nothing about Gods... I have not yet attained the salvation to answer your profound questions."

I was happy but a little shy seeing her smile from so close.

"No madam. Sorry for the trouble. I just have this small query about Gracie madam who joined few days back. She was my teacher when I was in Kerala. However when I met her few days back, she was not able to speak to me, nothing at all! Could you please tell me why has she joined this place and if she is fine?"

"Sure, meet me after the lunch break." She relaxed as I did not ask her some silly question.

I then went for my basketball practice and waited for the court to get free.

"Hey join in Om…" Surya shouted.

They were playing "half-court" as the other half was occupied by few students doing yoga. I joined in and for some time kept my brain focussed on the game. The climate was beautiful with light cool breeze flowing all around. After an hour of perspiration, the bell rang. The lunch time was already over. I ran to Shamita madam to enquire about Gracie madam.

She was still having her food so I waited in the medical inspection room attached to the place where she sat. I never liked the smell of the MI room. It was like Dettol all around. I could see glucose powder on the stool. I took a spoon of the glucose powder on my left palm and started licking it. I saw from the window adjacent to the staff room that Shamita madam was done with her lunch. I threw the remaining glucose in the dust bin and wiped my hand on my pant and walked straight towards madam.

"Good afternoon madam"

"Yes Om, I did ask about her."

"Is everything all right?"

"She now lives with her son. You must have heard of Capt. Ryan Gautier who presides over the school sports committee?"

"Yes madam. He is a nice guy and sometimes comes here to in the morning to play basketball"

"Gracie madam is the mother of Mr. Ryan and she is living with him in the Cantt. Let me also tell you that she is not a permanent teacher here but she has joined here for just few weeks, if it all works out with her son."

"All works out means all is not well? What is the problem? Something very serious?"

"Om I am not sure if you would understand this but life isn't as simple as we think." She opened her purse and took out an even small purse to comb her hair. Her hair was straight but some patches fell in steps, so beautiful that it was difficult to look away. It did not curl up but looked just like a field used for terrace farming.

She combed her hair and said "The problems that we face in life have to be dealt with strong heart"

"I am sorry madam but what is the exact problem?"

I really wanted to help Gracie madam.

"She is alone." She then took out her spectacles and wiped her eyes with a tissue. "This world if full of mess, exactly opposite to what she teaches."

"Moral science... she used to teach us that in Kerala" I completed her sentence.

"Yes, she is a good person at heart but there are some personal issues with her son and daughter in law due to which she is living alone in Pondicherry now."

"Oh! She has no job?"

"Our world works on a theory of retirement and she is well over the retirement age."

Shamita madam was quiet; she wanted me to ask no further questions. She also looked hurt by something, but I was in no position to directly ask her.

She then continued. "...She just wanted to stay here, but that is not looking possible due to some unavoidable circumstances with her son."

Shamita madam kept the books on her shelf and continued "She tried to pursue her interest of teaching in our school but her hidden expectation was staying with her son."
"Thanks for telling me all this."
I left for the classroom with confused mind and heart full of complications. How can such a good lady not be allowed by her only son to stay with him? How can a lady who is a champion of moral values be a victim of such an immoral behaviour? No answers were found.

It was Monday morning, start of a new week. I had decided to find and talk to Gracie madam today. I did not attend the assembly prayers and was waiting close to the kids sports ground to catch her.
"Good morning madam!"
"Om!" She could barely talk and her walk showed that she needed rest.
"Madam I am not sure if you will understand all that I am going to say. I just want to request you... please come to my home. My mummy is very nice and she will take good care of you. You can visit your son whenever you wish to."
I could see a big NO as the answer with her eyes and said "I'm going."
She replied as if my request was not an option at all. I could not understand her departure from Danapur.

"Chap, want to join us for the match?" This was of Capt. Ryan Gautier.
"Sure sir!" My inner self was pulling my legs back to the place I was sitting as I had developed a negative feeling about Mr. Ryan. Why should I call him "Sir"? I should rather refer him as just Ryan, the Insensitive, and ungrateful Ryan.

He was as usual wearing his black tee-shirt with big logo of his unit, the Punjab Regiment.

"Focus! Where are you Om?"

I had missed the pass, but what was I thinking, am I out of my mind?

"Sorry."

My pivots were not working that day; my shots were often coming back from the ring. I was frustrated...

"Hey Om is there something which is bothering you?" He asked

"Nah, I am all right. I would leave for now and will catch up some other day." I wanted to run away from the situation. Mr. Ryan took me in his team as I could play well. He had seen my game and loved my performances.

"Come, let us talk for a minute" He kept his right hand on my shoulder and was wiping his sweat with his left hand.

"Now tell me what is actually making you lose your focus?"

I had thought of keeping quiet but I don't know why I just said "Gracie Madam"

"How do you know her? And how could she ever be a reason for your worry man?"

His face suddenly changed from brownish red to yellowish white as if his secrets had been made public, as if he had been caught red handed.

"She was my teacher back in Kerala"

"So did she say anything to you? Did she hurt you? She is ageing and may have spoken ill to you. She has also become host to some serious bacteria... you won't understand so just ignore her man."

How mean he thought about the ill lady.

"I respect her more than my mother and she is one of the few odd people who don't hate me."

I rejected his assumptions and continued "However, I met her few days back and she has lost the charm, the smile that gave us confidence. The accent and command over her subjects on which she never got tired speaking hours. She looked feeble, vulnerable, she isn't that old." Suddenly I was gaining this thrust to talk more upfront with Ryan.

But then I looked in to his eyes and stopped.
"You need not worry as she is my Mom. We are taking good care of her"
Mr. Ryan was not able to see me in eyes while faking his sympathy for Gracie madam. I gave small whirl with my shoulder to drop his hand off it.
"I don't want you to console me over my bad game, but I want you to look after her bad health. She needs you. Why on Earth would you discard such a nice lady? I remember she often came up with allegory with you as the central character in her lectures. I could feel the warmth that she had and she still has for you. I saw it in her eyes" I wiped my wet eyes.

"Dude... keep out of this. You are just a kid, finish your classes and better watch out your career. I head the sports and you have two subjects of sports." He was just few inches taller than me, but had a good built. He also had a great stamina. The opening of his eyes had expanded sharply and his tone had a warning for me.
"Volleyball I am not sure, but Basketball you would get a big ball in your exams."

I wasn't afraid of his warnings. I further requested "She will be all alone in Pondicherry, she has no job, she has no money, and she has no companion…"
While I was completing my sentence Ryan turned to walk towards me with blood boiling in his eyes. He applied full strength and pushed me with both his hands.
The next moment I was seeing the blue sky. Ryan started leaving but I still stayed on the ground. Things were not static above.

The clouds were slowly going back home. Suddenly a fighter plane flew over me… it was so beautiful that I forgot I was hurt. I kept watching the last glimpse of the *Sukhoi* 30 MKI and closed my eyes. Was I tired?

When I opened my eyes it was a little dark and my back was paining badly. I somehow managed to hold the metal chair and get up. I touched my head and it had few bruises. I pulled over my pants and saw a cut due to the strike with the metal chair. I walked back to catch an auto rickshaw to my home as the school time was over long back. I could see no one in the school premise.

I removed the dust on my pants. The shirt too had got very dirty.

I tried to stop passing-by auto rickshaws to ask them to drop me to the cantt. I checked both my pockets and I was broke. I did not have a single rupee in my pocket. There was no concept of *pocket money* at my home.

I thought I would stop an auto and when I reach home I would ask mummy to pay the rickshaw driver. This idea needed some taxi or auto to agree to travel to my place. None of them wanted to go to that area, not sure what the reason was. I had always travelled by the school bus and had never tried the public transport.

I started feeling a little hungry too; however I had no option but to wait. I closed my eyes and did an akimbo to relax my body. Suddenly I realized that I had forgotten my bag in the classroom.

I was too tired to walk back. Also if I did go back to get the bag, then I would be wasting another half an hour due to my slow walk.

My first decision was to collect the bag next day as there were no valuables inside it. After a moment, I changed my decision and walked towards the classroom.

I turned back and walked slowly towards my classroom through the school playground which would bypass the regular avenue to the class and save some time. I never crossed any ground mid-way considering that action to be inappropriate and insult to the ground that teaches us discipline. I walked on the circumference of the court and wasted some more time to reach the classroom. I could see my old green bag present on the second last bench in the same position as it was left. I hung it on my back and started walking back to the main gate.

While I stepped out of the room, I heard a whisper. I was tall and could see two heads moving just behind the almirah. What the hell would that thing be? I was wondering if that could be a goat which had trespassed the school boundary. Or it could be a cow, there are plenty around.

I walked close to the almirah and was shocked at the sight! Rajlatha cuddling a boy!

I immediately turned back to ignore what I saw and started to walk out slowly.

"What the fuck... who is that?" Came some male voice... did sound familiar, but maybe I was out of my mind that evening. I did not know what to respond so I kept quiet.

"Come over you pervert... I'll thrash you down..." That guy shouted with so much of frustration.

"Hey Sorry..." I moved close and added "This is Om; I just came to collect my bag." I was least interested in knowing who this guy was, hiding behind Rajlatha.

She was best in studies and most of the teachers had some or the other expectations from of her.

"Sorry Rajlatha, I did not come intentionally and have no bad regards for you guys"

"If you ever open your mouth, I would peel your balls and roast them... yeah!"

The guy came in front of me and now I could recognize that he was the infamous guy from Twelfth grade. He was always seen playing cricket and then picking up fights for some petty score issues. He was the captain of school cricket team and was an arrogant piece of crap. He had a hefty build-up, almost double my size.

I had no reason to jump in the fight. I had my bag and I should leave, was the call from my mind. I could recognize him by his thick eyebrows and that thin French beard.

I wasn't getting his name. I stayed away from cricket due to the hype created around that sport in the school.

"Stud, I've seen the big orange ball you play with and throw it with all the fucking power in your ass. Bull shit!!" He was now acting smart abusing Basketball.

He pushed Rajlatha back and her head hit the almirah. She might have hurt badly. He then charged towards me.

I moved back and shouted loud with all my guts "STOP!"

Unexpectedly that call worked. He was in some shock to hear that loud opposition and the way I was standing in front of him. I then added

"And about the balls... the bigger the better... you must know the purpose."

He walked to the blackboard and picked up the duster. I alerted myself for a defence, but then he threw it on the floor and went outside the class.

I then went close to Rajlatha to check if she was fine.

"Look I am not your enemy. I have my bag and I am leaving. I assure you that I have not witnessed anything that was happening behind the almirah. I promise"

She thanked me and got up to walk back. I was wondering how she was keeping a balance between her studies and that badass. Anyways I took a sigh of relief and was replaying the whole drama that happened today. I laughed at myself and took support of the same eucalyptus.

"*Bhaiya*, can I take you somewhere?" There was a honk which brought me to the real task of going back home. This driver agreed to drop me to my place with double rate of the actual fare. I was fine with it. I could see photographs of several Hindu deities, *Sai baba*, and other colorful figures. He even had a cross on the left side of the auto-rickshaw and there was label under it that read '*Jesus is coming back*'
I was surprised and asked him the reason for all the graphics. He explained that by birth he was a Hindu and worshiped all the major deities. He also had a strong faith in Jesus. He said that he often visited church with his Christian friends and that gave him peace.

"Don't you get peace by just visiting a single temple or just the church?" I wanted to see whether his asking for benediction had a limit.

"How can I leave the deities I have worshipped for ages?" He adjusted his mirror and seeing me he continued "but if something new too gives me satisfaction, why not grab it with both hands?"

I was processing his reply, but could not understood how he preached the various forms of faith, without any conflict of interest arising out of either of them. I thanked him for dropping me to this area and went inside to collect money from mummy.

When I came back the road was empty. I walked a little on both sides of the road, but found no trace of the vehicle. He helped me and did not take the fare. I felt bad for not being able to pay him. That day I realised that pocket money is indeed a good idea. From where and in what precise time did that auto rickshaw driver arrive, I could not recall how he looked. I would forever be indebted to that guy.

CHAPTER 6

Migration Towards The Truth

Things moved with almost the same pace until next year when I was surprised to see Principal Sir even before the first lecture had started. He had come to the class with some new person. "Good morning children, meet the new Sanskrit teacher, Mr. Ram Avtar Trivedi. He is a Ph.D. in Sanskrit and has written numerous articles on Vedic secrets.

He had also translated Vedic books in Bengali and English." The Principal then kept the piece of paper back in his pocket and added "Interestingly Mr. Trivedi would also hold the charge of the school library."

After few days I started interacting with Mr. RAT, I gave him this nickname and we all started calling him by his initials.

In our social studies class, we were recently taught about the four *varn* or classes in the early Indian civilization. I then waited for my Sanskrit class so as to ask this to RAT.

"Look Om, the answer to your question could be pretty straight forward but I think it would take a lifetime to learn and understand how ancient India was."
He was right, but I wanted some clue. He then added

"...the best part is that you may still not get the answer." He smiled.

"I was just telling that ours is an ever evolving culture and what you are referring to is a very ancient practice which was designed by people of that age for the society to function the way they wanted to."

"Yeah categorization was fine till a certain limit. But why forcing son of a priest to be a priest and give him the respect which that person may not deserve, sometimes?" I took a pause to see him nod his head and continued "and why ridiculing daughter of a *shudra*, who may be very intelligent?"
"I see where you are going. In civilization, people create rules and limitations for the good. If the people sitting at the top of the civilization are not ethical, they may mould the laws as per their wish and hence the stigma attached to four *varn* remains"

The second part of his answer was too complicated to understand, thus I thought I would let him complete the topic he was teaching. That day he was teaching us about *Tulsidas* and his writings.
"By the way Om, the current syllabus of civics may not be teaching you the fifth varn which was there in the Vedic era. Have you read the Rig Ved?"
"Not read, but yes somewhat heard of its hymns from my father" I replied as I had not learnt that book, but had the memory of few hymns that were often recited by papa. I wanted to learn as much as possible from him, so I was sitting in front of him with zero knowledge. I added
"... but I don't understand it all due to my incompetency in Sanskrit"

"Don't worry now that I am here." He was confident. He then continued "I would recommend you, infact all the students to come up to me and ask me about any doubt they have regarding understanding of Sanskrit or for that matter *Pali* language or the *Prakrit*"

He was taking us to centuries ago and the local languages spoken then. I found this quite interesting but when I looked around I did not see happy faces.
"Thanks, I sure will."
Coming back to the fifth varn he recited hymn 7 (9) to the class

Ya ekaschrshaninaam vasunamirjayati. Indrah panchhva kshitinaam

"This means that lord *Indr* who rules everybody poor or rich and the five races that exist on earth"
"So here we are talking about five classes of men or the five *varn* at that time of civilization." One of the boys explained his understanding. I did not turn back to see him, but sure had good knowledge of Sanskrit.

"The four you've already read and the fifth ones were the *Nishad*." RAT said
Oh! That was the name of my buddy in Kannur? I was talking to myself. I tried to find some correlation between my buddy Nishad and the Vedic *Nishad*.

"Interesting, who were they and are they still here, are they extinct...?"
He cut me short and said we can discuss further but for now understand they were the tribal men existing in those days per Vedic literature.

Now I had a reason to attend the school more diligently due to the presence of RAT. He was open to discussions. He had some good analogy and references of whatever he talked about unlike any other Tom, Dick and Harry saint wearing saffron dress we used to come across on the banks of rivers or on TV. I was tired of the Godmen clad in saffron or white dress speaking on various TV channels.

The Sanskrit classes were conducted in library. I moved back to the classroom as it was lunch break. I was hungry and had the bad habit of not bringing the tiffin box.

"Hey Om" This was Rajlatha trying to talk something to me. She opened her tiffin and showed it to me. She moved her head asking me to have it. Jackpot! She was a south Indian and would bring rice every single day in one form or the other. When asked what she had in her tiffin box, she would reply in two words, the first word would be a variable while the second word would always be rice!
Like tomato rice, tamarind rice, lemon rice, curd rice and so many other prefixes to rice.

"Yes Rajlatha, something important you want to discuss?" I asked moving closer to her lunch box and while she was babbling I would just open the tiffin. It was a white paste of yogurt with black pepper and mustard seeds giving a soothing flavour to the rice she had brought today.
"Thanks for coming that evening. I was very afraid and this guy who is a senior always stalks me?"
"Do you mind if I have this?" I asked her, filtering her long story.
She nodded her head and continued explaining how that guy was always behind her.
"You mind if I talk to the Principal about this and solve the matter."
"No, leave it Om. After that evening, he has stopped thanks to you. God had sent you that night; else I would have never been able to get rid of him."
"Thanks Rajlatha, but you should not worry about any other thing except you being hungry" I showed her the empty tiffin.

She was surprised with my speed, but I couldn't help it. The food looked plain but it was tasty and there was hardly anything to chew. So I finished it no time.

I thanked her and moved out to the playground to see Surya.

Surya was a 'sweet-guy', not because he gave me lift all the time but because he would do anything to eat sweets. That day, he stopped at *'Laalji ki mithai'* an eatery famous for sweet dishes in whole of Patliputr. I felt like spewing, seeing him eat so much of sweets. One after the other, that too so quick! He loved sweets so much that if I gave him a spoon full of salt with a topping of few sugar granules to disguise the salt, he would gulp it down in no time. Sometimes, the sugar syrup or *chashni* as we call it would be spilled over his shirt and face and he would lick all that.

"So what was she saying?" He asked.

"Who?" I was ignoring his plate as it was giving me jitters

"Rajlatha"

"Don't tell me."

I was taken aback when Surya enquired about Rajlatha as he always avoided any discussion about her.

"She was just talking about the food. I was interested in how her mother had prepared the dish"

I knew Surya. He would have felt very bad hearing about that senior who was stalking Rajlatha. It was quite possible that he would have invited some quarrel over it. I thought it's good to keep the matter under the carpet. He was showing signals of a crush on that girl. She looked good, but she certainly had a complex character to decode.

"*Saale*, she dislikes me because of you and now she was offering you food"

I could see envy in Surya's eyes but that was a good moment to laugh!

"I will talk about you only if she is not too crazy about me" I said which gave Surya big smile as we both knew that no girl could fall for me owing to my nature.

Next few days I spent time revising Rig Ved.
I was finding this Vedic book so very close to praising nature in many different forms. Most of the hymns talked about how the sages in Rig Ved offered their respect and *somras*, the Vedic drink to various natural forces. Normally, the boons asked were good rainfall, sufficient cattle, good health and good cultivation. I was preparing myself to learn as much as possible from RAT and ask him precise queries.

"Good morning Om"
RAT would always reply to my wishes. I liked that quality of him, unlike other teachers who would ignore or just answer by smiles. I had reached before the class could begin and opened up my queries, as documented.

"I was revisiting Rig Ved and came up with this query about hymn 45 (2) where *Hrishi Kanv* says:

Shristi vanohi dashushe deva agne vichetasah.
Tan rohitshrav girvanstryastrinshatam vahh

"This, per my limited knowledge of Sanskrit means:
Oh Agni, Oh understanding God, give ear to the worshippers. Lord of the red horse, who loves song, bring three and thirty Gods." I completed.
"Yes somewhat correct" He replied. "But what is your doubt?" He asked then.

"Sir the query I have here is that my father and many other priests say the last word to be thirty three crore Gods." I stopped now.

103

"Both are correct. It literally could be thirty three types of Gods per Ved or thirty three *koti* meaning thirty three crore per legends." He gave some confusing answer so I expressed to know it in greater detail to which he added.

"I would say it's like... hmmm... they are all natural forces, as you already briefed... then it hardly matters what unique name you give to each. Does the count matter?"

I liked his logic of giving names to natural forces could be countless but I further asked "True. In any case, I mean be it thirty three or thirty three crore, I strongly believe that Agni is one of them right?"

"Yes Indeed!"

"Then why would Hrishi Kanv ask Agni to come with thirty three and not thirty two. Or for that matter, one less than thirty three crore?"

"You are not only curious but adamant too." He smiled.

"Om, the essence of that hymn is not to tell the count of Gods as it's a matter of perspective of who translates what. I would say it is un-denying fact that fire is preached in Hinduism from birth till death and so the respect."

Though I did not get my answer, but his statement made sense to me. Why should I be worried about the count? I should rather focus on what I understand about the nature in my own way.

"Is Agni so worth of worshipping that Hindus offer their body to it? I mean why do Hindus, who constitute one eighth of the world population burn their body for so called salvation." I was now focusing on why so much of respect for Lord Agni that the dead body of loved ones are offered to him?" I then continued.

"How can Muslims, Jews or Christians be not going to heaven due to their act of not burning the dead? Parsis have an entirely different way of offering the dead back to nature"

Students had slowly joined in and some were eagerly waiting for the actual class to begin. Most of them had started the murmur;

I could hear the noise behind my back. I had aberrated so very much from the topic that coming back would take more time. I was also hearing some "ohhhh..." and some "yucks..." from the girls' rows may be they took the discussion of dead as a matter of shame. I wanted to take back my question, but now the arrow was already out of the bow.

"Culture is propagated and observed only by the people of a defined area. It can't be forced on anyone else just like faith. Now this place where we stand has witnessed numerous changes starting from Stone Age. You agree?"
He was stern and I agreed very much.

"So Om to answer your query I would recite the shlok from hymn 66 of Rig Ved again where *Hrishi Parashar* while offering prayers to Agni says"

Tam vascharaatha vayam vasatyastamm na gavo nakshantt iddhwam. Sindhoorn kshodhah pra nichirainonavant gavah svargadarshike.

And he was very subtle in explaining the meaning.

"Like cows return to their home after sunset, we go back to Agni after getting cattle and bringing kids in this world. Agni drives the flames as floods. The flames of Agni rise up and guide us to the heaven"

He then added "Now by saying that Hrishi Parashar isn't boasting of how expert Agni is in taking the souls to the heaven, right?"
"Yes." I smiled
"Instead he describes how during those days, the respect for Agni existed that people offered their loved ones after death to him. Now this is again subjective and may vary from one part of the world to other within Hinduism. However the most

important point would be that burning the dead prevents any form of pandemic due to a lifeless decaying body."

I agreed. I just sat down, thanking him. I was now questioning myself as to why should I stick to just one interpretation of the Ved. There are many older or newer religious practices prevailing in the world. But which is the true path, who knows? We are just seekers! After discussions with RAT, I got more curious to understand what the Hindu scriptures mean. We then continued with our regular class on Sanskrit literature.

During a chat with Papa, he had mentioned about his maternal uncle named Umesh who had migrated long ago to Ohio, United States. He was a *pujari* there in a Hindu temple. He had called Papa last week to invite us to attend his grand-daughter's wedding in Cincinnati, USA. I thought let me talk to papa and get some details about his uncle. That evening Papa was in a good mood and was singing some old song of 70s.
"Papa, are we going to *dadaji's* place?" I asked though I knew it's next to impossible.
"No. Why are you suddenly interested in the relatives?" Papa asked this as he had never been fond of any relative.
"Nope, I was just thinking we could meet them. I've never seen him or my grandparents." I looked at him and added "... we never visit the village."
"Yeah" He said. But on further conversation, I managed to get the email address and phone number of dadaji, who happened to be very active in the Hindu community in the US. I had a reason to take the details.

Next day after the school, I went to a nearby internet cafe and thought of sending an email to him. I wrote an email introducing myself and apologizing that we would not be able to come due to some important commitment of Papa. I was not feeling good that we were invited and we were not even responding to his call. I also requested dadaji to send me Hindi translation of some scriptures. The best sunset was always visible from papa's cabin. It was on a little altitude and guarded by nothing but green pasture everywhere. No fence, no trees, just a slope ending in a marshy pool which later merged into the sewage and then finally dumped into the river Ganga. A small flock of the birds was seen from this point as well. They were slowly reducing in number and some making a V shape while flying back to the top... they were trying to cover the huge reddish yellow ball, which was slowly landing on the horizon. They knew its pace and thus were coming right between my eyes and the Sun.

"What are you looking at Om?"
I wanted to reply, but then I was facing the window. This was the last point of the arc diving in the river.
"Hmm...?" I asked
"Why are you here? Seeing the God set?"
"I am not seeing it, just feeling the sunset."
"What? Have they added philosophy as one of your subjects?"
My father smiled.
He then added "It's always an awesome experience to see *Pratyusha*... you know her?
"No."
"It's supposedly the last ray of sunlight leaving earth." That was a good name to that soothing light.
"She is the wife of *Surya bhagwan*... what a beauty!" That sentence of Papa did surprise me. How would a God marry her own light? That might again get added to the list of my unanswered questions.

We started moving out of the office. It was the ration day. I remember Papa handed me the bag full of cheese, butter, eggs, health drinks and other stuff. I sat in the back-seat of the jeep and was reading the contents of this new product in our ration.

"What is this new product in ration?" I asked showing him the shining white plastic box... *Chyawanprash*" I read the name and then continued

"...It sounds like a medicine" I opened the cap and it did not smell good. It looked dark like some grease mixed with rotten fruits.

"It's an Ayurvedic product, very good for health"

"Who on earth would name a product *Chyawanprash?*" I was wondering but this came out as a statement. I then looked at papa and added *"It* sounds like some chewing gum."

"Son on the wooden almirah in the kitchen, have you noticed the red book wrapped in a yellow cloth?"

"Yes, I've seen that"

"That is the *Rig Ved*. I used to recite that to you when you were a kid."

"Oh yes, I too read some of its excerpts when it's not covered and placed open.

"Nice! I did not know that."

Then he added

"In Ved, lord *Ashwini* who happens to be the doctor of all Gods is appreciated as"

jujurusho nasatyot vavrim pramujwatam drapimiv chyavanaat pratiratam jahitasyayurdastraditpatimkrinutamm kaninaam

My father was very fluent in Sanskrit. He was brought up in a society where being a Brahmin was synonymous to knowledge of Sanskrit. I had seen him conversing in Sanskrit with his colleagues and some close relatives.

He then explained how there was a sage named *Chyawan* who had grown old and Ashwini, the official doctor of all Gods prepared a paste for him. That *prash* or the paste made him everlasting youth and health. Thus the medicine was named after him.

"How is that thousand year old 'secret' recipe available to the present day scientists?" I asked with a puzzled mind

"Not exactly the same." He replied quickly but then added "Researchers might have done experiments with Himalayan herbs to make replicate the good *prash*."

I wasn't convinced how such a Godly medicine can be recreated without its secret recipe documented somewhere. May be that was documented at some place and I was not aware of it? Or no one else would have been efficient enough to decode that old extinct language. Then on second thought I realized if God had prepared that paste then the recipe must be in his own language, that was Sanskrit... hence it could be translated well. I was talking to myself...

We had almost reached home. I kept the Chyawanprash inside the bag and prepared myself to get down. Papa looked at me and could see my puzzled face. He wanted me to respect the books, so he said.

"Look no one in this world knew we could fly, we have references in Veds where we actually had submarines, flying machines... again hymn 116 says"

*tugroo ha bhujyumashvinodameghe rayim na
kashchinmamrivan avaahah tamuhathurnaubhir
atmanvatibhirantarikshaprudbhirapodakabhih*

I was impressed by the literature but not the story behind it, so papa continued.

"We had never thought in our dreams that anyone else except for God can create a life... see the clones. Scientists are studying and they are getting to know various secrets. You understand what I mean?"

I had partially got his point, but the clones were happening due to a detailed understanding of reproduction mechanism.

I just nodded my head, ran out of the Gypsy to avoid any arguments and kept the bag inside. Papa might not have liked my rebellion attitude. Or maybe he had started losing hope in me.

It was a sunny Sunday morning, so I felt too lazy to pull my body out of the bed.

"Om, see who is at the door" Mummy asked responding to the knock at the gate.

I got up and walked to the door to collect a parcel. It was addressed to me so I got excited. It was becoming difficult to slowly unpack so I took the scissors from papa's shaving kit and shredded the entire envelop. Slowly the golden imprints looking familiar to me showed up.

Aah! it was a set of Geeta, Ramcharitmanas, Manusmriti and Rig Ved which dadaji had sent us from the US. He had written a short letter as well.

Dear Aum,
Give my love to all in the family.
Not sure if you know this, but during your naming ceremony, everyone was thinking of some sharp and beautiful name for you which would best describe your features. The name should add its qualities in you.

Your red cheeks were oscillating up and down, owing to their heavy weight. You looked at me; I was just overwhelmed to be grateful to you to have chosen me for this. I am glad your name Aum, proposed by me was accepted by all.

I could see that light in your eyes, that curiosity in your smile when you looked at the big neem tree in the atrium of our village temple.

*I have moved to the US for a mission, I have travelled a lot. I am
still travelling. I want to educate people and give the rich gyan of
love and respect through Hinduism.*
Sending you few copies believing it would enrich your soul.

Never stop any form of gyan to not enter your brain!

Hari Aum
Your Dadaji

I did not understand why he had addressed me as *'Aum'* and
not 'Om'; he would have saved an alphabet and meant the
same.

But I finally knew who named me, though it may be a very
Vedic kind of name but people think hundred times before
abusing me as they would have to first abuse my name which
all my Hindu friends find difficult to do.

Thanks dadaji... I said in my mind then quickly hid all the
books in my room as mummy never allowed me to read them.
She felt that reading such books takes away kids from family
responsibilities. She wanted me to hear about the hymn written
in them, but not read them by myself. What was her fear?
She would often ask papa to keep all the religious books away
from me. She had once mentioned how one of our close relative
had left his home in search of salvation to Himalay. That guy
never returned. Maybe that was the fear... but why would I
runaway from such a caring family? I had no answer coming
from within.

I was very happy to have my own copy of the scriptures and
thus I need not steal my father's books in his absence. It was
tiring to pack it back in the yellow cover and then place it at
top of the almirah.

Next few weeks I started reading the Rig Ved and when I got bored then I used to pick any one of other books. This was one of the best times of my life when I was developing the habit of reading books word by word. I used to enquire about possible meanings of each word, thus changing the whole sentence. Sometimes I had so many interpretations and it was giving me that feel of going thousands of years back in the rich history of this land. Sanskrit truly was an amazing experience to read.

"Hey Om, school time man... come out quick" Shouted Surya while honking his bike.
I raised my hand requesting him to stop blowing the horn and called him in. While he was busy seeing the plants outside, I got ready and jumped to drive the bike asking for the keys.
We had this understanding that whoever sits first on the bike gets to drive it.
He yelled at me for cheating and threw the keys towards me.

"Aur bataa?" His style of asking if I had some updates. I should say it was kind of an idiosyncrasy which Surya had developed more recently.
"Nah, nothing new... your side?"
"I met Rajlatha on Sunday, we..."
"What? You are seeing her... I mean seeing outside the school... why, where?"
"Relax *yaar*, she is just a friend"
"Hell crap man, there is nothing called as friendship, don't give me that shit"
"Ohk." He agreed.
"I took her out; you understand this new bike is used now."
"Meaning what you slept on this bike with her? Bloody..."
"Hold on, I mean I always wanted that a girl sits at the back of my bike and I have that feeling of lady-pillion you know. In that ways I am saying the bike is worth..."

"I don't understand that feeling, using bike, pillion... you are dating the bike while riding that girl or dating the girl while driving this bike... tell me *Saale?*"

"Drive slow yaar, you are frightening me, please..." He cautioned me. He was losing the excitement now, so I reduced the speed and then he kept on talking about his blues and dreams about Rajlatha.

We kept talking about his last day's ordeal and the lover boy was pretty excited.

In the school, I had least interest in what was happening in other subjects and would wait for RAT's class to hear him. Days were moving fast now. I couldn't find him that day in the school. Was I missing him now?

Surya had some other plans so I had to ply using the school bus that day. But it was a good day to see my friend happy and sharing his light moments.

"I would be coming late... sorry man" Surya said

"I have a bus pass" I replied with a smile. I was getting his intentions but I had no interest in staying late. I caught the bus that was leaving early and reached home early.

"Good that you came early today *beta*. Come fast with me" Mummy did not even give me time to change my dress.

"But where? Why?" I asked opening my tie knot.

"We will visit Anirudh Gyani Maharaj" Mummy asked me happily. After a lot of efforts, I have got that appointment for you. She was worried since last so many years after I had stopped participating in religious activities.

"Leave her *bhagyawan*, he is not into religion. He has said so many times." My father spoke for me.

I don't know what made me say yes, maybe I did not want to hurt mummy, she looked very serious that day.

Papa did not like Godmen but he was ok that whatever be the means, I was trying to rekindle my faith. We drove to that place. It wasn't very close, but I was lost in my thoughts and time passed quickly.

I could see people waiting outside this hall. This guy had done it big. He had assistants. The receptionist looked like a schoolgirl and must be earning some pocket money from her efforts here. The place from outside looked dilapidated mostly made of mud and some fragile bricks. The receptionist asked us to enter quickly. May be mummy used her influence to get us in quick, though there was a long queue of people waiting outside.

To me, they looked like fools who were in search of alternative ways to die. One of them was sleeping in the lap of his young daughter. This guy who looked like a farmer was shivering. He must be having fever I thought. There was another guy with a fracture and he had come here crying out loud with his friends to get it fixed by this *baba*.

What was I seeing? How would he fix a fracture? A surgery? That did sound so bad. I wasn't seeing any bed inside, nor was I seeing medical instruments to perform surgeries.

Their cases looked emergency to me and hence they should have been allowed first but mummy had no intention of obeying the queue. For her the biggest problem was her son becoming atheist!

"Pranam.... Guruji" My mummy said bending her head and I was surprised at her respect. She never bowed with respect to anyone else, not even my father or her in laws. Why does she need to bow down by the way? This baba should be her favourite in Patna.

"Sit down *beti*." What? This guy looks to be around forty years old, a little younger to my mother and still he called her *beti*? "Thanks a lot Babaji. He is my son." And she stopped for the baba to give some blessings and do some divine comedy with his flowers and pot of water. The baba did not.

He also had ashes and some red liquid, possibly blood of the hen which was seen dead at the entrance of the gate. Some *voodoo*, he may want to call it, but it all looked so funny and weird.

That baba stared at me, made his eyes more broad. His eyebrows had a connection with his side buns and they were at some point meeting his black and white beard. His face was hardly recognizable. However his upper half was tall and the body below that was folded in multiple layers of fats. That made his lower half look very short. He must be suffering from some vitamin deficiency; hence his knees had folded inside making it short and curvy.

He then started shouting few words, some words which did not sound sensible or were coded in his special language. His *mantr* was more like some stone constantly put in a quiet pond; *dip, dop, dip, dop* sound was mixed with common Sanskrit words.

"Very heavy.... *beti*, the dragon's head is in Saturn and the dragon's tail is passing by Jupiter. This is very slow and this boy needs an urgent help... *huck hoo, swaha, aummmm.... phatt phatt... bdooom!*"
What was he saying... is he kidding, dragon... I am not in China? I kept quiet for mummy to be satisfied.
"Baba please help him... I am worried about his nature nowadays. He doesn't even believe in God." My mother took a lot of time to say the second line to describe my problem.

That was a sin and she did not know how offended baba will be hearing that.

"*aummmm... phatt, phatt... bdooom doppp dipp dhoom*!" Did he just repeat that garbage?

"The oscillatory motion of the dragon on the moon can be controlled in time. You've come here just on time" He assured and made mummy smile.

"Today he will see God, he will feel God. It's not his fault. He is ignorant. He doesn't know the power of Goddess Kali." He then went quiet and closed his eyes. Maybe he wanted to show his best, so he took a sharp knife and placed it on my head. I was thinking *what the heck*!

"Babaji.... some other solution... please don't cut his head" My mother was now afraid of the *darshan* I would have. She wondered if the solution could be made easy and non-violent. Meanwhile I was waiting for him to do something, say something and I was controlling my anger and smile both. It was a difficult task.

"Someone has to die and leave his soul to show this boy the presence of God in this world. Who is that someone? Are you that person *beti*?"

He pointed the knife toward my mother and my mother gulped her faith and said no to his option. She must be now happy to have a living atheist son than a dead religious son.

She then kept some more money inside baba's bowl. She requested the baba to be generous on us and show the light to me.

"Difficult.... very difficult. Are you sure you want to do this *beti*?" He asked my mother

"Yes"

"*aum phatt phatt bdoom*.... bring that lamb to me"

116

He asked his follower to bring the baby sheep to him and I was now able to guess what he had in mind.

"The soul of this lamb says it wants to spread the light of God in your son's mind. This lamb is divine."

He then continued after a deep inhale "O Mother, you are the purest energy; I now take the ownership of creating you here for this ignorant child. Forgive me mother and bless this child" He took the clay from his bag and prepared dough. Then he hit the knife on lamb's neck. It bled bad… fine blood vessels spurted out blood like a shower. It spilled projectile jets all around, some of which fell on my mother and she moved to her left.

Most of the blood was directed to the fire in front of us. The lamb shouted and the cry slowed its intensity, baba was trying to make the lamb unconscious and go to some other world smoothly. He was rubbing its face as if it was his child. How fucking caring I thought!

He then took out the last drops of blood in the clay and mixed it well. It looked like some flour being mixed to prepare chapati. He stood up and looked in all directions, from all windows if there was any one who could possibly have hindered the process.

"See no one…" He shouted and sat again. He then asked his disciple to take away the dead, may be to prepare a good feast for the evening.

He smeared some blood that was collected in his hand on to his face. I feel he was doing all this to make him look dangerous and frighten us. How is fear connected to realization of God? I saw that it's directly proportional. The more fear you have, the closer you are to your fictional powers.

I was seeing the drama and my mother was now looking scared.

"O Mother, let me start from your beautiful eyes.... aaaahh..."
He turned his eyes upside down and the brown iris was lost.
How did he do that? He was shouting with both his hands now
covering his eyes and bringing his spirit back to this world.

He then mashed the clay well with blood and formed three
small balls, looking like eyes. He pinned them at the center
and shouted again "O Agni God, give her the powerful eyes...
to burn all the evil"
He put his hand and the clay in fire for some time and then
took it out.
I was seeing such a big evil sitting and doing such hilarious
acts in front of me. He should have been burnt by now by
Lord Agni?

"O lord Brahm, give her the powerful pair of feet" and he
rubbed the clay on his head. Why did he rub it on his head...
Oh! Maybe he thinks he is a direct child of lord *Brahm* so he
is personifying himself as the creator?
Now I was seeing two feet and long legs. He was bad at
designing.... very bad!

"O mother earth give her the hips to sustain her powerful body
and sit on the most evil in the air around" He looked all over
again and rubbed both his hands with some clay back to the
muddy floor. I was now seeing half body.

"O *Indr* God, please give her all your powers to build her
strong waist." He took out few drops of water, which he was
referring as *Gangajal* all the time and poured few drops on the
clay. He then built the waist too.
"Now this is the difficult part... please move little back" he
asked us.

I thought he is not yet done, what will he do now? My mother
had stopped thinking and she quietly moved four feet back.

"O lord Moon you are so calm, so cold, so quiet, so beautiful... give all your beauty and power to sustain the mother in lord *Kali*, allow me to build her motherhood" I was staring at him, what is he building now?

I saw him making the clay big hemispheres and he placed it on the chest part. He then kneeled down before the clay and cried to forgive him for any mistake which he would have committed while preparing the motherhood. His eyes were wet and his expression of sadness was looking more like a smile. That was funny and he proved he was very bad at acting too.

"Lord Vishnu, you are seeing everything, you look after us, and you are in all the forms I see around. I beg you to give me the power to build her mighty arms. Mother Kali, get this arm as a gift and kill every demon in this world"

He placed two cylindrical looking arms of clay which did not bind with the rest of the body and fell frequently.

"Lord Shiv, you are so simple, yet the most powerful, so angry yet so calm, you have given us the energy to build the life on this universe. Give me the power to build the most beautiful face on this planet" He created a circular lump and two dots to signify her eyes and a small nose with a lip mark to make it look like face.

"Finally *Yama*, give her the hair with which she can pull the evil and kill them, she can tie the life and sustain them, she can hold creatures like us on her scalp."

He then plucked some hair from his own scalp and fixed them on top of the clay idol he had built.

It looked like he was making it for the first time. There are several Bengali artists who prepare exemplary and beautiful clay work for Goddess Durga, Kali etc. This guy was doing real time pass and blasphemy for those who are actually preached Goddess Kali.

"Let me give life to her to protect us" He finished his sentence and then took the same knife with which he had cut the lamb and rubbed it on his arm.

He did it slow and so fine that it started bleeding drop by drop, very fine cut.

My mother now bent to ask for forgiveness and show her respect to this fraud.

"What did you see son" He was expecting me to reply with some exhilaration and give him a standing applause. I was thinking of hitting my boots on his head.

I kept quiet and did not reply.

"See the power of mother Kali, all the evil... I see them"

He ran towards the window and closed it tight.

"Everything is gone now and your son has been turned into a true disciple of lord Kali."

My mother offered her five hundred rupee note.

"Baba I have one more problem." I thought of giving it a try to bring my mother out of this man's net.

"Yes my son... now you are connected to me... we are sons of the same mother." He was giving his fake logic out of his stupid experience.

"Babaji I smoke a lot."

The moment I finished the sentence, my mother stared at me and held my hand to give me power to take that evil out of me.

"Ha Ha Ha... I saw your black lips.... I guessed the smoke in your lungs was stopping you to believe in Lord. Now you will feel light and free of congestion" He smiled at his achievement.

"Baba I smoke after every hour. I want to quit it." I made a serious face and continued... "I resist myself but fail.... I've been detected with a very serious problem in my lungs. Doctors call it Cancer! I have hidden that problem since last one year from everybody. I wanted to tell that to a conscious person like you."

Hearing this he rubbed his fingers on his beard that was coming from his chin till his big fat tummy.

"I can see that very well…. It will be cured." He then rubbed the ashes and called back his disciple to offer me some meat of that lamb.

"Don't finish it fast. Have it slowly and cook it without salt… everything will be fine"

My mother had tears now and she was thinking of taking me and admitting me in the Military Hospital right away. I could see a change in her approach for the cure of the disease, but for cure of spiritual ailment, she still had faith in this fraud. She did not show slightest of respect for the current healing procedures and now she wanted me to go so she started pulling me.

"No mother, I will stay here with babaji and mother Kali" I bent my head and my mother stood up and tried to lift me and asked baba to leave me so that I can be taken to the hospital urgently.

"Don't worry beti… he is fine… he is my next successor… I knew since ages that a person born in Himalay and who has travelled through the banks of river Ganga will come to me today and become my heir, the next *Anirudh Gyani dwitiya…*" He was happy and he had now given me a name… I was bloody baptized as a guru!

"I will have it daily baba… I will stay here with you" Hearing that several patients waiting outside and some of his disciples ran towards me and touched my feet. Some patients were obliged to see a new babaji born today and gain consciousness. Now I was seeing a crowd of around fifty to sixty people in this hall and all his disciples too. I then asked

"*Guruji*, I just have few queries before I attain the lotus of your feet" I requested.

"This is the true nature of a disciple; test your guru…. very good. Ask me son…"

He stood tall to answer my queries.

121

"You talk daily to every God in the celestial system... You know their location and presence and the whereabouts of their movements... everything about the planets, the stars... right?"
"Yes... hundred percent."
"So lord Agni must be also in touch with you?" I simplified
"Yes, he resides with me here in this cottage. *Akal prajwalit*"
He was loud in saying the last two words to indicate that his cottage had 24/7 Agni dev customer support.
"So I request you to ask him the temperature on the surface of the Sun?"

Everybody started talking to each other and my mother was not finding a way to take me out. She had closed her eyes and was asking for forgiveness, maybe to the various known forms of Gods?
"Very good." He then answered with confidence.
"You should know that lord Agni is different from lord Sun... You will learn this slowly my child"
"So the fire on Sun is not Agni? Is it something else? So I request you to ask lord Sun about his surface temperature?" I asked again.

He started sweating and felt trapped. He rubbed his sweat and closed his eyes to read his mantr and ignore my question "Aummm... phatt.... aummm phatt...." He continued the mantr for some time and then replied

"God's temperature cannot be measured by any thermometer. God created the measuring units and you want us to use that against him, how funny"
"Thermometer was not invented by any God... but Mr. Daniel Gabriel Fahrenheit." I gave the due respect to the person who did the job and continued...
"Also you are correct to say that the temperature on the surface of Sun can't be measured by a thermometer" This puzzled him. I then added "The electromagnetic radiations emit unique

colours, which in turn have a particular wavelength and can be mapped to temperature. For the Sun's surface it's somewhere around six thousand degree Kelvin. Ask any eighth standard child and he will be able to answer it."

"You are an ignorant fool. You are asking about the heat of the mightiest planet... the Sun?"
I interrupted his poor knowledge about the planets "Sun is a star... not a planet and definitely not a God with seven horses."

He then closed his eyes and read some mantr and threw the water in his hand.
People were now confused at the exchange of dialogues.

He thought that he would make me a mouse or some other animal, but I was there intact, a human. He ran from one point to the other and looked very disturbed now.
His impatience could be seen by the way he was rubbing his hand on his belly.
"You have now become very powerful and my powers are not working against you as you took all of them... you *mayawi* cheater" He shouted and addressed me as a magician, I was laughing.

"I hope your gyan is still with you?" I asked if losing power had not taken away his knowledge from him.
"Yes you may have taken my power but no one can take the deep *Brahm gyan* I have" He was back with his false pride.

"So tell us all what was the name of your great great great grandfather and which religion or God did he preach?" I asked him to look back in his magic box.
He again went dumbstruck and started babbling "No... No one knows. That is a very old thing, how would I know. They were best of the best, Brahmin for sure" he assured.

"So if you don't know the details of your great grandfathers who were alive just few hundred years ago, how can you fool and treat the patients by narrating them about celestial objects created millions of years back? The sun, the moon, the earth, the stars…. they got created millions and millions of years ago. Stop fooling the people around!"

"Go away you ignorant mouse… runaway!!" He shouted with a cry and I saw his eyes getting red and wet again.

"He is correct; this babaji has been calling me since last few months to give a son to my wife. I haven't seen any change or positive sign. I rather see her getting ill due to the raw meat and ashes he offers. I will visit a doctor now." Said one of the patients.

There was soon a great protest built around this fraud baba's *aashram* and he was calling numbers from his cell phones. He had many phones, some under his seat, and some in the jar. The people ran towards him and some started hitting him. I took my mother out from the mob and we sat in the Gypsy to move back to our quarters.

My mummy was sad about what had happened, but she somewhat agreed to the fact that I was not a demon. I explained her that whatever I talked about my disease or smoking habits was a white lie, just to trap the fraud baba. She did not look convinced. She would sometimes call me '*Hiranyakashyap*' who was a very famous villain in the Hindu mythology. I had no other option but to ignore that name.

CHAPTER 7

Gives Up Flight Course

Today RAT was teaching about how to write essays in Sanskrit, usage of grammar. When we were almost done, I stood and thought of asking a doubt which was killing me since last few days.

"Sir, I have small query..." I was about to complete the sentence when he quickly responded
"After the class please."
I was getting bored here as grammar and that too in Sanskrit was least interesting to me. I still sat and was kind of mugging up the things taught by RAT. The class went off and he then pointed his finger at me.
I interpreted it to be my turn.
I was not sure how to ask but I said let me vomit everything I had in my mind.

"I have heard that the job of creation was first given to lord Shiv. Is that true?" I asked
"Yes lord Brahm had asked, I mean requested lord Shiv to create living beings" He replied.
"I don't remember the references of *Puran* but I have heard this story" He added

"So why do we call lord Brahm as the creator?"

"Because he created the Universe, all of us." His reply was killing me

"So what did lord Shiv create?"

"As far as I recall, he ended up creating his own images, which were all immortal and blessed with his goodwill"

"Oh!" I exclaimed... "then?"

"He refused to create any living being with disease or ailments or some other problem. That would have never ended the life" He added.

"Okay then it got re-created, a new version I mean? How did he do that... all at once?" I asked.

"I don't remember exactly again... but from his thighs the demons were born"

"Great and?"

"From his mouth, the Gods were created." He looked at me and continued.

"Cows were born from of his stomach"

"Which is why Hindus preach them?"

"Yes and there are other stories too... will tell you later" He then shifted to the main question and continued

"Animals who run and are tamed for travelling like horses, donkeys, deer etc. were born out of his feet."

"And all the trees and herbs, shrubs were born out of his body hair."

What a description... I was feeling amazed at the literary work of the writer of these stories.

"So who created Brahma? I mean how was he born?" I asked out of curiosity to see what the texts say.

"I don't know. I have never come across a scripture which talks about his creation. Maybe I am unaware as I haven't read them all."

I understood his point. We have numerous references and remembering them all would be a tedious job.

"Sir, I was just reading *Manusmriti* and at one point I read that Brahma from his own body became half male and half female and later produced something called as *virag*"

Before I could elaborate RAT smiled and said

"Just before that reference, in the same chapter did you read the statement where it's explained that the divine resided in the egg for an year and he himself by his thought divided it into two halves?"

"Yes I did read that. You remember that?" I was surprised to his ability to randomly access a topic from the scriptures.

"So this is one theory of how the creator was created. You would find not very different theories in other religions as well. Creation of earth, the planets, life and so on"

I could now relate to other theories I had heard earlier. All had certain things in common; Miraculous, unbelievable and illogical.

"I had some more doubts, only if you have time."

"Sure."

"The book says that those Brahmins who are thieves, outcasts, eunuchs or atheists are unworthy of oblations to the Gods."

"So?" He asked the exact query

"I am coming to that... Further it's written that during *shradh*, the death ritual, we should not entertain people who have braided their hair, who are afflicted with a disease, a gambler or a student who has not studied Ved."

"Look Om, first of all Manusmriti is taking reference from the Ved and is just an ancient jurisprudence. These books were not written by God; consider these to be legal procedures written by some scholars of that time."

"Okay." I agreed as that did sound valid.

"We keep evolving and hence laws change. Same place, if governed by different rulers, can boast of different laws which were accepted by one generation while the other generations might find them taboo. If you've read history, you may be well aware of it. Right?"

"Yes certainly."

"The law of the land in various parts of ancient India was based on how the priests and scholars interpreted texts from Ved, Manusmriti and similar books. No civilian or common man could get up to verify or was capable enough to validate whether the priest was interpreting the law correctly or not."

"Right."

He further added "You may find that for a deity, people offer flesh in one temple while in a second temple, such an act is strictly prohibited"

"Like?" I did not get his statement

"Well in some parts of West Bengal, people offer fish and decorate the fish as a bride. Also in some parts of Assam, devotees offer flesh of buffalo to the goddess. Thus they keep alive traditions prevailing since ages. While for the same Goddess, other parts of India can't even imagine offering flesh"

"You are correct. I remember our Kashmiri neighbours used to offer mutton to some *Bhairav baba* on the occasion of *Mahashiv ratri*, which I haven't seen anywhere else. Also I remember devotees offering dried fish to lord Muthappan in Kerala"

"Hmmm…" He agreed.

"One small doubt again about the sacrificial food." I requested.

"Sir may I please go out, I am having a head ache..." said one of the students. I knew the reason and felt sorry to bother that guy.

"Yes, I know where you are going, that is interesting. Complete your question."

"We also read in Manusmriti that ancestors can be satisfied for two months with offering like fish, three months with meat of gazelles..." I took out the notebook and started turning pages to find where I had written this query. I just remembered those two points.

"Let me complete it then... four with mutton, five with flesh of birds, six with flesh of kids or the lamb, seven with that of spotted deer, eight with that of black antelope... and so on" He spoke before I could reach my reference.

"Yes indeed"

"Okay, I would go back to my point where I explained that law is made by few and obeyed by numerous."

"Right"

"I or any other person may not have the best explanation for this other than the writer." He then continued.

"All priests are not saints, so it cannot be ruled out that there could have been some priests and scholars who would have added these laws to get alms in the form of live animals so that they do the sacrifice and offerings."

"Possible... but not sure, should I just judge it by the literal text"

"You are free to do so or think beyond it"

"In chapter 5, you should have also read that there is a specific clause which says eating of meat is permissible only when you have no other option and your life is in danger."

"Yes I read that."

"Also the book clearly says eating of flesh, especially by a Brahmin, is not allowed unless it's consecrated with Ved."

I was quietly observing his logic; he was very flexible in his explanations and was very cautious in using English words as they might not be the best translations for the exact Sanskrit word he wanted to tell me. He then added.

"Now I don't blame anyone for this. Various other civilizations across the world may have similar or different laws depending on the scholars and animals available in that region. Like offering of fish can never be mandate by a place where there is no sea, lake or river."

"Correct, I understand what you are saying" I smiled at his reasoning.

"On a second thought I would better switch to a different book, as this is a subset and may be this book has been tampered and mis-edited or misquoted by some invaders on Indian soil who wanted their own culture to prevail in the masses." I tried to conclude my understanding.

"Can't be ruled out... Just keep the doors of your mind open." He took both his palms over his head and created a bulb like image on his head. Funny he was, but worth listening.

I thanked RAT and walked out of the class thinking of what I had presumed and how incorrect I was interpreting the law. I took a deep sigh and decided to abjure the law book and move on to other texts, which are given more respect in the faith professed by my parents.

I moved towards the staff room where the clerk was registering our names for the board examinations and now we were supposed to be extra cautious to check all our details like name, father's name, age etc. The information that we gave now would be considered as a legitimate proof for our name, age for all future academic or professional purposes.

I stood in the queue thinking about my discussion with RAT. Things never went out that easily out of my mind. They always came in quick but the exit for ideas was always slow, especially if it came from my area of interest.

"Fill here... here" I heard a shout.

It was my turn and I was day dreaming or day thinking whatever. I checked my pocket and I did not have a pen so I borrowed the one from a girl standing behind me. I don't know what clicked my mind I filled first name as '*Ohm*' and kept last name as all blank as my mind was blank right now. What should I put? The girl behind me was almost putting her weight, and pushing me down. I turned back and out of agitation asked for an excuse.

Oh! She was Rajlatha and co-incidentally the owner of the pen. "Sorry, I was not…." I wanted to say something but held back my thoughts. Why was she forcing her on me? May be it was done unintentionally but she was not bothered by my shout, rather she was staring at my form.

"What Om… this is not how you spell it no? O H M, it should be O M right?" she asked pointing to the form I had filled.

"Yeah I know. But that is me, may be due to the resistance I see in myself. I chose this name, just like that. Ohm suits me better than Om" I smiled and returned her the pen.

Rajlatha was puzzled, so was the clerk. "No last name, no title?" He asked.

"No sir, I want to give up the caste label…" He pressed his eyebrows down and must have cursed my action.

"… and I just want myself to be called by a first name which is short and easy." I am not sure if I was rude, but let it be. That was the impression I always gave to teachers and students, so why change it at the end of the season?

I walked towards the playground, where I could spot Surya sitting above the guava tree. I too climbed one level up.

"Surya are you really serious about that girl?" I asked him.

"I am serious about all the girls, which one you are talking about?"

"Oh, stop that man. Tell me about Rajlatha. How is it going? Don't tell if you don't want to."

Before I could complete my sentence he cut me midway "Some other time, sure." And then he gave that whimsical smile which left me wondering about his feelings for that girl. It was his personal matter and he was a free human. So I did end the discussion at that point. We discussed about the exams and meanwhile plucked some guava from the tree to enjoy our evening snacks.

Days passed until I got another interaction to learn about the diversity of superstition. There was a couple from Ahmednagar who had come to our neighbourhood. The husband was from a different Army unit but the lady was in good terms with my mother. She was a Marathi speaking lady and she followed a lot of fasts. She also did some good amount of prayers which made her in sync with my mother. One day my mother came to the house around eight in night. She had come after her evening prayers from the temple and the new neighbour accompanied her.

"This new lady, Sheela ji, is very knowledgeable" She said.
I looked at my father and had guessed that she must have chanted some mantr or narrated her new stories to mummy, which charmed my mother.

"What happened *Bhagyawan*?" My father asked while chewing his evening dose of peanuts and holding the glass of whiskey in his left hand.
"Did you know that *Shani dev* is the most powerful planet?" She looked at me and asked.
I was now used to her queries and my reply hardly mattered but I still gave it a try
"Yes I've read about it mummy. It's called Saturn in English. It completes one rotation on its axis in around 10 hours which means one day on Saturn completes in just 10 to 11 hours."
She just looked at me and was trying to understand why I was referring Saturn or the Shani as some non-living thing.
"What?"
I continued…"It has beautiful ring of gases around it. Oh yes, one more thing, I remember our science teachers telling us is that it takes around 29.5 years to complete one revolution around the Sun. And thus your *Shani* is also a servant of lord

Sun, which's why it goes round, and round and round…" I smiled and looked at papa.

"Forgive him, he is still in his books" Papa did override my logic and gave some weight to my mother's new discovery.
"I don't know what they are teaching in books nowadays. Previously it was so good. Kids used to learn just about various types of planets, *nakhsatr*…" She rejected the whole education system and I kept quiet to just hear her logic.
"She is from some place in Maharashtra, she called it… *Nagar*" My mother was finding difficult to recollect the name or she was confused how it could be the name of place. It sounded more like an address in a city.

"Yes, I have few training day friends from Ahmednagar. The localites call it just Nagar" Papa said
"Why? Is it due to the first part sounding Muslim… Ahmed?" I asked.
I did not like the idea of shortening or ignoring a part because it sounds Muslim. Maybe I was wrong.

"Let's hear what your mother wanted to tell first."
"Oh yes, she told me a story about Shani dev. That story clearly tells that Shani is the most powerful planet in this world." She had a belief now.
"But mummy…" I wanted her to stop as I also could not see my mother getting brainwashed. She was already over loaded with fasting four days a week. I still continued.

"Don't you think that earth is the most powerful planet? We have life here. We breathe oxygen, drink clean water; we have plenty of food, good humans, trainable animals, so much of entertainment and beauty?" I wanted to speak more but stopped seeing her unconvincing expressions.

"Yes *Prithvi* is our mother, but the strength I am talking is spiritual power. Shani seems the strongest owing to his powers." She certainly was fed with some new knowledge about Saturn. "Okay mummy I agree. But still Shani is the second strongest planet even if weight or size is considered. Jupiter is much bigger... I mean *Shukr*."

"Oh, you are not getting me. I am telling about powers, miracles not the size... understand?"

Now for this angle of powers, I did not have much in the books so I gave up.

I thought of keeping quiet now. RAT often said I was a bad listener and maybe he was right. I often deviated from the main discussion.

"Have you read about king *Vikramadity*?" She asked. This was certainly a history question so I said yes.

"Such mighty king Vikramadity was also forced to go through bad times due to *Shani dev* coming over him for seven and half years. Shani dev was dishonoured by the king once and that led to Shani dev's fury when he had visited the Earth once."

"What? One planet coming on a different planet to meet a king?"

I asked and my mind was blowing out while asking this question.

"Om, you will not understand this. Lord Shani stays in the zodiac for two & a half and seven & a half years, so powerful!" She now did not want me to listen now. After that she focused on papa completely.

"The point is, we need to observe fast on Saturday... every Saturday."

Papa approved with the blink of his eyes.

"I've got this booklet as well. It has the *stuti*. Even lord Ram were not spared from the sight of Shani dev, we should do fasting for lord Shani... *Om shanti, shanti...*"

She had a new reason to pray now, or a new reason to fear from?

Next few weeks, I would see her busy just in getting mustard oil and coins which had to be offered while reading the booklet. I had got a new reason to stay away from home for longer hours. I would often spend more time roaming around with Surya.

There was a school trip organized for our class and we were supposed to visit forest areas of neighbouring state Jharkhand. Everyone was pretty much done with the packing. That was a much needed break for me. Papa had given me some money and also a big kit with necessary articles.

The bus started. I was excited to see the wildlife in proximity of nature.
It was the Betla National Park in a place called Palamu. It had already got dark by the time we reached the point.
I didn't know which all teachers were accompanying us but felt happy to see RAT as it would be good to talk to him in the absence of any wildlife.

Teachers made a bonfire and some '*lumberjacks*' of my class took out their guitar and started playing the usual romantic Bryan Adams stuff.
The voice of the singers and the string both were annoying to me but seldom did the girls feel that way. They were like "Yeah! Wow!! Sing hotel California please."
Surya too looked occupied with some new girls. I looked at him, but he couldn't shift his focus from the ladies. I couldn't understand if I should really breach that privacy, so I decided to move alone.

Our trip planner had taken special permissions for us to stay inside the wildlife park and for the fire to be done with utmost precautions. He was explaining all the dos and don'ts but I wasn't hearing.

I would better take a walk; I thought and went alone before anyone could spot me near the cottage. I heard a little about the *'old fort'* which was about a kilometre away per the map I had. The sun had set already. The guide had said that during this time the tigers don't come out in this region. Thus I had no reason to be worried about.

I opened the rucksack and took out the mosquito repellent. I applied the cream on most of the exposed parts fearing the malaria more than any beast.

Though there weren't any large trees in this part of the park, the area was full of shrubs and thorny bushes. I then started walking towards the Fort following the distant tip of it. I wanted to reach till that point and come back by dinner to meet the group.

A cold gush of air suddenly touched my neck. I could hear someone breathing on my back. I wasn't that afraid as tigers don't come here, I was assured and other animals don't look that harmful on Television. I paused for a while and tried to feel the surroundings. Let me take a look at what it could be. What if it's a real tiger and wants to jump over me? Should I sit or should I run? There is no tree to climb over.

Despite of the cold breeze, I could feel sweat running down my forehead. I thought of slowly sitting and simultaneously turning back to see what is coming by. I did manage to get hold of a bamboo stick which was just a foot far.

Swishhh! I turned and there was..... nothing!

I was even more terrified now. How could I be so scared? I had completely lost my focus and started running to reach one of the boundary walls of the fort. The moment I felt like touching the wall, I felt some liquid under my feet. It was a little warm and somewhat sticky liquid between my shoe and my feet.

I opened my shoes and the right foot was bleeding. I couldn't find any glass, metal which could have cut this. It was pretty dark now so I opened the kit which had a small torch in it. When I switched it on, I could spot a sharp stone which was stuck in the right shoes sole. I pulled it out of the sole and threw it away. Further searching inside the kit, I got *tincture iodine* liquid using which I washed the cut.

Now I was definitely not feeling good about this Fort. I thanked papa for keeping such handy things for me without my knowledge. I managed to walk more around the old fort to see anything abnormal or any wild animal. Paranormal activities never created fear in my heart but I was scared now. I continued my walk with this bamboo stick in the hand and collected few fruits which had fallen by themselves. Some looked like lemon and some like a cross breed of orange and guava.

I did not eat them, just collected them. As I took turn to go back, I saw smoke and a light source few yards away. The luminance wasn't bright to be seen from long but like a small candle. The fire was placed above a broken branch of an old shrub which looked like a dried up tree about to die. But the vent inside the branch was all black due to the light. The fire couldn't go for long by itself as there was no wax, no oil which would keep it burning. I wanted to see who had done it. I had switched off my torch and waited.

I sat beside the wall to see if anyone visited to light it up again. There wasn't any bird or bat, but lots and lots of cricket and similar insects which were completely out of sync. The boy of my class on guitar was much better than the cricket orchestra I was hearing now.

When no one came, I felt like checking the site. I moved pretty fast towards the tree.

I climbed the first strong branch and lifted my right hand up in the air to hold the light source with my thumb and the index finger. I didn't see what I was holding but it was some obsequious object which might have been covered with some natural oil from the branches. Slowly I jumped down with the light source in my pocket. I ran till the boundary wall of the fort and sat for some time. Now I thought of checking this item from close. I took out my torch and the object. I held the torch in my left hand and the light emitting object in the right. "*Wooouck!*"

I immediately threw the light in my hand away from me. It was a group of fire flies emitting their natural light. They all were pinned together to form a circular chain like structure supported by a dead lizard. I was holding the lizard's tail all along. I wiped my hand on the floor.
Could this be an ornament of some tribe we don't know yet? Could this be a garland for some deity the tribes have? Could this be a trap by some smarter mammal to catch up fire flies and eat them? I had no answers.

I was done with this short unofficial excursion so I started moving back. I thought I will walk fast this time instead of enjoying this place. While I was limping with my bleeding feet, I could hear pressing of shrubs and some footsteps that were a little faster than mine.
I ignored considering it to be echo of my walk or some monkey passing by. I started running this time feeling the weight of the rucksack on my back. The sound from the grass was more prominent now and I knew I had to speed-up. I then gave full throttle to myself. This run reminded me of the school athletics. After a very long time, I was running. This time I wanted to win, the motive was huge.

Then a big hand approached me from my left and it finally managed to hold my shoulder. I stopped now as running away was not in scope. I bowed down in surrender with closed eyes. Then I opened them to see a tribal guy too thin but painted well with some natural white paste all over his body. His teeth were shining more than his white paste. He said something to me which I couldn't hear well, neither understand.

I raised both my hands to say sorry if I had hurt his faith.

This guy was thin but had long hands and a spear made of metal. His expressions and hand now looked like some understandable formation. Was he enquiring? I could not decode his question but kept asking for forgiveness.

He then ran his hand all around his neck and made a flower like symbol using both hands and lifted them up. I was focused on his hands as his tongue was nothing less than Morse code for my ears.

Finally it seemed to me that he was asking about some flower which had just bloomed or was it some light... Oh yes!

I managed to smile a little and gestured to follow me to the boundary of the fort. I started searching the place where I had thrown the garland of fireflies. The guy now lost his patience and started shouting at me in his language which sounded much like Bengali. Good that the abuse was somewhat familiar!

I managed to ignore him somehow and kept the search running. It was dark now which had made it even more difficult to find it. Then suddenly, close to the boundary wall of the fort, I saw one bead shining like a small bulb toggling on and off. Its light was reflecting due to the white brick behind the firefly. I was relieved that I finally found it.

I lifted it up and presented it to the tribal guy. He started rejoicing with laughter. He was in no mood to stop soon, so happy... with tears tumbling down his eyes. The white paste under his eyes was getting wiped off and a new line had built to connect the other white paste on his cheek.

He then started jumping all over the place and finally took out a fruit from of his *dhoti* like garment and gave it to me. The garland was a precious gift for him. I also gave him the fruits I had collected in exchange of his gift. He was busy enjoying and I thought it was time for me to leave the place. I walked back and could hear him singing and shouting with his pride possession.

"Where were you man? We searched you all over the place" Surya asked me.
I did not elaborate but gave an excuse for my outing. Then both of us headed to our tent for dinner.

While we were talking, I could see someone wanting to excuse inside our tent. It was Rajlatha; I looked at Surya and smiled. "Surya do you have something for mosquito?"
I understood what she meant but I did beat Surya on this and replied "Yes for mosquito, I just have blood. I can feed the female."

"Please Om; I am not talking to you." I said sorry and left the matter with Surya.
He was having a hard time searching for a mosquito net which could be given to his lady love. I took out the ointment and pointed towards Rajlatha. She looked at Surya and got some telepathic approval. She came close to me and collected it. Then with all unthankful expressions on her face, she looked at me, turned back and again looked at Surya and said thanks and went away.

"What man, why do you pull her leg always?" Surya said with efforts to control his laugh.
"She is dusky hot, but... What will I get if I pull that fat leg?" This forced Surya to jump on me and hit me with the pillow. I laughed while he continued hitting me before we finally settled for dinner and nonsense talk. Don't remember when we slept.

It was a beautiful sound of some small sparrow chirping close to our tents that woke me up in the morning. I walked out to check the noise.

I was happy to see RAT and some other students busy early in the morning practicing postures similar to yog. I took tea being served there and sat beside my tent.

I was enjoying this time.

"Sir I have a question?" I asked aloud.

"Om, not now... we are busy in *Pranayam.*"

Oh, so that was Pranayam. They all look same to me. Various postures up and down, bending, curving, and breathing in and out.

I enjoyed the cup of tea. Every sip was much more refreshing than any form of morning exercise to me. So soothing!

RAT did not have tea rather a glass of water with some red liquid mixed in it. I enquired about it and got to know that it was water and honey with few drops of lemon in it. He said it kept him fresh and healthy always.

"So you were asking something Om?"

"Yes sir, only if you are interested in my boring questions."

"Shoot!"

"I was wondering if you have read about any *adivasi* culture or any tribal form of worship."

"What makes you ask that?"

"Nothing I was just thinking about what God, faith and ornaments could mean to a tribal person who has not read Geeta, Quran, Bible or for that matter any scripture which guides how to lead life"

"Very good question. But don't they already have some form which they worship like the trees, the rain, the river, the animals..."

"I think that is much better than taking rules out of any book written by humans and then follow each and every line by heart."

"But they do worship the almighty right?"

"Yes I agree, but by what name, creed would we force them to register if they come to school for admissions? Hinduism... *Sanatan...* what?"

"Look Om, I understand what you are saying. I think there are numerous classes of tribes, who don't know how and what to pray. All they know is that nature is the source of energy and it should not be destroyed or exploited. We call ourselves civilized and are exploiting this world as much as we can. They use the nature's gifts just in as much quantity as required." I couldn't understand where he was going with that. He continued

"...but you should not forget that we too were tribes millions of years ago. We underwent various forms of civilizations and chose the most convenient for us to live. We migrated all around the globe to finally reach this stable state of civilization."

"I have read about the tribal conversions to Christianity. How do you explain that?".

"Yes that is sad. The people who have just one motive in life, that is to propagate their faith in all corners of this world, do not look at the larger picture. The poor tribes of Eastern India are lured not just by money, but jobs."

"You are right; I've seen idols of Mother Mary in traditional Saree, which is worn by tribes of Jharkhand.

"Finally what they need is any X, Y, Z religion that will give them job. Right?" RAT made a very valid point.

"What about the procedure adopted by few to revert their religion? That sounds funny" I asked RAT

"Yes, and I wonder what caste they are put into once they are brought back to Hinduism; Brahmin, Kshatriya, Vaishya or Shudra?" RAT's last statement was satire mixed with the truth faced by eastern parts of India.

I could relate to what he said.

"It was a very slow procedure. What we have right now is a set of societies, with each society having time-tested and well balanced list of rules, be it religious or the constitutional. It does have scope of amendments though."

"You mean there could be adaptations from one civilization to other?"

"Also, understand that there are a lot of similarities in various civilizations which have developed within and outside India. One small example is *Doppa* which means hat in *Uyghur*, people of central Asia spread across Russia, China, and Turkey. In hindi we say *Toppa*..."

"Okay?"

"Persians mixed with Punjabi call it *paihe* for money while we call it p*aise*. Why go so far, let us see within the subcontinent. Heard of *Bohag Bihu*?" He asked

"Nope"

"It is celebrated in Assam and nearly on the same date as *Vishu* in Kerala. The sounds 'va' and 'ba' seem interchangeable in some dialects and 'sha' and 'ha' also hold that logic, thus Bihu becomes Vishu or vice-versa."

"Yes Vishu; I have celebrated with full enthusiasm while I was in Kerala."

The logic seemed reasonable.

He took a long pause and then suddenly asked

"Have you read the holy Geeta?" He asked.

"No, but should I?"

"Of course yes! You may go through it and understand life better as you are a Brahmin by birth." Why did he give a reason for me being a Brahmin? He left me puzzled after that good reasoning. That was in my To-Do list while travelling back from the trip.

I took out the book and for the next few weeks, soaked myself in reading the Sanskrit *shlok* and their translated literal meaning to understand what they mean.

I was reading it line by line and did not to misinterpret or miss any shlok. It was the 13th day of my reading and I was done with all the chapters and preparing notes for all my queries. I found the answers of some of them myself, but for some I wanted a Phd to attest my assumptions. I was feeling good but empty as I did not get many important answers. Instead several new questions were born.

I was now curious to talk to RAT and get a clarification on my doubts.

I skipped my first lecture and directly ran to the library where I would find RAT. He was taking some other class, so I waited reading the newspapers and some sports magazines. I was constantly looking at him to see if he had got free so that I could catch him at the earliest.

"Do you have some time? I mean a little more than 'some'?" I asked as soon as the pupil started leaving.

"I would have but right now is the time for parent-teachers' meeting; I am the class teacher of Eighth grade. I hope you know that?"

I nodded and thanked him while heading out of the library disappointed.

Next day too, I did the same, came to school and ran to the library. I watched RAT come and place all his files and books right where he placed them every day.

He smiled and asked me to sit next to him.

"How was the meet sir?" I wanted to make some small-talk before I irritate him with my questionnaire.

"You can come directly to the queries" He smiled.

"So I did manage to read Geeta hiding it from my parents." I explained him how my mother was wary of me reading Geeta and the reason for her fear.

"So how did you feel?"

"I have some queries as always. Allow me to ask you from the beginning"

"Yes, everything should start from where it started. Right?" He always looked happy and ready to answer.

"I would try to speak as it is in Sanskrit. Please correct me if it is wrong or my interpretation is wrong. Chapter 1 Shlok 41 says"

Adharmabhibhawatkrishna pradushyanti kulstriyah
Strishu dushtasu vasharney jayate varnasankarah

"This I found a little demeaning for women. Here I interpret it as intermixing of castes and women wedding out of so called *'varn structure'* might lead to destruction of the whole lineage. Am I correct?"

He scratched his beard and thought for an answer, but I had another similar query. So I then added, "Shlok 42 says"

Sankaro narkayev kulgnanam kulasya cha
patanti pitro hyesam luptpindodakakriyah

"I feel this can be translated to a statement which means promiscuity destroys the whole race and those committing that sin are deprived of *shradh*, which is ritual act to satisfy the spirits of ancestors?"

I was seeing RAT smiling at my curiosity and he did not utter a word. He now thought it would be good to answer all similar queries, so asked me to go ahead with more shlok by raising his right hand. I continued.

"Finally the 44th shlok of the same chapter says..."

utsanna-kul-dharmanam manushyanam janardan
narkey aniyatam vaso bhawatityanushushrum

"Here *Arjun* presents before Krishn his understanding that, the men who have lost their family traditions, dwell in hell for an infinite time."

He took a sigh. I too was reading it fast, so I tried controlling my breath. After few seconds I elaborated my doubt.

"My common questions for all these hymns are that why the caste system given so much of emphasis even during the time when the almighty Krishn, who is supposed to be the most loved and preached God of Hindus, himself was present."
I stood up and added "Why would that civilization treat people on the basis of caste?"

"Your translations have been literal."
"Yes."
"First understand that Geeta is a special portion of the epic Mahabharat. The rules prevailing in those days were mostly taken out of Ved which were much older than Geeta. Agree?"
"Yes."
"I have no scientific proof, other than scholarly articles to calculate correctly the age when these were written. There are pundits and scholars from Hindu religion who say it's much older than 3500 BC."
"Wow!"
"Then there are some who are just followers with no intent to question who say Geeta is since millions and billions of years."
"Agree" I said with a smile on his last logical satire. I had seen many such followers.

"So if you read your history books of NCERT, the *varn* structure was very much prevalent in those days. The write-up may be inspired from the society structure and laws of those days. I still feel that the message the shlok wants to convey is that no person shall breach the rich heritage of his clan and should abide by the traditions and virtues of their lineage."
"Possible" I somewhat agreed.
"Also never forget that whatever civilization it is, women have always been deprived of several basic liberties." He added.
"I couldn't agree more with you on the last statement of yours. But I don't find a reason why a lady becomes so bad in words of the above shlok. Also I am partially worried about such tradition still prevalent"
"True"
"We have had much abominable practice like *sati pratha*, *purdah* system, hatred towards so called lower castes, which eventually got abolished due to our mixing cultures and fight by reformists like Raja Ram Mohan Roy, Jyotiba Phule and many others whom I might not know."
"Indeed."
"I also thank the education and the Europeans who brought equality to women."

"More questions?" He asked seeing my notebook. I think he wanted to know how long I would keep him busy.
"Yes another query I have is from chapter 4 shlok 5 where lord Krishn talks about rebirths"

bahunime vyatitani janmani tav charjun
tanyaham ved sarvani na twam vettha parantap

"I assume here lord Krishn says to Arjun that he and Arjun have passed through many births and Krishn remembers them all."

"Yes. The shlok was an answer to Arjun's question about how Krishna could have imparted the knowledge of *Yog* at the beginning of creation. So this shlok is actually glorifying the timeless presence of Lord Krishn."

"Okay"

"And to answer rebirths, it has no answer" RAT looked helpless while answering the second part. He continued "...as we don't know what happens after death."

He was right, though I didn't believe in rebirths but I was not sure what must be happening after death, still a big mystery.

"Can we take a short break, as you seem to have few more queries in your list?" RAT smiled and moved out of the library. I waited for him thinking about this great book which has given peace, strength to millions of people. I was searching for the reason for that peace.

"So, where were we?" He asked looking fresh now. He had combed his hair. Maybe my questions were hair-raising for him?

"I am still in the confused state, full of queries."

He smiled on this.

"So my next query is about same chapter 4 shlok 13 where Krishn himself admits that he is the creator of the four varn prevalent in those days. He has created and classified them as per their qualities."

Chaturvarnayam mayaa shrishtam gunkarmavibhagashah
tasya kartaramapi mam vidwayakartaramvyayam

"Yes Geeta does state that. Lord Krishn here wants to convey that he has thoughtfully understood and divided the classes and given them work per their potential and talent. A not so good warrior can become a good merchant. Similarly a person not great in business cannot go to *Vaishya* class, but if he is strong and courageous then he can go to *Kshatriya* class" He elaborated.

"I agree to that at level one. But the question is why the complete family bears the same work forcefully. Son of a Kshatriya can be a good artist or salesman. Son of a so called *Shudr* can be a good scholar. So why give *Shudr* less respect. I mean why respect is directly proportional to the hierarchy in the *varn*?"

"I think we've had discussion on that or is it the *deja vu*?" He smiled
"Maybe..." He was correct; even I could recall my discussions with him on this topic. But what answer did I get, I had forgotten that.

I then continued "...but let me add that in chapter 18 shlok 41 as well lord Krishn says the duties have been assigned to all four varn as per their inborn qualities... which I don't understand."
"I know what you want to ask. However this shlok nowhere states that Krishna gives less respect to Shudr, Krishn himself was not born Brahmin?"

"Yes the scriptures say that, but I still don't understand why the respect for Shudr is less than others if Krishn himself had designed and put people in that class. The duties they were given was equally difficult in those days. Lord Krishn would not have wanted such hardworking clan to get offended by the upper class, right?" RAT did not answer but just bobbled his head.

"Ramcharitmanas?" I asked if I was allowed to jump to other book for a quick reference.
"Yes sure." He smiled at my quick jump from one text to the other.

"Thanks. In *Uttar Kand*, we read how *Kaliyug* is described"

Badahim shudr dvijanah san hum tumah tey kachu ghati
janayi brahma so biprabar aankhi dekhavahi daanti

Before I could ask on this RAT replied "Yeah as I've said the writer is living in that era where the four varn might have been at its peak. There might be some exaggeration of the ill-effects of Kaliyug; this is used as a reference. Here it's stated that Kaliyug would be so bad that even a so called *shudr* would be debating with twice-born breed."

"But what mathematics would have come up with that formula... twice born?"

"I am not sure, the birth procedure must be equally complicated for both the castes" And we laughed at his light hearted condemnation of the disrespect for Shudr.

This time I could see RAT was feeling a little uncomfortable in continuing this topic. So I thought I should move to the next point.

"My next query is about how society respected people who worshipped other deities in those days. In chapter 7 shlok 20 Krishn says"

Kamestayystayyrhattgyanah prapadhyantey anyadevatah
tam tam niyamamasthay prakrityah niyatah swaya

"Here I translate with my limited knowledge of Sanskrit that people whose wisdom has been lost due to various desires start worshipping other deities."

"Yes, you are almost there" He asked me to come to the point.

"So what other deities is he referring to?" I asked as I doubted it to be other religion?

"I am not sure, but this may be a way to prevent people from approaching false Godmen who loot simpleton by luring them with quick solutions using sacrifices. I interpret that lord Krishn wants that people stick to deities as described in the Ved."

"Could the other deities here mean any other form of religion, present in those days? Or was it written to stop the outflow of people from Hinduism to some other religion, prevalent in ancient Rome or Greece? I am not sure, just a guess."
"Possible, but which religion doesn't want its people to stay together and not scatter here and there in search of salvation, when the self is an answer to all."

He was right. That always remains as the most important factor binding people in a religion.
He then continued. "Hope you have read chapter 3 shlok 42 where Krishn compares senses, body, intellect and self" He looked at me expecting an answer.
"Yes I liked that shlok. Very interesting comparison between the four and how self is described as the ultimate" I agreed but then added
"Sir, I am not here to say that Geeta is incorrect, I am here to understand from you what has been written and why it has been written. I take it as a good scripture and part of ancient Indian literature."

"Good" He felt happy now, I was slowly clarifying myself.
"My next question is about the mystery of God, in chapter 10 shlok 2 Lord Krishna himself says"

Na me viduh surgana prabhavan na maharshyah
Aham adirhi devanam maharshinam cha sarvashah

"Here lord Krishn says that neither the Gods, nor the sages know secret of Krishn's birth. Then how do I believe any book, any scripture which talks about Krishn or about creation or about life. How do I believe that the writer, sage Vyas understood Krishn's secret to write Geeta, the way he wanted?"

151

"Very nice question. The reference here is to Arjun and the context is to build confidence in Arjun. The prime motive could also be to tell Arjun that what is happening is decided and Arjun has to obey what *Dharm* says. Arjun should not worry about mundane and love for his brothers in the rival group."

"Okay, but I still don't understand completely, how a writer could understand the supremacy and greatness of Krishn and write his sayings" I wasn't satisfied as that shlok was the most complicated and contradicting shlok, putting a question mark on the understanding of the supreme lord by the people who have described him in the form we pray his idols. I thought of not stretching the topic, so moved ahead.

"My last query on Geeta is…"
"Finally the last one, it was a short affair. I thought the discussion would last till the end of the day" and RAT had a sigh mixed with his signature smile wiping the sweat over his moustache.
"Sorry… the last query is directly hitting me in some ways. In chapter 16 shlok 8, lord Krishn says about the non-believers or should I say the atheists that"

Asatyam pratishtham tey jagadahurnishavaram
Aparasparsambhootam kimnyatkamhaitukamm

"Correct me if I'm wrong but here lord Krishn says that there are non-believers who feel this world is absolutely unreal and Godless and that this world is brought by mutual union of the two sexes."
"Correct"
"I am a student of science and I respect the concept of evolution more than any religious theory of creation of earth, be it Hindu or non-Hindu." I wanted to describe my query more, but RAT understood my point.

"Okay. The *shlok* you just said is for people with demonic nature. Are you an atheist? Needless to ask, but still?"

"Yes I consider myself one."

"Are you a demon?"

"I don't know, I may have hurt many through my arguments, but I am certainly not sadistic. My mother calls me *Hiranyakashyap*" I smiled.

"Don't worry, there are people in this world, busy doing destruction and fear no God. They are occupied in lust and ruination of life. You are certainly not the target of the shlok" RAT smiled and stood up to leave for his lecture while seeing his watch.

"Do you have some more time?"

"Yes, I am paid to teach you." He smiled and this time few others who had come close listening to the discussion also smiled. They also looked interested.

"Can a person convert; I mean upgrade or degrade to a caste per the books?" I asked

"Yes there are references about that in *Puran*. I can narrate numerous but I will tell just one."

He then briefed me about some person called *Prishadhru*

"He was the eldest son of Manu. You must have heard of him?" He asked

"No, I am sorry. But I would love to hear it more..." I went a little close to his chair as his voice was now becoming too low to hear.

"One night while he was required to protect the cows, a tiger broke in to the cattle shed. *Prishadhru* had very strong arms and equally capable sword" He paused

"Then did he kill the Tiger?" I asked

"It was too dark and he did attempt to... there was lot of fighting and bloodshed."

"Then?"

"Next morning when he checked the cottage... he was left shattered"

153

"Why... what happened?"

"He saw that he had actually murdered a cow. That was a heinous crime" RAT completed

"Poor boy! It was dark, what could he have done? His intentions were good."

"Yes, but the result... cow murder is a sin per Ved and thus he was cursed to lead a life of a *Shudr*" He now came to the point.

"So you mean killing a cow can degrade a person of so called higher caste to a lower caste?" I had a reason to ask

"Yes the story does tell that. Moreover it's not a decree... it's just that he now had a role which was more difficult in the social life of ancient India."

"Okay. So we have people in this world who eat beef. We also could have a scenario where someone accidentally kills a cow on the highway. So such people need to lead the life of a *Shudr*?" I asked in more straight forward way, which was not liked by him.

"I don't know if a person of different religion can be put under this law... as we had only ancient Indians then. But such accident by Hindus, if you visit villages is still considered as a big crime. They serve severe guilt and penance."

He stopped now and again looked at the watch.

"May I take a break for a lecture?" He smiled and went out of the library.

I was still blank as RAT gave his interpretation of every shlok and I was reading it from the writer's perspective. The more I read these scriptures the deeper I went into confusion. I then thought it would have been great if I could start practicing the worldly affairs and gain knowledge out of experience. With that final thought I threw the list of questions I had for RAT.

I thanked him for being patient but was cursing myself for coming across no solutions to the wars and poverty in this world. Was I over expecting from the book or maybe I did not understand that great book at all?

Whatever happened, it gave me a feeling that no book, no scripture if read and consulted can be interpreted in just one best way to lead such a complex life. There were numerous ways of interpretations and then there is the context why the book had been written, which only the author could best explain. I henceforth pledged not to read any religious scripture.

CHAPTER 8

Nesting In The Wild

The school education was over and most of the students, unlike me had a clear goal. Most chose to prepare for IITs, some went to the Armed Forces, some joined their family business. I was still wondering thinking about my next step.

"*Aur bataa....*" came a pat on my shoulders.
"Nothing man, just thinking about the future. What should we do?"
He looked worried about something.
"I don't know, have you thought anything... I mean anything?"
I was clueless what is done after school education. I was clueless what career was.
"Where is Rajlatha going, did she tell you?"
Surya had the typical sadness in his eyes right now; he looked here and there for few seconds and then started laughing.
"Hey, gone mad or what?" I asked.
"Om, she is going to some architecture college in Chennai. She had always had a goal to become an architect. She didn't even ask me. I got a call from her last evening when she informed me."
"Why Architecture! Does she want to renovate the Adam's bridge?" I wanted to keep the mood light.

"By the way, why does she need your approval... It's her choice, leave it." Surya was surprised on the way I tried to wrap up his topic.

"Bloody... you will never understand it man. You never are in this world. Maybe you will understand it when you come back from your lost world." He did not like my joke.
"Don't get annoyed at me *yaar*, come let's go for a ride and have some sweets at your favourite shop."
"*Saale*, I feel like crying and you are hungry?"
"Your bike's pillion seat must be missing her too. Let me give it my heat."
Saying that I had to run towards the bike, else Surya would have left me to walk.
I realized that to forget Rajlatha, all Surya wanted was '*mishti doi*' of Laalji shop.

It was 2nd April and this was the day when Surya would pack up. I went to his place and met his parents.
I gave him a tight hug and asked if he was sure to go for that B.Sc. course or was it the thought of Delhi which was pulling him to North?
He had no answers.

I had no money to buy anything for my buddy. I then went to the place where he had kept all his shoes. I removed mine and wore an old slipper of Surya and ran back to the cycle before he could see me clearly. He would see the shoes only when he comes out to go to the railways station. He always liked my new shoes but hesitated to ask for it. And I was not that attached to my shoes anyways.
Before I would hit the pedal of my cycle, He came out of his room and hugged me. He then looked at me and smiled for a while. I just waved my hand and dragged the cycle, as I then

didn't feel like riding it. The slippers were biting me but I was fine!

"Om, there is a defence quota in Birla Institute and the Director is a good friend of mine."
My father came close to rescue my career.
"He was saying based on your rank and the *defence quota*, you can get Mechanical Engineering."
"Quota?" I exclaimed in that irrevocable tone.
"What is wrong with that?" He asked why a privilege was being questioned.
"I feel a deserving student who is really into engineering should get that seat."

"Papa I've applied for few colleges and am optimistic about some."
"Good. If you ever change your mind, then don't forget I am still here."
I could see that eagerness to help me in Papa's eyes. I was unclear of what to do next, but was certain of what not to do. The latter was the root cause of my denial.

"Om, you should not sleep in the evening."
This was my mom. She started narrating the folklore that no good human sleeps in the evening time.
"It's a bad omen to sleep right after the sunset. Even the trees have just gone to sleep so we should wake up."
Aah I could never beat her by my arguments; she always won with her smile and affection. I hugged her and tried to go back to sleep holding her saree's pallu, but she was adamant.
"Okay, I am awake." I jumped up from the bed and walked straight to the bathroom.
While brushing my teeth, I could hear some talk in *Urdu* or was that some song?
It was evening and my father loved to listen to Urdu gazals when he would hold that glass of drink. Maybe it was Ghulam

Ali sahib, who was casting his spell on papa or was it his only guru... the bottle of drink, *'Old Monk'*.

"Some good news papa?" I wiped my face and sat in front of him. He pointed his finger to his uniform while pouring his peg. I walked to that hanger and lifted the dress to bring it to him. Midway, he gestured to check the pocket.

I checked it and found a pink cheque like paper. Reading it explained that it was my college's fee for the first year.

"How did you come to know about it? I mean how did you know the amount? So fast?"

"Don't forget, I am your father."

I could see mummy standing in the kitchen and facing us. She was holding that curtain of kitchen and smiling to see how papa had solved one of my big time problems. Papa was not only happy that day. He was smiling and the 'monk' in him was singing *"sarak ke dupatta jo gira, mai hosh khoya daffatan...* Om you know what *daffatan* means?"

"No, but I would like to know"

"It's what your eyes are feeling right now... it means surprise!"

I managed to reach my college and coordinated with the warden to get my room. I threw my stuff in the room. I was too tired to unpack the boxes as it was midnight already.

"First year!" This sound had some command. I woke up as someone was banging my door.

No not one but many hands were beating my door, "Aey *phasst* year" it was an accent from eastern India maybe from Bihar or Bengal. Before I got up and wore my slippers there was a bang! The people outside, they kicked so hard that the metal door latch collapsed and they were in front of me. It was one o'clock and I was just going to enter my sleep.

"Yes, how can I help you?"

"From where have you come?"

"Patna", I said.

Then a small chap looking like a tea vendor jumped up my table and held my head and said "Who will say Bihar? Say Patna city from Bihar" and they burst in laughter again.

"I stay in the Danapur cantt. Please tell me who are you?"

One tall guy then tightly held my chin and while moving it left and right said "Don't act smart. We are your fathers... seniors."

"Why you all want to do this? I thought we all are here to study about molecular engineering." I moved back and added "I want to stay away from this and if you guys are interested, you can carry out the complete drama with other guys standing here."

I was pointing to other first year students and expecting some outcry but I forgot this world is inhabited by majority of losers and only handful few who use their minds to find reasons.

Two hefty looking seniors approached me and pushed me back to the wall of the ground floor room.

"Repeat what you just said!" One of them asked.

"I have no time for this rubbish."

Next second, I was seeing the floor dust all around my eyes, the surface was parallel to my face and I did not know what happened. After few seconds, I realized someone had kicked my head from the back and I was flat on the surface.

One big fat senior came to my face and pulled me all over to erect my body.

"You are from Patna? Now tell what your surname is?"

"I don't believe in surnames."

"Then trust me, you would certainly believe this." Saying this he slapped hard on my face and for next 10 seconds, I could hear a low frequency in my left ear. It did sound like train initially but later took off like a jet

"Brahmin hai saala" shouted one of the senior who had a smart look-up table mapping face or colour to caste of a student. I could see that guy arranging all the first year students in

160

various categories. First it looked like it was alphabetical, then it looked like it was based on hostel floor. Finally I could see the segregation was based on state/region. They talked alike in north Indian accent with a B*hojpuri* in it. There were groups for Bengalis, north eastern guys, Punjabis, south Indians all segregated.

The guy referred to as Babu pulled me to the first group and said "These boys are all Brahmin, the next are all *Bhumihar*, then the *Kaayasth*" I could hear several new castes and I was so wrong to think the classification was based on language or state. It was instead based on caste, what a pity! I couldn't understand why some boys were isolated and cornered like unwanted.

Babu was fat and tall. He had short curly hair which was badly oiled. He had average facial features. The only thing which distinguished him from others was his arms. They were too thick and showed how he had reached at the top of the bully gang.
Babu pointed at them and said *"Saale neech hain ye sab."*
His statement did sound very derogatory, but his voice did not agree to what he spoke.

"Any person by birth cannot be superior to any other human. Haven't you read about fundamental rights?" I asked him
"Okay, what does it say?" He asked
"Article 17, per the constitution, we are all equal, untouchability is banned."

He wasn't happy with my lecture. This time I could see the blow approaching me and it was pretty fast, I tried to move left but my right jaws were hit hard by it and few shorter goons also jumped over me. They were kicking and slapping and seemed like they had this golden opportunity to mobilize

all their limbs on me. All kinds of accents were unanimously falling on my ears saying
"Hit him... maar saala"
"Hero banta hai..."

While I was trying to lift my body up, I could see other seniors bullying and hitting their juniors who looked like primary school kids. That brought smile on my face. They were all adults and how the hell were they accepting the victimization process.

I pushed some of the seniors and first year boys to make way for myself. I then started walking towards the warden's room. Quickly two of the seniors ran towards me and pulled me back, I resisted. I definitely did not want to waste my energy in hitting two and getting hit by hundreds of seniors. They were watching me like hungry vultures.

I had a transient anger which spiked suddenly. I held a tiny senior and kicked him hard just below his pride possession. Now he was now recalling his mother's touch.

I saw several seniors running back to ground floor and from the ground floor Babu running towards me. I had to run to the third floor where the warden had his room.

I shouted his name "Singhamare Sir! Please help."

I kept running and managed to climb first floor stairs before the first floor seniors could catch me and kept shouting. Within no time I was on the third floor but Babu and few seniors held my shirt tight and kicked me from the back which allowed me to reach the warden room a little faster.

I knocked it hard, but he was so fast asleep that he missed all the entertainment that was happening under his watch.

"Sir, please get up.... wake up! I need help!!" saying that I knocked hard and the door gave way as it was already weak owing to kicks it would have got in last few decades.

"What happened? How did you come here? You are not supposed to come to this floor... it's not for juniors."
I was astonished to hear that. The seniors behind me started laughing.

"Done with your FIR? Come down." saying this Babu placed his right hand around my neck to escort me to the ground floor. He showed his left hand to all other seniors as if he wanted to say that 'everything is under control'.
"You tried hard, but don't forget that you haven't come here for some BA or BSc. You've come here to become an engineer, we will make you strong." He then added "Let me introduce you to your boss for next 3 years. My name is Bihari Babu; you all will refer us as sir"
His speech was funny and I was agitated not at the pathetic behaviour of seniors but with the response I got from the warden.
"Excuse me... Sir, can you give me just one minute?" I requested Babu.
This brought smile to his face and other adulators near the lobby also laughed at me calling him sir.
"*Le lotta!*" That may sound French but it isn't. This was more like his word to express his surprise by such slang. However saying that he loosened his grip. I walked to the warden's room and banged his door to wake him up again.
"What does your name plate hanging out side say Mr. Singhamare? I mean what does it mean?"
He looked like a lazy camel with thin long neck. He took his time to come out of the room to read his name plate as if he had forgotten his name along with his duty.
"Son, My name plate reads M.C. Singhamare meaning Manikrao Chetan Singhamare."
"We all know what *MC* means. By the way, I am not your son"
Everybody in the lobby laughed.
I then added "By the way, what does Singhamare mean?"
While I was talking to this guy venting out my anger, I could

see seniors coming closer to me. They were interested in how the warden would hit back.

"Shut up!" He shouted but with no feelings.

"I carry the pride lineage of warriors. Legends say that we hail from a community who once killed a lion, thus the name Singhamare."

"Feel ashamed for calling yourself a warrior. Forget killing lions, I am sure you haven't even killed a mouse. You don't deserve that surname. You are nothing but a coward."

"Bloody... "He wanted to abuse but controlled. Then shouted "Boys, take this first year out of my sight, he has gone mad." He pointed to the second year wing and while saying this, he slowly approached the door to close it.

I was having a tickle in my hand since last few seconds and finally the itch was becoming hard to resist. I took my fist close to his face which frightened him. I quickly took my fist inside his pants and ran back.

"Aah... help help!" was the cry this warden got dead frightened by a small cockroach I got from his table. I was holding the creature since long. He then ran like a hedgehog towards the bathroom to undress and get rid of the cockroach.

This sight was hilarious and everyone including Babu started laughing.

Babu came to me and said *"Maar liya!"* In real sense, it meant my reply to the warden was liked by all.

Suddenly the seniors started giving room to me and Babu to walk. Then Babu took me to his room. His room was good. It had a computer, many books, and an almirah which was open. It was so full of clothes that it couldn't be closed.

He took out his cigarette pack from the pocket and searched for a matchstick.

Before he could run his eyes in all directions, one of the flatterers brought matchbox for him.

He made an attempt to light the matchstick but failed owing to a gush of wind. Another stooge jumped to the fan regulator and switched-off the fan. Babu asked all to sit and discuss about a plan to complete the ragging cycle smoothly. He was discussing when and where to take the first year boys. He also discussed how long a first year is to be ragged and which senior can have the power to interrogate. Finally he completed his plans by mentioning a list of first year guys who needed special attention. While ending his statement he looked at me.

"*Saala tassaan…* what is your name?"

"Om"

"Hmmm… I think Om is right. We will have to think about ways to end the physical ragging and bring fun to the activities" He had an authority, at least in this room. But what fun meant to Babu, could mean pain to the fresher's.

"By the way, why did you say that you don't believe in surnames?"

Babu asked while extinguishing his golden puff on a full size picture of Sharon Stone on his wall.

"Are you not a Brahmin?" He clarified his question.

"No, I am neither a Brahmin nor a Hindu. My parents call themselves Brahmin. Also, there is nothing called as low caste, all are equal by birth." I replied quickly.

I sat close to him and tried to explain the seriousness of matter. He seemed shocked with his mouth open.

"We are educated and only leaders like you can stop it. Others will follow you." I continued.

"*Bass…* you speak a lot." This time he was not happy though.

"Take him away… no physical hitting for anyone"

I was taken out to first year wing and I could see all first year guys coming back to their room and some of them looking at me and abusing me.

"Why did you act smart? Because of you, on the first day itself, we had to face the wrath of seniors." One guy from the lot said.

"Else you would have enjoyed this beating, had it happened on the second day or later?" I was sarcastic now.

"*Tassan...?*" He pointed to my attitude using that slang.

I went inside the room, looked at the clock. It was three. I looked into the mirror and saw that my left cheek was swollen and the chin was bleeding. I went to the washroom and washed my face.

En route I met a young, highly tensed and a feeble looking boy looking around. I think he was searching for his room. I checked the piece of paper he had and guided him to his door.

"What is your name? And what is your room number?"

"Thanks man. Kabir, room number 224."

"Oh, you are my neighbour! By the way, your parents have given you a very nice name." I smiled and made him comfortable so that he could forget the torture.

"I am alone here and rest all of you have roommates?" I asked Kabir because I was seeing multiple boys getting out of all the rooms on the floor.

"Did you closely see your room number?" Kabir asked. Was there some puzzle to it?

I stared up for a short time and watched the room number lit brightly under the CFL which was making it difficult to read it for long.

"Yes it's 223. So?"

"You are missing the star." He was quick

I looked back this time and I could see a star etched at the end of the number. So this was not a temporary label.

"I talked to the mess guy Govind and he was telling that this room is never given to anyone. There is some reason to it which even I don't know." He said

"So let's go to him tomorrow." Kabir agreed and then went back to his room. I finally could give myself some rest.

Morning was pleasant as it had taken away the fear from all the first year students. There was a great amount zeal and interest to attend college. Everyone had some or the other reason to join the National College. The day was passing quickly and I came back early to the hostel room to have a short power nap. Maybe the temperature of Nagpur was making me lazy.

"*phaast yeaarrrrrr….*" It sounded familiar this time. It was evening already. Different seniors this time, but they used the same phrase, the same abuse and the same tone.

We were all asked to gather in the lobby and this time it was driven by Babu. He looked at me and said "Now we will have fun first year". His smile had an authority and his voice a command.

"Line up!" He shouted and put his arm across my neck.

Babu was shouting aloud beating the drums inside my ears hard. He was literally giving me a walkthrough. He made me stand second in the queue.

The rule was simple; every student would hold the phallus of the person ahead of him and the person behind him would follow the same to make a chain.

This was referred to as *Train* by Babu.

"Hey, loosen your grip man…" I requested the person behind me, not knowing who he was.

"No the senior will beat me" He cried.

"What! They can hardly spot what you are holding. Just hold the garment and keep it loose man." I tried to convince him.

"Nope, please keep quiet. We are not supposed to talk… please"

This guy was pathetic. I tried hard to get away from his clutch.

"No one is seeing or listening. Just keep it loose yaar, I guarantee."

He finally loosened the grip. The guy in front of me was listening to this and was controlling his laughter. He was the engine so he was made to hold his penis with both hands. I was holding the tip of his *undy*.

"Run!" was the call from one of the seniors.

Before I could realize what was happening, we were all moving. Slowly we were moving...

"Aah... it's paining *saale*! Leave my dick." I asked this guy behind me.

"No please, the senior is running just behind us."

He was so frightened that he wanted to obey it 100% as if there he would get some reward for his honest performance.

After the ordeal, I went to the mess with Kabir to solve the room's mystery.

The mess guy was already asleep.

"Hey Govind" I pulled his hand and shook his shoulder to wake him up. He was startled and threw away the blanket and woke up as if he was in the middle of a nightmare.

"What... who are you?"

"I am Kabir, remember? I talked to you last day about the garbage in my room. This is Om, he is my neighbour."

He wiped the sweat on his forehead. I felt bad to have disturbed his sleep.

"Oh 225. What is the matter?" Govind asked.

"No it is 223 where I stay..." before I could complete my sentence he stood up and ran to wash his face. While wiping his head, he asked looking scared

"Why are you staying there? That is not good. Please meet the hostel in-charge and shift to some other room."

"Come on Govind. It hardly matters. Moreover there was no room left and the occupancy of any room would be disturbed if I become the third student in that room."

"Change it... please change it!" he said and then looked as if there was someone behind us. He then went towards kitchen windows and tried to shut down and lock the windows.

"Is there a... ghost?" asked Kabir with a candid smile but from within he looked frightened.

"Don't use that word, please go back. I will tell some other day, not at night. Please go back and sleep in some other room." Govind said and went back to sleep.

We stayed there for some time though he tried hard to ignore us. I don't think he would have had a quick sleep that night. I couldn't understand the reason for the guy's panic and went back to my room to sleep.

I was sitting in Kabir's room next evening and having tea when one tall guy with grey hair and moustache came in. We were seeing him for the first time since our batch started.

"Hi, my name is Amar Tiwari. I am from PTPS."

I looked at Kabir if he knew this boy. Kabir's face was blank, so I stood up and greeted by handshake. I did not like this guy. It looked as if some new joker had come up disguised as senior. We introduced ourselves and continued the discussion.

"I was behind you in the train. Sorry for the trouble *bhai*." He said. I wanted to get up and hit him for his stupidity. I controlled myself and recalled his introduction.

"What is PTPS... some nearby school?" I asked.

"Nope, it's a place's name - Patratu Thermal Power Station." Amar replied with a confident smile.

"Sorry, now what does that mean? You are from some coal mine... where is this place?" Kabir asked.

"Oh, sorry! It's a place in Ramgarh district of Jharkhand."

"Don't tell me you are from that famous *Sholay* place? Kabir was curious now.

"No, sorry again. This is a different Ramgarh, but has almost similar topography and ambience" We all laughed to hear the word 'ambience...' who would love that ambience I thought. We asked him to sit and have tea with us.

"Why have you kept this moustache, some reason" I asked to Amar.

Before he could reply I saw a pride which ran from his chest towards his face. His chest got broadened and his smile lifted his moustache.

"You understand what masculinity is?" While asking this, he moved his hand to the tip of left corner of his moustache and started twisting it. Whatever he did certainly made him look like a chimp itching his lips.

I looked at Kabir and we both smiled at his false pride replying with a plain

"No"

Before we could move ahead with our discussion, there was a call for first year students' gathering outside. Babu came in and saw the three of us sitting and chatting. We stood up and I was now enjoying this routine task. The activities brought out various interesting characters both in my batch and seniors.

"Who is this?" Babu asked holding his collar with his right hand.

"Hello *bhaiya ji*." Amar greeted Babu.

Babu slapped Amar and repeated the question.

"Kabir, who is this guy? Since he is your roommate, you should explain everything you've understood about him so far."

"Sir, he came today to my room. He had joined few days back and was temporarily living with his distant relative in the city."

Hearing this Babu hit Amar with a light slap and said "Fucker you live in the city? No first year is allowed to roam around in the city. Just stay inside this hostel."

It looked as if Amar too was facing such challenging situation for the first time.

"Sir, he doesn't know about the procedure yet, so please forgive him. His name is Amar and he has come from PTPS." Kabir gave a quick intro, hearing which Babu slapped Kabir and the color of his cheeks turned yellow instead of turning red. Maybe that was the wavelength of fear? Kabir was intimidated.

I was closely watching Babu. He didn't hit hard but was creating a scenario of fear. His intention was to prove his supremacy and remove the hesitation inside Kabir and boys like him. I was wondering why the slap to poor Kabir... did he say something wrong? Next statement from Babu's mouth clarified my doubt.

"I don't want to hear any short forms. Hear it up boys... no short forms. I don't want you guys to mumble up just any abbreviation and show your smartness." Babu looked at people outside and continued with his questions to Amar
"So where do you stay Mr. Amar? A boy with a moustache... err... should I call you a man?" Babu shouted hard with his mouth wide open covering the diameter of Amar's left ear.
"No sir... sorry sir..."
He continued the complete postal address but was stopped by Babu
"What is the PIN code of your place?"
"Sir the PIN code is 829118." That reply called for another slap in no time.
"What did I tell few minutes back? No abbreviation, what is PIN then?"
"Sorry... PIN... ppoo... postt... India.... number....."
Amar was sweating and his moustache was collecting all the sweat to protect his lips.
"It's the Postal Index Number Code." Babu moved ahead and while going he turned around for a second and signalled something with his index finger, moving past one end of his upper lips to the other... interesting! He wanted Amar to shave his moustache.

Amar was introduced to a soft version of bullying. He was petrified at the thought of shaving his moustache.
"My father will kill me."
He was weeping. He was afraid of hurting his father and the ritual which might have not yet been broken maybe since

hundreds of years. Most north Indian Hindus are not allowed to apply razor on their facial hair or scalp, unless there has been death of an elderly and in some cases specifically the father. There are millions like Amar who don't want to shed superstition not because they like it, but because they have a fear of hurting their dead or may be the living relatives.

Next day when we lined up for what was called as the half-naked parade, amidst all the chaos, I saw few laughs and for a moment my eyes stopped on this new face... familiar though. This was Amar and he had come out of fear at least this time. I felt good to see his new *avatar*. Babu held Amar's collar and took him to every single first year guy. He explained the lessons to be learnt by all. Babu knew how to convey without using too much of energy. Seeing the continuous ragging and bullying, Amar got more scared.

"What happened?" I asked Amar as he was standing next to me.
"I don't want to do all this stuff. I have never been abused by anyone and these seniors are constantly using foul words against my mother and sister. I am feeling very bad *yaar*."
I could see a child in him.
"Don't worry; this is to take away inhibitions from you. It's all for fun but if at any time they cross the line, then do come to me or approach the Principal."

Days were passing slowly, but the ragging didn't slow down. One day a huge crowd of seniors had gathered to rag us. Suddenly, someone from the crowd jumped in and brought his punch close to Amar's face and stopped.
"Aaaaaa.....!" was the shout. Amar was not hit but the fear mixed with lethargy was very prominent on his face.
"Sir, I am 20% blind sir." Amar pleaded.
Was he serious? I could not stop my laughter hearing this. That was a strangely unique disease or ailment. I mean how

could somebody calculate the amount of blindness? Last night everything was fine. He was watching TV in the mess, reading books without spectacles and now he was 20% blind.

Before we or the seniors could make our minds, we saw a slip in Amar's hand about his condition. The senior read and was confused, but gave it back. I was wondering what the doctor had examined, was it that Amar could see just 800 meters if we could see an object placed a Kilometre away?

Babu gave Amar a new name, "20%" and everyone started calling him by that name. Amar now had an exception from any kind of activity which would hurt him.
"Is it true that you can't see?" I asked him in a low voice.
"No man, I wrote this letter last night and signed it myself. This is the letter pad of my father; he is a doctor in Patratu." Great! So he was not as dumb as I thought.

Days had a fixed routine now and nothing was exciting me much. My hair had grown really long hair now as I didn't get time to cut them. I walked till the salon and there was a long queue for it. I then thought of calling my mother.

"What? At least listen to what I say when you are not near me" She cried.
"What happened? Why so much fuss about this mummy?" I asked.
"*Panditji* says and it is written in our religious texts that if you cut your hair on Thursday, then you lose your wisdom, money... everything." She completed
"I don't have either of them *maa...*" I joked but she was serious and asked me to go back to the hostel without the haircut.
"Okay, but you say the same thing for Saturday and Tuesday as well." I protested.
"No, on Tuesday the haircut results in reduced lifespan by eight months" She warned.

"Is it?"

"Yes, it's true. I've seen bad things happening to people after hair cut on Tuesday. Some met with accidents immediately."

"Maybe the hair would've gone in the eye. They lost focus and hence the accident." I explained, but could not make her laugh or ignore such beliefs.

"Don't be a fool, there are several people who believe in it, the astrologers, and they are so much educated. Forget about me, just listen to what they say" She pleaded and she was making me run away now.

"Okay then what about Saturday... why do you stop then?"

"I don't remember but *Panditji* said that reduces the life by seven months... no I think Tuesday was seven months and Saturday was eight months." She got confused and I was giggling at the other end. Her superstition did reduce my ragging pressure.

"Okay whatever *maa*, but I normally get a haircut on Saturdays only. I am free that day."

"You are ignorant."

"Okay consider this logic mummy. I would have got my haircut on Saturdays for almost fifty times so far... roughly." I said and she was quiet

"So per cut eight months, means I've lost almost one fourth of how much I've lived. At that rate I would be dying soon?" I presented some calculations which were outright rejected by her.

"Please don't talk about death. You will never understand me. Please don't do it Om. Promise me?"

She made me helpless and I had to postpone my plan of getting a haircut or next time I would not inform her.

One Friday, I wasn't feeling good so thought of coming back to the hostel room. The lectures were too theoretical to make sense and I was feeling overdosed with bookish corollaries of professors. I just pushed the right door and went straight to the bed. I covered my face with the pillow and could hear whispers.

Who was that? I covered my ears with the second pillow and ignored the whispers.

But who could be whispering when the hostel was almost empty. Now the noise became a little clear and it seemed to be some hymn. I was sure, I was not hallucinating. I woke up and went out to see through the atrium to find no one. Slowly the voice stopped. I went back and applied balm on my forehead and covered myself back to get some sleep.

Within a minute I could now hear somebody walking past my room, it was very slow step. This was certainly not an illusion, so I woke up and wiped my face with the towel. I then opened the door and saw a boy dressed in black and white, but the white shirt wasn't that clean, it was yellowish as if it had never been washed since purchase.

This was the first year uniform and this boy had handkerchief tied on his forehead like a bandana.

"Hey first year... can you hear me? Please stop."

I tried to shout but the boy was lost from my vision. His walk looked slow but his movement appeared fast for my sleepy eyes to track.

I lost him. Who could that be? His untidy shirt would have called for scolding from seniors. How had he managed to escape for that long? I had lots of questions and no answers, so sleeping was the best solution. I went back to sleep.

It was evening and I had to get up to entertain myself and the seniors. I could see some new faces in seniors and they were looking pretty old to me. Babu was looking extra vigil and shouted.

"Meet your grandfathers. They are all very experienced and respect worthy. You can learn a lot from them."

Why was Babu so worried?

Oh! These boys were super seniors and they were in a position to drag second, third and final year students, if the ragging wasn't up to the mark.

"Who is Om... come out" shouted one of the super seniors.

I could see few second year guys smiling and feeling happy over this call.

"Yes sir, it's me." I stepped up.

"Don't call us Sir. Call us *Bhaisahab*" and while saying that he took me for a walk.

This guy was almost 6'2" stout with belly fat burgeoning till his thighs. We were not allowed to see directly into the eyes of a senior unless we were told to do se. Hence, I kept staring the third button of my shirt per the protocol.

"I've heard you frightened the warden. Is that true?"

"Yes sir, I did interact with him for a while."

"I've heard the second year boys have now amended few ragging rules, no hitting etc. Who made that rule? Was it for your comfort?"

"No sir, I don't know what are the rules here, neither do I have an interest in their amendment. I've just come to study and learn..." I then added "from seniors like you."

"Hmmm... My name is Ajay Nagpal and I am here since 1988... how many years?"

"Almost 15 years, *Bhaisahab*"

I caught a glimpse of him while he was looking at his mobile. That guy looked young but was far more experienced. His built was just as good as Babu's physique. While Babu was a regular gym guy, Ajay looked like a body built with pure *ghee* and *desi* exercises.

"I used to be known as Cobra, Bond and many names which even I don't know. I was the king of this college." He was lost in self-praise, he then added

"...and I now own a furniture showroom and transportation unit in Nagpur. This city boasts of the highest numbers of millionaires in India and I provide them the best cushion for their ass, ha ha ha..." He laughed rather artificial.

"You've come here for just one thing... degree. Take that and go away. Don't do anything other than that."

While he was giving his life lessons, I lost focus. I saw in a corner of a room, some of the seniors were hitting Kabir and some other boys. There was hue and cry all around.

"Sir... I mean *Bhaisahab*, they are hitting those two boys badly. Look there." I showed the plight scene to him.

"The boys must have done something wrong. So, where were we?"

How could he ignore it?

I requested him to intervene as the two boys looked badly hurt. Despite all the persuasion and pleading, he was not at all interested.

"Sir, sorry *Bhaisahab,* people like you have laid the foundation of this college. The discipline, respect that we have is all a small chapter of syllabus drafted by you. How can you do injustice to the name Cobra given to you?"

Ajay thought for a while and asked to me see in his eyes. I was seeing his face for the first time. His beard was almost white and he had a clumsy hairstyle with yellow canines.

"Come, let's see."

He took me to the room and shouted "What is happening here?"

The second year students could hardly ignore Ajay, they were all shocked.

"Bhaisahab, this boy is trying to be smart, he is not co-operating. We were just teaching him how to behave." said the most feeble looking senior.

"Leave him, he will learn slowly. You guys also took time, right?" Ajay was logical, he then started moving back.

"*Saala…*" was a low voice abusing Ajay Nagpal, the Cobra. It came from a second year guy, unfortunately he made it audible. Ajay got furious. He turned towards the guy and lifted him around 5 inches above the ground holding his neck. I pulled Ajay from back and requested him to leave the guy.

"Bhaisahab, please forgive him... please. Hitting a senior in front of juniors will leave a very bad image."

Ajay was convinced that such an action would degrade the whole disciplinary fiasco but he was burning with anger. He then slapped the second year guy and with the other hand, then held the collar of the other senior and took them both to the second year student's wing.

That place was forbidden for any first year, but I still kept following Ajay. People came out of their rooms and I was seeing their faces, which conveyed sheer anger and plight with false air of superiority. Hundreds of second year and third year guys came out and many of them started coming to the area of action. I had never come to this lobby and was in dilemma as to what should I do.

I held Ajay and kept requesting him … "Bhaisahab please forgive him; think about your legacy, please."

He looked back and asked for a towel from the closest room, the third year guy ran and brought a towel. Ajay put the towel around his neck and then from the left corner wiped his face and started walking towards the end of the lobby. I was left alone, so I had no plan of action to defend my presence. Ajay knocked some of the doors that were closed and asked everybody to stand in a line. I moved away as I was not a senior and the command was for seniors.

Ajay then held the jaw of each and every senior in the lobby and asked if they knew him.

Those who said yes were safe and those who did not got a tight slap and were asked to repeat his name with appropriate suffix.

This was becoming the scene of my life, first year life... what a moment!

Soon I was seeing more than fifty red cheeks, some who had never met Ajay and some had forgotten the Cobra. After the entire session was over, Ajay got tired. His right hand had lost senses, maybe due to hyperdermalfriction?

Ajay threw the towel towards me and I passed it to the room from where it was taken. Ajay then walked towards the parking. "Come for a drink, I am tired." Ajay asked
I did not know how to respond to his offer as he was pretty eccentric. His mood could not be trusted. It was very likely that after the fifth peg, he would start hitting people in the bar... including me?
"I am sorry sir, we will certainly go sometimes later as this is ragging period and during this we are not allowed to enjoy that ways. Also we have an exam of Nano Patterning tomorrow."
"Hmmm. Take this card and call me whenever you feel the rules of the land need to be changed."

He gave me his visiting card and sat on his hefty Royal Enfield. I could see some seniors looking down when Ajay started his bike. Last few hours were imprinted in my memory forever.

"Hey, what happened? Who was the person with you and are you alright?" That was Kabir.
"It is fine, will tell you some other time... by the way, why were you taken to the corner room? Are you running around the seniors' girlfriend?"
I wanted Kabir to lighten up as he was very timid and often cried thinking about his home. He was bashed all alone, and bad times often become worse without a company.
"They hit me really hard yaar... thanks for coming" He cried, but then wiped his tears to add further information

"It was some senior. His name was... Shaukat. I don't know why he just rammed inside and took me away from all and hit for no reasons. I gave him all answers as expected and did follow our norms."

"Why would that Shaukat or whatever his name is, take you? What could be his motive?"

"I don't know *yaar*; I just know that there were few other seniors who asked me if I offer *Namaz* and lead my life like a good Muslim."

"What? Why would you read Namaz? Wait a minute are you a …?" I was startled to hear that.

"Yes, I am a Muslim and as far as I can recollect, all the seniors hitting me were Muslims too. I often come back to my room on Friday afternoon and offer my prayers."

Then I looked at his shirt. It was the same yellow shirt I had seen one afternoon. Then I realized that it was Kabir who would have come in the afternoon to offer Namaz that day.

For all this time, I wasn't aware of such an important thing about Kabir. I never bothered about Kabir's religion. But why should I enquire it? Religion A or B, it hardly made a difference to me.

"I think we should talk to Babu. This is some serious segregation happening here." I asked Kabir to excuse me and walked straight to Babu's room. I knocked his on the door and went inside. There were five other seniors sitting inside the room. They all turned their faces towards me. One of them was the same guy, Shaukat who was hit badly by Ajay Bhaisahab. I ran my eyes quickly over all the expressions and it was not pleasant.

"Why have you come here? Aren't you afraid of the consequences? We can bury you here and no one will ever come to know" said Shaukat, with red angry eyes just wanting to kill me.

I moved few steps back. I recalled my purpose for coming here and that gave me some confidence to start the conversation again.

"Sir, if you all permit me then I can explain. I mean it all just happened and I did not know that this would go that far. My presence during the whole ordeal was just a coincidence."

I wanted to explain more but this wasn't the place to give logic.

Babu got up from his bed, threw the butt of cigarette and came close to me. He held my collar and shouted something which I missed as I was thinking about... I don't know what.

"Speak out! Do you understand that your life can be put in grave danger if you obstruct more?" He then stopped to watch my face and then lowered his voice to continue. "Please don't put your ass in anything wide open, you getting me?"

I smiled as I saw no anger in Babu's eyes. It seemed that he was pretending hard to abuse me, provoke me and force me to oblige to the seniors. I did not know what to say but I knew Babu wanted me to apologize and stay out of something big... some big danger.

"I am sorry, but it was not intentional." I said. Then there was silence. No one was speaking anything about any happenings. "If you allow me, then I have something to say here... something very important."

"Speak." Shaukat said with a tone filled with vengeance.

"I would not take names but I saw that few Muslim students were segregated and ragged more brutally than others. It was all physical and such type of group formation would actually divide the first year."

"See... he is back with a controversy. He has forgotten his apology done few seconds back" Shaukat said to Babu.

"Look Om, things are not as simple as you think. I lead the second year group and I can guarantee you my words to keep you all united but there are a lot of sensitive topics which cannot be touched"

Was Babu's use of '*you all*' explicit, referring to the Hindus. "Sir, with due respect, I feel that continue your ragging procedures and tasks that you give to us but if the complete batch stays together, only then can we know each other, help each other during bad times." I tried my best to convince them. "This is not possible, please go back" asked Babu.

I went out of the room. I could hear Shaukat's group jumping over Babu and demanding apology from me. I had added more fuel to the fire that broke because of Ajay Bhaisahab. I had also started developing some fear, some premonition that something was going to turn out really ugly for me.

This was referred to as '*Class*' where the alleged culprit who had broken some ragging norm was paraded in front of all seniors and a public apology was issued with hundreds of abuses and warnings. I was feeling trapped and getting deep into this bog created out of nuisance.

Next day was the longest day of my life. Few seniors, who came with rods and bats, held my right hand and took me to the terrace. It was a terrifying view as I was seeing almost all the seniors, super seniors or Bihar, Bengal, Gujarat, South India, Punjab and yes not to forget, a special lobby of Muslims, from all corners of India. It all looked so united and diverse.

I was placed in the centre and one by one all the seniors came and nagged me, pushed me towards the wall of the terrace abusing me and then moved ahead. Everyone asked me the reason to bring Ajay in the corridor. The discussions clearly said that Ajay Bhaisahab had no authority to hit a Muslim junior and I had provoked him.

I was tired due to standing all along. When I tried to give an explanation, I was asked to keep quiet. Babu was trying hard to defend me from any senior or super senior and diverted the matter to some other talk. The *class* had started in the morning and it was late afternoon now and the heat in Nagpur was burning my face and drying my mouth.

"Why have you come here? To become a Don... Mangal Pandey? What do you think of yourself?" That was Shaukat, his anger was legitimate but he was not ready to listen to anything. I had no prayers to say. I had no other option than to listen to all the abuses and scolding. I was occasionally being hit from all corners with some rod or wooden stick, the series of strokes gave me no time to guess who was hitting that to provoke me or hurt me?

I think on first year's floor no one was aware of any such special *class* being held on the terrace. There were some seniors who were constantly keeping a watch on me from second and third floor lobbies, blocking any possibility of an exit.

Meanwhile, Kabir came to my room to see me, but found nothing. While he was leaving, he saw a card and considering it useless, threw it outside the window. When he walked out of the room something flashed on to his mind. He had read something on the visiting card. It read 'Call urgent.'
Without losing a minute, Kabir ran downstairs and started searching for the card. Few yards away, he saw the card in the shrubs. It was Ajay bhaisahab's cell number and behind it, I had written to call him urgently to help and also my friend from the gymnasium, Jai.

Kabir did not know where I was, what problem I was into and why did I want him to call Ajay Bhaisahab?
He ran to the main gate and using an auto rickshaw reached a *basti* where he used to visit the *Dargah* to offer prayers. This

place was abundantly populated by Muslims. Kabir went to a PCO and stood in a queue for his turn to call Ajay.

His fingers were shivering while dialling the number but he tried hard. He started wiping sweat from his forehead when he heard a voice on the other end

"Nagpal Transport... who is this?"

"Hello Sir, I am Kabir from National College, Nagpur."

"Okay what's the matter?" Ajay asked.

"Sir, I think Om is in some problem and he has asked me to call you for help."

"Om... Oh first year! What happened? Need money?"

"No sir, I think he is in some danger. He is missing since morning and he did not attend any lecture. He is not in college, I checked twice."

"Hmmm... Don't worry much, note these numbers and take my name. I am in Ambala, so would not be able to come there. But don't worry. Call me in the evening."

Kabir noted both the numbers and dialled the first one

"Hello"

"Hello sir, Ajay Nagpal gave me this number and ..."

Kabir narrated the whole drama again. From the other side it came out that it was Ajay Nagpal's furniture company workers who were mostly from western UP. The boys promised to come to the hostel and narrated that they had been to the hostel in some previous fights as well. However the way they answered sounded more like a false promise. Kabir was not sure if the boys would turn up. That frightened Kabir more. Kabir recited some prayers and asked for strength from God.

Zabbar Qureshi, this was the second number Ajay had given. Kabir had heard this name earlier. The name would often come up in the local newspapers and the old *basti*, where Kabir went to offer afternoon Namaz. The local boys would talk about the bravery and larger than life stories of this local don.

Zabbar had his hand and commissions in any activity happening around the central Indian belt. He had a chain of hotels, parks and hospitals.

"Salaam wal-e-kum bhaijaan... This is Kabir. I got your number from Ajay bhai"
This time, Kabir narrated the episode to Zabbar bhai again and mostly in Urdu, with more confidence. Zabbar seemed to have a lot of time. He listened very patiently and finally spoke *"Jo sahi hai woh sahi hai."* His statement made him sound like a man of principles as he was adhering to *'what is right is right'* philosophy.
"Jee bhaijaan" Kabir affirmed expecting more.
"Shumare me hoon... take this number of Imran, put 0092 before dialling. He will settle everything. *Allah Hafiz"*

He was in some meeting so he gave the number to Kabir. It was relayed to a new character now and Kabir was exhausted narrating the tale with same zeal.
He realized that Imran bhai was the right hand of Zabbar bhai and 0092 meant he was in Pakistan. Kabir thought to him how would Imran help? Would he give another number? This was a battle with time as well.

Back on the terrace, I had experienced a very heavy dose of lectures and some contusion in parts below my thigh. I was also hearing stories of how the groups were divided, how they were governed and managed since last few decades. Any disturbance by me to that would cause a resonance, which would have been extremely dangerous.
"Yeah sure... consider it done... I will personally come... yeah sure... not a rupee less"
I was hearing one of the seniors talking to someone on the phone about money, around 2 Lakh 25 thousand Rupees to be deposited and everything should be looked after.

"Oh! this is a plan…?" a web set up by the seniors, they have funded local police station enough notes to keep quiet about any incident that may happen here and not to patrol in this area for next two days. How can a matter of ego lead to such a big plan?

After the call I was seeing more seniors getting physical and slapping me.

I was taken to a room now and there some super seniors reiterated the whole philosophy of ragging and its need and what blunder I've done by breaching it.

Kabir had now talked to Imran bhai who was sitting in Pakistan. It came to light from Imran bhai that Ajay bhaisahab and Zabbar bhai happen to be classmates and childhood buddies.

He was happy that he was knocking the right door but sad that there was no clue of my whereabouts.

Imran bhai called few numbers while Kabir was on the line and asked his men to leave for the hostel and accompany Kabir from basti till the college.

"Boys will be armed, so don't feel scared" Imran bhai told Kabir

"*Jee zaroor*" Kabir replied short as he was petrified by the scare of local mafias.

"Ajay bhaisahab and Zabbar bhai are like elder brothers to me"

"Yes"

"Zabbar bhai have asked you to call me, consider it an order for me…"

"Hmmm"

"If at all anything serious happens, we will make sure to cover-up the dead and take out your friend… what name did you say?"

"Om… He is a nice boy…" Kabir wanted to cover the Hindu name with some good qualities, to make the case more sympathetic.

"Don't be afraid if you see blood around, or if we need to take severe action"
"Yes" Kabir was stopping his tears
"Even if we need to kill the bad while doing the deeds of righteousness, God will forgive us... such small fights will give you strength to lead a right life" Imran gave some serious lesson to Kabir and frightened him more.
"Sure" He wanted to cut the phone and go back to the point where *basti* boys would have gathered to escort him till the hostel.

Here on terrace, I asked for an excuse to get fresh and came to the toilet on the ground floor. I was escorted by few seniors and reaching the ground floor toilet was like police escorting a serious convict and on both sides of road people are abusing and pelting stones at the convict. All my talks did not yield any results as no group was ready to listen to any argument. At this moment, bringing a reform to the ragging process was a futile talk. I closed my eyes and just relaxed while passing the liquid out of my body. As the stress inside my bladder was releasing, I was feeling relieved. Suddenly, I felt someone's hand on my shoulder. I felt "what the heck... just leave me free for a minute. Peeing is my fundamental right?" I turned around and was elated to see Kabir. He came as surprise oxygen for me!

Kabir had tears in his eyes and hugged me and started crying. "Where have you trapped me yaar?" He said quietly wiping off the blood on my face and touching the swollen parts of my neck.
He had so many things to say and that too in so little time.
I was happy to hear all his efforts and felt good about his approach.

"Finally you called Pakistan. I knew you would have some relative there... *Saale* terrorist." I joked to make him smile.

He then pointed from the window towards main gate where I could see few trucks and almost all the trucks had hundred to two hundred people.

Some had swords, some sticks, some iron rod, some had unseen weapons, self- made it looked.

"Now come, we will go out of this place."

Kabir asked me to come to the main gate, but I wanted to face that class and attempt one last chance. It was difficult but I moved up and this time I was very happy and confident seeing Kabir's efforts.

"He has brought the gang... hurry everybody" That was a shout from the door outside the toilet.

"Listen to me please." I stopped Shaukat's hand and looked into his eyes.

"I have no plan, rather I see you planning with cops to create a furore out of nothing. Open your mind." I reacted loudly.

"That timid friend of yours, Kabir he now has wings?" One senior behind Shaukat replied.

"And you..." Shaukat pointed his finger towards poor Kabir, who had just fought one of the most challenging battles of his life. Shaukat added in anger

"You've sold your loyalty to a *kaffir*" He wanted to light up that hatred in Kabir.

I don't know from where, but that was a new version of Kabir. He looked very confident and knew what he was doing.

"There is something called as humanity... people like you may not understand it" Kabir replied and came close to me to avert any backlash from Shaukat.

"Okay now that all of you know, so what will you do? Kill me, hit me and bury me. But what after that? There are huge numbers of boys in trucks and with weapons" I was seeing the group in some worry so I added more.

"They are all from local *basti* so for them hitting you all is never going to be a big task."

I went close to him and took a sigh to say "But we can still work this out."

Many of the seniors had now lost their courage. By seeing the swords and rods, they all got very scared. On the main gate, Kabir now saw few more trucks and this time it was loaded with North East boys from the *akhada*, the Gymnasium.
Great Kabir had called Jai as well. He did it well in time, I thought.
These were my friends who often played basketball with me. I went to their place to use their swimming pool and gym.

Kabir looked at some unusually shining sharp weapon with one of them.
"This is Rambo knife." and the boys laughed showing how it went in and brought out the soft human tissues. It was too much for Kabir to handle. But he was happy with the army of boys he was able to gather. So, smile was pasted on his face continuously.

It was almost night and the drama was still going on. I was explaining them the need to have religion-less ragging. How it was accidental that Ajay bhaisahab hit seniors and my presence was to stop him.
No one was convinced but no one now had the courage to hit me seeing the crowd outside. The air was now filled with foul smell of fake courage.

Escaping was not the plan now; I was running from one super senior to the other.
I tried to bring a conclusion to the discussions and finally all of them had to unanimously pass a verbal resolution about no ragging seclusion based on religion and caste, to give first year better opportunity to bind. None of the seniors wanted this but it happened and I thanked all and walked back clapping to

meet all my friends outside. I shook hands with all the seniors but some did not react to my handshake.

Some abused on my face but got a smile from me. Their plan was all screwed up.

The super seniors passed a decree and hence I was brought out unscathed with a new resolution for ragging.

I ran towards Kabir and hugged him. I thanked the boys and asked them to go back as the job was done. I jumped to the truck in which Jai was standing, hugged him and thanked him with some tears. We then moved towards the a*khada*. I wanted to swim. Reaching there, I did not remove my dress and just jumped inside the water. It was so very beautiful and peaceful. Outside world was full of chaos and inside the water; it was all blue and quiet.

Due the whole drama that took place, I was suggested by my North East friends to stay with them in the *akhada*. I took Kabir with me as well. Kabir had never bunked a class even in school days and he narrated that he was so obedient that he even attended the school when he was ill.

The *akhada* was situated at the opposite end of the city and it had very old dormitory, where the terrace was almost up to 30 feet above the ground and one big room was accommodating 6 people. Though I knew almost all of them, but one of them, Jai Singh Thokchom was a very close friend of mine. Kabir had synced up with him for the whole drama.

Out of the six people in this room, three were Manipuri, one was Lepcha from Sikkim and one was a Presbyterian Christian from Nagaland.

They were all pretty simple and innocent boys.

There was a new boy in the room as well. He had a stubble and fair skin with curly brown hair. It did not take more than 5 seconds to guess that the boy was a Kashmiri.

"*wa-ray chuv...*" I approached him to say hello.

He was not interested.

"Where is the toilet?" I asked, as this was a new block. These boys used to previously live in the *Rajguru Block*, and this was a new block named after *Lachit Borphukan*, a brave hero of Assam.

"*Kho-vur*" was the reply, he pointed towards left. Vijay Koul, I read his name above his bed; else he was never going to waste his energy in introducing himself.

I went out and to my left I could see no toilet but a thin avenue which was muddy. I obeyed nature's call right on the boundary wall and walked back after finishing the job.

When I opened the door, I saw a small creature lying dead with all four limbs facing the sky. On a closer look, it looked like a big frog and Jai was doing his medical surgery on that poor creature.

I sat close to him.

"Is this tasty?" I asked with a smile.

The frog had his eyes staring at me and a green skin with rifted scales which gave it a look of bitter gourd. There was no flesh on it which made me wonder about the quantity of the servings.

"Not tasty, but I am hungry..." and then everyone around started laughing and even I could not stop me from laughter seeing the dissection by Dr. Jai or should I say Chef Jai.

"*Muji dand!!!*" was a soft but repelling voice that came from Vijay Koul calling Jai a moron for eating a frog.

"What?" asked Jai who was weak in every language except Manipuri.

"Nothing, he is not feeling good." I did not tell the truth trying to prevent any altercation between the boys. I was then able to sense what the problem was.

Vijay was a Kashmiri pandit and non veg for him mostly meant nicely cooked mutton. His roommates were voracious non-vegetarians who ate almost anything, which had developed hatred in Vijay's mind for these boys.

After few minutes, I saw the other two boys also coming in and placing their black polythene bag on the bed.

They then got the aluminium vessel and poured the things out of the black plastic. It smelt different.

The vessel was filled mostly with intestine and ribs. Now I could recognize that this was raw beef, which was a favourite cuisine of the majority here.

Seeing that, Vijay immediately covered his mouth with his fingers. He wanted to puke, so ran out of the room.

"Saw it?" He shouted

"What?" I asked

"I could not get a room as I joined late and this is the punishment God is giving me."

"How did God come in picture now? It's just food."

"Aah, it's not food. Cow is our mother, we drink its milk."

He was angry with tears shining in his eyes and almost going to pop-out.

"Oh! But we drink the milk of goat, camel and sheep as well. Many countries use their milk to process and form cheese. Right?" I asked.

"C'mon, I am a *pandit*. How can I see or live with someone who eats beef?" Vijay argued feeling helpless.

"If cow is your mother, then that animal with beard...?" Jai asked me pointing his fingers to his chin.

"Goat?" I replied.

"Yes, goat is my mother, my Goddess and you eat goat... mutton, why?" Jai asked. He had a point, though there was a huge possibility of a lie to support his satire.

"*Payee tratth...*" Vijay ridiculed in Kashmiri and walked out of the room.

I signalled Jai that all will be fine and ran towards Vijay heading to the football court.

"Don't worry too much *yaar*; they are having the food which they have always had since ages. Also, it's not that we Indians never had non-veg since evolution. Right?"

He did not react so I added more.

"It's all part of civilization that we started with eating, then taming and finally exploiting every other species in the most convenient way possible."

"But these *chinkis*... all are uncivilized. Bloody villagers!" Vijay had now lost his calm and was venting anger by calling the North East boys as *chinkis*.

I knew my philosophy won't work on him but I had to try, else they would someday chop Vijay and eat him. The visual of Jai dissecting Vijay's body like the poor frog was overwhelming, but I controlled my laughter. It was difficult to explain Vijay.

"That's not the point. They are as much civilized as us. They have a sense of right and wrong too. They have a set of beliefs and they also come under the same constitution as us."

I continued.

"Look buddy, food is a matter of preference. Food of one community becomes bad for others. It's all in the mind. For instance you eating a goat or a chicken is a big 'crime' for various communities around the world just as others eating beef for you. So does that mean you are wrong?"

He gave me a look where he somewhat agreed.

"No" He replied.

"Correct, it's just how the person has been trained since childhood and his preferences." I had made my point and Vijay seemed convinced.

We then walked out towards the playground and discussed about his personal life and his days in the physical education college. In some time, we walked back as I was hungry. I assured him that after eating the chicken prepared by me, he would forget all the worries. We enjoyed the dinner and were unaware of when exactly did midnight pass and brought sleep in our eyes.

Vijay was still trying to adjust. So he spoke minimal to hurt the room mates.

Next few days went smooth. Coming here gave me time to do some physical activity as I was putting on some weight, especially around my stomach and arms. I was getting chubbier due to oily food, imbalanced diet and lack of sleep.

It was a nice sunny morning but I looked around to find the boys sleeping. I walked to the shop outside the main gate and watched students doing their morning exercises. I also upgraded my walk to jog to let my body know the real speed of my blood. Running did open up the pores and I had a sweat bath.

I bought some cigarette, milk and biscuits for the breakfast and did small amount of jogging on my way back to the dormitory.

"Get up Jai. Jai... get up my hero."
I shook his shoulders and took the cigarette close to his nose. He came out of coma. Since last so many days, I too had developed a taste of the cigarette smoke. It was soothing but I limited myself to the passive role.
"What Om, so early?" Jai looked at the watch and covered himself back with the pullover. I uncovered him and gestured with my hand about the time. The clock in their room always showed 10:12, not sure if it was set that way to show a smiling face or the battery had drained. The boys were not bothered about the time that morning.
Vijay had his own watch and various other articles, properly organized on his table. It seemed that he never relied on the items of that room.

We all had morning tea and biscuits and sat under the tree which was on the other side of the hostel fence but its branches and shadow were benefiting the boys.

After some time a stray dog passed by the wired fence and wanted to pee on the shrubs close to the tree. The dog was looking cute and healthy and it looked like the boys had tamed it and fed him tonnes of frogs.

"chh chh chh chh…. chhhuaaah…" was the calling from Jai. Jai had a very small face and pouted lips. His eyes looked like blue marble and he would always keep his head bald. I would see him going to the salon every week and get everything cleaned up. Maybe that gave him focus for his sports.

The dog came close to us. Jai hugged it and played with it for some time.

I too sat close to the dog and could see that the dog had its front portion pretty clean and brown with no hair. Its back including the tail was full of fur and off-white in color, so it looked like a cross breed. That dog somewhat took me decades back to the days when I used to roam around with Tipu as my tail.

Jai looked at me and said "You are fat now. From all sides looking *motu.*"

"The universe is expanding, so my expanding shouldn't be that big of a problem?" At this, I and Vijay laughed, but rest of the boys did not understand the joke. They might not have learnt about related theories in science. They were all into sport.

I was lost in my thought when suddenly I heard a smashing sound. The noise brought me back to the shade under the tree. The dog was lying flat on the ground with its head bleeding.

"Fuck Jai! Do we have some medicine? Something to cover the wound?"

I was hurried towards the room to find a bandage or an old cloth to cover the bleeding.

"No no, stop it man…"
Jai asked me and lifted the dog and brought it inside the room. He placed it on the boundary of a closet which was used as storage.

He took out his *khookhri* and started cutting the dog in to two halves. It was for the first time that I was saw the fresh red flesh of the dog. I had only seen badly distorted bodies of dogs on the highways. But this was seemed gruesome, just as we see at a mutton shop. Why was that scene difficult for me, when I had never complained about mutton hanging in a butcher shop?

Jai behaved like an expert in this act. I tried to hold my breath for some time and then closed my eyes too.
"What… aah… sorry" I don't know why, but I was not liking it.

Vijay came to me and saw the feast division and held my hand to ask
"*Lazmey mayel*… Now what? You accept this too? I can't… I am leaving."

Vijay was furious now and he packed his items and went out to check with the warden if there is any availability in other dormitories.
I couldn't stop him as this might have been a little too much for him to focus on other things in life. Maybe that was the threshold of his tolerance level.
"This is *haram*…" Kabir said looking disgusted. I raised my shoulders to show that I was least bothered about it. I was neutral and had given up reasoning. I then picked the pack of noodles which I had bought last day.

"Why did you divide it into half?" I asked Jai. I asked that while spitting out the saliva that had gathered in my mouth, not due to the urge to eat that meat but to show the rejection of that food by my taste buds.

"Rest for tomorrow."

Hearing that statement, Kabir covered his mouth and went outside the room.

"Call me when this is done." He was not able to stand any further.

The boys did not have any freezer or storage system. So I doubted if it would be edible in next few days.

I hugged Jai and other boys and thanked them for their 'Rambo knife'. We returned to hostel where everything had calmed down now. We came back to our normal routines.

While I was resting quietly in my hostel room, my eyes got stuck on the corner of the slab. I could spot an abandoned trunk. I quickly jumped over with the help of chair and pulled it down.

"Hrihaan Mutreja, first year...1989. What the heck?"

I showed it to Kabir and took out few other charts, small calculator and some other personal belongings. We both went straight to the mess boy who was here since he was a kid as his father used to work here as a cook.

"Govind, who was Hrihaan?" I asked.

Govind went cold feet and turned around to clean the vegetables.

"Tell us else I will report that you steal food from the mess. I've seen you many times putting expensive items like butter, oil, sugar in your bag when you leave for home." I tried to create some fear to get things out of him.

"I was 12 year old then and I had come to spend time with my parents in the hostel mess during my summer holidays." He opened up, slow but effective.

I offered him a chair and asked Kabir to bring some water for him to make him feel comfortable. All of us sat down and waited for Govind to break the suspense.

"Go ahead. What had happened? How long was your leave?"
"I came here for a month and it was all going good till one night." He stopped and his face was pale now with no expressions. Kabir shook his shoulder to bring him back.
"Hrihaan *dada* was a very nice person. He used to give me some English books and offer me items he brought from the city. One night it was almost past 11:30 PM, the time for me to lock all the doors of the mess and the boundary wall. As I passed by Hrihaan dada's room, I heard a lot of noise from inside the room. I peeped through the small opening between the doors."
"Was there any problem…. ragging?" I asked
"No, Hrihaan dada was a jolly person. He would stand for truth, but never start a fight. He would sing, dance around and often joke about ragging and enjoy with his mates"

"Okay then what did you see?" Kabir asked
"Before I could see anything I was spotted by Hrihaan dada. He called me to join their celebrations. They were all first year students and were playing cards and drinking some alcohol too."
"Oh, then did you sit with him"
"Yes I sat for some time and but did not understand the game they were playing. They were all speaking in English about the game."
"Then?"
"He then asked for tea so I went back to the kitchen to prepare tea for everybody."
"How long did they play? And did you join them back with the tea?" Kabir was curious
"There was no sugar in the mess, I searched all the places but couldn't get any."
"How would you get it? You steal it always…" Kabir tried to bring a smile to his face
"I kept searching in my father's almirah, but the moment I opened the almirah door…. I…"

"What happened? Did you see anything inside the almirah? What shocked you?" I held Govind and asked.

"No... I heard a loud cry and some noise as if someone was breaking the tables or chairs. It was coming from Hrihaan dada's room. I ran towards the room and when I opened his room I did not see anybody except Hrihaan dada"

"Was he alright, why was he crying... shouting?" Kabir asked

"He was sitting idle, very quiet and none of his roommates were there. I thought he was sad as he must have lost in the game he was playing."

"So you mean you heard the sound, still everything was organized in his room."

"Yes, seeing everything rightly placed shocked me. I apologised to him that there was no sugar and I would not be able to prepare the tea... but I was not sad, rather I was frightened"

"Of what?" I asked

"Some energy was sucking all the happiness from my body. I was feeling blank and exhausted, though I had hardly done any physical work. I had just climbed up few stairs."

"I would have taken the tea without the sugar. The quench for tea needs to be satiated even by a bad tea" Kabir joked, but Govind could not understand his humour.

"He then asked me to go by signalling through his hand. His eyes were so quiet and his body looked boneless. I went to check the neighbouring rooms for any furniture which had been broken due to some accident"

"Are you sure, he asked you to leave the room? Did you find any broken furniture?" I asked

"I don't know... maybe I assumed. And yes about the furniture... No, not at all"

"So you mean in that chaos, no one was around?" Kabir asked

"Yes. Instead I had to knock neighbours' door and wake them up. They were in deep slumber as if they had not heard the noise. It was loud enough to be heard kilometres away, especially at that quiet night"

"Then did you go back to prepare tea, I mean, to add sugar?" I asked.

"No, I went back to ask Hrihaan dada if it was fine to add jaggery instead of sugar. That would give a natural sweetness and color to the tea."

"Jaggery in tea... yuck!! Did he agree to it?"

"I opened the door and then...."

"What did you see? C'mon don't worry, we are with you."

"Yes, but there is someone else as well with you in that room."

"Which room?" I asked

"223, the room with star. It has a reason to be marked... go away, please go away!"

Govind was not crying but I could see tears in his eyes. None of his facial muscles had folded, they were all still. He was not blinking but the inflow of tears was very consistent as if he was crying. I wiped it with my handkerchief and asked him to continue.

"I saw Hrihaan dada hanging from the ceiling fan. His eyes were popping out. His shoulders were crooked down and his neck seemed to have broken and stretched abnormally long."

"C'mon, how is that possible? You had seen him few minutes back and talked to him about the tea. Now either you are hiding the truth or you were dreaming then?" Kabir did not like this story.

"Please believe me. I have spoken to you about the incident which I have never spoken about in years."

"I trust you Govind" I offered him water.

"Why did you join this college hostel when you had seen that accident... or suicide, whatever it was?"

"I will tell you, but before that listen to this."

Govind was had more to add. It looked like he was speaking the truth, though it was hard to believe. Maybe he was partially correct.

"Though I did not tell the whole drama which I had encountered, but next day Police did come and performed a thorough check up. They cleaned the room and took all his belongings. They forgot one small trunk which was on the slab above the door."

"Yeah we found that trunk in our room today. You mean to say it hasn't been cleared ever since?" I was puzzled.

"Yes I was doing the final clean up and the police asked me to check if something was left, I saw that black trunk but I was very afraid to lift that. It could have had the spirit of Hrihaan dada, so I did not tell about it to anybody."

"What was in the reports... the post mortem... if you have any idea?" Kabir asked but he was not sure if Govind knows what post mortem was and if it was done to Hrihaan.

"Yes" Govind replied

"That is great, what did it tell?" I was happy to hear that positive reply from Govind

"I don't know all the details but it said that the death was due to some word I am not able to recall but it said something like *car... cardeck... ritha... miaa...* something like that"

"Cardiac Dysrhythmia... you mean?" I asked

"Yes... correct dada! Same name." He then continued. "They said it was heart attack which I never believed as I had seen him twice, once while he was sitting quiet and second he was hanging. I am not sure if that can lead to heart attack."

"The second point which made my doubt even more clear was the time reported by the Police"

Govind's tears had dried now and he was in a state of shock. However disclosing the heavy burden after years, he looked comfortable in narrating further events.

"What did they say?" Kabir asked

"The Police said the death took place between 10:00 PM to 11:00 PM and I am hundred percent sure that I had met Hrihaan dada and his friends at 11:30." He opened his eyes more and searched for a watch here to see the time and continued

"There is some spirit or some ghost which killed him. I don't know why and how, but I am sure he was alive during that reported time."

"Could it be that the clock was not working or its battery must have drained?" Kabir asked a valid question

"No, on my second visit to dada's room I had a glimpse of the clock and it was 12:35 and it seemed correct as I should have taken that much time to search for sugar while preparing the tea."

"So you should not have joined this hostel again after seeing so much right?" I asked

"After my father had retired owing to his age and weakness, I was given this job and I had to discontinue my studies. I left everything and gave full time effort here in the hostel. Side by side I started a small canteen close to the college ground" He continued...

"The room was vacant and was never given to anyone but as the college was becoming popular and started admitting international students as well, the rooms were not sufficient to accommodate all"

"You mean it was later allocated to someone else too?" I asked

"This was a tall and fair boy from Afghanistan or Iran... I don't remember"

"Please don't tell me something happened to him too... I mean what are you trying to say?" Kabir was anxious now

"I have not narrated this incidence but just heard of it. He was also given room number 223"

"What happened to him?" I asked

"There was a peculiar thing about this boy. He never came down to have food. He always asked me or any other mess boy to deliver the food in his room during lunch"

"Ok, then?"

"One day the story repeated…"

"Repeated means?" Kabir stood up
"Same noise of breaking of furniture and things falling on the floor... finally a second mess boy saw him hanging from the fan" Govind had less tears this time as he had not actually seen this death but had fear about the incident for sure.

"The room was then marked with a star and never allotted to any student."
"Yeah I remember that the management was keeping it vacant. They were adjusting me with few other boys, which would have resulted in a very congested stay. I saw this vacant room in the chart and forced them to assign this to me. I don't know why they did not even tell there have been not one but two suicides here."
"They were not suicides dada. Please leave that room... you are a nice guy and that room is cursed by some evil spirit."
"Thanks Govind, but I am not very nice, especially for evil spirits. Actually, I am finally happy to know that I too have a couple of roommates, though I can't see or interact with them."
I tried to keep the moment light, but it hardly brought a smile to Kabir or Govind.

I didn't believe in the good spirits and the bad ones equally, so I was undeterred and decided to continue staying in the same room.

One fine day when we had a break after the exams, we relaxed from the ragging trauma by discussing things with each other. I tried to ask Kabir about his personal life but he did not open up much. One thing ragging had done well to Kabir was the loss of his shyness. He was now more open and participated in almost all the garbage we fantasized about. He looked less afraid of the slaps and approached fellow victims with fun.

"Hey, who is that in your wallet, some retro queen, you never told me?" I pointed to the picture in Kabir's wallet. She looked like some village queen but dressed decently in saree, so I was amazed.

"This is the solo picture of my mother. This was taken just after her marriage"

"She looks beautiful... but" I did not know how to ask so I moved my fingers with pinch action towards my forehead.

"Oh the vermilion. She was a Hindu. I mean she is still professing her religion. My father is a Muslim"

"Oh, bloody you are from such a dramatic family... I mean sounds great. So I've never seen you going, but do you go to temples as well?"

"Yes I do. I am actually very fond of lord Krishn. I adore him; I mean I respect him as much as I preach Allah."

He was reluctant in using both the names in the same sentence but he did it, which brought a smile on my face.

"Okay, I understand. So you don't do that in the hostel room. I mean you haven't kept any idol of lord *Krishn*?" I enquired

"I visit KRISHCON. It's on the way to Kamptee, just 18 KMs from the city."

"What is that?"

"It is a new concept, where all followers of lord *Krishn* gather and we do charity, *kirtans* and we all dance and enjoy... we call it Krishna Conglomerate Of Nobility."

That I heard for the first time.

He then added "I have not kept any idol here in my room as that may lead to several questions by seniors. You know there are some other folks of my community who sometimes visit my room. I just don't want to complicate the ragging tenure. I don't know how seniors of my community would take it."

"I understand man."

This also came to me as a surprise. I knew him for more than 6 months now and still there were many things about him that I did not know. He had that fear in him to place idols but was balancing fine by visiting some Hindu temple which may be complementing his faith. Though it didn't seem very logical, but I was cool as long as he was happy with his style of prayers.

"Utho re bokachoda…" That was some voice asking me to get up, but I was seeing his shoes and was not able to recollect if I had ever talked to him. I got up at midnight, finding it hard to recollect his name but as he approached I was finished with my puzzle. This guy used to come and often pick up Bengali and north east students to his place. Bengali seniors were considered to be the most frightening seniors and I had never faced any one of them. Maybe because of some level of diplomatic immunity I had due to my closeness with Babu. Most of the Bengali seniors lived outside the hostel and they preferred ragging outside the premises. They took enough time to get introduced…

"Take this" saying that, the senior placed a letter on my table. I flipped it both sides to see if anything special, but it was just a plain letter from my father.
"Yours?" He asked
"Yes, the 'from' address reads my father's place… I mean my new place in Gangtok."
"So let me update you if you are not aware that North East India and Bengal have been merged and we now have a common group, a common ragging policy. So technically you are coming to my place today evening."

I had no other option but to approve. I wanted to see what happened there. I was a little excited with a small fear of uncertainty. But that was a good opportunity to travel around the city.
"My name is Shobeek Bhattacharjee… and I will fuck your happiness for next one month…"

I smiled and sat behind his bike. I could not hear much of his bluff as I was busy enjoying the breeze flowing past my ears and through my hair. We reached a place which was almost 10 KMs away from the hostel.

His room was filled with smell of socks and sweat. This smell was worse than any form of toxic gas that might have been used during World War I. I could see some other boys from neighbouring colleges; they all were talking in Bengali. I was asked to get to the room to the left of the main door. This room was little clean with a small desert cooler and an earthen pot placed close enough to the bed, infact just above the pillow cover. Few seniors had come in from outside to watch us.

One more boy was brought close to me and that boy looked like a cute panda. He was crying and not understanding what the seniors were talking in Bengali. He looked simple and innocent, thus an easy target. He reminded me of the way Kabir was on the first day I saw him. This new boy was round with short spiked hairstyle. He had a clean pinkish white skin and four or five hair on his chin. He must be calling it a beard? The senior who brought me stood right in front of me and started boasting about his girlfriends and his achievements.

He held my collar and started pushing me to and fro. He placed the picture of a lady close to my eyes and asked me to see clearly.
"I visit *Ganga Jamuna*, everyday... understand... everyday"
He was briefing about his hard work in the red light area of Nagpur. I had no words to say, so I kept quiet.
"She is not just a harlot, but she is my girl friend now... I love her."
Saying that, he asked me to sit on the bed. While I was thinking about his relation with the prostitute, he suddenly burst with tears. He was drunk and hence the mood swings were causing him to either abuse me or recall his lady-love and cry.

"One day when I had no money to eat, drink, buy anything; this girl gave me fifty rupees. I did not even have petrol in my bike to drive back and this girl... she is your *bhabhi*... understand?"

That level of commitment brought smile, but I restrained my lips and smiled within, thinking how this idiot had money to visit prostitutes daily but no money to eat.

"She is an angel... see her."

Her photo was zoomed in to my face and my eyes were not capable of understanding the figure in the photo.

While the drama was on, I saw that the short guy from northeast had removed his lower and was half naked. Few seniors, who were done lighting up their smoke came close to the boy and handed him a new match stick.

"Put it in your dick" The senior asked. To this, the boy was not sure how and what to do. He looked around with his small round eyes.

"What is my name? Shout!" the senior asked me.

"Shaovik Bhattacharya..." I replied and before I could double check the correct pronunciation in my mind, I had already received a tight slap.

That was pretty hard. I blacked-out. All I could hear was a high frequency noise running through my right ear. The slap had left me disoriented, though I was feeling my ass being kicked every now and then by feet of different sizes.

"My name is Shobeek Bhattacharjee... you forgot it so soon..."
I was finding it hard to balance the left-right recording of my ears. I was sure that there was some problem. So I pulled my ear to see if everything was alright. However, it filled my palm with some warm liquid, which on closer observation looked like blood. I could not see it clearly as my head was spinning and everything was blurred.

I did not know what to do, how to stop the blood flow from my ear. It had now spilled on my shoulder. I then saw that Shobeek and his friends getting frightened as well. He started searching for some cotton or cloth to cover the ear. He was drunk and so not able to balance his mind about the whereabouts of the first aid box, if any.

I did not say anything to this and asked him to pull the curtain. He did so and gave it to me quickly. I folded the curtain and covered the ear to wait for some time.

The north east boy saw the bleeding and he went into shock. I saw him pulling out the match stick from his penis. His pain must have been unbearable. The phosphorus in the match stick must have burnt his penis.

Few other Bengali seniors now joined in and asked the same north east guy to stand up on the chair behind him. A new Bengali junior had recently joined us. This boy was asked to stand on the chair opposite to the north east guy.

The tall Bengali senior was not from our college as I had never seen him come for ragging. I assumed him to be from some medical college as he was wearing a white apron. He had yellow teeth and his hair was wavy while the side buns were straight till center of the cheek. He was confidently mistaken about the cool look he possessed. He took a chain which is used to lock the suitcase when we travel in the train. I thought he would frighten the boys with his looks and his bad breath but he went a step further and splashed his chain like a hunter. It ripped out some flesh from the poor boy's skin. Even I was hit it a couple of time, but I couldn't feel the pain after the hangover I was put in.

The second Bengali junior who was standing on the chair jumped down and started crying tightly closing his eyes. I didn't like that, so I thought of stopping the senior or at least talk to him. The north-east boy's skin was swollen with marks of the chain over his back printed diagonally in red.

Collecting all my energy I stood tall and went close to the senior.

"Sir, I request you not to hit us with the chain. I mean what will you gain with such an attack?" I requested.

He came to me and Shobeek followed him. He started abusing me in all the languages he knew. He pushed me back to the bed, but I managed to stand up again, bending my head to let blood flow and collect in the curtain.

"I know this is not at all enjoyed by you too, so please stop this." I requested again.

That request wasn't appreciated by some other seniors who came close and pushed, one of them kicked me from the back and I fell on the pillow, thus breaking the earthen pot.

I got up and kept requesting that this should be stopped; it was looking futile until one of them was little convinced and asked his mates to stop.

"He is right; there is no fun in this. So let me make this funny" He had a very bad smile with grey teeth. His mouth was more of exhaust for gases coming from his lungs, all having the smell of *beedi*.

He took the chain from the senior and in one end of the chain he put some copper wire which he got from under the bed. There were extra cables placed on the TV set, he then cut another piece of wire and peeled off the plastic cover over the cable using his teeth. He then made a ring like structure.

He came close to north-east guy and tied the end of the chain in his penis forehead. He then started rotating the wire to tighten the grip "aah... sorry sir... please sir..." The poor chap was begging and I was standing helpless, my arms and my waist being held by three seniors.

This senior then tied the other end of the chain to the Bengali junior and drew a line on the center of the floor.

He then acted like a psycho referee and asked them to play a tug-of-war and pull each other's weight using that chain tied to the penis.

It must have pained terribly bad as the weight of the chain and the copper wire gripping the foreskin of the penis.

I tried hard to get away and shouted and cried to leave us but they kept hitting and punishing the boys. My bleeding had given me an excuse from further hitting so I was just being thrown from one end to the other. I knew they would not hit me more, my quota was already over.

I was waiting for the day to get over; it was a very long day again. By the time the play was over, I could see that the boys' skin was all red and looked swollen. What that north east boy must have experienced could not be even thought of. Finally the moment came and we were dropped back.

Kabir came to talk to me while I was opening my room's door, but I had no interest in talking to anyone. My body was also paining due to the hard massage I got from the seniors, but that was nothing when I recalled the face and the plight of that boy. Such exercise would run for next several months if not stopped now, I thought.

Next morning I went for the shower pretty early and did not wear black and white dress. I took a tee and blue denim and while all the juniors were moving from the hostel till the college in a defined queue, I was walking alone.

I was being abused by many seniors but the irony was that several batch mates joined them too. The scenario was that the fear of wrong and right was superseded by the fear of offending the senior's decree. I kept walking with a focused mind to reach the college and meet the Principal.

I was waiting outside the Principal's office and was spotted by some seniors who made few calls and I could understand that they were all united now to stop me from entering the Principal's room. I did not talk to any professor or lecturer or any staff member as I wanted to remain focused and firm. I sat outside as the principal had gone out to take a lecture for final year students. I was in no hurry so I sat with all my patience. I closed my eyes, but closing the eye was bringing the flashback of the nonsense that we had faced last day.

"What are you doing here?" That was Babu's voice; he then took me towards the water filter area and asked me what was going on. I did not have much to talk about but now I was building that confidence to face the Principal.
"Nothing, just wanted to talk to the Principal."
"I know it must be about Shobeek. He is an asshole and often does stupid things. Please ignore him Om."
There was some fear in Babu's voice, was he sent by the Bengal group seniors? Before I could explain anything to him, I saw Shobeek coming out of the washroom; he still was in some hangover.

"*Saala*, if you open your mouth then you will not go alive from here. Forget the degree, no education in life. I know you are under loan... your father will be screwed up!" He was trying hard but his efforts were making me smile now.

"And... What else?" I asked. Babu gave a tight slap to Shobeek and asked him to leave the place or hide in the hostel. He then said something to Shobeek which even I could not hear.

"Om, leave him, forgive him. You must understand his state of mind, he is still under drugs. He is not normal"

"Then please send him to some rehab. Why should we suffer? We have paid immense amount of fees and tried hard to reach here, not to see this bullshit, but to study."

Babu was just trying to save his batch mate. He was leading the second year boys and several other committees of the college. He pretty much kept everybody together and that was the time for him to use his brain and not strength.

"If you say anything which may go against him, then think what disaster could that cause to his career. Shobeek scored 98% in 12th Std. and in first year engineering too he topped the branch and came 5th in the university. He is from a very poor family and they have paid enough money for this dumb-head to study and they have just this boy to look up too."

I was seeing that urgency to help Shobeek in Babu's eyes but I could not mellow down at this point. I asked Babu a glass of water and sat back on the chair.

"I will not let you down, don't worry. I too want the same change which you always have in your mind" Babu smiled hearing this and went back towards the hostel. I was seeing that some first year boys and few Bengali seniors were closely observing me from the Chemistry lab and one of them abusing me and showing gestures through his fingers to warn me.

"Please come" said the Principal.
The principal's room was D shaped arrangement and I was standing at the center of this D. Above his head was his photograph with Mr. Varghese Kurien, for whom I had immense amount of respect. I had read about him in my school books and got some confidence after seeing him.
"Good after noon Sir."

"Yes? Don't tell me you want to change your branch." He asked.

"No sir. When I joined this college, one thing I made sure to carry with me was a copy of notification which I had downloaded from the AICTE website. It was the supreme court's decree on the prohibition of ragging." I said

"Good, and in my college I assure you that we oblige by those guidelines... what else?"

"You believe in revolutionaries, sir?" I asked.

"Yes of course, I not only respect them but I tend to obey and follow them as well. My grandfather was a freedom fighter and he has built my childhood on the great anecdotes from the freedom struggle in *Champaran, Bihar*. So what is your point?"

"Thank you sir, I can see a great revolutionary right above your head."

He understood that I was talking about Mr. Kurien, who played pivotal role in a revolution that made India self-sufficient in milk and dairy products.

"Oh, the father of the white revolution! He was my batch mate, long back in Loyola College, Chennai and mind you, that man still has the spark which I appreciated and respected years back." He paused for some time and asked me my name.

"Om... my name is Om sir."

"Om, Tell me what is the matter?"

Then I narrated him the nexus between the warden, second year, third year, final year and pass out students. I also tried explaining him how this was developing like a cancer within the system. I narrated him the hardship which were given to first year students physically and elaborated every scene that came to my mind. They were all fresh. I requested him to not just pity about the pain felt by us, but take all necessary actions. He looked moved by the victimization descriptions.

"I will set up a committee and call you back to hear from you."

"Sir I am sorry but I am not leaving until any assurance or any action is taken against the culprits. We are weak juniors suppressed by the faculty, seniors, curriculum and pressure of getting a job. I don't want any batch-mate of mine committing a suicide due to this."

"I assure you Om. We will have a panel which will analyse and do a thorough investigation. I also request you to not approach any guy from the press or leak this matter in the open"

I was finding it difficult to trust him, but he gave me a certain timeframe and asked me to come after two days to explain everything to the panel. I thanked him and moved out to see a flock of seniors staring at me as if I had committed a blunder.

"Today we will teach him a lesson."

"*Saala* Mangal Pandey..." Mostly these were the statements coming out from the seniors gathered outside. I pushed some of them and then moved through the thin passage between them.

I packed some of my items and informed Kabir that I would come directly after two days. Kabir was afraid of another big problem, so he requested me to be safe and come directly to the college. I was about to leave when from the window I saw few trucks loaded with men armed with baseball bats and hockey sticks getting inside the main gate of the hostel.

The hostel perimeter was fenced by wires and had only one gate for entry and exit. The gate was the only way to get an auto rickshaw. Behind the kitchen was the cricket ground and that was fenced with trees and shrubs. But if that jungle was crossed then one could directly reach the next square in the city.

I packet a light bag so that I could move fast past the fences. I started running fast to cross the play ground. I turned back for a second to see if I was being followed and there were some eyes on me. I kept running and when I had almost reached the end of the ground, I started hearing few motor bikes approaching me. That was the time to gear up. I threw my bag across the fence and started climbing the fences. The wires had been rusted but were still thick enough to sustain my weight.

The gap between the wires was too small; hence I could not cross it by bending my body. I had to climb up. While I started getting down my shoe lace got stuck in the wire. I bent to solve the knot to get rid of the shoe. I could hear the bikes coming very close to me. I looked up and now I was clearly seeing hundreds of seniors having hockey sticks just running amok.

I left the shoe and continued the run. I now had the shoe only in my right foot. The balance while running reminded me of three legged races I used to have during school days. My boot was thick and heavy making it difficult to run. So I removed the second as well. It was a slope and the jungle was getting thicker.

The sun set had never been so fast. I could see sun running from over my forehead and getting out of my sight so fast. I ran touching one tree and holding the other and finally reached a place which was very quiet. The other end of this was a square, which was visible but was around a Kilometre far. I was now trying to differentiate between the noise of cricket and other nocturnal creatures but whenever I closed my eyes, the harmony broke and I was just seeing the darkness. I barely managed to walk, limping through the shrubs. But when I finally reached there, I saw several seniors standing at the parking places.
They all looked like predators waiting for their prey to land in front of them. They were also staring at the jungle as if they had sent their search party inside the jungle?

I could not have risked an exit through this point, so the only way was walking back. This time I was slow and took time. I was now hearing no one. I had closed my eyes for some of the journey towards the barren land covered with shrubs and trees.

Beautiful! was the word to express what I was seeing... a serene piece of land which was not more than 2000 Square feet? As and when I was moving close, I could smell fragrance of flowers which were blooming at night and their scent had created a sphere of tranquillity around this plot.

I was tired and had no water to drink. I looked around but could not see evening dew on the green grasses around. I sat on one of the stones, which were all shining white; the moon was kind to show me some light. There were several cuts and bruises on my left leg. I started picking the thorns out one by one and wiped off the sweat around the cuts.

The salt in the sweat was burning the cuts even more, but I did not have the option to howl or groan. Every small cut was gave me a burning sensation. I calmed myself for some time and laid-back.

It was not more than few minutes since I had let my muscles to relax, and I was clearly hearing people walk close. The dry shrubs and sticks sounded an alarm to signal me the danger. I could see flash lights and torches. I hid behind one large stone and kept a watch on the people approaching the periphery. Suddenly the moonlight got intensified and it fell directly on the stone.

It read "*Mohiuddin Sagir Ahmed, 15 Dec 1976*" and it had some other lines written in Urdu, maybe to appreciate or condole that person?

I was happy and sure of the safety which this place could provide. I thanked Mr. Sagir's cemetery and searched for a corner which was hidden from the end of the jungle. I plucked the flowers around and created a bed from its leaves and petals.

I had the bag to be used as a pillow. The footsteps were now heard clearly but I was more than very sure than the seniors searching me would never visit the cemetery that was pretty much secluded. I was happy that for the first time some superstition or fear had worked in favour of a person who didn't believe in them.

No dead man would walk and disturb me and Mr. Sagir, as far as I knew since I first met him 20 mins back, looked like a gentleman. Not to forget his hospitable nature. I was lost tossing and turning but the soil was fresh and the grasses were blessed with that natural fragrance. I plucked some grasses which were young and milky and started having them. I was thirsty and that was keeping me busy and I did not know when I went into my dream world while chewing one of those milky grasses.

"Craw, Crawww…" was the call, that wasn't a good alarm. I was seeing few crows, accompanied by few sparrows seeing me from the branches on my right. To my left the trees were filled with vultures. They were shouting hell. Some of them were plucking the hair on my leg, may be they were eating up the insects stuck in my wounds.
"Get off… I am not dead!"
I shouted and stood up to clean up my pant and shirt and ran my fingers through my hair to take out small insects who were missed by the birds. I turned back to salute to Mr. Sagir and ran quickly towards the main square. That was too early for the hostel boys to get up for patrol. I crossed the fences and ran towards an auto rickshaw. I asked him to drop me to Government Medical College & Hospital, where that north east boy studied.

I reached the hospital gate and the resident doctor's hostel was attached to the med college. I ran inside and asked some resident doctors about some north east boy in first year. Most of them did not have a clue of who he was but one of them directed me to the class room. I walked there and searched inside but could not find him. I moved out and saw a water cooler. That increased my thirst and I ran close to it to grab that tasty mineral. That was the sweetest water of my life. I forgot my breath while having it. After long time I took a deep sigh, a sigh of relief. I turned back to see the same northeast boy walking slowly towards his classroom.

"Hey... stop!" I was so happy to find him. He got frightened to consider me as some Bengali senior. So he increased his speed to enter the room. Now he could recognize me. I did not know what and how should I greet him, so I just started narrating him what I did in the college. I wanted to talk to him more and explain him that we could together approach the Principal of his college and the University to take stronger action. He was appalled by my action and wanted to get away from me.

"Please go away man. I can manage the ragging, I am sorry." He turned his back and walked towards the left lobby. I followed him and kept requesting him that the change would come only if we unite and strongly bring the issue in front of specific people in the University.

"No change would happen. It could get worse if we do anything. You know I've come from *Lachen*, Sikkim and coming to a medical college is like a dream for me. I am the only person from my entire village who has taken admission in MBBS"

"Oh, I thought you are from Manipur. Well I am also currently residing in Sikkim, precisely Gangtok"

"Good, that is nice." He now showed a smile, with compassion. His eyes got pressed in and then it was difficult to see his iris. His cheeks moved up when he smiled and this wasn't a fake smile as he looked happy, at least for first few seconds. He then continued...

"Please understand that for me coming this far is a very difficult task. I did not choose drugs; I did not choose to become a hooligan like my friends. I have chosen education and whatever it takes to become a doctor and go back to my village. I will go through the pain"

He started crying again, elaborating his difficult choices.

I did not know the best way to show my sympathy to him, but I wanted a change in which his testimonial could bring drastic turn to the malpractices inside the University.

"My name is Om, what is yours? I am sorry for asking so late." I asked with a smile to relax him.

"Chumbi Gomchen... sorry I am not able to help you. I understand your point, but I am afraid to take that big step."

"Just imagine it's more than 30 years now since Sikkim became a state of India and from your village you are the first person ever to reach this place... why?" I asked

"My hard work, labour"

"...and the most important thing is acceptability." I cut him short.

I then added "You've broken that cage finally and opened it for many more youngsters who can now know from you the procedure of admission and further about jobs here in the mainland?"

"You are right, but what is your point?"

"Not my point, but my request. You would be sad if someone, especially if some young sister of yours comes from your village and is tortured by the people here. What if she is not able to continue her studies or the worst case, she does something very wrong... something like suicide. There is hardly a senior from North East India who can fight on your behalf."

His expression was now sad and he had started feeling why I was requesting him so much.

"You are right." He thought for a while. "But if even I am not able to complete my education, then how would I spread the education to others. What you are suggesting would even close my doors."

"Can you please get me a glass of water?"

I asked controlling the gullet with blow of oxygen as it was getting dry and the friction was tickling inside the throat. I think I should have had the water in small instalments. The swift gulps exerted some pressure to the lateral walls inside the vocal cord and my gullet had developed a pain with some irritation.

"So Chumbi, my simple request is to please come with me to my college and identify the culprits"
"Yes." There was a pause. "Okay let me think about it Om."
"Don't worry, you are good." saying that I hugged him.
He was hardly reaching my shoulders, but he gave me a warm hug.
"I will always be thankful to you." I gave him the details to visit my college and requested him to contact Kabir if at all any help was needed.
I then took his leave. I marched towards Jai's akhada to spend my night there. I had to hide till the day when I would see the principal.

"Good Morning Om." The Principal advised me to have a look at the panel, comprised of professors and lecturers from different colleges in the university and as well as the trustees. I did not know how trustees would react to the dirty games inside the hostel since its inception. Would it back fire on the staff?
I ignored the repercussions and greeted everybody.

"So explain in detail, what happens inside the hostel. Feel free to take names, don't be afraid" said one of the panelists. He was bald and had white moustache. He had the typical Marathi accent and was polite in asking me the first question. I read his name but the important part of his name was the designation that said '*Trustee*'.

I narrated one by one the ragging rules, procedures and booklets which had the syllabus of dos and don'ts for first year boys. I presented the dossier which was a photo copy circulated among the freshers.

"Why should I believe you Mr. Om?" This was another trustee looking like a shrewd business man. He was smiling and busy with his cell phone all the time, while I was narrating the activities date by date. He did not look interested and considered it a waste of time. He was rather interested in rejecting the whole meet.

"What would I gain out of this? I am not here to settle personal scores or ruin my career by playing this blame game. I just want a safe environment to study. That is why we are here, right?" I replied.

"Wait a second..." The trustee then showed the paper to the principal and some panelists sitting close to him. He then had that sarcastic smile and asked

"I see this paper which reads *'Ohm'*. Why is it spelled wrong? Also you don't have father's name or a surname. Isn't that weird?" The trustee jumped back and that time he wasn't in a mood to get an answer but was ready with another question before I could answer his first question.

"I am sorry, but I fail to understand how the ragging activity is linked to my name. This has been happening inside the hostel since ages and now when I have approached you, then what I hear is the description of my name" I wasn't happy.

"You haven't answered my question" the trustee smiled back cunningly.

The Principal looked at me and signalled with his hand to calm down and come to the point quick.

"This is how my name is spelled, it is not wrong. Also surname and father's name need not be carried forward because the moment someone hears it, he or she starts thinking what community I belong to, which place in India I can be mapped to, how must be my upbringing, what caste I can be associated to and so on..."

"So?" He asked

"So I thought of keeping just a first name. That is permissible?"

"I see a rebel in you" the trustee flung the file back on the table. Was he provoking me? I took a deep breath and thought of keeping quiet.

"Do you know about the educational background of the boy whom you've accused as the prime culprit?" the Principal asked.

"Yes I do but being educated, as per my limited experience, doesn't make a person civilized. We have examples in history where illiterate people have proven to be great leaders and built up good civil norms and greatest of literates committing homicides."

After a minute's silence, I heard the door open and somebody walking close to me from behind. I looked my left and right and saw all the accused seniors standing just next to me. I was seeing the seniors from medical college along with Shobeek. They did have some fear in their eyes but no shame at all.

I was asked to see them and clearly say who did what.

I looked them into the eyes and at this very moment they all looked down, they had no courage to look up into my eyes now.

I explained the individual contributions of the seniors. I tried to recall minute by minute details of that day.

The accused were asked their stand and my statements were denied by all of them, as expected.

"Now how can we punish them? Do you have some proof which we can see and understand is a result of the ragging?" the person to the right of trustee asked.

To reply that question, I closed my nose with my right thumb and index finger. I walked close to the person and blew air from within. This was gushing out wind through my right ear. I was in pain but this was a clear proof of the fresh wound.

"Have you gone mad?" The trustee moved back. He wiped his face with his handkerchief.

"This can be an accident... while you were playing games, cricket?" the trustee raised his shoulders signalling a gesture of 'I am not bothered'

"Some of the seniors are not from this college. How should we believe that they even met you? Do you have someone else who can say he was a victim as well or has seen these boys victimizing you or other juniors?" The principal was hinting me to be more specific and bring evidences. I had none. I had a feeling of despair and the final thought was loud in my mind that '*I've lost it*' All the running and shouting went futile. I lowered my neck and closed my eyes.

"Sir, May I please come in?" was the voice from behind. I turned back to see Chumbi. Great!

He had experienced so much of pain that he had lost his entire hesitation. While he was introducing himself, his hands were busy bringing up proofs without wasting time. He opened his shirt and showed the marks of the metal chain. He showed the scratches on his chest by the nails of the seniors. He opened up his small eyes and they were red and blue from inside. He was attaching visible proof to the actions. Finally, he started unzipping his trouser and simultaneously described the tug of war to show the inflammation caused due to the match stick insertion.

"Stop!!" the Trustee stood up and called the peon.

"Sir I am just showing the marks on my private organs which are still red with bruises."

"Oh, heck!" Said the principal and few other panel members too agreed to his call. They repeatedly asked the seniors if they had committed slightest of ragging or was it exaggerated.

"Sorry sir we did ragging, but these boys are lying. We did not go physical, we just asked for introductions" Shobeek defended.

The chemistry teacher was a very senior teacher in our college. He was since the beginning trusting our testimonials. He also knew what harm phosphorous could cause to the sensitive foreskin. But the panel were still not satisfied due to the lobby of the trustee not wanting to publicise this issue.

Suddenly when I had lost all the hope, I heard Chumbi's voice again.

"Sir, I remember one thing which might be unique in this case"

"Go ahead" asked the chemistry teacher.

"Sir, the matchbox the senior had was *'Agni patta'* with a picture of two swords and a fire. That company is a local manufacturer of match boxes in Eastern India." The chemistry teacher asked all the seniors to take things out of their pocket and display what matchbox they had. The peon collected all the items and fortunately the idiot senior who had tortured Chumbi had brought the same matchbox.

This brought a smile of hope making the case clearly in our favour.

Now the seniors started taking names of one another and things came out in light. With this, things were sorted out and all seniors involved in such organized and unorganized ragging activities were punished. Some of them were barred from the University exams for next two years. It was ordered by the trustees and the principal to place five more vigilant security guards inside each hostel building and the mess.

We thanked all in the panel and I hugged Chumbi hard "You were great buddy. Thanks for coming here!" Kabir was standing just outside the office and hugged me the first moment he saw me.

"We won it yaar!" was my reaction with some tears rolling down my cheek on Kabir's hair. Kabir seemed so delighted that he lifted me. We then dropped Chumbi to the auto stand and thanked him again for his courage.

Next few days, we all enjoyed fearless days, button less shirts, sports shoes, denim and the best was entry to the canteen, which was till date prohibited to freshers.

Without ragging the days were passing so fast. I hardly got to see any unhappy face, until one day...

"Om, open the door. You there?" I recognized the voice as 20%. Why has come up bothering me late night? I walked carelessly and hit the table. It bruised my big toe. The size of blood droplet on the edge of my nail was just going to overflow when I spotted my handkerchief.

"Wait I am coming, just hold on." I requested 20% who was banging the door continuously. I tied a tight knot with the hanky after applying the after shave over the wound.

"Yes what happened?"

"Come out and see. He's back, please come quick!"

He took me to Kabir's room and opened the door. I was shocked to see Kabir all dressed in orange. He was sitting in front of a big Krishn picture. His head was shaven, leaving behind a small *shikha* which was around three inches long. His room was filled with sandal fragrance, which took me back to my school days when I used to visit the Krishn temples. I ran to him and tried to pull him up by holding his shoulders and arm. "Get up *yaar*, where were you since last 4 days? We searched you everywhere. We called all your seniors, local numbers from your diary. I am sorry, but I even called your mother. We were all worried"

"Please go back and remove your shoes."

He wasn't happy with my encroachment into his *pooja ghar*, it seemed. I was stumped by this sudden change. What was happening?

Few more boys gathered around the door.

"Sorry, but please say where you were man? Your parents were so worried and your mother was literally crying. We were going to lodge a police complain today for your missing report."

"I was in Pune. I had gone to KRISHCON annual meet. I now know what I was missing, what I did not know since last twenty years. I was so ignorant. I was a fool but now..."

Saying that he looked up and with his hand touched his eyes and then he kissed his hands. He finally kneeled down in front of the picture.

"What!! Pune? You travelled that far and you did not inform me?" Kabir wasn't bothered at all. I tried to be harsher.

"I am your friend. Remember me? Look at me!" I was shaking his shoulders to bring him back.

He pushed my hands and sat back attaining some peculiar *aasan* to continue his worship. He looked lost. I could see him starting sentences with open eyes and ending them with his eyes closed as if he understood the divine meaning of what he was speaking. I was feeling bad for him now. I was not against his new form of worship but against his complete dedication and blind faith towards the religious group.

"I stayed with so many learned people from across the globe and I finally have understood that all efforts, all actions lead to one and only one place."

"One place? Which place?" I asked

"The immanent, the immortal, the supreme soul, the primeval lord... Allah... Krishn."

Then he stood up and continued...

"Lord Krishn in Geeta clearly says that he is the creator and universal truth and we are just pawns obeying him and the same thing I've read in *surat-al-baqarah*, the *pak Quran*, that the whole religious system and lifestyle we enjoy is designed by Allah, there is no one who is better than Allah in religion and we are his worshippers."

"I don't understand the theory and adjectives you have been using for the supreme, as you know that I stay away from such..." I replied, but went soft to not hurt him right now...
"But still I feel you are getting a little too much into the whole religion thing. I am sorry but you should not neglect the whole scientific temper to just stare this picture." I pointed to the picture of lord Krishn which was all red and did not look like a conventional lord Krishn's image as seen in the posters.
"Mind your language Om!"
"This is not just a picture. It has been painted by all the devoted followers of lord Krishn not by color, but by their blood."
"What?" A boy behind me closed his mouth after the shout.
"We all contributed to this holy picture" Kabir replied with folded hands.
"Blood! Get up Kabir, open your eyes." I went close and added "Remember, you used to talk to me about completing your course and joining a good company for research? You wanted to help your parents in getting your sisters married; you wanted to take your family's responsibility after your father has retired. Please open your eyes and get out of this." I was pleading before Kabir to recall his real purpose of joining this college.
"Nothing happens without the consent of God and if my prayers have the power, then my sisters will get married. I won't have to waste any time to think about that." He then turned his face to the picture again and said "Lord please give me the power to focus."
He was not moved an inch by my logic.

"Kabir, please listen to Om. What we want to say is that we have had sages since Vedic times and they have done prayers and offerings, which is good. However there is some family responsibility which you as a student and as the only educated son of your family should never forget." 20% came in with good logic to persuade Kabir.

"Please don't indulge in small talk. I have bigger things to do; lord will take care of smaller problems described by you. In Vedic times, the sages were so immersed in the love of Krishn that they lived ages and thousands of years. Small issues like family get solved automatically in few years. I want to live for thousands of years and become one such sage."
Kabir broadened his chest and took a deep sigh. I was not going to take that so I quickly responded.
"Did you say thousands of years? I am sorry, but have you read Rig Ved?" I thought of trying some reference in his language to stop him from getting deep.
"No, but I've read Bhagvad Geeta."
"You agree that the four Ved were written previous to Bhagvad Geeta and the knowledge in them is much older. I am not saying that Vedic books are better than Geeta, but yes the Ved helped ancient sages to preach various forms of natural forces?"

"They were *devta*." He wasn't happy with me calling the Gods as 'natural forces'.
While he was warning me with his broad eyes, I tried to give him a reference
"Sorry, so just consider hymn 89 (9) of Rig Ved, Hrishi Gautam says"

Shatmin nu shardo anti deva yatraa nashchakra jarasham tanunaam,
Putraso yatra pittro bhavanti ma no madhya reerishataayurgantoh

The shlok ended and everyone was quiet, they looked at me and Kabir came closer to me and expressed his will to know what it means.

"Oh God, We live for hundred years. You've given the ageing on this body of ours, by then even our sons become fathers. So please try that our age doesn't limit in between."
After translating it, I expected some response from Kabir to which he kept quiet and gestured with his eyebrows to infer. I then tried to make it simple
"I just wanted to say even when we were in Vedic ages and had the best of our ability to preach and love the creator; we still lived for 100 years. This fact is not said by a common man but a much respected sage."
"So what do you want to say?" Kabir asked.
"Please remove that misconception that Vedic age-limit was thousands of years. Come back to normalcy yaar. Whatever be the age of a life, live it to fullest, enjoy it and work towards your goals."

"Don't trap me in your words." He then thought for a while and continued "May be the year then was too long, not like present day and hence they may have lived for thousands of years. May be the revolution around lord Sun was slow."
I was now seeing an arrogant and haughty phenomena developing on his face.

"Forget the age boys, we are here to request Kabir to be normal and bring him back to studies. You scored well in the first semester and we have a lot of expectations from you" 20% tried to bring us back.

"He is right, we all request you to get normal, before it's too late." I continued.

"*Hare Ram…. Hare Krishn…* you guys are stopping me from practicing my faith. You understand what level of crime is that?"

"No, we want you to continue with your faith but as a normal follower. Continue both ways of prayers but don't leave your education, please!" Someone said from behind.

"Normal… Normal? What has happened to you all? Did I ever come to your room and peep into what you've been doing. You guys drink and roam around with girls and what not" He was getting annoyed.

"I apologize for everything Kabir. Just understand that we all have full faith in you as a student and I personally have strong confidence in you. It doesn't matter if you baptize to Christianity or become a Jew or obey any other religion."

"Then what?" He asked.

"For us what matters is your focus, which should be back on your education. Pursue your faith as much as you want, but come to college as well."

"Oh, baptize… now I see. Go away and leave me alone. Why did I come back? I should have lived in the temple itself. This is real *Kaliyug* where a non-believer is teaching me what to profess." He was hitting hard on me, which brought a small laugh. He did not enjoy the smile, so I covered my face with my palm quickly.

"In every *yug*, people like you and me are born and we fight against each other through our thoughts. I have set a goal for me and studies hardly bother me now. This *yug* is for me to gain that level of consciousness." He was feeling elated thinking about that goal.

"I am sorry. I am not a demon and have a small question for you."

"Ask"

"Do you really know about what a Yug is?" I asked him politely.

"What? It's too big for your science to understand right now. It definitely has millions of years" He said that without confidence but wanted to ridicule science anyway.

I wanted to take clear his misconceptions, but at the same time didn't want to hurt him by any means.

"Per ancient Indian scriptures, the temporal division of this Universe is referred to as *Kalp*"

I paused to see some reaction from him, but he was plain and the expressions were shielding my speech. I still continued.

"432 Crore revolutions of Earth around the Sun have been divided into 1000 *chaturyugs.*"

"Yes I know the four Yugs. I see Kaliyug now, you demon!" Kabir reacted.

"Please continue" 20% asked and few others did nod their heads.

"Sorry... so each Chaturyug is made of four Yug; *Satyayug, Tretaa, Dvaapar and the Kaliyug.* The age of Kaliyug is the shortest amounting to just four lakh thirty two thousand years. So don't worry I am here for very small time to bother you."

I tried to make him laugh, but he seemed irritated with me.

"So you mean in my small life, I can't attain that level of nirvana?" He asked.

"Per mythology, you may find several references of people directly meeting the supreme lord. I don't buy that logic though, be it any religion. However what is going to give you satisfaction, you might find that, when and where I have no clue."

"What does that mean?" A voice came from the back.

"I mean I am not stopping Kabir, he must keep doing things that make him happy. But he should be careful with the people posing as 'gurus'. Rather than believing in their bluff about various Yugs and their ages, we should understand the actual division. This is not done by me. Though I am quoting it, I don't subscribe to this formula."

"Om, I know you will pay for all this when the time comes." Kabir said with some anger in his eyes and I was now feeling hopeless.
"Om, I request you to please get out of my room with these pseudo Hindus."
Kabir shouted and seeing no response loudly continued.
"This is my prayer time and if you guys bother me further, then I would go back to Pune" He warned us.
"Kabir, can you get ready for the college at least and we would not stop you from prayers?" I requested.
"I would not be attending the college... for some time." He slowed down and started thinking, or maybe lamenting why he joined this college. We were finding it difficult to bring him to his regular routine but the unlearning of his recent knowledge was going to take time. I moved close to him and tried to hug him.
"Get off! Please go away... *dushtt Nastik!*"

He shouted and I was taken aback at his strong words. Though the word "atheist" used by him to describe me was correct, but the adjective he had prefixed with that was colouring all atheists as demons. I had immense respect for Kabir as my friend and how he managed his studies so well during the ragging days. He used to study late night whenever time permitted him. He was and will be a good pal, I said to myself. I had nothing more to say, so I apologized and went back to my room.

Next morning I woke up early and walked towards Kabir's room to see if he was alright. I decided to go inside the room without knocking and apologize again. I had decided to listen to whatever he said. I was a little harsh last day and I really wanted Kabir to get back to his world.

The room was dark and my eyes were not yet acclimatized to this, so I turned left and saw that he was offering his prayers. Oh! I had come a bit too early. This was the time for his morning prayers and I was seeing him offering Namaz for the first time.

Normally he would come and wake me up after his morning prayers and then we used to go out for walk. We used to jog around the college ground and enjoy the morning breeze. I was missing my buddy since so many days. That day, I kept quiet to avoid any act of offending his prayers, be it Namaz or his Sanskrit chants.

I stood there watching him all the time. He offered his prayers and when he was done, he was the first to break the silence.

"May the almighty forgive you for your ignorance?" He said that in a very low voice and then closed his eyes.

"Sorry yaar." I had planned not to speak anything but apologize as Kabir was a great friend. He did not reply and sat on the bed for some time. He asked me to sit close to him, on the chair.

"Om, please understand that this education, job, running around money and all such stuff is not going to bind me now." He was now speaking up his mind.

"So, what have you thought?"

"I would visit places and spread this information. If I am able to make one person of this world understand the true love of Krishn through KRISHCON, then the purpose of my life is served" He took a sigh and smiled as the exhale ended.

I wanted to keep quiet and say nothing on that topic. I wanted to stitch my lips or block my ears as the more I listened, the more I was tempted to respond. I kept quiet and looked into his eyes.

"We are all going to die one day, so we should just finish that one task which is the reason for our birth... that one important job."

"Can I help you in any way... money, arranging your travel in the cities you travel? I have few good contacts and my father's friends who can support your trips" I wanted to help him and not stop him.

"No, Om. You have still not understood that now I just want to see that beautiful face of my lord all the time. It gives me energy to walk, dance, travel" saying this he suddenly stood up and circled twice in front of the same picture. He threw his hands up in the air and jumped back to the bed. He was still dressed in the same orang coloured dress which now smelt bad. That dress was not enough to cover his body. It was like a short towel running from his shoulders and then covering his body under his waist.

"Kabir, I just came here to tell you that you are one of my best buddies and a very talented student. You've performed so well in studies and I just want my old friend back. Remember how you balanced between ragging and studies. Can't you do that with your worship as well?" I asked as politely as possible

"No. This is my life and I have learnt lessons for my wrongdoings. How can you even understand my pain? Do not come between me and my faith."

He raised his voice and gestured with his palm to get out. I moved out thinking how I could help him better. I was not a counsellor but Kabir would never have agreed to visit one with me either.

The routine was fixed now. We used to see him engrossed in his offerings and prayers all the time. The music sometimes went loud, disturbing us but we never complained. I tried to counsel him time and again, but in vain.

One day, when I came back from the college I saw a note stuck on my door. It was Kabir's message. He had packed his bags and left for Pune. He had also asked me to inform his parents. He did not leave any contact number of Pune. He was knowingly cutting off himself from studies, family and friend. He wanted to be aloof immersed in his devotion. I walked inside the room and looked at the mirror. I had nothing but pity on my failed attempts. I couldn't stop a future genius. May be he would come back some day. I consoled myself.

CHAPTER 9

Compass Aligned To Heart

Years passed and we were slowly reducing in numbers. Very few students were left in our batch. Many had failed to progress till the final year and some had left the course to choose a different track. I was busy learning the new trade and kept myself busy in the dedicated lab assigned to me for my project work.

"Hi, you are Om? Hello!" Someone from my back was trying to call me, with a request in her voice.

"Hello" I looked at her and just... kept looking at her!

She was very beautiful. I went few seconds back and found her voice to be even more soothing. She had long black hair tied in a half ponytail with fringes, small ear rings and an even smaller *bindi*, stuck just in the center of her forehead. She was wearing a *rani coloured kurti* and a *ferozi choodidaar*. She was very fair, but it did not look like a natural fairness. Her fairness would be considered as a disease by most of north Indian people. Many may even go to the extent of calling it a disease which would have triggered by having milk immediately after fish.

"Hi, my name is Sayali. I am from the Government Biotech College."

"Hi, I am..." I kept looking at her.

She now started adjusting her *kurti*; meanwhile her *dupatta* was blown away by the wind. She held the latter and tried to speak out. I took a deep breath and focused on her eyes now. She had big brown eyes with her *kaajal* underlining them to enhance her beauty. She had that random eye movement so I was not able to focus back on her eyes for long. I then switched to her small forehead.

"Sorry, what did you say?" I tried to come back.

"Sayali... I mean. I am..." She repeated and bowed her head to continue

"I heard you talking about the implementation of Moore's law trajectory to design new age mobile processors with minimal space utilization and...

"Optimal removal of patterns from integrated circuits?" I added before she could complete her sentence. She nodded her head. She was speaking about my project.

"Yes, I had come to your college when you have given a great seminar on this topic. I mean other speakers were good as well."

I took a pause from listening to focus back on her eyes. They were moving less now and slowly started looking even bigger!

"What is your question madam?"

I asked and it was difficult to talk anything to her except the words to define her beauty.

"I would love to work with you for my University project." She said.

"Do you really think so? I mean I have no issues with that, but are you sure?" I asked to which she replied.

"I just have my theories and I have no means to execute them due to lack of infrastructure in our college. Do you think the idea you spoke is really possible?" she asked

"Yes, I do feel that the way we discard ICs can be reduced by thousand fold if we learn how to remove the pattern and etch them. Hypothetical, but I need to work more on it." I just gave a brief scope of my project.

"I am actually a doctor." She added

"A Ph.d?" I asked

"No, medicine. My interest is more in planting the smallest sized ICs in human brain to gather as much information possible. Even better would the ability of the chip to clean its data, so that the chips don't need to be plucked back from the body. We have not invented such chips yet which would serve their purpose and finally dissolve amicably in the brain." She was talking good about electronics. Was she really a doctor?

"Yeah, this could have an application in medicine as well. I had never thought of it from that angle." I smiled and thanked her through my eyes.

"So, why have you come here? Some conference?" I asked.

"I have enrolled myself under Dr. Shashi Patil. He heads the neurology department in our college. I've completed my MBBS and have good hands on work in neurology."

I wanted to ask her if she could take that bug out of my brain. The stupid bug that I had had since birth, which diverted me to weird thoughts all the time. She then added

"I was not interested in sitting in a cabin and prescribing antipyretics with antibiotics to the patients. I don't want that life."

"Wait a minute. You don't like Rx or do you have a good handwriting?" I joked

"No, I like that too but I want to continue my research in the application of nano-ICs that we implant in the brain. I am making it simple for you."

"That sounds cool, especially from a doctor's mouth." I thanked her for not using her medical jargons.

"Okay this is my bio-data. Please feel free to call me if you are ready for this proposal"

She gave me her resume and attached her visiting card to it. It was pink visiting card and had a logo of her hospital. The resume elaborated her papers on similar topics to some very serious institutes. The visiting card was a soft plastic but the font was hard and bright. The black italic fonts were contrasting the card and I found it hard to read it except her name that read.

"Dr. Sayali Pranay Thorat"

I was holding a visiting card for the first time and I did not know the convention followed in those days or by doctors. So, I ignored the further analysis of its design.

"Pranay…" I smiled but soon felt bad that I did it upfront. I just couldn't stop my smile.

"What is so funny in it? That is my father's name."

While saying it, she raised her eyebrows and bent her upper half closer to mine. Though she was yelling at me, it sounded like a melody.

"Nothing. How well-versed are you in Hindi? I mean, do you know the meaning of the word Pranay?"

I couldn't believe I asked that question to the lady on my first visit. I was cursing my sense of humour but the arrow was well past the bow already.

"My father is an IPS officer and I've travelled many places, mostly in North. So I know Hindi, may be not as much as you do but I sure can speak and write it. What is so funny about the name?"

"Had I been a euphemist, I would have said it means Romance, but its literal usage in Hindi translates to the *act of sex* between the partners. I was wondering how someone can name his son Pranay."

"Really? Oh God!" While giving me the expression of displeasure, her eyebrows moved up and her oval face became reddish pink. She was mad at me and she turned around to walk back to her car. She wanted to walk fast but with her sandals, which had a heel of almost three inches, it was difficult especially in the grassy area around the parking lot.

"I am sorry, I will call you soon Sayali... Ma'am."

I tried to shout to let her hear my apologies. I was stupid enough to have talked like that. Her face was flashing in front of my face and I did not want to open my eyes to see the lab. I let loose myself on the table and placed the water bottle on my forehead to balance it. I tried to balance it with closed eyes and now I was seeing the bottle see-sawing left and right just like her *dupatta*. It took me a week to get normal. I was finding it hard to ignore her image on the etching boards. The tool for micro fabrication had just evolved into her soft palms.

"Sorry Om." I turned around to see her standing near the lab door looking remorseful. I couldn't believe it. Days had passed and I had focused back on the work ignoring her face with great difficulty. But what was that? She was there, standing near the door of my lab. Before she could say anything, I ran towards her. I didn't know what to do, so just apologised to her.

"I am sorry Ma'am. I shouldn't have..."

I folded my lips hard inside to show my lamenting face. It felt good now. I couldn't recall when was the last time I had collected that much courage to ask for forgiveness. Why was I tendering down? Was it the 'lady charm' running some chemicals inside my brain? Whatever was happening, it was making me feel really happy.

"No, I am sorry I should not have... Also, just call me Sayali." Why was she apologizing?

"Please don't. So, how are you?" I then asked her the reason for her presence in my research room.

"I have chosen this topic of CMOS Biosensors for neural signalling, but as you know I am from medicine and I had never learnt the basics of such chips. I mean I have never seen how a CMOS looks. I really need your help on this." She smiled after speaking the truth.

She was correct, she could have sat and minted money by prescribing medicines from internet, but she chose not to. She wanted to learn and contribute towards human life-saving engineering. Did I like that girl? Why did I want to help her understand everything about my theories and related concepts? I agreed to help her whole-heartedly.

In next few days, I prepared an induction plan for her, hour by hour contributing to teach her direct practical applications of electronics. I had the resources. We started with basic molecular structures then moved on to fundamental quantum engineering. I had less time as it was my final year but I could explain all that I'd learnt in past four years. The best part was that I was not going to judge her through theoretical papers. While explaining her basics, I was living all my years again with Sayali sitting beside me in all the lectures. That was a lovely view.

I then wished if there was some technology through which I could transfer all my knowledge to her brain and all my fondness for her in her heart...

Next few months, we met quite often. I would wait for her all day long. She would come dressed in a new *kurti* daily and bedazzle me with her sense of aesthetics. I would see her hair, falling delicately on her cheeks which she would tuck behind her ears every now and then. In all these days she never repeated a dress as far as my memory goes. Her dupatta would always compliment her dress and would be light enough to fly away at the slightest of breeze. I did not know what texture do they call it?

Was I falling for her? The moment she entered the room, I would search for a base or support to hold. My knees went weak, and I would gaze her all the time, even if she said something or not.

One day while she was typing something on my computer, I was compelled to ask her...

"Will you..." I don't know why I had that fear in me which suddenly stopped my tongue. Asking her out could have led to a confusion that I had been teaching her all this time for the sake of being close to her. Should I? I asked myself.

It might also look as if I wasn't helping the girl but being selfish. I was already so unpopular; especially with the ladies. I ignored most of them but for some, I was diabolic who never socialized. I had heard many such groups talking about my attitude issues and how I was engulfed in my 'own' world. I had no hard feelings for them but I never liked a girl until I saw Sayali. She was always in a slow motion.

Whenever I thought of her, I would see her walking slowly, dancing slowly, and speaking something which I never understood but the words came out slow and sweet.

Sayali had briefed me with her 3D models of brain and did the dissection so many times. I never watched her hands. My eyes were always stuck on her lips. She opened it so well and closed it just in time to bring those syllables that would enchant my ears. She had now started understanding and operating on my computer and using the brain mapping software. She knew how to link synaptic travel and explained me the points in the brain adopted for safe surgery. She also explained me various signals carried by different types of neurons and how it assembled in forming a message. It all looked so beautiful on the screen. I somewhat understood it on the laptop but felt yuck when she did that with the real model. She carried a synthetic brain with her and she opened it like a walnut. The route looked difficult in real life, but on the computer I knew the defined path to reach a portion of the brain and had the facility to zoom. I was finding it hard to learn the real model.

It happened most of the time that I would finish talking and then wait for her reaction to continue. She would not speak up but chew her dried lips, which was her habit to signal *'yes please'*. I would then forget what I was talking about. I had a lot to learn from her but I could hardly listen to her voice. It used to get lost midway. I sometimes felt like sleeping in her lap and see her eyes blink every five seconds to help me realize that I was alive.

"Sir, there is a call for you." Said the lab assistant and asked me to come and pick it.

"Hello."

"Aur bataa... saale?" Was I dreaming? I was able to hear this voice again after so long.

"Surya, how are you *Saale?*" I asked and the talking went for long. I had several questions and things to talk to him and he was slow... with emotions deep within which he never shared or expressed.

"Hmmm, tell me did you ever get to talk or find that south Indian girl of our school?"

I candidly asked, as I had never been able to understand the fabric of their relation.

"Rajlatha? Forget it yaar, many *Rajlatha's* came and went away screwing up my life."

I laughed out at his spirit.

He continued. "Now I don't know what I am doing with it." He paused

"Am I that bad? I mean every time I express all my love for a girl, she just fails to understand it." He was sounding utterly dejected.

"You've called after so long and..." We both kept quiet for some time and wanted the other party to bring a new topic.

"Sorry yaar, just forget about any other thing. I mean for now. I am feeling so good, so happy" I wanted him to not feel alone.

"Come to Nagpur, I have a big room... a lab. We will have fun. I will take you to places around and will show you my college"

I had nothing else to offer as I had an empty pocket and could give him nothing but my affection. He was my brother and we shared so many memories.

"I will try to come, but you too promise me that you would come to Delhi and stay at my place. This place certainly has more things to see than your Nagpur." He joked.

"Yeah Delhi has beautiful girls and my best buddy too." I replied quickly.

"What? Did I hear 'girl' from Om!" He exclaimed.

"Yes, what's wrong with that?" I tried to play it down.

What the heck! A girl meaning a girlfriend? I mean two hands, two legs, a pair of…

"I don't know about what image you are building up for her, but she sure has a big heart and she is a beauty. Her name is Sayali." I described a little.

"*Saali*?" He was puzzled.

"Nope. It's Sayali, a common name here in Maharashtra, but the girl is very uncommon"

"So is this love? You are gone. I have lost my friend. Where would I get the old version of Om?" And we laughed again.

"Come to Nagpur and we will discuss in detail what all has changed for good."

I then gave him my address, but I don't know what made me realize that Surya was engrossed in competitive studies and he might not ever visit me.

The research required me and Sayali to spend a lot of time together. That time was used by Sayali to complete her thesis and the simulation model. For me, it was a different project; I took initiatives in researching Sayali's heart. She often talked about her dream to complete this project and send it to the *Human Brain Map Project*, France.

It was led by some eminent Nobel laureate and had best of doctors and scientists. Entry to the elite group was her dream and she would often talk about her dream to meet such stalwarts. I would then ask her jokingly to travel to Paris for this research and once it's done, she should contact some modelling agency owing to her charming Indian look. I was sure she could be hired by any company; at least I had that notion.

We had a single electric kettle used to prepare tea and she would always say no to my tea. She was a *'coffee-only'* person and had a peculiar habit of leaving half the coffee. Even if she prepared half mug of coffee, she used to leave half of that half. I loved her so much that anything tasted by her, could not be left to go waste by me. I would mix the residue with my tea and finish up the *'Toffee'* to see her laugh at my act. But even while laughing, I would see that shine in her eyes which sent current in my veins.

The lab door wasn't closed as nobody came there during the day; it had the least probability of getting robbed. I went to the water filter and started the tap to fill the glass and when I turned right towards the window, I saw Sayali sitting inside the room.

"Free now?"

She said and she was angry. She had the every right of getting annoyed at me. No arguments worked today and I was seeing tears in her eyes.

Sorry Sayali, I have not been picking up your call due to the heavy workload my recent assignment demanded from me. That is my prime motive, you know that?

"And what about me?"

"What?" I asked".

"Nothing, I am here to just make you laugh, sit beside you, listen to your jokes and understand whatever you type or draw. Right?" She was getting mad at me and I tried to calm her down by moving close to her. This was my first fight with her. I had no idea of how to tackle the situation.

She was dazzling with her dress and her voice was now modulating into soft violin notes. I held her left hand with my left and her right palm was crossed by my right hand. I couldn't hug her, so I just made her feel I was a mirror and emulated her moves. We moved from one action to the other. Slowly the moves evolved as dance steps. It was so easy to dance with her.

"Thank you Sayali!" I folded her hands placing them just above my waist and hugged her. I went close to her eyes and saw her tears which had created a smooth road map on her cheeks. My hands were busy, so to wipe off the tears I just had my lips; I went close and kissed her lips.
She had very soft lips and perfectly thick to form a stair of love with my lips. I was having the best time of my life now and with every kiss that she offered, she looked even more beautiful. Her eyes emitted that glow back.

She rubbed my head again and apologized to which I just kissed her back. That feeling of oneness can never be expressed in words. She was beautiful all throughout and she had that whole stock of love for me which flowed from all parts of her body and then the heartbeat had crossed Neil Armstrong's rate for sure. She slept on my chest and then looked up. Her eyes were bright and wide open to see my feelings.
She was slowly going into sleep. I kissed her head and slept sitting with the table's support.

From that day, she started staying with me in the lab, day and night and I also thanked the college for giving me Sayali. Though this was unofficial but my heart had approved her stay.

We were almost done with the research and she had come up with a signal optimal way of placing the chips inside the hippocampus. She could see it was working on the computer. I could hardly differentiate the before and after actions in this software. She explained me the flow of emotions and its obstruction in the brain. I was happy for her.

"I am leaving tomorrow, my father is ill."
Sayali was tensed that day.
"Ok, I will drop you don't worry." I wanted to ask her when would she be back but I was afraid. I was having that weird fear from inside.
I dropped her to the station and gave her all the necessary articles needed during the trip. I gave a CD with the details of my research for her and the hardware I had prepared. I jumped inside the train and gave her a tight hug. I did not know what had happened but she did not smile at all.

The stipend wasn't enough to pay back the loan and my research was going in no direction. I then had a bad feeling of looking for a job.
"Did you read the notice board?" Mr. Sonare asked. He was the Training and Placement head for our college.
"No sir." I replied and expected some positive news for my research work or fellowship through his network.
"*KoolConcepts* is coming for an interview in our college. I have high expectations from you Om." He said.
"What is that company into?' I asked.
"Don't tell me you haven't heard of it? It's the biggest offshore product development and engineering company of India." He said so many big words that I couldn't grasp all of them.
"You mean a software company?" I asked in simple words.
"Yes and not just any company. It's the highest paying Indian IT firm. You better try for it boy."

He then walked into his cabin. I was feeling bad. No core company had come and I had a lot to research. But then I thought about the time it would take to complete it. I was seeing no less than two years more for any solid research to be done by me. I had no backing, to continue that research. IT was the rising Sun and I had to salute it like every other engineering grad. I ran towards him and entered directly to his cabin.

"Sir what is the syllabus which I need to learn? I mean KoolConcepts subjects…" I had lost my athletic attitude so was losing breath soon.

"See the notice board and prepare well. Just two weeks are left." I thanked him and moved out to search for the info.

"C, C++, Java, TOC, DBMS…" What were these subjects? I did not even know the full forms. I saw a computer science guy of our college moving past the notice board and called him close to the board.

"Hey, what is this buddy?" I pointed my finger on the letter "C".

"It's a language, for programming. You haven't ever heard about it?" He then asked.

"First year? You will learn all these important subjects soon."

"Nope, final year. Molecular engineering. I am more into nano-thermodynamics and quantum calculations?" I replied. He looked puzzled and his head would have gyrated hearing my subjects. He then asked in a low voice.

"Condom… calculations?"

"Go fuck yourself! Idiot." I shouted and he ran away like a hyena. I was losing hope. I went to the city and got the books for all the subjects written on the notice board. I tried hard, but could not understand a line of what was being explained in the books. Those abbreviations and flow diagrams looked more like a nomenclature of amino family.

The interview had started and it was a bloody long procedure. We all waited since morning and the result was boring lectures from women dressed as executives and they called themselves as HR managers. We were divided in several groups and sent to various classrooms. I wasn't sure why I was there? But I could not have given up the opportunity to face my first interview. I looked at the question papers distributed to us and was happy seeing the pattern. They were all analytical questions and mostly required logic and physics to solve, to which I was pretty happy. I answered them and submitted the answer-sheet back to the invigilator.

After the paper, I moved out to have some water. I met students from other colleges and they had come far away colleges. They all looked smart and mostly talked about the computer programming languages which I had never heard of.

"The palindrome program was asked last year." One lady said to the boys.
"See this; I got this from my senior who was selected last year. This company has a trend of asking questions on pointers and linked lists" One of them was very excited and I was thinking what I was doing there.

"The circular linked list, I have learnt that program." The lady said. She was happy to have mugged the same program and was now confident to go through.
"Don't tell me, we need to learn that memory thing. What was that?" one of them asked looking tensed.
"Calloc and Malloc?" the lady replied again

I could not find any non-computer science candidate and felt fooled by the T&P.
"Hey Om!" I got a pat on my back and this was Babu. I had completely missed that he was a computer science guy. Though he had failed a year but he was good at programming. We were more like friends.
"Read about sorting algos. These are the examples of bubble sort, heap sort and merge sort." He gave the book with pages opened to me and stood by the window to smoke.

"Do you think I'll be able to make it? I mean I see people here who have been spitting out language jargons that make no sense to me, working on projects based on languages I don't understand. Do I have any chance, at all?"

He had his second puff and stopped his breath for some time and looked back at me
"I don't know." I was okay with his blunt view as I was zero when it came to computer programming. But he then looked back and said "I am still pretty sure that you will convince them" and he smiled and threw the cigarette, which whirled in the air.

The HR came out and announced names of the people who were selected for the second round of written exams. I wasn't very surprised to hear my name but felt sad that Babu's name wasn't called. He was so good in his subjects and he shouldn't have been screened out so early.

Meanwhile I came to know that I was somehow called for interview, irrespective of being a non-computer science graduate.

There were two people in the room. One of them looked very senior or maybe he was young and bald and was wearing sports shoe on his formals. The second was in his mid-thirties and wore a half-sleeve shirt and a pair of jeans.

I remember I was asked a series of non-stop puzzles and analytical questions, which were answered in no time. But owing to my aptitude inclined more to science, the interviewers thought of challenging my basic physics.

"So you are in a lab" The *bald and the beautiful* both looked at me, I could not see who asked me that.
"A science lab sir?" I asked.

"Yes, a physics lab to be specific."

"Great, nice place" I tried to stop myself from speaking any further.

"How do you calculate the height of that building?"

"I could apply Pythagoras theorem seeing the shadow of the building and a parallel stock and its shadow but that may take time." I said.

"Then?" The senior asked.

"I would drop a ball and based on the time taken, I would estimate height from the formula $h = ut + 1/2gt^2$" I said confidently.

"You don't have a ball." He then limited my options.

"I would then drop a stone or my belt or shoes." I was just eager to drop something.

"You have nothing and are standing nude. Be quick I need the height" The older one was in too hurry to find the height as if he needed to jump from the top.

"Sir, considering that no one is around, I would just close my eyes and …"

"And what?"

"Pee."

"P stands for?"

"Sir, 'pee' doesn't stand; it goes parabolic until it hits the ground!" I showed the little finger of my left hand.

I smiled within but saw no expressions on the other side of the table. I continued

"I would then measure the distance where the projectile has landed and calculate the height" I raised my shoulders with some confidence now.

"Are you telling me that you know the speed of your pee?" The younger one asked, controlling his laughter.

"No sir. But I can definitely control, I mean, adjust my urination speed to the best suitable value to make the calculation easy."

"Forget that. Think more." The elder guy was adamant about the height of the building and I was thinking he came in to the wrong profession. He should have been a builder or an architect, definitely not a software architect.

"Then I can run from the top of the building till the bottom with a stopwatch and based on the time taken, I can roughly calculate the height" The second guy smiled again and moved the discussion further. I was not sure if I was answering their query the way they wanted, but I was glad to be a part of this interesting interview experience.

I walked back slowly towards the hostel with the offer in hand. I was really exhausted. To my surprise, I saw everyone, irrespective of branch, group and seniority coming and hugging me. They even lifted me in the air looking really happy. I was seeing this sudden flair around. Those were the same people who had always wanted to hit me or tie me with some rock and throw me in the ocean. I was the only one to have got a job now and this was a respected company. The batch was united again. I was missing Kabir. He would have felt so happy for me. I was not sure where he was.

It was break time and final semester did not have much to offer. I was already placed and had nothing much to learn. So I got all the relevant books issued from the library and got my tickets to Gangtok. Though the journey had been really long and tiring, I finally was glad to have reached in the last lap of it. It was very beautiful but scarcely populated area. The roads were not that good, there were twists and turns all over and some of the roads were covered by rocks that had fallen from the top. The arrangement of local governing bodies was unexpectedly agile. A crane like structure came down from the slope and cleared the road and went back to its parking up the acclivity. It looked so smooth and easy, however I saw the crane very much in the air most of the times.

This place was different from rest of India. It looked organized, traffic rules were obeyed and it had not lost its countryside feel. Wherever we drove, we saw a long stretch of Teesta River following us. I was seeing people rafting and rowing their kayaks through the river. That mere look made me so happy. I made up my mind that I would ask papa to settle here after his retirement. The best part was the amount of oxygen I was getting. After coming from Nagpur which had really bad summer, it felt like heaven.

"What is that?" I asked the driver pointing towards numerous orange and white flags on the top of the hill and on the borders of several roads in the valley.

"That one?" He confirmed with confidence as he was from the same place.

"It's the resting place of the dead. We feel that once the person is dead, the soul needs to go to its final resting place. We write *mantr* on the flags and when the wind blows, it takes the spirit to its destiny."

That was a nice philosophy. I did not ask much as he was driving in a difficult terrain.

My mother was very happy to see me and ran to the gate to receive me. We had regular discussions and I checked the beauty around this house. Orchid flowers blooming all over, right till the bottom of the valley and giving me a feeling of a botanical garden. I had a good sleep that day.

"Get up everybody and be ready to see heaven on this planet." My father woke all of us and had already packed our bags.

"Where are we going papa?' I asked.

"Can't tell you the name but you will be glad to see that place…. *jannat*" and he took a deep breath.

It was too early and difficult for us to get up, but this was a surprise plan by papa so we all felt happy too. We kept our bags and sat in the Gypsy. It moved slowly and the drive was giving me a second round of sleep.

"This place must be having some name... I assume" I joked.

"Lachen... then Gurudongmar" He said.

I had heard this name, but from whom? After some time I recalled, Chumbi Gomchen, the medical student from Nagpur. "North Sikkim. I have a friend from this place in Nagpur." I said and people inside were surprised. I did not reveal the story of how I met Chumbi but it felt good to see his place.

"All of a sudden, this plan?" My mother asked and she was happy that we were together out for a vacation.

"Today is the day I married a young and a beautiful girl from a remote backward village in *Banaras*." Hearing this we all had some reactions. I had never asked my parents about their marriage anniversary date. I had never seen papa celebrate his anniversary or birthdays.

I was shocked and this was news for me. But for mummy this was a big gift. I was seeing tears trying to tumble down but she covered her eyes with shawl.

"My village is not that backward. My father had elephants even then, while your parents were taming some cows." She said with pride and attacked papa.

"So did the elephant give better milk?" Papa joked and mummy was too happy to reply with her smile. We all gazed at the beauty we were seeing and it felt so nice to breathe and see freshness at the same time.

This was an earthquake prone area and the roads were in a very bad condition. It was just muddy patch many a times but the people driving here were organized and disciplined. I was not seeing anyone breaking the lane or overtaking from left or exceeding speed unnecessarily. It took us more than six hours to reach the place. I could see gradual change in the hair structure of the livestock. They were evolving with hair to become a yak from bull to protect themselves from the freezing temperatures.

"It's all snow-capped. What would be the temperature outside?" I asked papa.

"Close to zero, but at night it may go negative." He rubbed his palms feeling the chill already.

We stopped in front of a double story building and this place had very few such high rise buildings. It read "Mr. T. Dorjee".

"Do we know him?" I asked as this looked like someone's home and not a hotel.

"This is Dorjee's house. We were together in training days and then in Lucknow posting, when you were not even born. We got our first posting together, same place." Papa's eyes were filled with the same nostalgic happiness which I felt after meeting Surya recently. I could recall that long back papa had mentioned Mr. Dorjee while describing Gurkhas.

"How did you meet him?" I asked

"He had no place to show himself than the Army Hospital and I caught him there. He came there for a check-up and couldn't escape my eyes."

"Is he still serving?"

"No he took voluntary retirement and focused into full-fledged mountaineering."

"Oh! He is a mountaineer?" I was thrilled to hear that.

We then got down. The place had a wooden gate locked from the inside. Papa jumped over it to ring the bell. Within few seconds, I saw a short heighted person with pink red face and very little, opening the door. He said something to papa in the local language to which papa did not reply. He had spectacles and removed it to see who was standing in front of him. Now he could see it was his old friend. He then hugged papa but he could hardly come till papa's shoulders.

He then looked at us and called us towards the room by both bending his arms. He welcomed us and asked his wife and children to take our luggage to which my father resisted. From inside, this place was no less than a hotel. It had everything. It was built mostly of wood but it had heater, good bed, carpet, nicely painted walls and western toilet. I moved towards the washroom window and saw; through a gap the mountain range. It looked so beautiful! I wish I could reside at such a place forever.

After changing, I went down to see what papa and Mr. Dorjee were talking. It was more of English but in some local accent which I was difficult to understand. It looked like they were recalling all their good memories. Mr. Dorjee's daughter brought warm water and some bottle which looked to me like brandy. There was another transparent bottle which may be vodka or wine.

"This is the best brandy here. Please have it." He offered me as well, but I had never had a drink with papa. However, how could I refuse his closest friend?

"This is special Sikkim wine." He poured that too in a glass. I brought it close to my nose and enjoyed its smell. It was more like a mix of breezer and vodka.

My father and he went back in their training days. I was able to connect with their stories and enjoyed them with every sip of this new drink.

"You know Om; my friend has climbed the Mount Everest. It was published in the International Defence Journal, though the Indian newspapers did not respect his feat much"

I looked at Mr. Dorjee's feet and they were too small but he had a thick strong calf like a football player.

"Sir, do you still climb?" I asked.

"No, I teach now in a nearby school." He replied and then looked at me again and continued "There is only one school here in a radius of three kilometres." His accent was more like Nepali being stretched and sung with soft tempo.

"You know Om; my friend climbed the Everest, the majestic mountain, around 9KMs without an oxygen cylinder."

My father gave this info which took me out of the mild intoxication. Was he repeating the info or was there something new for me to grasp? The drink had increased my reaction time a lot. But then I realized what he had said.

"Without oxygen cylinder?" I was shocked at his achievement and felt bad about the press or our books not talking about his work. Mr. Dorjee then continued telling his mountaineering stories by placing fictitious characters on his way and the hardship he overcame during the entire journey. I stood and bowed my head to show my respect to him. Before he could reply to my respect, I sat back and showed the empty brandy bottle to him.

He smiled and signalled his daughter to bring a second bottle. "It's nice and you're awesome" I said. I don't remember much of what I had asked but I was feeling sleepy. I then looked at his daughter and she looked to me like Chumbi with long hair and in female attire. Then they brought some food which certainly did not look vegetarian.

It looked as if it was prepared the way Jai prepared chicken, that is with minimal oil, less spices and more of water but juicy and properly cooked with some local flavours erecting the hair inside my nose.

"Have it. It has been made especially for you as promised." He looked at my father.

"I had it with rice and it tasted so well. It was fine like mutton. Though the fiber content was little less, it was cooked well after marinating it with ginger, garlic and lemon, each giving its distinct flavour...

"Nice mutton sir. This is my favourite." I said.

Then my father and Mr. Dorjee looked at each other and laughed. My father said

"This is Yak meat. Don't tell your mother, please." I stopped chewing and looked around for my peg. The glass was empty, so I poured some wine and then equal quantity of brandy and some cold drink. I had the drink in one gulp to take everything inside.

Then I asked myself, why my father considered it a sin to eat beef when Yak is almost the same species, tamed the same way as Cow, maybe it's slaughtered the same way as well. Why was I hesitating? May be the body was sending some signal to be cautious not knowing how to take Yak's meat. I don't know when did we stop our conversation and when did I go to sleep.

"Om, we need to go there before the sunrise. We will see the best part of North Sikkim now. Get up beta." My mummy kissed me and moved her fingers through my hair. I had no mood to get up so early again, but the plan was something special. So we all loaded back in the Gypsy and moved ahead with Mr. Dorjee becoming our guide. Slowly we were feeling the rise in pressure and seeing lesser and lesser of vegetation. There were some check posts where visitors were stopped and their documents were verified. We moved quickly as we had some one in the uniform sitting beside the driver. Now both sides of the road were plain light brown and the peaks snow-capped. It looked like what papa called as *jannat*.

"How are you feeling?" Papa asked mummy as she was covering her face again and again with the shawl. She was surely not well so we stopped for some time. She felt like vomiting but after a while again moved towards a place which was referred as the last point. There was no road now but due to army trucks crossing the same lane over and over again we could see some nice road like avenue. On both sides, there was ice wall up to a meter high. The local dog, we could spot were having some fur and they looked like wolf. I watched the group look at us and some happiness in their eyes. I kept looking at the dog for long till the vehicle stopped.

We were falling short of oxygen and I stood there for some time.

"I can't breathe." I said.

"Take it slow and do not burn your energy... slow and steady." Said Mr. Dorjee.

"We've just 8% oxygen in the air, one third of what you get in the mainland. So don't consume all." Papa joked and I wasn't able to laugh properly feeling the scarcity. I held the barriers and climbed up the temple steps. I did not go inside that room as it looked like a temple. Some visitors were tying flags with hymn written in local script. It was not *Brahmi* or *Devanagari* for sure.

"What is this lake? It's so clean!" I exclaimed seeing the beauty of a placid and quiet lake with no wave or weed over it. There were several stones placed one over the other reminding me of *pitthhu* which we played when we were kids.

This was a temple and a lake called Gurudongmar. There was a board which said we were around seventeen thousand feet above the sea level.

"This is the highest lake in India, my boy!" Papa said and immediately after him Mr. Dorjee added "and a very pious source of energy and life for us."

"What you see there, the piled up stones" He said showing the *pitthhu* "They are out of respect by the people who had some wishes which got fulfilled." He then went ahead and in a bottle collected the water of this lake and continued. "Just as the water of river Ganga is holy, this water is holy for us." Saying this Mr. Dorjee looked three sixty degrees and enjoyed the divinity of this place.

While I was looking around, the caretaker came close and offered resins and tea to us. This place was no less than a five-star hotel now. That cup of tea, I badly needed. With the first sip, I wished mummy and papa on their special day. I could see that deserted and small plateau encircled from all sides by White Mountains. That image was captured in my mind with all the feelings it generated in me. We drove back dropping Mr. Dorjee and thanking him for his hospitality.

Soon the trip ended and so did the vacation. It was time to travel back and finish the last exam.

After reaching Nagpur, the first thing I wanted to do was calling Sayali and letting her know my first employment. Then I realized that I had never asked for her number. I checked the resume she gave to me and the visiting card, which again did not tell the contact number of her native place. She had not shown up since months, which was worrying me. I then thought it would be better if I give her a surprise. I did not have her address but I knew Ratlam as the station I had to reach and after that, I had no plans.

I boarded a train for Ratlam. Thinking about the days spent in Sikkim and imagining Sayali in that wonder, made the time fly quickly.
"Sir what are the big places around Ratlam? I mean where I can travel within an hour and a half?" I asked one of the passengers in the train.
He had a big belly. One thing which was distracting me was the fact that he was clean shaven, but his side buns were very long and dense and looked badly unorganized. His shirt buttons were open and his vest was wet due to some water that would've fallen out while drinking.

"*Beta*, there are many places. All are very nice to visit….
Naagda, Jaora, Banswada, Neemach." He spat outside the
window and said "You are in Malwa, just eat and enjoy."
He replied with a smile. I did not know there were so many
places close to Ratlam. I then recalled during our first meet
itself, Sayali had described that her father was an IPS. Yes how
could I have forgotten the name which led to the argument?

"Sir, I wanted to visit the place where IPS officers have their
quarters. I mean I am visiting my acquaintance for the first
time, so don't know where he is posted right now" I asked him.
Hearing IPS, he started to button his shirt and wiped the extra
water on his neck and chin.
"*Beta*, there is a lot of police here. Neemach is the head quarter
of CRPF that is a possible place. However every adjoining city
here has few officers or a battalion"
He was right. Every city has hundreds of senior police officers.
Within a radius of ninety minutes, I was seeing the options
getting increased by at least four folds.

I then went to the washroom for some time to take a break
from the puzzle. While I was peeing, I heard some quarrel
outside the toilet. I tried to finish quickly and run out to see if
someone needed help. I came out and saw the ticket examiner
was holding one person. That guy was wearing rugged cloths
and had unshaven facial hair, since ages it looked. He smelt
bad. After some time, I realized that the thing in his hand was
actually producing the smoke, causing the smell.

"Sir, any problem" I asked the TTE.
"This fellow was having *gaanja* in the train." And then he
slapped the poor guy again. Smoking normal cigarettes is
banned and this guy was having *gaanja*. I was surprised with
the availability of that illegal weed to the poor guy.
"Sir, but how? I mean it's banned and not available in the
pantry right?" I joked but the TTE gave a mirthless look.

"Mandsaur is a place where they get it from illegal vendors. He must be looking poor. But if he grows even one plant of opium in his backyard, then just think how much money he can get by selling that illegally?"

"How much?" I asked as I wasn't aware.

"Per gram, this stuff sells for thousands of rupees and if refined properly from raw opium to cocaine and similar drugs then lakhs." The TTE replied and I was shocked to hear that making money was so easy in that part of India, though illegal.

I went to my place and saw that the cute fat fellow passenger had combed his hair. He had also shut the window down and was ready with his bags. He informed that Ratlam was about to come. While I was packing, something suddenly clicked my mind. I remembered when Sayali was in the hostel, all the girls used to ask her for some *'packet'* out of fun to pull her leg. That packet could be nothing but drugs? I thought to myself. Oh! I was a fool to have never asked her about that. I ran back to the TTE and he was gone from the spot. I started searching him in the neighbouring coaches and finally caught him.

"Sir, what place was that?" I then clarified "... the one where plenty of opium is grown?" I asked him and everyone in the compartment gave me that look of doubt.

"Mandsaur" He replied and moved ahead to examine tickets. I thanked him and got down with the guy who was sitting beside me. I enquired to him about some trains that may ply to Mandsaur.

"Catch *demo* train in the afternoon, which will take you directly to Mandsaur." He then lifted his luggage and walked outside the platform.

I was wondering what he meant. Was that some train which was running on trial? A 'demo' train? I asked few other folks and they too gave the same suggestion. After some time, I heard the announcement for the train and as the train approached I gave it a closer look. That was a Diesel-Electric Multiple Unit called DEMU train, which had been tried in few places in India and is a subset of EMU trains. I had read about that in my first year electrical engineering subject. I laughed at how everybody was pronouncing DEMU as demo and had thus left me wondering for so long.

Finally, I had reached Mandsaur to meet the love of my life. I walked out to look for a conveyance. It was a very small platform and hence the count of auto rickshaws waiting outside wasn't great. I boarded one and asked the driver to take me directly to police line. I was going for a blind bet as I did not know if she even lived in this city. There was minimal chance of her living here, but if she did then the element of surprise in her eyes, when she would see me would be worth hundred such trips.

I could see the city to be a quiet and rarely populated one. Few people were wandering without a purpose, it looked. Maybe they were all sleeping or intoxicated by the opium flavours in the air. Suddenly, I saw a big pothole right in the middle of the road and there were few heavy machines running till next five hundred meters. It looked like some serious repair was in progress. I asked the driver, if there was some alternate route. He thought for a while and replied that he had an alternate option, but that ran through the old city. I was okay with that option. We moved again and this time very slow, through gullies running from within the old city. While we were passing by, I saw a huge statue standing right in the middle of the road. It was a giant idol carved out of a stone. He certainly looked like some warrior from the past.

"Who is he?" I asked the driver.
"*Ravan.*" He replied in a word and then turned back to see my expression.

"What?" I was taken aback. I had never read about some place in India having a statue of Ravan and this looked like an open temple and not just a statue. He is considered to be the biggest villain by many in India.

"How and why?" I threw more questions at the driver and this was so bloody interesting that I asked him to stop. I went close to the idol and felt the hardship the sculptor must have gone through building that face which seemed so ready to just talk to you. I could not find any detail of when the statue was built. The driver had no answers to describe its origin but he explained that Ravan had been worshipped in Mandsaur since thousands of years. I liked the answer. We started the journey again and within no time, he turned back to ask me another question.

"You know *Mandodari*?"

"Yes, she was the wife of Ravan"

"She used to live here in Mandsaur. So in that sense, Ravanji is our *jawaee*. I mean Ravan's in-laws lived here."

Oh! Did he just say *Ravanji*? I exclaimed and thought of how fortunate I am to share that one link with Ravan and smiled at myself. I then thought that Ravan chose a good place with abundant opium store. But was this soil rich in opium cultivation since the age when we had Mandodari or we started farming opium after Persians invaded us? I had no answers, but I was very happy to know that my mother wasn't aware of this. Else she would, no doubt promote me from H*iranyakashyap* to *Ravan*

"Sir, we have reached the police line. Where should I stop?" He asked

I kept quiet. I then started having goose-bumps running from the hair on my hands till the central part of my chest, close to my heart. I had developed a sudden fear too.

It was late in the evening and I looked around the name plates outside the gates passing by. I could not find Mr. Thorat's residence.

I asked the driver but he was also not aware of Sayali's father. I got down and saw a person jogging in the evening. He wasn't really jogging, just walking fast. As I approached him, I saw his tee soaked in sweat.

"Excuse me sir, do you mind telling me where Mr. Thorat lives?" That fellow lost his lethargy and started jogging again. He turned back and asked me to follow him. He had suddenly gained some extra energy, I did not know from where.

"See this young boy." He smiled and showed the name on the gate. I got down and took out the bag to pay the driver. I was very happy that the assumptions made were right and finally, I had reached the place about which I had no clue at all. I then started thinking how Sayali would react seeing me, how excited she would be to hear about my job placement, how glad she would be that I had managed to find her address without any information. I opened the gate and started to move in.

"Whom do you want to meet?" The person jogging wasn't leaving even after I thanked him twice.
"Sir, I need to meet my friend who stays here." I ignored him and tried to close the gate.
He held my hand and said "As far as I remember, I have no friend who is as young as you." He pointed his index finger to himself and then to the name on the board. Oops! The first meeting with Sayali's father wasn't very good.

"Sorry Sir. Actually I am a friend of Sayali and have come from Nagpur. We are doing our research together." I gained all the confidence scattered within my guts to bring those sentences without fear on my lips.

"Come in young man." He escorted me and asked one of the batmen to arrange for chairs outside in the lawn and bring some juice. I followed him till the drawing room and could not see Sayali. I saw a lady in her fifties, but she looked just as beautiful as Sayali. I discussed with her about Sayali and the place. I liked them, but was looking around for a glimpse of her. I also managed to brief them about my parents and in general, the life in Nagpur. They looked at each other and to me. It felt like all's done. They were smiling. Was that some kind of approval? I did not know, but one thing I knew was that Sayali did make me wait for long.

"She is out for tennis and would be back in some time." Her mother could see the anxiety on my face and gave me a cup of tea. The aroma of the tea relaxed me.
"I hope, this is just plain tea and not any by-product of opium." They laughed just as Sayali did on my jokes. Her mother would lift her head a little and cover her mouth while laughing, exactly as Sayali did.

After an hour or so, I saw Sayali coming from the gate. She had gained a little weight in so little time. She looked tired as well. She had perspired a lot and as she entered the room, she threw her tennis racket out on her right. Then was the moment she saw me. She stood there for almost thirty seconds and I kept seeing her, waiting for that one smile and hug. I moved close to her and she took few steps back and her expressions did not change at all. Perspiration has gained the velocity and this was not due to her workout. Was she worried?

She lifted her left foot to itch something on the right calf. She looked for her napkin and wiped her face again.

"Why are you here?" She asked me arranging her hair; she couldn't look into my eyes. What did this question from her mean? It had been months, since I had heard her voice. I had so many things to say, but she looked so indifferent.

Her father had gone for bath now and her mother went to the kitchen to bring some snacks.

"How are you?" I asked trying to press the floor beneath my feet to feel that surface. I was trying to get a grip of mother earth. It felt as if the gravity had multiplied a thousand times and the ground below was pulling me down, sucking my body down to some abyss.

"Please go. I am sorry but you should not be here." She turned her face towards the lawn and walked out.

Was she explaining something which I had completely missed understanding?

I had a glimpse on the calendar. This was a Hindu calendar which had the diagram of full moon for today's date. I then recalled one day Sayali and I were in the lab, when she told me one weird thing about her. Were we discussing about the tides then? I don't remember. I had started to feel that weird difficulty in recalling things from my episodic buffer.

She had asked me about how different I found her, to which I had replied that she was the most beautiful and amazing lady I had met in my life. I explained her how warm she was and her love always generated a bliss in my brain. Hearing my opinion, she hugged me from the back and started explaining the reason for her uncomforts that day. She was having her periods and she then confessed that she sometimes got a super natural power in her by which she could make anyone fall for her. I was left confused. Then I recalled her exact statements.

"My periods coincide exactly with the moon cycle. You know, that gives me the power to control anyone?" I had reacted to her thoughts with a smile and then her expressions did not change. She was serious that day. I was taken aback by her look and was in no mood to get into any argument that could hurt her. May be she was stressed? Her statement had ruled out all my efforts to be her miraculous trap owing to her full moon day.

I rubbed my eyes and was back in Mandsaur.

"I know today you would not be working out. So why are you being dishonest to yourself and your parents?"

"You remember that thing?" She asked and without waiting for a response from she continued.
"Actually, I have someone. He was with me in MBBS."
"Please stop. I can't hear it." I kept quiet for some time and then took a long breath. I continued to ask her.
"So you never loved me? You stayed with me for so many months and we experienced the best moments of our lives. Have you forgotten everything?" I asked her with tears in my eyes.

"Please go away, you will not understand." She was very clear. She wanted me to leave and then suddenly took me to her room. She offered me a glass of water and said

"Remember when I asked to you about the marriage plans?" She was angry now and I was failing to recall what had I said then.
"What about that?"
"You often talked about being irreligious and prefer a registered marriage under some marriage act and bullshit." She walked back few feet and then came forward to continue.
"You never understood that marriage needs religion. I knew that you would never agree to me getting a good bridal wear and taking vows around the fire. You don't respect marriage." She was weeping now for the bad choice she had made, but how did she come up with such a sudden realization?
"You are just good for love." She ended her reason.

Hearing that, I recalled the day when we had that discussion of marriage. I think it was more of a serious argument? I visited her place in Nagpur one day when she was alone. She had invited me to spend some time. I was ready after a cold water shower. I had managed to reach her home without failing. I went in and saw her dressed in a beautiful western outfit. She wore pink top and blue denim that day. Her cheeks were shimmering with pink blusher. I hugged her and started to open her hair. She had dense brownish black hair, some of the strands looked light brown matching with her thorough fairness. She threw my arms away from her hair and asked not to open her hair locks.

"It's forbidden." Was her short reply.
I did not understand her point. I ignored her mood swings and entered the kitchen as I had thought of preparing some really good snacks for her that day. I searched for the utensils in the kitchen and asked her from inside.
"So, are we going out?" I had a doubt so thought of clarifying. She just said yes to my query. She was keeping all her replies so short that day.
"I am a good cook. I mean people say that I can cook well. It's my hobby." I tried to persuade her and added that qualification to my profile. She then gave her magnificent smile and I fell for her again.

I had warmed the bread in the microwave and cut it in triangles. I couldn't find *besan*. I had then requested her to come in and find it for me, but she wasn't moving from the drawing room. On repeated requests, she walked till the door of the kitchen and directed me to search inside the third drawer on right side. I managed to find it. I ignored her behaviour and warmed the oil to deep fry the item. While she was looking at me with all her love, I went close to her and pulled her in to hug her and kissed her forehead.

"Wait... leave me!" She shouted and I was shocked and fingered her lips to keep the shout a little low.

"What is the matter Sayali?" I did not understand the situation.

"I already told you that today is the forbidden day for me to enter the kitchen." She said and I was blown out

"What?"

"You are a doctor and you understand this design. Such prejudice and rituals were made centuries back to suppress women and keep them confined within the household work." I gave a justification.

"It's a matter of faith and I have never entered the kitchen during..." She shouted back. She looked more like a defence lawyer.

"How can you still follow it? That is a natural way of cleansing and a new life formation can't be connected to impurity. Don't tell me, you don't visit the temples as well during your periods?" I asked but I knew the answer

"Yes I don't. You know why?"

I kept mum.

"Because I respect my culture. I love my elders, unlike you. I can't be against everybody in this world." She was now attacking hard.

"Please Sayali. It doesn't matter a bit. It's normal just like any other biological process. I am not questioning your faith; I just want you to be free. Please understand." But I was cornered as an ignorant and sinful person. I did not like that curse coming from Sayali's mouth. I tried hugging her but she went back to her room and closed it from inside. I requested a lot but she did not open it and after sometime yelled at me to leave the place.

We sat for some time and then I did not know how we ended up discussing about marriage. My idea of registered marriage and my speaking in high voice against the rituals made her anger blow out of proportion. Her eyes went red and she was so furious at me that she pushed me hard, making me fall on the ground.

"Om" Why are you always lost?
She was there, in front of me, in Mandsaur. Beautiful as ever and again had two heavy drops of tears waiting to dive on her cheeks. I moved close to her mirror and looked at my reflection. I laughed at my expressions. I had never seen myself like that... so helpless! I had no one to express that feeling of despair. For the first time, I had a girl whom I respected so much. She gave me all the love, I longed to get. Now she wanted to leave me, just like that.

I gave her the key to my lab and decided never to enter the lab again. I also explained her to see when in doubt and how to assemble the simulators. I explained her in detail the papers and CDs which had theoretical explanation of my work. She sat down in her room and tried to interrupt me a couple of times. But I had to complete my task and finally I just said "I am done Sayali. I loved you and had only loved you." Was she worried about her project? I did not know but I did not look back and walked towards the exit. I then heard her voice.

"Please stay tonight and leave tomorrow. Did you have anything, I mean food?"
She was too late in asking that question. Why was she caring about me all of a sudden? Was she being grateful?

I walked and kept thinking about every moment we had spent together and her expressions when she looked at me. She was so beautiful and I never understood why she liked me. Maybe she did not even like me?

I had walked till the station. The road was pretty short, but how had I reached so fast there? The return journey started soon while I was busy thinking and occasionally wetting my eyes. I was fighting with myself now. Why was I not just an ignorant person who takes birth with closed eyes and finally dies without raising his fingers on the things he sees around? That was the day when I had realized how true the saying is, that ignorance is bliss.

I boarded a train and closed my eyes to think, rewind and process my mistakes. Maybe I could undo some of them to have her.

While I was juggling between my thought and Sayali's response, I was staring outside the window, but not seeing what I was looking at. The train suddenly stopped with an emergency break.

"What is that?" I saw a crowd just besides the road pulling out their kids from cow dung or it looked like a ditch full of livestock excreta.

I stood up and tried to focus more on it.

"Today is the *pooja* day of the cow dung?" The person next to me replied.

"I have seen people using the cow dung and urine in prasad so often. But this is like pulling the kids from a well full of dung" I asked

"We, in Madhya Pradesh observe this festival. Per ancient rituals, the mother herself throws the kid in to it" He replied.

"What?" I had always thought of a mother to be lifesaving, but yes even my mother sometimes did crazy things for my safety and hurt herself or kept herself hungry for days to satiate the age old rituals. I was nobody to question this faith then.

"What is the gain out of this?" I wanted to know.

"The kids who bathe in the cow dung today..." He stopped and spit outside the window the beetle he was chewing and continued "... remain healthy always"

"Always means till next year?" I asked

"Yes, the women do it every year. You are right sir." He smiled and while he did that few drops of beetle spit fell on my pants. I wiped it and he moved a little back seeing my reaction. Thanks to the ladies, I was back in the real world. My eyes were seeing some major problems, much bigger than what my heart had just lost.

In no time, the day arrived, my first day at office.

"Welcome Mr. Om." I was welcome by the HR and saw several fresh faces in the office. The office had a beautiful logo in bright blue and it read *"KoolConcepts"*.

She then continued "From today, you all will belong to the top five percent of the Indian population. You can get whatever you want, good infrastructure, comfort, best of resources, machines, technology and above all, the freedom to think."

She was doing well. I found her statistics fake but most of joinees were pretty excited to hear that they were at the top of the phony pyramid.

"You've passed through one of the most difficult recruitment processes in the industry. Only zero point zero three percent of people who come for the interviews are finally offered a job at KoolConcepts." Now I was hearing lots of 'Wows' and folks were pretty excited to come here. Some had developed so much respect for this company in this first look itself. While I was doing my analysis of this company, I heard a voice

"We will work hard and make you proud... ma'am. This is my dream come true, my dream company" And I smiled at that silly pride.

I did not find anyone interesting and focused on learning the new skills of software development. I had given up what I had learnt in last four years and was slowly forgetting the books as well. Next few months, I would wait for the salary and then stand in the bank queue to send as much as possible in the loan account. The loan was compounded such that the interest was adding up every month and crawling the balance sheet to make my EMI look like nothing. I then decided to give up the luxury of staying alone in the independent house and found a smaller house which was in the outskirts. I started commuting by the local train. My office was in east Pune with world class buildings right at the center of *Pune* city. That required me to commute using local buses. The monthly passes were economical. My boarding point was far enough to privilege me a comfortable seat in the bus. I used the travel time to talk to my parents. I updated them about the city and the job; internally I cursed myself for the work I was doing. I had left my project back in the lab; I had dumped it with Sayali's memories.

My immediate manager was a real bad ass, the one with two legs. He had well-versed in English and thought the whole world runs on English grammar. He was one of millions in India who value English more than any other skill.

"Paritosh, you should've used *'because'* and not *'since.'*" He conveyed politely to one of my colleague. Paritosh bowed his head down with embarrassment. He was losing his hair and most of the hair loss was due to his indefatigable efforts. He would wake all night sometimes. I saw him start the work too early in the morning. He was taking the work way too serious. His eyes looked red due to lack of sleep and his cheeks were getting thinner, so thin that the jaw-line became very prominent. He was technically very sound, but when it came to writing emails or beautifying the code, he always had sweat moistening his forehead.

The manager continued "Why am I saying so? Do I have some personal gain? No!" He paused for a while and opened his mouth again to give some crap logic. He could have corrected the email in few seconds, but he was creating a scene by shouting this hard publicly.

"You have a cause, you understand Paritosh. The sentence has a cause, hence *'because'* and not *'since'*... so easy?" and poor Paritosh had nothing to say but yes to his explanations.

I approached Paritosh to hear from him. After talking to him, I realized that he had put a lot of effort in completing his education from a remote village which was some thirty KMs away from Amravati. His father was a retired postman and Paritosh was the only earning person in his family. He had to look after his parents and his younger brother.

"In future, just show me any email before sending. Ok?" I found a good person in him and assured him to help and prevent the harassment from his manager.

It was months since I saw him getting lectures from the manager until one fine day. He had solved a major bottleneck in performance owing to his sharp analytical skills. The CPU utilization was running hundred percent after users uploaded heavy images.

He had spent one week in doing this analysis and found some hot-spots where the code had the possibility of tuning. I was also not very good in English as well, so I approved his email but within a minute we got a reply from his manager about the 'blunder' he had committed. The excerpt from the email which led to the drama read *'seventy thousand lines or less'* and was sent to everyone in the project including the delivery managers. Instead of appreciating his work, the manager *'replied to all'* about the use of *'seventy thousand lines or fewer'*. The manager did not speak a single line to appreciate the hard work Paritosh had put day and night. I slowly understood the reason why Paritosh was bashed verbally. I asked Paritosh to escalate the matter but his timid nature reminded me of Kabir when I had first met him. I could hardly put me in his shoes, so I left it to him to fight the battle. His efforts went unnoticed.

Paritosh and I were called in a conference room by the project manager. We were assigned with our Key Responsible Areas and we both thought we have done justice to the self-evaluation. I did not evaluate myself much but I was seeing Paritosh wiping his sweat.

"What happened?" I asked.

"I have worked hard this year and expect really good results, but this manager. I am sure he would come up with something or the other to degrade me." He was now anxious to get out as soon as possible.

"Keep calm. Why are you afraid? He will not take away your life. If you are happy with your work, then let him say anything, the documented facts will speak for you." I tried to boost his confidence but did not see much of a change in his level of anxiety.

My father used to talk about the Annual Confidential Report procedure in the armed forces and that used to be very straight forward and disciplined. Here in the software industry, there was a rather hazy show-off of some procedure which was actually not in place.

"Om, you are a team player and mind you..." He combed his hair by his fingers and continued "... there are very few members like you who can take up the complete ownership as you've done. You are an asset to this company." He spoke more but they all sounded synonym to me. Moreover it looked like he was adulating me. Why, I did not know. He ended up reducing my numbers to a decent level and I did not expect much from him, but I saw him reducing the ratings sharply.

"Excuse me sir, why did you reduce the overall ratings from 5 to 3. I think, I completed all my tasks well in time and you just appreciated it."

He gave a sarcastic smile. His canine flashed to show that yellow tar on its tip.

"It will be difficult to explain, but consider this. Give yourself five out of five only if you have got a Nobel Prize."

What the heck? Was he kidding? Seeing these deductions, Paritosh too felt doomed. He was now thinking what four and three would be compared to... *Bharat Ratna* or the *Padma Bhushan*? He looked tensed.

"I take your point." I replied expecting some more elaboration on the reduction but he was quiet. I then added.

"So how many employees in *KoolConcepts* have won the Nobel prize?"

"C'mon, it's a big deal. No one." He replied.

"So why don't you take the initiative with the HR to remove that option and let the ratings be out of four?"

This brought smile on his face. He was a seasoned manager so he chose to ignore my query by a smile.

"So, coming to you Paritosh." He was now blank; he had forgotten all his efforts, his achievements, and his good work. He was just sitting quiet and time after time, he was wiping his sweat.

"Technical capabilities" He read "You've been doing well and have come up with some solutions to complete the desired work. So you completed the desired work."

Why was he stressing so much on the word *'Desired'*?

"But where is the innovation?" The manager's eyes became big and his face now resembled some lost African zebra, laughing at himself.

Paritosh had no answers.

"Had you been good at communication skills, you could have done some level of 'farming' from the current client and got us some other projects too. You are technically good, so you should have done that right? So 2 out of 5?" He asked and poor Paritosh just shook his head.

"Quality Delivery" He took a pause again and continued "You have been delivering a good quality... a very good quality product to the client. He has never escalated against you."
Paritosh was now happy and expected somewhere around 4
"Had you been good at communication skills, you could have built a very good rapport with the client. You could have forced him to call you to the US. The company would have got extra money in dollars. But sad, your communication skills...2 out of 5" Paritosh felt lost.

"Team Player" He now had a smile and looked positive for Paritosh.
"All your teammates come to you for help. You often sit with them and I have seen you solving their problems too."
"Right sir." Paritosh said with some hope of appreciation through ratings.
"They all boast of your efforts and the help you extend to them. However had your English been a little better, I think you would have groomed all your juniors to one level up. They would have learned the skill of verbal communication from you. You often talk to them in Hindi. So 1 out of 5." This manager was crossing his limit. I sat quiet to observe the new drama.

"Punctuality and Self Learning" He continued.
"You have been coming on time and there has never been a case of delay of even half a day due to your time logs." Paritosh was confident about this point.

"Never has your immediate manager or anyone from your colleagues raised a voice about you coming late or skipping a meeting. However..." Now was the googly...

"Had you been more interactive and intuitive, you would have passed on this behaviour to other members of the team. You should take company level initiative and teach this habit of punctuality and its benefits to all freshers. They would then look up to you. Who in the company knows you by name? Tell me." He asked

"Very few." Paritosh replied.

"Why? Have you ever thought about that? Why no one from other projects. We have hundreds of projects."

"I don't talk much..." He ate his sentence and gave an opportunity to hit.

"Gotcha!" The manager stood up from the chair and went to the white board with to explain diagrammatically how Paritosh is making loss for the company.

"Sir I have a query." I asked.

"Yes Om."

"Sir, we have a section exclusively for Communication skills. Is that correct?" I asked.

"Yes."

"So I suggest you give him minus 5 in that and give proper ratings out of five for other options. Will that not be a fair judgment?" I said and Paritosh shook his head to stop me from saying anything. The manager did not like me and my idea.

"I think you are done and you should not intervene in this one on one meet."

This meeting had suddenly become a covert operation. I left the room and wondered how he would have finally rated poor Paritosh. He was putting pressure that would take out confidence out of Paritosh and in long run might hinder his interest to contribute with full dedication.

One memory that I recollect often was the drama created in the so called largest IT company with multi-national ethics due to me having eggs in the office.

"Come in Om." She said.
"Thanks." And I sat on the chair.
"I hope you know the reason of this meeting?"
"No."
"Okay. Did you not go through the company policy? This is a purely vegetarian company." She was commanding through her voice. She tried hard but she could not give me that positive feeling of being a matured person. Her short hair and brown eyes added to her manipulative nature and shrewd talks.
"This company does not allow any kind of non vegetarian item." She continued.
"No, I had missed those 'Terms & Conditions', may be due to the small font sizes?" I joked.
"This is not funny Om. Such things are not documented. You are a very good resource and have done great for your project. Mistakes like this can cost you big." She broadened her eyes.
"Thanks. My manager doesn't reflect that in the appraisal. I would request you to please tell him this fact." I wanted to keep the moment light but she was taking it in wrong sense.

"So you say that we should not eat egg at all?" I asked her
"Yes, it's killing a life." She replied.
"Why does the government of India, through National Egg Council spend crores of money on the advertisement of benefits of eating egg, especially for the kids and expecting ladies?" I asked her.
"That is the government's job to sell their product?" She replied.
"But government of India has more important things to do than selling eggs to its citizens." I was quick.
"Whatever it is. We are a private organization and per company rules, it is not allowed." She said and then called few other HRs

in the cabin. She also called my manager in the cabin to make the scenario look even more complicated.

They came and settled. One of the junior HR sat on the table to be close enough to observe my responses. My manager sat next to the senior most HR and he was briefed about my 'blunder'.

"I just have this small query to the people here. How do we ban an egg considering it to be alive? How do we understand if there is a scope of fertilization in it or not?" I asked.

"It hardly matters if it has some freaking zygote in it or not. What matters is that it smells bad." This was my smart manager.

"That smell may be accepted by my nose. I find that smell soothing." I replied.

He then stood up and walked closed to me and then walked back to sit on the chair.

"What is an egg?" I asked all of them and maintained my calm

"It's something to carry the species of hen forward." The junior HR was quick to show his IQ

"So can I call it a seed?" I said and everybody looked ok with this.

"Don't we eat sprouted gram, beans, kidney beans and several other pulses which have their seeds grown." I asked.

"C'mon Om, they are all plants." The HR said.

"So was Dr J.C. Basu a fool to prove that plants also have lives. My mother always taught me not to pluck flowers in the evening, as the plants would be sleeping." I then continued.

"I was taught by my mother to collect those flowers and fruits which have fallen by themselves as plants also feel the pain"

"Yes she is very correct." My manager tried to show his respect.

"So what am I speaking here?" I asked

"Don't mix issues. Animals are non-veg and plants all veg." The junior HR said.

"Do you believe in the process of evolution? I mean the way we have evolved?" I asked.

"Yes of course. We are all scientific and most of us are engineers." They said with pride.

"So we evolved from?" I asked.

"Chimps. We all know that." My manager replied quickly.

"No sir, I request you to go back further." I was polite.

"Fish or maybe some kind of reptiles." The junior HR came in.

"Further." I moved my hands to bring words out of their mouth.

"Some micro-organisms?" The HR said.

"Yes, very cool. So plants are our ancestors. Right?" I was seeing everybody blank now and they were confused. They were now sure that I need to be admitted to some mental hospital.

"So, we now eat plants and thus we eat our own ancestors." I made it even clearer.

"C'mon, this is rubbish!" the HR said.

I stood up and went close to my manager and said.

"Sir, I think we all are hypocrite in some way or the other. We make rules convenient for us. Whatever bleeds in red or cries while slaughter becomes non-veg and whatever doesn't, becomes a veg. Poor plants can't even shout for their grievances"

"No that is not what we meant." The HR said.

"There are plants with whom our DNA matches to a great extent. They thus become our close ancestors and we eat them." I paused and tried to make it clearer

"Tea, coffee… You have it daily right?" I asked.

"Ridiculous Om. Sit down. I think you are out of your mind." The HR was now losing her calm.

"So you all, who boast of being a pious pure veg actually drink and eat your ancestors. Weird, isn't it?" I then continued "Is that called cannibalism?" I asked

"Om…. Om… Please sit." The HR tried to calm me down.

"Have you read Bhagvad Geeta?" she asked me. I had heard from some of the colleagues that when HRs and big managers don't have anything to say then their final call is to speak out some excerpts from Geeta and show their capability to guide us just as lord Krishn guided Arjun. I showed myself as a dumb and though I had read it all, I chose not to disclose it.

"No Madam. What about it?" I asked.
"Lord Krishn says that we should focus on our work and adapt to the culture to bring good to the organization and oneself. Please calm and control your senses Om, and oblige to the policies of this company to go higher. You are very good at work." She continued and now my manager also nodded in agreement. I did not understand what part of Geeta she was referring to.
"Sorry madam, I have not read it like you have read in detail" I appreciated her to make her feel happy and continued "But I had Sanskrit in my school and know one shlok of Bhagvad Geeta that says..."

Karmendriyani samyamya ya aste manasa-smaran,
Indriyaarthan vimoodhaatma mithyacharah sa uchyate

I looked at them and none of them understood a single word. So I translated
"Here the lord says that he who restrains the organ of action, sits thinking of materialistic objects in mind, he of deceived knowledge, is referred as a HYPOCRITE" and I walked out of the room.

When my education loan was almost finished, I started thinking seriously about engaging in a work that gave me more satisfaction and happiness. I did not find anything "*kool*" or any serious '*concept*' in the so called software engineering companies that were mushrooming all around. I really needed a break!

283

CHAPTER 10

The Moulting

I had saved enough money to look after myself and handle some emergency. I wasn't expecting much from life. I wasn't enjoying the job, so I started looking for an alternate career that could give me some satisfaction. Through one of my colleagues, I came to know about a social service group called *Insaaniyat*. I appeared for its interview which was pretty straightforward. Seeing my zeal, they hired me. The salary was not even one third of what I used to get, but here I had started looking ahead. I was seeing reason to work hard, I was motivated and I was seeing the result of our efforts. I gave my day and night to this organization and we focused primarily on bringing smile and stability to the life of widows and female kids.

All the time I had spent at this new institution was a collection of various hair raising experiences? Whenever I saw a widow or interacted with the kids, I was taken aback to see what was I missing all these years. It was the real meaning of life which I understood through the problems faced by others.

"Amma, apni kotha theke aschi?" I asked one of the oldest inhabitants where she was from. She used to wear a big nose ring and white saree and never missed to cover her head with her *pallu*. She also wore a beautiful big red *bindi*. She had a

clean wheatish complexion but her head was almost bald. She must be protecting her scalp from the sunrays; she was fighting hard against the norms. She had developed a lot of facial hair and she never bothered to remove them. The beard at her chin was all white, while some on her upper lips were brownish. I looked at her and held her knees. I shook her a little and asked her the same question again to which she replied

"Kolkata" She had no teeth, I observed. When she spoke the words, her head started trembling a little and her tongue tried hard to get out of the mouth. Had I been here few years back, I would not have collected the courage to talk to her. But now I was sitting with her, talking to her. She was answering my questions, but in her own slow and difficult accent. I watched the experience she had accumulated in her wrinkles.

I took her out in the open and walked with her till the swing to finally help her sit on it. After some initial momentum, I saw she was doing well. She was pushing it and raising her limits. She laughed and held her spectacles with her left hand.

"*Amma, maach bhaat khabe ki?*" I asked her if she was interested in having fish and rice. I held the swing and slowed it down. She looked up and held her eyes and replied with a smile.

"*Daya kore...*" and she signalled me to stop the swing and I walked back with her to the place on the porch where she spent most of her time sitting and watching the kids play in the garden.

In most parts of India, widows still don't enjoy the freedom and liberty they would get if their husbands were alive. Most of the restrictions come from the society and family members, but a part of inhibition comes from within. I brought fish curry for the lady and placed the plate of fish and rice in front of her. There was no family member of her relatives or staff from Insaaniyat, who stopped her. But still I saw her trying to push herself away from the non vegetarian food. The lady was forcing a self-imposed abstinence from having non vegetarian food or even veg food with spices especially turmeric. She kept looking at the fish from far. Then she walked towards the sand outside in the play area and spit the saliva that might have collected from her hunger instinct seeing the food she would have loved to prepare and serve for so many years. I went close to her and persuaded her to have the food with me.

I did not know why I was doing that. She would talk about food which she used to prepare for her husband and I found it difficult to place myself in her position. I then mixed the rice and the fish, carefully taking out the thin bones. I tried to feed her with my hand, but she was not ready to have it. I then requested her to try at least one small bite. I put the food in her mouth with my hand, and watched her chew it with her gums. She did it slowly and shivered while having it. She wanted to express her delight describing the taste but she had somehow decided to abjure such a taste. I sat with her till she had some more and finally she took both her hands on my head and blessed me for breaking her pledge.

I left the place and met the officials to see what work we had for the coming week. We normally travelled through neighbouring villages and would often stay overnight with the villagers to talk and understand their issues. The facts we faced were always depressing.

"Om, I think this assignment is never ending" Said one of the colleagues. We often met some new colleagues who joined temporarily and they used to go back to their old jobs. I never got time to bond with anyone in particular and that was okay with me.

"What do you suggest then?" I asked while gesturing another query using my fingers asking for introduction.

"Raghav Singh" Hearing the name, I recalled that he was the founder member of *Insaaniyat* and I had heard from the colleagues that he was expected to come to Pune. I was surprised that he knew me by name and felt bad that I couldn't recognize the Managing Director. He was okay with it as he had a bigger ambition which was suppressing his ego, it looked. "We are thinking of shifting some more people from Delhi to Pune. The place in Delhi is becoming expensive for us to rent, thanks to increasing number of politicians buying plots to increase the concrete jungle."

"So, how can I help sir?" I asked.

"Call me Raghav." He then continued "The Delhi branch had focused on rehabilitation of patients with critical illness."

"I am sorry for them. It would be good if they are shifted here. The climate here must appeal to them and may be the placebo effect gives them strength to continue their fight for some more years."

He kind of agreed to me and asked me to arrange for the stay and bifurcation of the place that we had rented in Pune.

I focused on the new project, pairing with local groups and some college students who would come as part of their National Social Service camps. The youth who came for the social work would often joke about the five marks extra they got from the university for their efforts with us. Some of them had even passed their papers just because of those extra five points. I was happy that we got enough hands and whatever may be the reason, we could see people around, else this place looked deserted and the inhabitants felt lonely.

It took a month's time to finish the setup. We had categorized the stay and food and special arrangements needed for the health and emergency of the patients suffering from various ailments. The medical college fraternity was more than helpful to extend the know-how of setting up specific units serving each illness. The list was huge, but I was never short of time or energy for the project.

Amma was now shifted to a new room within the same facility. She hardly showed up, but she went away with a new zeal urging her to not stop herself from whatever life offered her. She was seen smiling and engaging. There was one small chubby girl too who was affected from HIV. I wondered how such a sweet kid was facing the toughest fight of her life since she took her first breath. She would always occupy the place on the porch where Amma sat. I did not know if that particular spot was having some relation with me? Seeing her sometimes made me feel as if Amma had come back in form of the kid. The best past was her new set of teeth, tiny, white and cute.

"Hi baby. What's your name?" I asked pulling her cheeks.
"Sayali." She said and I was thrown in flashback. I tried to close my eyes, turn around and walk back. But then I started fighting with that impromptu reaction to know this kid. Within few seconds, I had started to find a lot of resemblance in her and the Sayali I knew. I opened my eyes and forced my mind to bring me back from the past. I saw this little girl looking at me with her mouth open.

I picked her up in my arms and took her to the park and talked about her friends and her house of which she did not have much memory. She might have been left by her parents who did not have the courage to keep an HIV girl at home. What else was I expecting? People in our country seldom take a healthy girl child home. They have easier options to kill the foetus or abandon the new born on some place close to garbage bin?
I ran around with her and other kids who had assembled there to play with me. It was a good day, like all other days I had spent on this project, full of content. I sometimes wondered why I was being paid. I was enjoying, not working. I was not able to recall when was the last time I had switched on my laptop or checked my email. I lived every moment by spending

time with the people who really needed someone to look after them rather than pity them.

After we were tired of playing, I thought of dropping Sayali and leave for my room.

"I know one more uncle who is very nice." She said.

I didn't know who else she would be playing with as the team here was new. The staff was small and mostly ladies. I asked her about the other friend she had.

"Come with me." She took to the last room occupied by people who had come from Delhi.

"Okay, so you know him from your old home?" I asked Sayali.

"Yes. Every Sunday, he used to take me to *Appu Ghar*. He has taught me the *Gayatri Mantr* and I know it by heart." She started reciting it immediately after she ended her sentence. She really had a sweet voice; however she often ate half of the words in the hymn. I was no one to take that spirit from her. I was now becoming more tolerant to religious talk. Had it been few years back, I would have asked the girl to not sing it. May be I would have taught her some other English rhyme, but now I had suddenly got this tolerance to all this stuff.

"Meet him. He tells me nice stories of lord Krishn and also gives me peacock feather which I keep in my notebook." I looked at the person. He was in his mid-thirties and looked very thin. He was wearing an orange *kurta* and a white pyjama. He had very short hair and some of them were greying out. He was busy doing some prayers in front of a set of pictures kept on the shelf. I heard some murmuring while he was whirling the incense sticks and then I finally concentrated on his voice with a clearly audible chant saying "*Hare Krishna…*"

His voice was familiar but I couldn't map a name for it as my mind was stuck with the fragrance of the incense sticks. I kept my hand on his shoulder; I was excited to see who that person was. He turned around. I was shocked to see this face.

"Kabir?" I couldn't help but shout his name. Yes, that was Kabir indeed, I tried to be certain comparing his picture in my mind to what was in front of my eyes. He now had a short beard. He had become very lean and his fingers looked pretty long to me. His nails were not cut since long causing black deposition in the tiny finger-nails of both the hands. His cheek had gone extinct it looked, and the eyes bulged out. I moved close to him without saying a word and he stepped back. Had he recognized me?

I opened my arms to call him close to me. But Kabir hunched trying to ignore me. I pulled him and looked into his eyes. I then hugged him and felt that there was enough space between my arms even after the hug.

"Sorry *yaar...* How are you?" I asked. He wasn't ready to reply. Then Sayali went close to him and pulled his *kurta*. He now smiled seeing her face and then looked at me and hugged me back. Now this was my Kabir.

"I was lost yaar. Please help me, I was lost." He started crying. He cried a lot but his weakness was so much that it was difficult for the tears to roll down. I was overwhelmed by his state. I asked him to sit on the chair and looked at Sayali.

"I know this uncle too. He is a very nice man" Sayali was confused as to why were we so sad even we were not strangers.

"Tell me what happened after you left. Did you meet your parents?" I asked him

"I don't know where they are. How would I go back to them? They may have left the place. They will not be happy at all to see me. I treated them very badly. By the time I realized, I was all alone."

"You've not lost anything Kabir. You were and are still my best buddy." I assured him and continued "This life is pretty long and we try to complete the journey as fast as we can. We should take some pause or stop at times to see if we are leaving others behind. Now we've met and everything will be same as it used to be."

I was very happy and wanted to give Kabir the hope of living life for.

"Look at Sayali. She likes you a lot and she wants to stay with you always. She treats you not just like her elder brother, but like a father" I caught his hand and held it tight.

"Yes you are right. She is so cute." He looked at her and cried. "I too want to see her grow and then send her to some good school. She would be a very ..." and he started crying again.

"I am sure that would happen." I tried boost to his hope.

"You still don't go to temples?" Kabir asked me recalling my arguments.

I wanted to give him strength. I suddenly realized that my mind was considering it ok to not tell the truth if the purpose would keep a faith alive in Kabir's mind.

"I do go to temples now. I visit once in a while." I lied.

"Nice. Finally we are all the kids of that almighty and we should not let him down by disrespecting his beautiful world. He has sent us all for a reason and I knew you would come back to God one day." He was very happy and he wiped his tears. Sayali went out to play with other kids and I offered Kabir a glass of water.

"So what all did happen with you?"

"It's a long story. You must be a busy man now. Is *Insaaniyat* your company?" He asked.

"No I am just a volunteer. Tell me, I want to hear whatever you say. I have a long; very long life just to hear people like you, whom I love so much." I added.

"I roamed around from one KRISHCON to another, from one city to another. I travelled a lot." He said and continued.

"I remember that you once talked how travelling makes us broad minded. I am a live example of that thought. Travelling did make me the space around me too broad to hold my life in it. I was falling in an abyss, which was created out of my ignorance."

"Don't worry. Whatever you see today is the reality. We are safe and together. What happened then?" I asked

"I was engulfed by the work I was doing. I was preaching morning till afternoon. We travelled in various *ashrams* and sold religious books and finally at night gathered to tell how much we had collected. I eventually became a senior *pujari* in the temple as I was educated and spoke English."

"Nice, so did they give some salary too?" I asked.

"No, there was a common fund of KRISHCON and we all had one particular passbook. Whenever required, we used to visit the treasury and request for some money. We were never denied of the funds." He was quiet now and had started breathing normally.

"So you are still associated with that institution?" I asked.

"No, things did not go as smooth as I had thought." He looked cheated now and his face had the expression of questions and regrets.

"One day, I saw our priests meeting some people in the central chamber. They were dressed nicely and had come in big cars. I had seen big cars coming previously as well but this time I could identify them as politicians." He went into his thoughts and was stuck there.

"So did they talk to you?" I asked.

"No, I went to clarify some miscalculations in the funds we had collected. I opened the door of the chamber and some of them were shocked to see me. They then quickly hid their briefcases and bags."

"Who were they exactly?" I asked.

"I heard them talking about some transfer of money and the amount they said was in millions of dollars. I was shocked and for a second, I did not believe my ears." Kabir looked shocked. "The treasury asked me to sit and introduced as a very hardworking and intelligent devotee. I did not understand how an intelligent devotee is better than a dumb devotee." I was glad to hear Kabir's mind questioning the false praise.

"Then the bags were opened again but the currency was not all Indian. Some fonts looked like Russian, some looked like American dollars." He took a pause and continued.

"One of them stood up and then made a formal announcement to add me to what they referred as 'the Core Committee...'" He smiled and looked down. His smile expressed how bogus was the respect given to me.

"Om." Kabir just called my name and said nothing. He was quiet for long time.

"Yes Kabir." I kept my hand on his shoulder to bring him back to our conversation.

"How good were those days? Though we had the fear of ragging and bullying but we were all so united? We roamed around, sat together and discussed for hours in the room."

"Right and it has not changed at all. I am here; you are also very much here." He smiled on my taunt of how absent minded he had become.

"I was then sent to Moscow. What a beautiful city!" He looked up at the fan. His eyes got stuck on the blades of the fan. Kabir was finding it difficult to shift his focus from things now. If he was in some deep thought of flashback, then his mouth was left open and for minutes, he would just stand expressionless until I moved him.

"I led a group of Russian devotees and several Indian origin disciples. We would wander in the city, from one corner to the other. I would also see the beautiful temples we were building there. My job was much simpler now. I was like a courier boy." He laughed at himself and he was loud. Looked like, some incident of Moscow was pinching him from within.

"What happened then? Met with some beautiful Russian girl?" I joked.

"Many" He replied and shocked me.

"I was strangled in the network of escorts and money. In the day, I would just see money, international currencies. I was the in-charge of the delivery of earnings we collected. In the evening, I would sit alone in my five star suite and spend time with girls. I never liked them. I would just sit with them. But why did I develop a lust for them?" He stopped. After few seconds stood up again and had his eyes locked with the picture of lord Krishn. While gazing, he again went physically immobile. But when I rubbed his head, he became excited. He had suddenly started repeating his words. Maybe that was the aftermath of severe depression? Sometimes his voice would modulate to mimic Sayali or his own voice, but the frequency would be low.

"It went for years. I felt like the CEO of a big company and had no shortage of money. CEO of the company... CEO of..."

"Yes." I swayed my hands in front of his eyes to help him come out of the anxiousness that led to the stutter.

"I don't remember the last time I had visited a temple." Kabir's statement puzzled me as he was supposed to be an official devotee and propagator of the faith for KRISHCON.

"Why? You were leading the group."

"Yes, like a builder or a real estate *mafia*. I would meet the engineers and contractors and talk with labourers about the progress of the site. But I never went to the temple, never worshipped the lord inside." He was sad.

"So when did this end?" I asked.

"Never... but it did end my conscience." He was depressed and the guilt was eating him within.

"Don't worry. Should I take you to a temple right now?" I asked.

"Do you visit temple Om?" He asked and this time he was smiling.

"Yes, I had said few minutes back that I go sometimes." I reiterated.

"Oh yes... sorry I forget things nowadays. You never liked our culture or books, right?" He was now recalling my words and I did not want to portray myself as the same adamant atheist. I thought of adding some values to his faith by quoting references which would give some positive feelings to Kabir.

"In *Balkand* of Ramcharitmanas, we hear the description *Kakbhusundi* of what he saw inside Lord Ram's body."

"Yes I have heard about a crow who got into the body of lord Ram. What did he see?" asked Kabir. I then explained the narration.

"*Kakbhusundi* was shocked and surprised to see countless stars, countless Suns, Moons, numberless Gods of death and punishment, innumerable oceans, lakes, seas, rivers. He also saw all the four classes of people; The *Sidhh*, the *Nag*, the human and the Eunuchs."

"What else?" Kabir was excited and he came closer.

"*Kakbhusundi* narrates that he stayed for hundreds of years in each of the universe and there were plenty of universe inside lord Ram. He went round and round from one universe to another and he found it to be of the shape of an egg."

"Yes, that is what we have read in science books too." Kabir was now justifying the literature with the science theories. I was in no mood to defend scientific theories as long as Kabir's morale was shooting up.

"*Kakbhusundi* said that each Universe inside had its own creator just like lord *Brahma*, its own preserver just like lord *Vishnu* and he saw demons too."

"What else?"

"...Gods, serpents, he also saw several creatures which were half human and half animal." I added.

"Amazing!" He was elated to hear all this.

"He also said that each universe had a different style, he was able to see different *Ayodhya* and complete life cycle of lord Ram inside each universe at different times. The only similarity in each universe, as per Kakbhusundi was lord *Ram,* who was gracious and wise everywhere."

"Oh Lord Ram! Your *maya* can be understood by none." He closed his eyes and appreciated the matrix of life created by lord Ram.

"He also happened to see the birth of lord Ram inside lord Ram's belly in one of the universe. *Kakbhusundi* was amazed by this and lost." I added.

"Then how did he come out? Did someone find him?" Kabir showed his sympathy for the crow who was aberrated inside the matrix of life.

"Yes. He then came out of lord Ram's mouth when the lord opened his mouth to laugh."

"Great, lord Ram is so gracious." Kabir was looked happy now. I was could see him getting normal. That day, I took Kabir to a temple. After years, even I was standing behind him in the temple. He hugged me again and cried for all that had happened in the past. We came back and suddenly Kabir realized that it was Friday.

"I will start offering Namaz again…. from today onwards."

Then I realized that the main reason for his weakness; both mental and physical, probably was a feeling of betrayal towards the Gods. That feeling of despair towards the almighty had got deep rooted like cancer in his mind. At that very moment I was seeing and realizing how the thought called 'God' becomes so necessary for people like Kabir. There are people who may go astray or may commit various types of crimes or hurt people without the fear of some 'almighty'. For me, it was an observation but at the cost of Kabir's life.

One day after finishing my routine, I came back to Kabir's room with Sayali and was surprised to see him dressed normal. He was combing his hair. He wore a shirt that fitted him perfect. He had shaved his beard and was trimming his side buns.

"Kabir if you don't mind, can I ask you a question?"

"Yes… *bolna*" He asked me so informally that for a second I thought I was in my college.

"When did you realize that you want to get out of the maze you were trapped in?" I asked him directly and Sayali looked at me with her innocent eyes. I did not know what did she make out of my question but she was eagerly waiting for a response from Kabir now.

"When? I will definitely tell you brother. But some other time, okay. Time... time." He was happy and excited but soon he realized that he had started repeating words. He threw his palm on to his mouth to stop his lips from uttering the same word again and again. Sayali laughed the way Kabir stopped his repetition. He then continued

"What if the right time is now?" I asked

"One morning, I woke up and went out of the hotel in Moscow. I didn't like the breakfast that was served in the hotel. It used to be very raw. I couldn't know why they did not cook the items?"

"Then what did you eat?" Sayali asked in her namby-pamby voice.

Kabir took her up in his arms and replied.

"I used to go to an Indian cafe just across the next street, adjoining to my hotel. I went there and gave my regular order."

"Then?" I asked

"When I was going to have the bite on the item.... on that item..."

Sayali again burst out laughing to hear the way Kabir's tongue couldn't control the words.

"I saw a small boy crossing the road with his mother. His mother was having some back problem or some issue in her feet, may be her bone was fractured. She walked very slowly and this boy was agile, he wanted to just jump over to the other side of the road"

"So did you help him?" Sayali asked.

"No *beta*. I was selfish and bad uncle then" He had tears again his eyes. Another good physiological development was the refill of Kabir's tears. The positive strength he had gained in last so many days had started sending out more and more quantity of tears, which ultimately reduced the load Kabir was carrying on his heart. He then continued.

"I turned my face back to the newspaper and in few seconds, I heard some noise as if someone fell or crashed. Yes, I heard that screeching sound of the brake applied on a bus. I heard a women shout loud in Russian. I looked at her, she was crying for help. I heard a nimble voice calling his mom."

Sayali was frightened and she hugged Kabir and I stood up to take Sayali from him. She had closed her eyes too.

"So what happened then?" I asked.

"I don't know what made me stand. I looked at them. The small kid had reached the other side but he was way close to the wall. He might have been thrown by the accident and might have hit the wall. The woman was in the middle of the road and was bleeding very badly. I went close to her and tried to lift her but she had given all her weight. I asked people to come close and help me lift her. We then took her to the place where kid was."

"Were they alive?" I asked

"The kid wasn't speaking now. I tried to shake his head and open his eyes but... He looked so innocent but now he had no voice. His white school shirt had now turned red. The blood was still leaking from the centre of his neck." Kabir cried.

"I lifted the boy and his back was wet and warm. I then looked all sides of the road... no help! I ran with the kid to search for a hospital and reached the next square"

"Did you find one?"

"No I then ran back towards the other end, crossing the woman... his mother; she looked at me and asked to help her. I gave her support and other people also gathered."

"Did the ambulance arrive?"

"No... I don't know. I had the kid in my arms and the lady was limping with me showing me the direction to the closest hospital. Then a van stopped, it was a van of some bakery I remember."

"Nice" I said while tapping Sayali's back. She was getting fast in to her dreams.

"There are good people in this world. He stopped and helped us to climb inside. It felt nice to sit inside the van. I was hoping the kid to get up and smell the confectionaries in the van. He did not. I kept watching the kid and then shifted my focus to his mother. She was begging me to help the boy. I did not know Russian; her eyes had spoken more than her tongue. I kept looking at the kid and pressing his injury hard to stop the bleeding. Believe me, that was the longest felt journey of my life, longer than my flight to Moscow. The van stopped and we came out to run into the emergency ward."

"Good, what happened then? Was the kid alright?" I asked.

"They took him in. The kid had bled profusely. His weight had reduced since the time I had lifted him on the road. It felt as if the whole liquid has come out of his body. His face now looked white. No more rosy pink."

"Then?"

"The mother was taken to some other ward and the kid needed blood. I heard the doctor shouting *Hh* antigen blood group in the open area. He was continuously ringing places" He took a deep breath of helplessness.

"I went to the doctor and said that I have Bombay blood group. He did not understand. I did not know Russian. I pulled a nurse; she had a typical South Indian face cut. I asked the lady in Malayalam and repeated the request in English that I had the blood group the boy needs. She then explained it to the Doctor in the Russian."

"Great Kabir! You saved his life?" I sighed in relief and saw that Sayali had slept. I put her on the bed and covered her.

"No Om, I could not. I don't know." He seemed dejected.

"They tested my blood and the nurse asked me to get up and move to sanitation area quickly. I was given due cleaning and then they asked me to leave the place immediately."

"What... why? Some police case?" I asked.

"No, I had tested... tested…"

"What?"

"Positive for HIV." Kabir burst out in despair.

"What? How... oh the escorts?" I was sad and sat on the bed besides Sayali. I couldn't control my tears hearing this. All this time, I was considering Kabir to be an abandoned person to have come here for shelter, not knowing he was also suffering from the killer virus.

"My life was over. I walked out. I don't know what happened to that lady or that kid. Maybe they survived or succumbed to heavy bleeding. But I got the punishment for my wrong doings." He cried.

"Oh Kabir!" I went close to him. I tried to give him my support. "Did you double check?" I asked.

"Yes. In Delhi, but all the reports were positive." He stopped. "There are hundreds of scientists doing research on this Kabir. I am sure soon we will have some good solution for this problem." I know I was just bluffing, but what else could I've done. It's also true that people were fighting hard to find its cure, however I was in no way touch with the research results. Kabir was having the medication but that was not going to cure him. I had interacted with HIV patients but had never thought a person so close to me would be infected by it. I was feeling very bad and had nothing to offer to Kabir except my false assurances.

Kabir used to spend time with kids and play around with other inmates. He looked confident but at times, he used to go back in depression. One fine day, I went close to him and surprised him with my request.

"Come, let us go to Delhi." I asked. He initially resisted and then started packing his thing.

We met *amma* and asked her to look after Sayali. I asked the kid to look after Amma too. She was smart and in her soft voice she assured me that *amma* would be alright.

CHAPTER 11

Flight Sees No Fence

In Delhi, we directly went to search Surya at his old address which I had noted when he had called me years back while I was in final year

I knocked the door of the new address we had. The door was finally opened by a familiar face, Surya's mother.

I touched her feet and asked if she could recognize me. She looked clueless; thanks to my weight and the clumsy hairstyle. I was not being recognized by even the people who were too close to me. I had also grown some beard. I did not remember the last time I had run the razor on my cheeks. I then smiled and introduced myself to aunty.

"Om... Patna... Surya's friend!"

"Oh! You were such a short and smart kid. What has happened to you? Is everything alright?" She sounded happy first and then worried.

"Yes…" She too had put on a lot of weight. I remember mummy often talked about Surya's mother undergoing some thyroid treatment. Maybe the extra fat was its side-effect on her.

She met Kabir with same warmth as she met me. She tried to offer us a lot of things but I wasn't hungry to have them. I was rather excited to meet Surya.

"He is in the Delhi Police. You can wait for him. He will be here at five in the evening." She asked us but I was in no state to wait. I took the address of the *chowki* and ran there with Kabir. While we walked till his place of work, I saw the newly renovated face of Delhi. This place had drastically transformed from what I had experienced long back.

We had reached the police chowki. I asked Kabir to get inside and gave him some dialogues to talk. I went to the corner where visitors were seated. I saw Surya from a distance. He had grown tall since I last saw him. His hands were looking long and thin, so were his legs but his tummy had grown big. He was wearing nicely ironed uniform. Also, he had a thin but neatly trimmed moustache. I tried to control my laughter. I wanted to observe my domineer buddy who was a cop now.

"Excuse me sir." Kabir requested Surya.

"Yes?" He did not even look at Kabir, as he was busy seeing his file. Surya then called up on his junior.

"Rathore, please ask *Chhotu* to bring my tea. I need to go now." Surya was behaving like a typical cop I had seen in movies, he was enjoying that spirit of ordering subordinates!

"Sir, my friend is missing. He has not returned home since past four days." Kabir said.

"What is your name?" Surya asked raising his head.

"Kabir."

"Hindu Kabir or?" I was completely out of my mind. Surya, being a public servant, asked a direct question which showed a new trait of him. Not sure if that was developed recently.

"Muslim" was the reply.

"Bloody Pakistani." He wiped his face with the towel hung on his chair.

"You Muslims always cause trouble; you don't want us to live free. I run around you guys all the day. You don't spare us even at night with your processions and we need to forget our sleep giving additional security to your areas. I am tired of all this." He threw his file on the table and continued

"Then I see people like you coming and lodging complains about their missing accomplice." Maybe Surya was annoyed at possible suspects who kept him on his toes 24/7. That might have piled up in his mind as venom against the second major faith in India. Kabir looked at me and pressed both his lips to hide his shock. He still waited for Surya to complete his sentence.

"Give me his picture. Mehta, bring the files of recent unclaimed bodies that we found this week." Surya didn't want to lodge the FIR. So he was trying to find a reason to send Kabir back. Kabir now seemed a little frightened and he looked at me. I smiled back to encourage his acting skills.

Surya got the file and turned the pages one by one "Mahroof Khan... Amjab Iqbal... Anwar Hussain..." He continued and was expecting some answer from Kabir. Surya stared at Kabir, but he was quiet.

"Say Yes or No if the name is what you are looking for." He was stiff now and Surya's anger forced Kabir to gather some courage and reply "No sir. He is alive. I mean he must be alive. I am sure." Kabir looked trapped.

"How do you know he must be alive? There are people dying every day in Delhi, murdered and thrown away in Yamuna. How can you be so sure? Are you lying? Malhotra come here." He ordered his colleague to come closer to Kabir.

"Maar dandey..." Surya ordered his junior to hit Kabir with stick and seeing Kabir's expressions I was not able to stop my laughter.

"No sir, I was just saying..." Kabir had forgotten his lines, so he quickly took out my passport sized photograph and showed it to Surya.

Surya saw the picture and then signalled Malhotra to stop his baton in the air. His facial expressions were changing from anger to sympathy.

"Where? How do you know him?" He asked Kabir.

"He is my friend" and Kabir made a poor face to show his tension for the loss.

"Malhotra, call the headquarters. Now!"

"When did he come to Delhi? Bloody fool! He should have informed me when he was here. I will find him, don't worry." Surya now looked here and there and then he suddenly found me. He broadened his eyes and kept looking at me. I tried disconnecting his contact; however my peripheral vision showed that he was approaching me. I turned around to look at the notice board. Someone held my collar, when I tried to see who that fellow was, I saw some other cops jumping close from left and right to help. He kept pushing-pulling me until I looked him into his eyes.

"Om?" He quietly said my name and hugged me.

"*Saale*, how did you recognize me, even aunty, I mean your mother couldn't guess me?" I asked.

"I am your friend first and then a policeman. You can't hide your face under that beard, *motu!*" He laughed calling me a fatso owing to my increased diameter. Kabir also jumped in and we all sat on the empty chairs in the visiting area.

"Why so much of anger against the..." I wanted to ask but was feeling afraid of how Surya would react.

"Against the... whom?" He asked

"Muslims?" I somehow asked it, while enjoying the breeze blowing past my hair. Surya was more focused on driving his office jeep. He did not reply and his face showed some hardship he might have faced recently, maybe that could be the work pressure he had. He might have inadvertently conditioned his brain to see every Muslim as a suspect. I did not see the old Surya; I tried hard but could not make him happy during the short trip from his office to his home. However I had a reason to be happy, seeing him settled well.

After reaching home, we spent a lot of time relaxing and discussing our stupid activities done during our school days. Kabir was hearing a different side of me; he was surprised to hear how I troubled the teachers and the classmates. In the college he had seen me always a patient and diligent student, never arguing with the professors. Surya pulled Kabir in the game of cards and asked him not to feel frightened. There was no end to which direction the talks went. We were covering the map of India with all the silly things we recollected. Surya had a heavier voice now, may be shouting and chasing goons all day had deepened his voice.

"Don't you use your office jeep for a daily commute?" I asked him next morning seeing Surya cleaning the dust over his bike. "It wastes too much of fuel. I prefer this. He rubbed the final patch of grease under the bike's oil tank. I asked him to apply for leaves in the coming week for some vacation which I had planned and he couldn't say no to my request. I further requested to leave the bike for us and go to his office by the four-wheeler.

"I love this RD350 and have kept her young like a princess... do not hit her to some wild bison on the road" Surya gave us a quick warning for his old, deprecating motor bike.

We drove around Delhi to revisit the first set of memories of my life, that special place where I was brought up. We reached close to Palam. The place used to be deserted and now it was so densely populated with apartments all over, touching the sky.

We finally reached the exact area where I stayed when I was a kid. The stairs, the park, the wide open playground, the route to go to the milkman, everything was looking at me. They were expecting me to play or walk over them. I did not know when I reached the floor where I stayed. The flat wasn't locked from outside, so I rang the doorbell. A lady in brown saree opened the door. I introduced myself by my father's name. I told her the story of my childhood and how the memories I had of the place. She called me in and made me sit. The furniture was almost the same, made of robust and durable sal-wood.

I walked close to the window and felt so happy to see the pigeons still coming to the window. May be they were the second or third generation pigeons. But I felt that they knew me, which was why they were coming so close to the small opening in the window. I remember I had managed to trap some, but later I would let them fly away. I looked into their eyes; they had so much to talk to me. I was no longer that small kid, but the eyes... they never age.

The lady brought some refreshments for us; I passed it on to Kabir. I was not going to waste even a single second. I kept thanking the lady to permit us to check inside, letting me see the old Om who had so much of acceptance. I then looked at the door from inside. The drawing of lord Krishn was intact. I was in love with the portrayal of lord Krishn and I got so much of appreciation for my faith and sketches. I showed it to Kabir and explained how I drew it with so much of love for that face. I was overwhelmed with emotions. Back when I was a kid, the painting meant faith to me, but at that very moment it was much more than faith. Before I left, I turned around to ask the lady for one more favour.

"Madam, by any chance do you remember if there was a dog named Tipu who stayed here when you moved in?" I was hopeless, but I couldn't stop myself from asking the whereabouts of Tipu.
"No" I looked all over and apologised to Tipu for not being able to find him, and more apologies came through my tear ducts for deserting him as a small kid long back.

"Where is the bike?" Surya asked.

"I have given it to a friend" I saw him getting tensed, to reduce which I added "just for some days." I said.

"Oh Om!" He wanted to say more, but I limited him to just say "can't you say NO to anyone asking help from you?" I smiled back with my eyes replying non-verbal 'no' to his query. For next few days we travelled using Delhi buses and the more I travelled, the younger I felt. Surya was engrossed much in to his government duties that we couldn't meet in even at night for next few days.

I got Surya's bike back and was eager to see his expressions on seeing what I had done to it.

"Surya, can you check if your bike is in good shape?" I raised a doubt in Surya's mind.

"Don't tell me! I asked you not to give it." He then ran towards the parking and uncovered the bike. Kabir and I stood behind him to hear his first reaction.

"What did you do to this?" He exclaimed loudly.

The petrol tank was polished red and it had a beautiful lustre. The guard, silencer and various other parts were sparkling silver in a new stainless steel-look. The light was glowing bright and the metal parts at bottom were painted black. The visor and the missing tail light were fixed. The logo and branding was properly aligned on the tank. The restoration was so perfect that it looked as if the bike was just out of showroom.

"Is this the same bike Om?" He questioned with shock.

"Yes Inspector *Sahib...*" I replied and the smile on his face was all that I needed.

Surya sat on the bike and could not express his happiness. His old kick was also tilted which had been replaced, so the bike was completely new from outside. When he gave a kick, the bike produced a new thrust. He could see the exhaust gases coming out with boom and a bass. Surya just kept saying 'wow' and he was glad to drive it.

Days passed and I was now planning to get off from Delhi to a longer flight, to reduce a burden which was on my shoulder since long?

"Come, we will go to meet a person." I said and asked both to sit behind the bike.

"Okay, we will go but you don't have a driving license, so let me drive." Kabir had a good memory about me having no license. "What? You still don't have a driving license Om! It takes just few hundred rupees. Come; let us go to the RTO. I will get it made quickly." He requested me to let him drive. I apologized. "I see people with valid license driving so badly that I have lost faith in the licensing policy." I joked and only Kabir smiled. Surya was forcing me to come to the RTO.

"It's so close boys. Come on, sit behind and get ready to experience the greatest time of your lives" My loud cry did not lead to any reaction, so added "Moreover I don't need to be afraid now as I have the Delhi Police sitting behind me." Saying that I accelerated the bike and it did sound good in pushing me ahead.

"Let us not do triple at least. I will get the office jeep" Surya was suddenly so law obedient after getting into the police forces. I liked it, but he couldn't over-rule me. "Where are we going to meet that special person?" Kabir joked.

"Punjab." I replied quickly to help them mentally prepare for the extensive drive we were going to cover.

"Om... you've gone mad. No, we can't go to a different state on this bike." Surya replied with worry.

"Why? Is this a stolen bike?" I replied.

"No jokes Om. It's very far."

"We will take some stops. Don't worry." I assured.

The road was so smooth and beautiful; it felt like a black carpet rolled out just for the new bike. The journey started so smoothly. Plantation on both sides of the road and green open paddy fields made me want to stop and stay over.

"How am I driving Surya?" I asked.

"Good so far. But we should stop at the next *dhaba*. I don't want you to drive at night." Surya looked concerned but was enjoying his break from the duty. He couldn't hide his happiness after sometime. I could see his hands stretched to feel the air in the rear-view mirror.

"You are free Surya. No officer over your head... no FIR, no chasing around terrorists." I tried to express what he must be thinking, but heard no response from him.

We were driving since four hours and Kabir was stuck between the two of us. I took a stop in Sangrur to let everyone stretch out. The *dhaba* we could see was very much inside the farm. The farmer looked sun-tanned owing to his hard work in the fields. He did sound friendly though. He washed his face with the water outside the dhaba and cleaned his beard and eyebrows as he approached us.

"Where are you boys coming from?" He asked

"*Dilli*" Kabir replied and the dhaba owner looked happy hearing that. For the people of Punjab, Delhi is like a second home. We had the delicious food followed by a glass full of tea. It was fun to take a break at such a beautiful place.

"Kabir, do you remember that during first year, we had a technical conclave for which we were almost prepared to go to the site?" I asked.

"Yes. But we could not make it due to your ear which got burst."

"Yes, it was supposed to be held here, in Sangrur... this very land." Kabir wished that we should have visited it then.

"You can't hear?" Surya asked

"My eardrum is no longer a virgin." Hearing this, Kabir burst out laughing

Surya was out of his seat and he started behaving very concerned for the problem in my ears. He pulled me to pay a forced visit to a nearby doctor.

"I haven't come this far to show my ear drums to a Hakeem" Kabir smiled and tried to convince Surya about the problem which was somewhat auto healed by my body. I too denied as that rupture was no more painful.

The *dhaba* owner not only gave us good food, he also gave us cots to sleep in the open. There were some mosquitoes, but we covered our body with some oil, which we got from the experienced dhaba owner. The mosquitoes did not like the smell of that oil, so did Surya. He felt like vomiting a couple of times.

"Surya, remember I once gave such a paste to your girlfriend to let her apply it on her sexy body... long back in jungles of Jharkhand." Hearing my satire Surya held my neck tight and this frightened Kabir. He jumped in to plead on my behalf, but before he could start his arguments Surya looked at me and we laughed at how silly those days were.

"I am seeing the sky after so many years. See there." Surya pointed up in the sky and added "*Ursa Major*, I used to search it daily when I was a kid." He kept gazing up in the sky like a child.

"Om, you were good at science. Can you answer what animal it forms?" Surya was now taking a quiz and I was glad he had paid that much attention while in school.

"I thought you just looked at the 'ursa major' and 'ursa minor' of the girls in our school." I replied ignoring his question.

"Bear" Kabir replied, who was also lost in the beautiful sky.

"Bingo*!, bear se yaad aaya... Veerji, kirpa karke ek beer pila do... hun*" Surya now asked for a beer from the dhaba owner.

"*Loh jee, chilled.*" He threw one at each one of us.

Surya was overjoyed to get the can of beer in such a remote village. Kabir had never had a drink in his life. He now thought of breaking that sainthood. He started with the first sip and did not like it. But seeing Surya's speed, he too started swallowing it gulp by gulp. Then came the Belch...

"Such a horrible burp!" I slapped Surya's back and added "I am afraid it would mutate the paddy crops, cover your mouth!" I asked Surya and I don't remember if he replied. Even if he did, I was lost in my sleep to see much better things.

The cot was not very comfortable, physically some parts of my body were jammed, but mentally I felt fresh, very fresh in the morning.

"Good morning" I tried waking up the boys and it was hard as they were tired and were enjoying the sleep. They must be experiencing such a quiet sleep after a long time. Both were exhausted by the challenges which life threw at them. After having the morning tea, I went to the owner and thanked him with all my gratitude. Initially he did not take money from me, but later on requesting and assuring that we would not visit again on his denial, he took it.

We then started our ride again and this time it was for the entire day. After every few kilometres, we saw Police parties patrolling. We had reached Ferozpur; that was what the milestone said.

"My ass is paining boys. Om, how much more is left? We've already entered Punjab." Surya did sound exhausted. "*Saale*, how did you get selected in the Police?" I asked. I had to stop again at a place which looked a little populated. The village board read '*Kundhe*'. This land was so flat and looked fertile with green and golden crops flourishing over it.

"I can't see any house. Don't people reside here, in such a beautiful place?" Surya asked. He then walked to a public phone booth to inform his chowki about the extension of his short trip.

"Take these T-shirts" I threw one to Kabir and the second to Surya.

"Afridi!" Surya shouted with an element of ecstasy, and continued "I am not playing cricket here in this village?" Surya was puzzled.

311

"The land is so plain; it can be a very good pitch by the way. Akram, mine is good... I like this fellow" I had seen Kabir playing cricket. He often gave a tough time to the batsman by his fast pace. So Akram was good choice for him.

While the boys looked confused and wondering where we were, I took out a small paint box and a brush. I opened the bike's tool kit and took out the screw driver.

"What are you doing? Is the petrol leaking? I had already requested you to take the office jeep. This is an old bike yaar, you never listen to me Om." Surya started grumbling.

"I took out the number plate and turned it around and it was all white. I then asked them to speak any one alphabet.

"G... but why?" Surya asked.

Before I could reply him, Kabir immediately said "F". The letter 'K' came to my mind quickly, so I randomly wrote "KFG 9554" and then drew a small crescent and a star just above the numbers.

"From where did these numbers come?" Kabir asked.

"See the pillar close to the fence" I asked the boys to see the pillar just in front of them, which had the serial number.

"What is this?" Surya repeated.

Kabir understood my intentions and he had no fear, it seemed. One great thing that had happened to Kabir's life after Moscow trip was the loss of his fear.

"You always cry that the petrol is very expensive here, right?" I asked Surya.

"Yes, it won't be much different even in Punjab." He replied

"Who said I am talking about this place?"

"Meaning?" Surya lifted his shoulders as he was clueless.

"I am taking you to another Punjab. I need to meet someone across the border."

"Oh my God!" Surya was now sweating. He went far and found a small rock to sit on. He held his forehead and in despair closed his eyes. He wanted to yell at me, but it was too late, we were almost there. After sometime, he walked to me and said

"Why didn't you tell me that we are going to Pakistan?"

"You know the answer" I replied. He was left poker faced and after some time, he ran towards the river, hitting the mud and some pebbles by his feet.

"Don't run… we have a bike. I did not hide the truth from you. I always clarified that we are going to Punjab. Which Punjab, you never asked." I shouted but he was in no mood to listen to us. He held the fence by hand and kept watching the flow of the mighty river.

I reached there with Kabir and we waited at the bank for someone to come.

"Surya you are in Delhi Police, you should not be frightened to meet your neighbours" I said. Kabir was giggling all the time.

The fence wasn't greatly designed. It had big space, broad enough to force the bike to the other side. But the other side was a little sloppy; hence I put the bike in gear so that it didn't slip down.

"You could have asked me, I am sure we would have got the Visa." Surya was now talking sense

"I did try that my friend, but the officer did not find it as a valid reason to visit Pakistan. Moreover it's easier to enter into India or Pakistan this way, than applying for Visa and coming through Bus or Train" I said.

We reduced the volume of our talk now. We were right on the edge of a sword that had taken the lives of hundreds of millions of people. The border area and forces from both sides thus were on red alert every second.

We started crossing the fences. It was easier for us to climb up but pushing the bike to the other side was the biggest challenge. We had now reached no man's land which was just close to the Sutlej River. I did not understand what ran into Surya's mind; he suddenly dived into the river. He was very fond of bathing in the river and this one was too beautiful to dive in. I had seen him jumping in full school uniform in the holy Ganga, when we would be stressed out. I looked at Kabir and he rejected the idea of a dip.

"Surya" I raised my hand.

"What?" He asked while spitting water he had gulped in his mouth.

"How are you feeling after taking your first holy dip in Pakistan?" I pulled his leg.

"This is our river. It flows from India to Pakistan so this is our river." He was now talking the same language which most of the Indians talk when it comes to giving air to their nationalist feeling; both the sides go far in claiming the resources created by nature.

It was a regular afternoon and the Sun was right on top of our head. We saw few movements from the Indian side. I quickly asked the boys to bow down. Maybe the splash was loud which attracted the Indian side of security personnel. We were much behind shrubs and I pulled both Surya and Kabir with me completely immersed in the water. The bank fortunately had few tall plants which were dense enough to hide the bike. The sun rays were falling on the side mirrors of the bike, so Surya came out of water and slowly rolled them out and threw the mirrors inside the river, fearing reflection which could have helped the border security personnel to locate us. The patrol party then moved away.

Kabir had never attempted even a snorkel under the river water and he lived up to the strength needed to hide under water breathless for almost the same time as we did. Finally we came out of water and took that deep, life saving breath. We were now idle and waiting for some clue to click our brains that may help us getting to the other side of the river. We couldn't see any long branches or tree logs which could be tied together to create a boat. Even I was felt hopeless and guilty for not planning about the river. I had assumed it to be narrow and still, which could be easily crossed by swimming. However the flow was very swift and it wasn't deep and broad enough to challenge our limited capabilities of breast-strokes. We looked at each other, hiding behind the shrubs waiting for the bulb to glow on either one of us.

After sometime, we saw a person rowing his boat. There was a kid as well, sitting inside the boat besides the old man and he was busy playing with the beautiful white current. The three of us got ready with our T-shirts. I asked the boys not to utter a single word which would give a hint that we were from India.

"*Salaam-walekum chacha jaan.*" I raised my voice and saluted the person rowing the boat.

"He could be a terrorist." Surya was haunted by his police instinct.

"Oho, *zehnaseeb... zehnaseeb...* Akram, Akhtar and Afridi, all three..." and he laughed. He asked us to jump in.

"How did you boys come here?"

"Bike stunts. Few hours back, we drove from that slope." Kabir showed the cliff to the person. The person stopped his boat completely and watched the tip from where the so called jump was done. Kabir then continued

"We drove from there and wanted to cover Sutlej. We almost succeeded in it but this side of the river is all plain and muddy. We were foolish enough to not plan the return trip." Kabir made up a quick story

It sounded like a bluff but I was fine as long as the boat owner was convinced.

"Triple?" He asked.

"Yes... it is fun. You should try it too? We always drive a triple ride" Surya suggested the idea to the boatman, though he himself wasn't entirely convinced of a triple ride.

"Don't worry boys. Very nice. I respect courage, very well." He asked us to sit inside and the kid was happy to see our bike.

Prakash Sharma

"Boo Boo.... Bruuuu!" The kid was surprised to see a very sporty
new bike which was shining high. He started accelerating his
fist. It was funny to see him accelerating from both fists.
"Your bike is not hurt at all. Landed smooth?" the boatman
asked. I appreciated the presence of mind the person possessed,
but I could not think of a reply.
"We do this all the time, we've done this over trucks, cars and
this time we thought of doing the stunt over the river and it
was thrilling. You must have seen our stunts on the TV." Kabir
added again.
"Oh! You might not recognize us as we have to wear helmets
all the time." I tried to amend the stunt story. Now, he was
somewhat convinced and glad that we were professionals and
not some college kids or spoiled brats running around for
weird pleasure.
"I've heard that Akhtar has started taking drugs. He was our
pride, we loved him so much." He asked, feeling sad for the
Pakistani star bowler. I could not get what made him feel
that wearing Akhtar's T-shirt would make us understand
everything that Akhtar had done?
"No *chacha*, it is all rumour. Please don't trust it." I replied
"Where are you boys from? I mean where are you camping
here?" He asked.
"Nizampura" I replied quickly. The boys immediately turned
their necks to give me that look as if I was some spy.
"See Sheikhpur has come." That was his stop. We got down
and thanked him.
Surya took out his wallet and put his fingers to take out a
hundred rupee note to give to the boatman. I immediately held
his hand and showed him the note in his hand.
"Gandhiji... gone mad?" Surya immediately put it back in his
wallet.
"Sorry, we don't have any money right now" I said and hugged
chacha and thanked him. Surya again took out his wallet and
gave something to the kid. The kid saw the small sachet and
felt happy.

316

"What did you give to that boy?" I asked.

"I searched my wallet and the only thing I found was the sachet" Surya replied.

"Was it shampoo?" Kabir asked with a smile.

"No it was... it was a condom." Surya replied.

"What!" We exclaimed. I then added "That kid's father saved our life and you gifted him a..." Kabir was holding his stomach laughing loud.

"That was the only thing in my wallet which I could have given to the kid." Surya was pretty bad at logic since school days. I was glad that Delhi Police took no aptitude test for inspectors. "He was a kid. What will he do now? Blow air in it and make a parachute from it to travel across Pakistan?" I asked which Surya completely ignored.

"By the way, I've seen during cricket matches." He looked excited now.

"What" Kabir asked?

"The girls of Pakistan. They are so bloody hot!" He was now making those filthy expressions and the way he shook his body gave an impression that some current just ran throughout his body.

"Bugger, we've come here for a very important task, to meet someone. Remember?" I asked and that made him forget about his plan of hooking up with local ladies.

"He is right yaar, leave it. Let us see the person we have come to meet. She must be special *yaar*. Where did you meet her? Internet?" Kabir asked.

"No I've never met that person. I have just talked on phone" I said.

"Love on the phone. Love is in the air, now I get it." Surya said.

"Boys that person is a male, I mean a man." I said.

"Are you gay? I should have sensed it the moment you kept yourself far from girls. *Saale* you did not find a boy for love in India... yuck!" Surya spit but it was fun to see his expressions.

"Idiot! I wanted to thank him for saving my life once." I narrated Surya the story of hostel and how Imran bhai saved my life.

"Thanks to you too Kabir for all the efforts you took to help me that day."

"You never mentioned it to me earlier..." Surya gave a serious expression to show his helplessness.

"You were not in Police then." Kabir replied which made us all smile.

We started back with our triple ride to Kasur through the bumpy roads. The terrain was much like any Indian village. The air that blew here had the same essence that we have in the western parts of India. The people were also busy with their daily life and we noticed the road-side shops serving almost the same items. It was fun to drive freely. I then stopped at a square and asked a young boy passing by.

"*Bhai*, which road goes to Bhalla, near Nizampura?" He looked at the three of us.

"Where did you buy the T-shirts?" Then without waiting for a reply he answered the query "Go straight and after two kilometres take first left, then again after few hundred meters there will be a board for Nizampura. Ask anyone there about Bhalla... it's very famous." People here had exactly the same accent as we have in the Indian part of Punjab. It was more than fifty years since the partition and there wasn't much of a difference here except for the sign boards in Urdu, which only Kabir was able to read, partially. The boy ran to the other side of the road and Surya shouted to thank the boy as a matter of courtesy.

I then drove full speed so as to return back before it was dark. We had reached the destination I had noted. I matched the address from my pocket and stood at the gate. I asked Kabir to ring the door bell as I was having some bad feeling about the place, something that was asking me to go back.

A lady opened the door and she did not wait to see or hear our greetings. She moved in and called another person who was around six inches taller than me. I was on the stairs and this person was in his drawing room, a feet below the entrance gate. He had kept a small beard on his chin and was wearing a *Che Guevara* tee- shirt. He had back brushed his long hair and applied *soorma* in his eyes, perfectly thin. Kabir then read the name plate and in no time recollected the day when he ran all corners to get help for me.

"Hello Imran Bhai..." Kabir offered his respect and added.
"Some ten years back you had talked to a person from Nagpur."
"I don't remember. Who are you?" He questioned with suspicion.
"We are from India." Hearing that, the people in the house stood and started approaching us. The old lady came to Surya and asked
"*Tussi kithhon aaye?*" She had the motherly affection. Surya replied honestly
"Dilli."
"Imran, *Mai Dilli vekhnaa chaunni... kinne saal...*" She was lost in her memories of Delhi. She must have moved from India to Pakistan after facing the wrath of partition. People of her age had faced the real pain of the division which was marked on the heart of a mother, so painful that it bled on both the sides. I could somewhat understand her emotions.
She pointed her index finger towards a picture on the wall. She was looking stunning in that black and white picture, standing right next to one clean shaven fair looking gentleman with neatly side partitioned hair. That must be her husband, who was sporting an astrakhan. I was seeing a modern youth of Pakistan framed on the wall, just the opposite of Imran who was dressed pretty orthodox, especially in his short pyjama. The generation gap had just reversed the modernity in attire, it looked.

She explained that she got married in Delhi but due to present day conditions she is unable to go there. Her in-laws were from Delhi and immediately after the partition she had to move to the other part. Listening to her story left me thinking how brutal her ordeal must have been, that had cost her the life of her husband.

Imran came close to his mother and took her to a different room. The bungalow was big and much like a modern day duplex, nicely decorated from inside. He then looked at our bike and closed the door.

"How could I have forgotten you Kabir? Stay here as long as you want to." He opened his mouth for exhaling the air that was stuck in his chest may be since ages.

"No *bhai*, we will like to leave today itself as we have some important work tomorrow, back in India"

"Why have you boys come here? Some college trip?"

I then narrated in detail how he had helped me get out of the trap. I thanked him a lot and said that the only purpose of visiting Pakistan was to thank him in person. He looked emotional hearing me. Imran hugged me and by the time we were discussing things, his mother had prepared all kinds of food, mostly vegetarian food. We were hungry since morning and wasted no time before cleaning the plate.

While having the food we had a look around the house and saw the beautiful paintings and engravings. It looked like we were in a fort of old Delhi. The floor was all white and walls had beautiful colors and some scriptures hung on them. After finishing the food, we relaxed on the sofa.

After sometime, I looked at the clock and then quickly got up and took out my wallet. I took out all the cash I had in my wallet and asked Imran to give me some Pakistani Rupees so that we could buy some stuff. He folded my palm back with the Indian currency I was trying to offer him. He took out his wallet and gave a bunch of Pakistani rupees.

"You've come to meet me from my India; risking your life. I can't accept this."

He then took his mobile, searched a number and continued "Drive to Kalyan and meet Maqsood Afroz Patel. Note this number."

"We've a Kalyan here as well?" asked Surya.

Imran bhai smiled and asked us to leave to board his truck that would leave with onions to India by road.

"Seeing you boys, I am finding it difficult to wash away the memories of my best buddy, decades back when I was in college."

He was speaking just like us, I mean he was known as a strong man, but he too had a friend?

"We spent the first semester together and all of us had such a good time then. I too was in National College."

That was a wonderful surprise; all this time he did not tell us that we were the products of the same alma mater. He had a lot of patience to hide such a wonderful connect between us.

"Where is he now? Can I take your message to him?" I asked.

"He is with Allah" He sat back on the chair feeling utterly depressed, and then he added "Ragging ate him."

"What?" asked Kabir.

"Some seniors came to our room one night." He then turned back, may be to wipe his tears.

"What happened then?" I asked.

"They were so jealous of this boy being liked by teachers, students, everybody loved him. He was very adamant though. He would stand against anything wrong. I learnt from him the courage to stand tall." He was happy talking about his learnings from his friend but then also looked very sad recalling such a harrowing incident.

Imran then added "I could not guide the courage in me to go in the right direction. See where I am now." He went quiet and moved his head to continue

"My room number was 223." He said and went back to his room.

"Hrihaan?" Kabir asked.

"Yes... but..." Imran came close to Kabir, who then narrated Imran about the trunk we got in the same room. We then discussed the developments about ragging policies. He smiled at the efforts we had tried to put in against ragging. The complete family came out to bid adieu. With overwhelming emotions, I thanked him and his family for the hospitality and drove towards Kalyan.

"The bike is giving some jerk." I asked Surya if that was a common problem he had faced earlier.

"Oh! The petrol." He replied.

"Now is the time to fulfil my promise." I replied jokingly to Surya.

We reached the petrol pump and it had a lot of trucks and bikes already. When Kabir saw the rate he jumped "Hundred and ten rupees... so expensive! It is seventy at our place." I asked him to be quiet putting my index finger on my lips. He then recalled that the Indian Rupee is almost 1.7 times that of Pakistan currency.

After sometime, Kabir calculated and said "The tank capacity is around 16L and per litre we are saving rupees 10."

"So?" Surya asked.

"So overall, we are saving just Rs 160, not much?" I looked at Kabir and requested him to keep quiet as the discussions would have hinted our trespass. Surya then asked me to give him the control. I was okay as I was also a little tired.

Surya had the habit of chasing miscreants in Delhi so he was driving way too fast in such a craggy road. He was often taking sharp turns and was going for wreck-less overtakes. Kabir and I requested him to slow down but by the time he understood us, I saw a Pakistani police vehicle following us. Surya then slowed down and followed the left lane. The vehicle overtook us from the right and applied a sudden brake.

The officer showed his hand from the window asking us all to get down the bike.

"Show me your driving license." He asked. This person had a big belly just like any Indian traffic police. But I was not able to figure out if he was a traffic cop or from the Army. We were little worried but had to maintain our calm.

"I don't have it." Surya said as showing his actual driving license would have invited a larger issue.

"Okay, do you have it?" He asked me and I also said was negative. Kabir also shook his head left to right.

"None of you have license!" He signalled few of other guys in uniform to come out and interact, meanwhile he went to pee on road side.

"Where is this bike from?" This guy was young and liked the bike. He was also a cricket fan so he winked his right eye to let us know that his senior officer would not cause a serious problem to us.

"Sir I've asked these boys. They are college boys from Lahore. They came here to see Sutlej river and do some fishing" This young cop tried to let us go with the excuse.

"Where is your net to catch the fish?" The senior was finished with his job so he asked while tucking his shirt in.

"Sir we cooked most of the fishes on the bank of the river and gave the rest to a small kid. He was a good boy. He helped us spot the place where fishes are in abundance" Surya said.

This reply from Surya made me laugh but I then coughed to control this laughter. How could Surya call the condom as fishing net?

"What is your name, *jenab*?" The officer had come close to Surya and he was now looking tensed. Surya's face showed that he wanted to retaliate as he was also a cop, but the situation did not warrant that.

"Shaist... Ahmed" He randomly said a name.

"How much did this bike cost?" The officer asked, but his eyes did not have that appreciation but some greed.

"Sir, this is second hand bike and we bought it from *chor bazaar* in Lahore. This had cost us twenty thousand and we further did its restoration from Javed bhai. He does good bike modifications." I said.

"Why are you answering, smart hmmm. What is your name?" He asked me.

"*Sagir Ahmed…*" This name came had queued in my mind with the picture of the cemetery, where I had spent one night in Nagpur.

"Ahmed… you also Ahmed?" He asked Kabir. He was safe as his name goes well in India as well as Pakistan

"Shah Rukh" Kabir replied after thinking for some time.

"Oh… *Shah Rukh* is a girl's name. Why did your parents name you like that? Your face doesn't look royal." He translated the name literally.

"May be I looked like a girl when I was a kid." Kabir joked. He had maintained his patience in this strenuous situation.

"Do you offer Namaz?" He asked and we were in relief that he asked to recite it to the right person, else we would have been in great trouble.

"Yes… I mean of course yes." Kabir was confident.

"Good. It does not matter how far you reach." He paused for a while and turned back towards his vehicle and continued "You should never leave your roots… Go, but do not drive without a license from the next time."

We waved at him and got back on our bike. He did not question once why we were triple? Not sure if triple was legal in this part of Pakistan.

I took the control from Surya and heard Kabir scolding Surya for driving bad enough to invite the cops. That was good to hear from Kabir, who looked timid on his first visit to inspector saheb.

We drove per the road explained to us by Imran. Before I could take the last turn to catch the truck, I saw a big structure to my right. It looked like a *mazaar*. I saw hundreds of people going inside. I then decided to check that out. To my greatest of surprise I felt some force, pulling me from the center of that tomb. I asked Surya and Kabir to wait for me and walked towards the main gate.

A dead person's tomb hardly mattered to me but I don't know why I liked that place. I went close to the main gate and lifted my right leg to step in, but suddenly one person with green dark gown came in front of me, stopping me from entering. He was whirling the broom which he held in his hand. Then he started hitting me with it, while speaking out some phrases in Punjabi and some couplets in Urdu. I was not able to understand if I could have been of some help to him. He had long white beard and was holding an *iktara* in his right hand. His cap was violet while his fingers were all black, exactly opposite to his clear white skin. He then looked into my eyes and shouted and slowly walked inside the tomb disappearing into the crowd.

*"Naa khuda maseety labdaa, Na khuda wich kaabey
... Na khuda main tirath dittha, aivyein paanide jhagein"*

I had heard this couplet, not sure when and where. I kept running my mind, checking the logs of my long term bucket. To make the search faster I closed my eyes. Suddenly I was able to not only understand, but also feel what he meant. Yes the couplet was one of Bulleh Shah's sayings.

Oh! How could I have forgotten my visit to the Gurudwara in Kerala. The *babaji* whom I met daily used to talk extensively about Bulleh Shah, his sayings, couplets. I clearly remember how babaji used to go into some mystic mode while reciting Bulleh Shah. I turned back and looked at the boys. They were just looking at me aghast. I wasn't very good at Punjabi, but I did understand that the fakir who was dancing in front of me recited a couplet which was not new to me. It roughly translated to a quest to the self to think where God resides, is it the Mosque, or the sacred house in Mecca, or is it the divine temples built at sacred pilgrimages. The answer from the self would always give a true reply. I may not have understood babaji's fight to seek the truth then, but today I felt as if I had not just walked to Kasur without a reason. I too had some mystical feeling which raised my hair. I searched for the fakir, but he was lost, I don't know where.

"What are you talking?" I realized Surya was calling me.
"What?" I asked coming back to the real world and wiping off my tears.
"It wasn't making sense. What language was it that you were talking right now?"
"Oh, maybe I was talking to myself... actually I make sense only when I talk to myself, and when I talk to others I am normally rubbish" and I smiled leaving Surya and Kabir confused as to what had just happened.
"I am not feeling great about driving, need a break" I said and asked Surya to drive it to the place.

Suddenly something clicked my mind, which had just happened and was running in and out.
"Kabir" I called to check if he was awake.
"Yes?"
"Surya and I both did not have proper credentials, so we lied about our names. But you are actually a Muslim, why did you hide behind the name Shah Rukh?"
"I don't know. Maybe I thought everybody is lying so I also should not speak the truth as well." Hearing his reasoning, all three burst back to laughter. I was hearing Kabir's laud laughter after a long, really long time.

We had reached the place where Imran had asked us to reach. We walked in three directions and asked every person we met about Mr. Maqsood. Getting no positive reply, we were tired and it was going to get dark now.

"Are you looking for someone?" asked a person. He was dwarf. He had a stubble and a thin moustache. The right side of his lower lip had swollen, may be due to his continual chewing of tobacco and his denture also was in bad shape and color. He was too thin and was wearing a red vest and a white skull cap but his *lungi* was clean, it looked he had just ironed it.

"No thanks" Surya said, ignoring him.

"Then go out. This is a private property and trespassing is not allowed" He now had commanding voice and all of a sudden it developed some fear in our minds.

"Bhaijaan, actually we are looking for Mr. Maqsood. By any chance, do you have any idea if we can find him?" Kabir made a polite request.

"You are speaking to him." He said and while introducing himself, his chest did pull in some extra air to increase its width.

"Oh great!" Surya jumped towards the fellow and introduced all of us by our real names. We updated him that we had come here to meet Imran and now we just wanted to go back to Delhi. It felt so good to hear our original names from Maqsood's mouth.

His expressions were showing his distrust and funny reaction towards our story.

He made a call to someone and went far to talk.

"What if he is not the Maqsood we are looking for?" Kabir asked.

"He just said he is Maqsood, but he did not tell if he is the same Maqsood Afroz Patel that we were looking for." Kabir added another valid point.

"What if he is an ISI guy and he now calls his men. We would be left to serve lifelong imprisonment here to finally be discarded as rotten unclaimed bodies." Surya was losing his calm.

"We should go to the Indian Embassy." He said and now he was showing up the confidence of a policeman. "I will update them my name, id and they will surely help me. I report to the Central Government of India, they will have to help me." He said with some more confidence.

"I hope you've forgotten that you were not sent here to execute your duties by the Indian government." Kabir brought down Surya's confidence level back to zero.

Then the awkward looking guy walked towards us and smiled to confirm his action after the talk he had on his cell phone.

"The truck that leaves now will go to Delhi but via Lahore so it may take some more time. I have another truck that will leave at 10 pm from Kalyan, directly to Delhi. Which one do you want to sit in?"

We looked at each other and jumped with happiness.

"The sooner the better" was the reply from Kabir and he was right. We were glad that we disclosed our identity to the right person. We ran towards the truck which was full of sacks. It smelt rotten and some of the sacks were wet. I pressed hard on one of the sacks and its fabric was too weak to sustain that much pressure. It broke opened and spread rotten onions smell in its surrounding.

"Surya, where are you going?" I asked as he was still on the ground while the engine of the Truck was running.

"I want to pee once" and he was running towards the wall with both his hands holding his zipper. How did he manage that run? He did look awkward running with both his hands holding his zip.

Maqsood drove the truck in full swing, hearing old Punjabi folk songs in his audio system.

"Dates, Walnut, Apricot... so much of dry fruits man!" Kabir showed both of us. Surya and I envied him for his area being full of dry fruits, while we were bounded by rotten vegetables. We adopted a position which was comfortable enough in that limited space. We then kept talking about the journey. I looked around and just above Surya's head I saw pack of cards; I held the sack with one hand and stretched my body to pull the cards. Meanwhile Kabir cleaned the surface.

We could hardly throw the cards but we were fine even dropping the cards to let the game run. We played for long but then the air in this part also pushed my eye lids with so much of warmth that I wasn't able to stop myself from sleeping. I requested the boys to be alert and wake me up when both of them go to sleep. Even in my dreams, I was listening to the folk singers jumping in green fields. It was so soothing!

"*Thak khataak…* thak" This was big knock on the gate of the truck. Hearing that sound, I woke up instantly. I rubbed my eyes and tried to see where I was. The back-door slowly opened to show us bright street lights outside, just above the truck. That place was like some road side dhaba and Maqsood asked us to jump out. My back bone had gone numb due to hours of pressure it had faced. I jumped down and stretched my body up in the air.

"This looks just like Delhi. The breeze, the smell of the food, the people, the trucks, the open tap, people on the terrace and dress up of cooks" It was great to hear such words from Surya's mouth who hated this place so much. He had now thought of comparing the two cities, which was a good change.

"*Chheti aajao mittro*" Maqsood shouted. A kid walked to where we were standing.

"Order… *Veerji*" The kid asked. He must have been eight or nine; he was wearing a torn vest which had perished due to days of sweat and oil. He had short hair and a small round face. He also had a small napkin on his shoulder.

"*Chhotu naa ki hai tera?*" Surya asked the kid his name.

"*Koi menu chhotu kahida, tey koi master… menu maaloo see nhi.*"
He did not know his name but offered Surya the freedom to call the kid by the name he wished.

Surya liked the boy as if he could find a connection with him. He rubbed the kid's head and kept talking about his village, his school. While we were stretching our legs on the cot, Kabir and I just looked at the innocence building up in Surya's eyes. He had a long discussion. Surya had learnt the basic difference between a so-called enemy state and the citizens of that state.

"Om, please go and order something yaar. I am very hungry. He is now too busy." Kabir giggled and even I did not want to bother him. So I walked to the kitchen and ordered the items. We had *keema, paratha* and that was by far, the best food I had tasted since ages. We thanked the cook and Surya gave all the money he had to the kid.

"*Khayal rakha*" He asked the boy to look after himself and also requested him to go to school daily.

Maqsood bhai then signalled us to get in the truck and offered us four big sacks. We got the reason for that luxury. He asked us to hide ourselves nicely and warned us to cover all our parts. His gesture translated serious repercussions, but his smile showed a confidence owing to his experience in this style of 'transport'.

Surya held the front portion of the bike and Kabir was holding the tyre. We together tried to push the body inside the large sack. I was battling between their understanding and it was a chaos. We would sometimes trap the sack in the engine or sometimes the handle would tangle with the bottom of the sack. I then requested them to stop and convinced them to just let the bike be erected tall and we could hang the sacks to curtain it. We could almost do the job well barring the bottom wheel. We then entered inside our respective sacks and it felt like going inside an egg. Though it was itching and difficult to move our hands, we covered ourselves holding the openings of the sack over our head. We then continued to talk and see each other through the pores.

"Yaar, whenever I am inhaling I am taking in some threads. It's causing serious itch inside my nose." Surya had a problem. "Break the thread" Kabir asked him and Surya managed to cut the thread with his teeth. I uncovered my head and went close to some other threads close to his face and managed to pull that long thread with its tributaries.

"Blow air from your mouth from time to time." I suggested.

We were fast asleep and then the drive did not let us feel any motion. Was the drive smooth or were we too tired to feel the jerks? The quietness was similar to the one we feel after switching off a generator, the buzz just vanishes leaving behind a serene silence.

"Open this." It hadn't been more than an hour and I heard a loud voice from outside. This brought me out of my sleep. The side walls of the truck were wooden planks patched between iron plates. I then pushed myself to reach a crack to peep outside the wall. It was the trade gate between India and Pakistan, a big gate with bright flash lights extending till the length my eyes could cover. It was beautiful, but there was long queue of trucks and ours was moving slowly to reach the actual check point.

I hit Kabir with my shoulders not to wake him up, but to stop him from snoring as it was loud enough to be heard outside. I kept pushing him and finally he was quiet. But soon, he lost his sleep after a beam of light fell directly on his eyes through the small aperture of the truck's lateral wall. We both started our communication, first through expressions, then moving to gestures through our eyes and slowly we lost that fear to continue actual verbal talk.

"Haakchooo!"

"Shhhh... Get up Surya!" I was now a little loud. Kabir then pinched him to give him a feel of the ground situation.

"Don't sneeze? Please keep quiet. There is a police checkpoint outside." I informed him.

"Why should I speak so low, I am an Indian cop too?" He replied.

Kabir then added "Haven't you seen animal life on the TV? Your territory is within just few meters, marked by Indians urinating on roadside. You are just a prey here." We laughed under a controlled noise. Now, we had passed through the Pakistani side due to the contacts Imran must have had, but were stopped by Indian side for a heavy checking.

"You bastards take all the money from us and bring in arms and bombs in our country" said an Indian cop.

"The story must be the same for Indian drivers entering into Pakistan. We do a trade of more than two billion dollars and still have so much of hatred inside as if we were never a single country once." I said on seeing the difficulty in travelling across to the other side. Surya was now advocating the unification of India and Pakistan and he replied… *"Saale Radcliffe ki maa ki…"* He was now angry on the person assigned to draw the line between the two countries, as if it was the hobby of Mr. Cyril Radcliffe to divide countries.

"Can we keep quiet if your history classes are done?" Kabir scolded. Actually he was right and we had to oblige.

"Sir, take this. We've all the papers, see." We heard Maqsood showing the papers and negotiating with the cops to let him go. He then pulled a sack from under his seat and gave it to the cops. That sack must be full of dry fruits. Few more cops arrived on the scene and demanded one more sack. Now Maqsood had to open the gate behind which we were hiding. Maqsood accidentally removed the sack supporting Surya.

The sacks were a little translucent and through the minute pores, we could see the deal happening. Surya's sack became horizontal to the ground, but he was well trained to keep quiet and be patient in such difficulties. He stopped breathing as well.

After few seconds... "Haakchooo!!" he sneezed again and this time louder.

The gate was not yet closed. My heart beat increased and I was hoping that no cop climbs up to check the source of that sneeze. Surya seemed to be seriously allergic to dust.

"Who is there?" This was the cop flashing his torch on the sacks close to us. The deal was almost done and we then heard few more boots running towards our truck. That moment looked like the end of our ordeal. There was a small chance of us fighting our legal case to prove we were not Pakistani agents but Maqsood would be in big trouble. He may end up serving life-long harsh torture which was difficult to imagine.

"Sir, it's the conductor, nothing is there" Maqsood said and then abused the conductor in Punjabi. Hearing the scolding, the conductor ran from the front seat and pleaded before the cops for causing 'inconvenience'. Just to add weight to the lie, he sneezed again and rubbed his nose. The other cop did not look satisfied.

He took out the knife bayonet attached to his rifle and started poking the sacks one by one. Kabir and I were safe but Surya's sack was right in front of the gate. One shot went so very close... *swoosh!* It just missed his stomach, but Surya was brave and he did not move an inch. He looked fine after a few shots. In his last shot, the knife went smoothly inside and when it came out, it spread that pungent aroma from the rotten onions. "Saale, you sell us these rotten vegetables." and he slapped the conductor. Maqsood again jumped in and started closing the gate while apologising for the bad products.

"Sir it got delayed in transportation. We will make sure to not charge for that sack."

The officer then hit his baton on the walls to hint our exit. There were lots of trucks honking and moving slowly, some accelerating again and again but with zero displacement. The gate closed tight and we had a deep sigh of relief. We came out of our sacks slowly rotating our bodies and pushing ourselves out to breathe the fresh air. We threw the sack and it looked like vacated snake exuviate. Surya was the one who was fighting his allergy and I raised my eyebrows to congratulate his efforts. We started playing cards again till the sleep permitted our eyes to be opened.

"Come out... get up!" I woke up and looked around to see where we were. I gave my hand to Maqsood who was standing in front of me. He pulled me to lift me up. He looked dwarf but had enough strength to pull my entire weight so easily. "Thanks *bhai*." I said.
"See the sign boards are in Hindi, we are back... alive." Kabir along with Surya, started jumping and dancing inside the truck. But suddenly he felt a pain in his abdomen and took his hand to feel that place.
"I thought it missed your stomach" I went close to analyse the red cut which was pretty thick and dark. The blood had clotted around the straight line just above his waist.
"Police did train you well, I would have cried in that big cut, if not the pain, then certainly the blood would have made me shout" Kabir appreciated Surya's patience.

I gave everything I had in Pakistani currency to Maqsood; he denied and claimed that our safe return was his duty. I forced and gave some of it to the conductor. This money was of no use to either of us. Kabir also gave his share and we hugged him and thanked him for bringing us safe in Delhi.

Surya was now thinking what he would say to his seniors. But he was so happy that he had brought something with him in this trip. I did not ask him what, but I was seeing a different Surya. The trip had brought back the empathetic and warm Surya whom I had always known. I could make that out by the way he hugged Maqsood. Finally, this trip was able to uproot the hatred he had for Muslims in general. He looked up to find no difference from the sky he saw from Lahore.

There was a positive change in Kabir as well. He was not afraid of the end anymore. He knew that life was too long and he had so much to give. He had many places to see. He was okay even if he forgot to have his medicines for a day, his confidence was there to keep him healthy. He looked young and free. He wanted to discover more instead of fighting for his existence on this planet.

I looked in to the mirror and then I asked to myself, as to what did I gain after risking my life. I had no answer that was prompt. But I did feel free of a heavy loan. There was no better way I could have expressed my gratitude.

Kabir and I soon left Delhi to get back to our routine work in Pune. I focused on giving more time to Sayali and narrating her stories which Amma often told me. They would be mostly from *Panchatantr*. In return, I would get selfless love from Sayali. I was trying to fill the love she was deprived of, in the absence of her parents. I was now ready to take up the responsibility of that kid. She was like a daughter to me and I wanted to do all that my parents did to for me, may be a little more.

I sat alone in my office room one day and closed my eyes to rewind things. There were so many events running in front of my eyes. There was this huge stock of emotions I had felt. They were tussling with the fantasies which could never be bounded by any spatial or temporal limits. I penned down everything that we did to reach Kasur and drafted to form a detailed manuscript. I then emailed it to British Bilateral Channel of Humanity, BBCH based out of London. It was extensively involved in peace talks with various nations. They also had a sisterly concern which published travel memoirs, mostly by war correspondents. I just wanted to bring down everything from my heart on this paper. I wrote a raw manuscript but requested the Editor to not consider it as a fiction or a provocation for illegal travel. I then felt relieved that I was conveying my emotions to a reputed and credible international committee that worked towards peace and brotherhood.

With each passing day, I saw Kabir getting healthier. He had started contributing more towards *Insaaniyat*. He would visit adjoining districts to meet people discarded by their families and help them with some medical and moral contributions. This brought a visible positive ramification in him. He had gained some weight too. Seeing him running around for days, I would sometimes forget that he was internally fighting against a deadly virus.

"Sir, there is a letter for you." Said the office assistant.
I just took the envelope. He went away. The letter had a logo of BBCH and it read…

Dear Ohm,

Our panel of journalists went through your letter titled:
Crossing the border to thank a friend

This was read and analysed by our team and me in particular. The article you emailed to us, dealt with anxiety and gratitude while the visit continued with fear of getting caught.

You were box clever and I personally want you to visit us at our office. We are thinking of starting a new series of documentary wherein the protagonist would ethically trespass inside a country, with an intention of building up a positive air.
We may want to begin with the neighbours of the United Kingdom.

I hope this summary has helped you explain our interest in this project. We should start it by next year and its details would soon be advertised on various channels and news dailies.

We would like to meet you in person and share your experience again. Plan your visit and you need not worry about your expenses. We would be more than delighted to have you in our crew.

If you have further questions or queries, please do not hesitate to contact me (details at the bottom of this page)

Many thanks again for sharing your ordeal with us.

Miss Rebecca Dyer
Sr. Editor
BBCH Network
445 Windsor Walk
London
AB2 9BE

That did sound awesome!

The most I had thought was my article getting published in some monthly issue of its stories. Moreover, they responded very quickly and I was still not able to believe what my eyes had just read. I kept looking at the letter and went into my thoughts.

Will the new task take me away from the real issues we were after? The current project had given me all the happiness I could have ever wanted to get from a career. I still had that slight apprehension of entering back into the world of wicked corporate and managers.

I called Surya to update him.

"I knew my friend. I knew you would reach heights" He was elated hearing the news. I updated him but I myself did not know if the new challenge would be just a trip or some long term project?

"I knew things will fall in place for you, just make sure that you stand whole heartedly for them when asked." I was getting what he meant. The image of London for him was nothing more than beautiful white girls.

"C'mon Surya, I am off for a new project, a new life. I am just in dilemma if this is really worth a shot?" I asked, cutting short his imagination of white girls dancing around me in London. "I am sure you will be all over on the TV, running from one part of Europe to the other." He gave some false assurance, but did not understand the real question my mind was after. Would I lose my happiness if I leave India?

I kept thinking if I should fly to London or not. I went for a bath to let my brain relax. After the shower, I think my mind opened up and I talked to Kabir about the new project.

"What? London!" He was happy about it and asked me to leave ASAP. He started assuring me of taking up the tasks I had scheduled for Insaaniyat. He looked confident and would always sit with me to understand the new assignments and areas we found to extend our help.

I still wasn't sure so I went to Sayali and held her in my arms. "Would it be fine if I go out to some other place for a long time?" I asked and kept looking at her eyes. She did not blink. She processed my request for long and finally asked

"Will you be happy there without me?"

She had so much depth in her query that the thought of London got a quick departure from my mind. I hugged her tight and went back to the office to think on other measures I could take to increase my efforts in other aspects with much more effect.

One day while I was relaxing on my chair in the office, I kept asking how I could make the life of patients like Kabir and Sayali more meaningful. I was brainstorming hard but nothing was easily coming up.

I then recalled what was it that such patients need badly; was it the financial stability, social acceptability or self motivation? We were already working hard through some other wealthy foundations to provide them sufficient support, but still I couldn't see that zeal in the inhabitants. We would also provide the inhabitants' occasional trip to public meetings and functions in schools that helped them mingle with the privileged healthy entities of the society, so where were we lagging?

"Could it be the support which I provide to Kabir, that shoulder and warmth which Kabir finds in me?" I finally could think one way to connect the have-nots to form a big group of smiling faces.

A dating-site for the people suffering from HIV wherein they could search the right shoulder to relax?

Yes! Something like *positiveindiadating.com?*

However bad the professional practices might be at my first organization, but one thing I could never take from them. They gave me the opportunity to learn all aspects of web development. I took out a pen and for next few days kept drawing the possible architecture which could help us build a robust web application in minimal time and using minimal resources. I asked few other educated inhabitants to sit with me and Kabir, while we thought about its design. I purchased few old machines and configured a set-up which would help each member take up assigned task and check-in their progress. I wasn't sure of the feasibility, so I purchased a cloud sample portal server which would render the requests.

Kabir had almost done one year of engineering so he could pick up user interface development fast. I had purchased few books to help each member understand theoretical knowledge of what they were into.

Next few months, I slept in my cabin and the moment I woke up, I would start going through the mess I would have coded while in my half-sleep.

Finally we could erect a simple framework which catered to the request from a web form and served well through internet. We spent next few weeks polishing it and making optimal use of open source community help. I finally called Raghav one day to give him a demo of what we had built. I showed him the progress and how the dating could be initiated between partners sitting in one end of the world to finally choose the best companion. I dictated him to type and access the web address word by word and focused on his expressions.

Unlike my previous managers of the IT industry, Raghav looked confounded by the web app and looked happier talking about the motive behind the idea. He congratulated the team in high voice and granted me some more money to actually purchase expensive, high performing servers to cater to actual load of millions of hits. We all were obliged by his help and that was a fresh breeze of oxygen as I had already finished all the money I had.

The website was up and we started propagating it through radio and pamphlets. It was interesting to see the reaction from the crowd. Many would utterly reject calling it a stupid idea, while some appreciated the efforts. We still had managed to become a known website in the city.

"Who is Om? Come out." A person around six feet tall entered our office with seven or eight vehicles fully loaded with his supporters. He had a heavy build and all of them had tied orange bandana covering their head.

"My name is Om, what is the problem?" I rushed to the guy before he could cause harm to my set-up and the machines.

"You mother fucker, you want our motherland to be full of virus infected people like you. Get lost filthy virus." He held my collar.

"We take full precaution and explain the risk to the users of the web application. Please visit the website once before you curse us." I asked him to sit and tried to explain him the measures we took in order to have a safe interaction between the two parties.

While I was requesting him, I felt a kick from behind forcing me to fall close to the almirah. I held the almirah and turned around to hear what he wanted to say

"People like you have done dirty things to get the curse from God and now you want to spread your disease through that website."

Hearing that logic I smiled and before say anything, I got another slap.

"We will not let you spoil the Indian culture." I held their leader and asked him to sit and hear the measures we had taken to make my point. We were finally having the database of all the people registered; hence any illicit trespassing was overruled.

"They have the right to live and enjoy the life as much as you guys have. We all know how much productivity you all have added to the GDP of India by spending hours in the arms of sex workers."

"Keep quiet!" Shouted their leader.

"He is right" Kabir came running and he was followed by around hundred odd inhabitants from our ashram. Kabir then continued.

"We all know that you never want the millions of sex workers trapped in Indian red light colonies to enjoy their freedom. We may be ill, but we are not weak."

I was animated seeing the huge support we had in the united force standing behind Kabir. The hooligans knew they could not do much, so went back shouting and warning us for the aftermath of running the campaign. I thanked all of them and this move confirmed that the efforts were really getting popular in the dark markets of Indian flesh trade.

"This can be cleared for review. Please start the work on this and the defaulters list would be double checked with the medical registers in India." I asked Kabir and I rubbed my back for small time pain which was now running inside like a current.

"What is it?" Kabir asked.

"It had started behind my right shoulder since we came back from Pakistan."

"So let us visit the doctor tomorrow." He replied.

"I did a lot of running and that must have caused it. Let it be. I will apply a pain relief ointment" and I asked him to leave. I focused on observing the response we were getting and that night, I had estimated to complete the analytics around our product. I wish I had got this as my project in KoolConcepts.

It was late night and this pain sometimes stretched from back to the shoulder and then to the back of my neck. It had increased so much that I was finding difficulty in laughing too. I thought this may be a good time to get a medical check-up. I started walking out of the gate to catch an auto rickshaw. I looked back and saw Sayali looking at me and she looked so beautiful. She opened both her arms and wanted me to come back and lift her. I had opened the ashram gate, but my mind wanted me to go back.

She was saying something and I was now not able to hear her. What was she saying? She was suddenly so close to me, so very close that I could clearly see her beautiful eyes. I always thought she had black eyes, but thanks to the proximity I had which made me distinguish the brown eyes which looked almost black from distant. How had I attained such short height?

I felt some sudden pain on my knees. My chest felt congested and I found difficulty in breathing. It gave the same feeling of obstruction inside when I had fallen from the cashew tree in Kannur. I could feel on my skin plenty of cold breezes, it was constantly flowing outside, but not a single molecule was entering my chest. I wanted to breathe...

"The left artery is blocked" I opened my eyes and I was seeing a torch right over my head and there were stainless steel equipments being lifted or dropped in some utensils. The noise thus produced, was echoed in my brain time and again. I opened my eyes again and there was a hazy picture of a person in sea green apron moving his hands very quickly from my chest, which was felt till my neck. What was he doing? I had no energy to move my lips.

"The plaque is now compressed, but the blood is not able to flow past it." He was feeling bad for something. I was breathing cool oxygen and this was now sending me back to my good world of dreams. I gave up my efforts to bother poor fellow working so hard digging inside my body.

I collected all the energy I had to change the direction of my vision towards the nurse and waited for her to see me. She was busy reading some magazine

C'mon, look at me. My request was loud from inside but my lips were blocked to bring out a word. Then suddenly she turned towards me. I blinked and stared at her to ask something. I then looked into the screen in front of me and asked through my eyes what that was? I kept blinking my eyes fast and then tried to focus her towards the screen in front of me. I was seeing some white cloth covering my head and my chest was almost open. The center of the chest looked bulged in and there was a vacancy.

"Everything is fine sir" She replied. On further requests through eyes, I managed to force her to pity on me and elaborate my condition.

"There was a clot in your brain sir. We are trying to remove that. The heart surgery has gone fine. Everything will be all right sir!" She repeated and I now understood that may be that clot was special. That clot may have blocked all the irrational theories supporting miracles to enter my brain. I smiled and had wasted enough energy to make me feel dizzy to go back to sleep.

"Om Uncle…" This was Sayali and I opened my eyes quickly to see her. I felt that I was running out of time. She then pointed her small index finger to her left. She had brought black roses for me. I used to take such black roses for Sayali in the college. It was her favourite flower. I had to run from one place to another in Nagpur in search of those. There was only one big vendor who used to import such flowers from Russia. How crazy I was, but that was worth the efforts after Dr. Sayali smiled receiving those flowers. Had she stayed with me, I wouldn't have had that big crater in my heart. Maybe?

I thanked little Sayali through my eyes and she looked back at Kabir and asked what had happened to me. Kabir was not able to explain. Kabir then put her down and came close to me. Meanwhile Surya kept hiding his tears seeing me in such a helpless state.

"Om… you can't…" Kabir looked at Surya to come close and help him complete his sentence. Surya still couldn't manage to stand up from the visiting corner. Kabir continued

"We have so much to travel. You are our guide, please don't go yaar." I was now not able to hear his words. I tried to speak out but in vain. I tried to put all the energy I had on my throat, but I collapsed again. I took a deep breath and opened my eyes to thank Kabir and let him know that I was fine. I then tried again to call him close to me through the index finger of my left hand. Kabir noticed it and brought his ears close to my mouth.

"Almirah…." I could finally utter a word, but that brought sweat all over and I had to lower my body for sleep, expecting Kabir to check the Almirah in my office room.

When I woke up, I would see the date and time running pretty fast. Sometimes, I would have taken a long leap of five days, sometimes just two hours. However I was not able to feel any pain which people standing outside were feeling.

"*Beta…*" That was my mother. She wanted to hug me and she then looked up and started praying to her lord(s) to cure me. She was asking for forgiveness for all my sins. While she was wiping her tears, my father approached me.

"Get up son…" He wasn't crying. He was trained to be tough. He would always stand stiff. He couldn't talk more, was he waiting for my acknowledgement? I owed a lot to him, everything I would say. I thanked him from my core for being my father. I had nothing which I could give to them. They gave me a good upbringing and in some way, the attitude that shaped me. I was proud of the way I was brought up. I closed my eyes and I saw my mother sleeping over my arms, coming close to my chest and crying loud.

Just say once "*Ram naam satya hai….*" She was still hoping for me to fall for those magical words per Hindus which hailed lord *Ram's* name as the only truth.

She then continued "Say it once, don't go away with a burden of that sin." How could I have left without asking forgiveness to her? If I had even the slightest of energy, I would have just replied to my mother that if there would be a truth it would never have a name. The truth could only be a beautiful life which we get once to achieve everything in such a short span. The truth could be the love which my parents had for me. The truth could be the respect I got while working for the underprivileged and many such versions of truth which I might not have known yet.

My father then started talking to me, looked as if that was his final commandment for my soul purification.
"Om, void your brain and just quietly take your own name. Listen to Chapter eight verse thirteen from Bhagvad Geeta, that says" and he was loud

Om itee ekaaksharam brahm, vyahaaran mam anusmaran
yah prayati tyajan deham, sa yati pramaam gatim

I did not need RAT to describe what it meant as I had come across that verse very often. It meant that by just chanting that one divine syllable called '*om*, a person could reach the supreme abode, away from the infinite cycle of life, birth and death. The person can reach that cosmic planet where there is no life and death, just happiness!

May be I never longed to get that level of salvation? Maybe I was happy in this beautiful planet placed just at right position, right spin, right gyration, with an appropriate gravity and the best suited climatic conditions to sustain life. Earth had so much of misery that leaving this place for the ultimate pleasure was never in my list. I replied to my father by my smile, may be that was my last act which my face could feel. This was my last sin?

CHAPTER 12

Is The Bird A Phoenix?
The Epilogue

I chose this life. I chose not to settle with ignorance!

I wish that Kabir got the will which I had placed in my almirah. That would help Sayali complete her education. It might also help Kabir travel to more places and get awareness on the research and new medicines for the cure of the virus.

I wish that little Sayali wouldn't develop my attitude. She may find it hard to survive then. But what if she becomes a girl chained by the social forces? She will be hand cuffed by bangles. She will be registered by her *managsutr* in neck just like a pet. She may be forced to put that mercuric sulphide on her head to show that she belongs to some greater species. But what If she doesn't do that at all? Then I am afraid she will be lost thinking and begging for answers from all corners.

I wish Kabir had clearly read my instructions and would manage to call the ambulance. They should not be late as I have enough to share with this world. I may have had a not so acceptable mind, but the brain would be healthy. I have eyes through which I saw Sayali and yes the little Sayali again. I saw my friends and my mother. She is a gem!

She would not let this body go to medical college; she would pull my legs to stop me. She would beg Kabir to not let me torn by doctors. But she would have to agree to that last wish of mine. I can't let this body feel the burn of Lord Agni. He already gets thousands daily. I can't let the ashes get mixed with the holy waters of Ganga. She is already transporting the bones and ashes of millions.

My mother often gave the reason that those who are born blind in this life had committed some serious crime in their past life and their eyes were removed in their previous birth. She believed strongly in reincarnation, she had to believe in it as she preached it. She did believe in 'last-wish' thus she will have to oblige by my final request.

My father would be fighting in high voice with the medical team who would have appeared to collect '*me*'. My father was a strong person. He would also show his Army ID Card to use his influence. He may force the medical team to step back and not collect me. He would want me to have peace when I am not on earth. He often looked at me and thought of the ways to bring peace to my mind. He could not; he tried so hard and collected the money to send me for higher education. He strongly believed in the good and the bad soul. What soul I had per my father?
Whatever it was, I felt its weight! It was too heavy to carry a life time.

May be I had some part of my lungs, still storing that fresh oxygen of Sikkim?
I also have a heart. But the nurse showed me its state... that was pretty bad. I apologize to the hospital getting this body.

This body was as simple as anyone else's but the life inside this body was just great.

I think the volume of thought reserved for me was all used up so fast that I had to leave. Sayali should see that clot. Maybe she could fix it? Oh! I did promise her that I would be her guinea pig. I have a good memory, so what are my final memories?

I have met a person who had climbed the highest peak without oxygen; I had immensely beautiful parents who in good or bad ways, helped me grow up like this. I've had amazing buddies to grow up at various stages of life. I've had unknown people helping me. I am a bloody trespasser who just happened to accidentally trespass in this beautiful planet called Earth. Fuck I should've consulted a shrink!